I0760329

Possession and Prejudice

A Magical Pride and Prejudice Variation

Catherine Bilson

Shenanigans Press

Copyright © 2025 Shenanigans Press. All Rights Reserved.

This book and all its contents are protected by copyright law. No part of this publication may be reproduced, distributed, or transmitted in any form or by any means, including photocopying, recording, or other electronic or mechanical methods, without the prior written permission of the publisher, except in the case of brief quotations used in reviews or other non-commercial uses permitted by copyright law.

For permission requests, please contact:

Shenanigans Press

PO Box 323, MORAYFIELD QLD 4506 AUSTRALIA

Email: admin@shenaniganspress.com

Contents

Chapter One

ELIZABETH MARCHED BACK TO the parsonage steaming with rage, her jaw clenched so tightly her teeth ached. The revelation Colonel Fitzwilliam had so casually imparted, that Mr. Darcy had deliberately separated Bingley from Jane, had congratulated himself on saving his friend from an imprudent connection, burned in her chest like a hot coal. She barely noticed the spring flowers nodding along the lane, the pleasant warmth of the afternoon sun. Her mind was too full of Jane's quiet sadness, of her own foolish hope that Bingley might eventually return for her sister, of Mr. Darcy's insufferable pride.

She had known him arrogant from their first meeting. But *this!* This calculated cruelty, this casual destruction of her sister's happiness, exceeded even her worst estimation of his character. That he should consider Jane unworthy of his friend, that he should take it upon himself to judge and condemn where he had no right, made her hands curl into fists at her sides.

The parsonage door stood open to admit the spring breeze. Elizabeth stepped inside, grateful for the cool dimness of the entrance hall after the glare of the bright sunshine. She needed solitude, time to master the fury that threatened to choke her, and marched briskly towards the stairs.

"Oh, Elizabeth!" Charlotte appeared in the parlour doorway, her expression apologetic as she saw Elizabeth's intended direction. "I did not expect you back quite so soon. We have visitors; Miss de Bourgh and Mrs. Jenkinson have come to take tea."

Elizabeth felt her composure, already strained, threaten to crack entirely. She could not, absolutely could *not*, sit through tea and make polite conversation when her blood was still hot with indignation. But Charlotte's eyes pleaded with her, and Elizabeth recollected that she was a guest in this house, that Charlotte must manage relations with Rosings as best she could.

"Of course," Elizabeth heard herself say. Her voice sounded nearly normal, though her throat felt tight. "I shall join you directly." Removing her pelisse, she yanked at her bonnet ribbons with perhaps unnecessary force, wincing as she heard threads rip. She made herself stand still for a moment, closing her eyes and taking in a deep breath, before resuming untying the ribbons more carefully.

She followed Charlotte into the parlour, willing her expression into pleasantness. The room seemed over-warm and too small. Charlotte's sister Maria sat perched on the edge of a chair, her posture painfully correct, her eyes bright with the importance of entertaining such exalted company. The companion Mrs. Jenkinson occupied another seat, her spine rigid, her hands folded neatly in her lap, eyes cast down as was her usual habit.

And Anne de Bourgh herself sat in the best chair, looking as pale and insubstantial as always, yet regarding Elizabeth with an intensity that seemed at odds with her fragile appearance.

"Miss Bennet," Anne said, her voice soft but carrying clearly in the confined space. "How pleasant to see you again. I trust your walk was agreeable?"

"Very agreeable, thank you." Elizabeth took the only vacant seat, on Anne's other side, accepting the tea Charlotte poured for her with fingers that wanted to tremble. She gripped the delicate cup too firmly, feeling the heat of the tea through the porcelain. The fury in her chest had not subsided. If anything, being forced into this performance of civility made it worse, a pressure building behind her breastbone.

"You must find Kent quite different from Hertfordshire," Anne continued. Her gaze never left Elizabeth's face, an unwavering attention that felt oddly improper. "The countryside here is perhaps less wild, more cultivated."

"The countryside is very pleasant," Elizabeth replied, taking a sip of tea she barely tasted. The liquid was too hot, scalding her tongue, but she welcomed the sharp sensation. It gave her something to focus on besides the roiling in her stomach.

"And the company?" Anne's lips curved slightly. "My cousins have both been pleased to make your acquaintance, and I hope you have found their company interesting. Colonel Fitzwilliam is considered quite charming, I believe."

From the corner of her eye, Elizabeth saw Charlotte looking at her with a concerned expression. Perhaps she could see the colour rising in Elizabeth's neck, the way her shoulders had gone rigid. Elizabeth forced herself to relax marginally, to set down her teacup with exaggerated care before her hands could betray her by shaking.

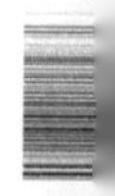

"Colonel Fitzwilliam is indeed amiable," Elizabeth said. Her voice had an edge to it she could not quite suppress. "He is very forthcoming in conversation."

"And Mr. Darcy?" The question hung in the air, pointed and deliberate. "You have spent some time in his company as well." Anne tilted her head slightly, like a bird examining something curious on the ground. "He has spoken little of your prior acquaintance in Hertfordshire, but then Mr. Darcy is not given to idle chatter. Do you find him agreeable?"

Maria made a small, nervous sound, half-hidden behind her teacup. Even she could sense the tension crackling through the room. Charlotte began to speak, some deflection about the weather or the roads, but Anne's attention remained fixed on Elizabeth with an unnerving focus.

"I cannot claim to know Mr. Darcy's character well," Elizabeth said. "He keeps his own counsel, as you say."

"But you must have formed some impression." Anne's voice remained soft, but something in her eyes had sharpened. "He is the sort of man who makes an impression, whether he intends to or not."

The pressure in Elizabeth's chest threatened to burst free in words she would regret. She could feel her composure fraying, thread by thread. Yes, she had formed an impression, of a man so consumed by pride and prejudice that he thought nothing of destroying another's happiness. A man who judged others by their connections and found them wanting. A man who...

"I find Mr. Darcy to be a gentleman of strong opinions," Elizabeth said, selecting each word carefully. "He is not easily swayed by the feelings or preferences of others."

"How perceptive," Anne murmured. Something flickered across her pale features; satisfaction, perhaps, or calculation. "It is refreshing to meet someone who observes so clearly."

Mrs. Jenkinson stirred, finally speaking for the first time since Elizabeth had entered. "Miss de Bourgh, you must not tire yourself with too much conversation. Remember what the physician said about exertion."

"I am quite well, Mrs. Jenkinson." Anne's voice remained pleasant, but her companion subsided immediately, folding her hands once more in her lap. Anne's attention returned to Elizabeth, that same unsettling intensity in her gaze. "Tell me, Miss Bennet, do you enjoy your time at Hunsford? Does it suit you?"

Charlotte seized on the change of subject with visible relief, launching into praise of the parsonage and Mr. Collins's situation. Maria added her own eager observations about the neighbourhood, the shops in the village, the kindness of Lady Catherine's condescension. The conversation became a flurry of social pleasantries, a familiar dance that required little genuine participation.

Elizabeth contributed little, but she remained acutely aware of Anne's continued scrutiny, the way those pale eyes tracked her smallest movements. It was the attention of someone cataloguing, assessing, measuring. Elizabeth had been observed by potential suitors, by disapproving matrons, by curious neighbours, but this felt different. This felt like being examined by a natural philosopher studying a specimen. This was a different Anne de Bourgh than the silent girl at Rosings, stifled by her mother's overbearing presence.

The flush in her cheeks would not quite fade. Whenever Darcy's name arose, and it arose with suspicious frequency in Anne's gentle questioning, Elizabeth felt fresh heat prickle

across her skin. Her posture remained too rigid, her responses too cautious. Anyone with sense could see she was barely maintaining control.

Anne, it seemed, had abundant sense. Each time Elizabeth struggled to master her reaction, Anne's expression shifted subtly; a small tightening around the eyes, a barely perceptible nod, as though Elizabeth had confirmed something important. It made Elizabeth's skin crawl in a way she could not quite define.

"You must come to Rosings again before you leave Kent," Anne said. "I should like to know you better, Miss Bennet. I find you quite fascinating."

Fascinating. As though she were a curiosity in a cabinet, something strange to be studied and understood.

Mrs. Jenkinson set down her teacup with a soft clink and cleared her throat. "Mrs. Collins, forgive me, but I wonder if I might have a word about the receipt you mentioned, the one for the tonic you mentioned that your mother taught you? Miss de Bourgh's constitution might benefit from such a remedy."

Charlotte rose immediately, ever the accommodating hostess. "Of course, Mrs. Jenkinson. I shall write it out for you. Maria, perhaps you might help me – you can show Mrs. Jenkinson the herbs in the stillroom while I write out the receipt?"

Maria nearly leapt from her chair, eager to be useful, to be noticed performing some service. The three women departed in a rustle of skirts and murmured conversation, their voices fading down the passage toward the back of the house.

The parlour door clicked shut.

Elizabeth found herself alone with Anne de Bourgh, and the room seemed to contract around them. The afternoon light slanting through the windows had taken on a thick, amber quality, illuminating dust motes that hung suspended in the air.

The silence pressed against Elizabeth's ears, broken only by the ticking of the mantel clock and her own too-loud breathing.

She should say something. Make some polite observation about the weather, about the quality of Charlotte's housekeeping, about anything at all. But her mind remained stubbornly fixed on Colonel Fitzwilliam's revelation, on Darcy's interference, on Jane's lost happiness. Her anger sat like a stone in her throat, making speech difficult.

Anne reached for the teapot with movements that seemed oddly deliberate, almost ceremonial. Her pale fingers curled around the handle, and she lifted it with exaggerated care. The spout hovered over Elizabeth's cup, and tea flowed out in a dark stream, the liquid catching the light as it fell.

"You have finished your tea," Anne observed. Her voice remained soft, but it carried a strange undertone Elizabeth could not quite identify. "Allow me. You must be thirsty, after taking such a long walk."

Elizabeth watched, oddly transfixed, as Anne topped up the cup.

"Oh," Anne said. "What is that bird, in the garden?"

Elizabeth followed the direction of Anne's gaze, though the window, but saw no birds. "Where do you mean, Miss de Bourgh?"

"It flew away," Anne said dismissively, and Elizabeth blinked, looking back at her. Anne was concentrating on the tea again, topping up her own cup this time.

"I find the gardens at Rosings particularly beautiful at this time of year," Anne said, lifting her own cup to her lips and taking a small sip. "The grove of oaks, especially. So peaceful there, so removed from the main house. Do you walk there often during your visits?"

"I have walked there once or twice." Elizabeth reached for her refreshed cup, grateful for something to occupy her hands. The taste seemed slightly different somehow, more bitter perhaps, or was that simply her mood colouring everything?

"You strike me as someone who enjoys solitude," Anne continued. Her gaze remained fixed on Elizabeth's face with unsettling intensity. "Someone who prefers her own thoughts to idle company."

"I enjoy walking," Elizabeth said. The words came out vague, distracted. Her mind had already wandered back to Darcy, to the image of him congratulating himself on separating Bingley from Jane. The arrogance of it. The casual cruelty. She took another sip of tea, barely registering the taste.

"And what occupies your thoughts during these solitary walks?" Anne's question felt invasive somehow, too personal for their slight acquaintance. "Do you reflect on books you have read? On conversations that have troubled you?"

Elizabeth blinked, pulled reluctantly back to the present. "I think on many things. Whatever comes to mind, I suppose."

"How vague." A small smile touched Anne's lips. "Surely someone of your evident intelligence has more specific preoccupations. Your family, perhaps? Your eldest sister, Jane, is she not called? Or your younger sisters, and their welfare?"

The mention of Jane made Elizabeth's chest tighten. She set down her teacup with less grace than intended, the china rattling against the saucer. "My sisters are all very well, thank you."

"But the eldest was in London recently, was she not? And did not see as much of certain acquaintances as might have been expected." Anne tilted her head, watching Elizabeth's reaction with avid attention. "How disappointing that must have been.

For her, I mean. When one forms expectations of a connection, only to find oneself... overlooked."

Elizabeth's hands clenched in her lap. How did Anne know about Jane and Bingley? The question surfaced through her renewed anger, but she was too upset to properly consider it. "These things happen," she said stiffly. "Not all acquaintances deepen into friendships."

"Indeed." Anne took another delicate sip of her tea. "Though sometimes the failure of an acquaintance to develop stems not from natural incompatibility but from interference. Do you not think? When well-meaning friends decide to protect one party from what they perceive as an imprudent connection."

The words hit too close to the wound. Elizabeth felt heat flood her face again, her pulse hammering in her temples. She reached for her tea, needing to occupy her shaking hands, and drank deeply. The bitterness seemed more pronounced now, coating her tongue.

"I am sure I cannot speak to such situations," Elizabeth managed. "I know nothing of interference in others' affairs."

"But if you did," Anne pressed, leaning forward slightly, "if you knew someone had deliberately separated two people who might have made each other happy, what would you think of such a person?"

"I would think them insufferably arrogant." The words burst out before Elizabeth could contain them. "I would think them cruel and presumptuous, no matter how good their intentions might be. To assume one has the right to judge another's feelings, to decide they are not genuine or worthy..."

She stopped abruptly, horrified at her own loss of control. Anne's pale eyes glittered with something that might have been triumph.

"How passionate you are," Anne murmured. "How deeply you feel injustice. It must be exhausting, caring so intensely about everything and everyone."

Elizabeth forced herself to breathe slowly, to regain the composure she had lost. But her thoughts scattered like startled birds, refusing to settle. Darcy's face kept appearing in her mind, his proud expression, his cold civility, his evident disdain for her family's circumstances. That he should have the audacity to judge Jane, to find her unworthy...

"Do *you* know Mr. Darcy well?" Elizabeth heard herself ask. The question emerged without her conscious intention, pulled from her by the swirling confusion of her thoughts.

"As well as anyone knows him, I suppose." Anne's smile widened fractionally. "We have been acquainted since childhood. Our families have long expected... but I am sure you are not interested in such tedious family history."

"I am not interested in Mr. Darcy at all," Elizabeth said firmly. "I find him disagreeable in the extreme."

"Do you?" Anne leaned back in her chair, apparently satisfied with some private assessment. "How interesting. And yet you seem to think of him quite often. His name keeps arising in our conversation, though I did not introduce it just now. You did."

Elizabeth's face burned. Had she? She could not quite remember. Her head felt oddly heavy, her thoughts sluggish and difficult to grasp. The afternoon light seemed too bright now, making her eyes water.

"I think of him only insofar as his actions have affected those I care about," Elizabeth said. Even to her own ears, her voice sounded strange, too slow, the words requiring tremendous effort to form properly.

"Of course." Anne's voice seemed to come from very far away, though she sat right next to Elizabeth. "You are devoted to your sister. One can see it quite clearly. You would do anything for her happiness."

Would she? Yes. Yes, of course she would. Elizabeth tried to nod but found the movement difficult. The room had begun to tilt slightly, or perhaps it was only her perspective that had shifted. She blinked hard, trying to clear her vision.

"I find you utterly fascinating, Miss Bennet," Anne said softly. "Your spirit, your health, your determination, are all quite remarkable. I wonder if you properly appreciate what you possess."

The words made no sense. Elizabeth wanted to respond, to ask what Anne meant, but her tongue felt thick in her mouth. She reached for her teacup again, some instinct suggesting that drinking might help, might clear the strange fog descending over her thoughts. The tea was cooler now, and she drained the last of it, tasting only bitterness.

Footsteps sounded in the passage as Charlotte and the others returned. The door opened, and Mrs. Jenkinson stepped through, Maria chattering behind her about the receipt and its ingredients.

"Miss de Bourgh, we really must return to Rosings now," Mrs. Jenkinson said firmly. "You have been away from home quite long enough."

Anne rose gracefully, her movements smooth and controlled. Elizabeth tried to rise as well, managing it only with difficulty. The floor seemed uneven beneath her feet.

"Thank you for a most enlightening visit," Anne said, her pale eyes meeting Elizabeth's for one last, lingering moment. "I do

hope we shall have opportunity to speak again soon. I feel we have so much more to discuss."

Elizabeth murmured something, she knew not what. The words were merely sounds, meaningless syllables pushed past her lips by habit and training. Her head throbbed now, a dull ache spreading from her temples to encompass her entire skull.

She was dimly aware of Charlotte showing the visitors out, of Maria's continued chatter, of the front door closing with a decisive thud. The sounds reached her as though filtered through thick wool, muffled and distant.

"Lizzy?" Charlotte's voice, concerned now. "Are you quite well? You look dreadfully pale."

Did she? Elizabeth lifted a hand to her face, finding her skin clammy beneath her fingertips. The room swayed around her, the furniture blurring at the edges.

Charlotte was saying something about dinner at Rosings, about the carriage that would be sent to collect them at five o'clock. The words reached Elizabeth as though travelling through water, distorted and slow.

"I cannot possibly attend," Elizabeth said. Or thought she said. Had the words emerged properly? Charlotte's face swam before her, concerned and questioning. "I have a headache. Quite severe."

That, at least, was true. The dull ache that had begun during tea with Anne had intensified into something demanding and insistent, a pulsing pain that seemed to originate behind her eyes and radiate outward in waves. Each heartbeat sent a fresh throb through her skull.

"You should lie down," Charlotte said, her voice seeming to come from very far away despite her proximity. "Let me help you upstairs."

Elizabeth wanted to protest that she could manage alone, that Charlotte need not trouble herself, but the words tangled in her mouth and would not come out properly. She found herself accepting Charlotte's offered arm, grateful for the support as they moved toward the stairs.

The staircase presented an unexpected challenge. The steps seemed to multiply before her eyes, each one requiring tremendous concentration to navigate. Her boots felt heavy, as though weighted with lead, and her legs responded sluggishly to her commands. Once, her foot caught on the edge of a riser, and only Charlotte's firm grip prevented her from stumbling.

"Perhaps we should call for the apothecary," Charlotte said, her concern evident in the tightening of her fingers on Elizabeth's arm.

"No." The word came out more forcefully than Elizabeth intended. "No apothecary. Simply a headache. I require only rest."

But even as she spoke, Elizabeth knew this was no ordinary headache. She had suffered headaches before; from eyestrain after reading too long in poor light, from the stuffiness of overheated rooms, from the tension of particularly trying social occasions. This felt different. This felt wrong in a way she could not quite articulate.

They reached the landing, and Elizabeth's bedchamber door seemed impossibly distant down the corridor. Each step required conscious effort, her body growing heavier and less responsive with each passing moment. The floor tilted beneath her feet, first one direction and then another, as though she stood on the deck of a ship in rough seas.

The afternoon light streaming through the corridor windows hurt her eyes, making them water. She squinted against the glare, but that only made the throbbing in her head worse. Nausea rose in her throat, bitter and acidic.

Finally, blessedly, they reached her room. Charlotte guided her to the bed, and Elizabeth sank onto it with a groan she could not suppress. The mattress seemed to undulate beneath her, rising and falling in slow, sickening waves.

"Let me help you with your boots," Charlotte said, already kneeling to unlace them.

Elizabeth tried to protest, to insist she could manage, but her tongue would not cooperate. She lay back against the pillows, closing her eyes against the spinning room. But darkness brought no relief; behind her closed lids, patterns swirled and shifted, making her feel as though she were falling through endless space.

She opened her eyes again, fixing her gaze on the ceiling beam as an anchor. The wood grain seemed to writhe and flow like water, the knots transforming into eyes that stared back at her. She blinked hard, and the illusion dissolved, but the sense of wrongness remained.

Charlotte's hands were cool against Elizabeth's ankles as she removed the boots, then drew a blanket over Elizabeth's legs. Her face hovered in Elizabeth's narrowing field of vision, creased with worry.

"I shall tell Lady Catherine that you are unwell, and give your apologies for missing dinner," Charlotte said. "She will understand, I am sure. And I shall have cook prepare some broth for you, something light that might sit well."

Elizabeth tried to nod, but the movement sent fresh agony lancing through her skull.

"Try to rest," Charlotte urged, already moving toward the door. "I shall check on you in a little while."

The door clicked shut, and Elizabeth was alone. The room settled into oppressive silence, broken only by her own laboured breathing and the relentless ticking of the small clock on the mantelpiece. Each tick seemed unnaturally loud, each tock reverberating through her aching head like a hammer blow.

She should rest. Charlotte was right, rest would help. Rest would clear whatever affliction had seized her so suddenly. She tried to relax, to let her muscles soften into the mattress, but tension gripped her entire body. Her hands clenched into fists at her sides, her jaw remained tight, her shoulders drawn up toward her ears.

The afternoon light through the window cast long shadows across the floor, shapes that seemed to creep and lengthen as she watched. The sprigged wallpaper appeared to shimmer, the small flowers detaching from their printed stems to float through the air like dying moths.

Elizabeth squeezed her eyes shut again, trying to block out the disturbing visions. This was wrong. This was all wrong. Headaches did not do this, did not steal one's coordination, did not make solid walls ripple like fabric, did not transform familiar objects into nightmare versions of themselves.

Fear crept through her confusion, cold and insidious. What was happening to her?

The tea. The thought surfaced through her fragmenting consciousness with sudden clarity. Something in the tea. Anne's careful pouring, her deliberate movements, the way she had watched Elizabeth drink...

But that was madness. Why would Anne de Bourgh poison her? They were barely acquainted. The notion was ridiculous, a product of her illness-addled mind seeking patterns where none existed.

Yet the conviction remained, settling into her bones with terrible certainty. Something had been in the tea.

Elizabeth tried to rise, some desperate instinct urging her to seek help, to tell someone of her suspicions. Her arms would not obey. She managed to lift her head from the pillow, but the effort cost her dearly. The room spun violently, and bile rose in her throat.

She collapsed back, gasping. Her limbs felt disconnected from her body, as though they belonged to someone else entirely. When she tried to move her right hand, her left twitched instead – or did neither move at all? She could no longer tell where her body ended and the bed began.

The throbbing in her head had become a roar, drowning out thought, drowning out everything. Pain and pressure, building and building until she thought her skull might split open to release it.

Darkness crept in at the edges of her vision, not the soft darkness of closing one's eyes but something absolute and hungry. It spread inward like spilled ink on parchment, consuming the room piece by piece. The window vanished. The wardrobe dissolved. The ceiling above her ceased to exist.

Elizabeth tried to fight it, clinging to consciousness with desperate determination. She had to stay awake. Had to tell someone. Had to...

But the darkness would not be denied. It wrapped around her like thick velvet, stifling and complete. Her last conscious thought was a fragmented confusion; why was this happening? Why did it hurt so terribly? Why had Anne de Bourgh's pale eyes glittered with such satisfaction?

Then even confusion faded, and there was only blackness, deep and absolute, pulling her down into depths from which she might never surface. Her body went slack against the mattress, her breathing slowing to shallow whispers.

In the stillness of the room, the clock continued its relentless ticking, marking the passage of time that Elizabeth Bennet could no longer perceive. Somewhere in the house below, Charlotte moved through her domestic duties, unaware that her guest lay unconscious upstairs, trapped in a darkness that was not natural sleep but something far more sinister.

The shadows lengthened across the floor, reaching toward the bed with grasping fingers. And Elizabeth, lost in the void, could not see them coming.

Chapter Two

PAIN ARRIVED FIRST, DULL and insistent, dragging her up from bottomless depths. Elizabeth became aware of her body in pieces – an ache in her skull, burning in her throat, heaviness in her limbs suggesting she'd been crushed beneath something immense. Consciousness flickered like a guttering candle, present one moment and gone the next.

Time passed, unmeasured. She floated between waking and sleeping, dimly aware of discomfort but unable to address it. Heat pressed against her skin, thick and suffocating, making each breath an effort. The air tasted stale, recycled through lungs that couldn't draw enough.

Eventually, Elizabeth forced her eyes open. The lids felt weighted, reluctant. Light filtered through in fragments, indistinct and blurred. She blinked, and the world remained stubbornly unfocused. Blinked again, and details began to emerge.

Heavy fabric surrounded her on three sides. Bed hangings, she realised slowly, her thoughts moving like chilled honey, slow and thick. Deep crimson velvet, pulled partially closed, creating a stifling cocoon.

This was not her room at the parsonage, the room she had been sharing with Maria these past weeks. The certainty settled over her with the weight of the bed coverings themselves, which pressed against her chest and legs with oppressive heaviness. Where was she?

Elizabeth tried to lift her hand to push the hangings aside. Her arm refused. The muscles trembled with effort but achieved nothing beyond a slight finger twitch. She concentrated harder, focusing her will on the simple act of raising her hand from the coverlet.

After an eternity, her hand rose perhaps two inches. The exertion left her gasping, heart pounding erratically, sweat beading on her forehead despite her immobility.

What had happened? Elizabeth's thoughts scattered and reformed, refusing to arrange themselves coherently. She remembered the parsonage, Charlotte helping her to bed, the terrible headache that had made the world tilt. And before that...

Anne de Bourgh. The tea. That strange, intent way Anne had watched her drink.

The memory surfaced through her confusion like something dredged from muddy water. She had suspected poison, hadn't she? In those final moments of consciousness, she'd been certain something was wrong with the tea. But surely that was impossible. Surely her illness-addled mind had conjured phantoms.

Yet here she lay, weak as a newborn kitten, in a room decidedly not her own.

Elizabeth let her gaze wander across what she could see without moving her head, which felt too heavy for her neck. The furnishings glimpsed between the bed hangings spoke of wealth and status far beyond the comfortable but modest parsonage. A massive wardrobe of dark wood dominated one wall, its surface gleaming. A dressing table stood near what appeared to be a window, though heavy curtains blocked most of the light. An ornate mirror in a gilded frame reflected back the crimson hangings.

The heat bordered on unbearable. Elizabeth could see a fireplace across the chamber, flames leaping high, sending waves of warmth that made the stale air even more oppressive. Why would anyone maintain such a fire on a warm spring day?

Her throat burned with thirst. She tried to swallow and discovered her mouth parched, tongue thick and uncooperative. Each breath through her dry throat felt like inhaling sand.

Everything felt wrong, foreign, deeply uncomfortable.

How long had she been unconscious? Hours? Days? The quality of light seeping around the heavy curtains suggested daytime, but whether morning or afternoon remained unclear. Her last clear memory was lying down in her room at the parsonage in late afternoon. Had she slept through the night? Multiple nights?

She needed to see more, to understand where she was and why she'd been brought here. With painstaking effort, she attempted to push herself upright. Her arms shook, muscles screaming protest. She managed to lift her shoulders perhaps three inches before her strength gave out and she collapsed back, gasping.

The exertion left her trembling, vision greying at the edges. For a terrifying moment she thought she might lose consciousness again, slip back into that absolute darkness. But slowly her vision cleared and her breathing steadied, though it remained laboured in the thick, hot air.

Someone must have moved her here while unconscious. But who? And where was here? The grandeur suggested a great house, and Elizabeth knew of only one such establishment near Hunsford.

Rosings Park.

The realisation deepened her confusion rather than clarifying it. Why would she have been brought to Lady Catherine's estate? If she'd taken seriously ill at the parsonage, surely the sensible course would have been to keep her there in familiar surroundings, where Charlotte could tend her. Or if her condition was severe enough, to send for a physician who could attend her at the parsonage itself.

Unless her illness had been so alarming that Lady Catherine insisted on her removal to Rosings for better care? But that made little sense. Lady Catherine had shown no particular warmth toward Elizabeth, had indeed made clear her view that Elizabeth was unsuitably connected and beneath her notice. Why would she concern herself with Elizabeth's wellbeing? Perhaps Colonel Fitzwilliam or Mr. Darcy had insisted... but if she'd been so dreadfully ill, why was she apparently now alone, without a maid to watch over her? Rosings hardly lacked staff.

The questions circled in Elizabeth's mind without resolution. Her thoughts felt sluggish, difficult to hold, slipping away like water through cupped hands. The heat pressed down, making concentration nearly impossible. She needed air, coolness, water for her parched throat.

She tried to call out, to summon whoever might be attending her, but her voice emerged as barely more than a rasp, a whisper that wouldn't carry beyond the bed hangings, certainly not beyond the door. Her throat ached with the effort, burning as though scraped raw.

Elizabeth let her eyes fall closed, conserving what little strength remained. Perhaps if she rested a few moments longer, she might gather enough energy to make herself heard, or better yet, to rise from this suffocating bed and seek help herself.

But exhaustion pulled at her, threatening to drag her back under. She fought it, clinging to consciousness with desperate determination. She wouldn't slip back into that darkness, wouldn't surrender to the weakness that had claimed her.

The clock on the mantelpiece, barely audible over the crackling fire, ticked away the seconds with maddening regularity. Each tick marked time passing, opportunities lost, questions unanswered.

Elizabeth forced her eyes open once more, staring at the unfamiliar ceiling, and willed her body to obey. She *would* rise from this bed. She would discover where she was and how she came to be here.

Elizabeth braced her palms against the mattress and pushed. Her arms trembled violently, the muscles burning with effort that should have been trivial but felt monumental. She managed to lift her torso perhaps six inches before having to pause, gasping, vision swimming.

She wouldn't give up. The thought anchored her, gave her something to focus on beyond the physical distress. Whatever had happened, whoever had moved her to this stifling chamber, she wouldn't simply lie here helpless waiting for answers.

Elizabeth pushed again, gritting her teeth against the weakness. This time she managed to raise herself higher, propping herself on one elbow while the other arm shook with strain. The heavy bed coverings tangled around her legs, and she had to pause once more, breathing hard, before attempting to kick them aside.

The simple act of freeing her legs took far longer than it should have. Her feet moved sluggishly, as though encased in mud, and the coverlet's weight seemed impossible to shift. By the time she finally worked herself free, sweat poured down her temples and her heart hammered so violently she feared it might burst.

But she was sitting upright now, perched on the mattress edge, the bed hangings pushed aside. The room swayed, the ornate furnishings sliding left and right in a sickening dance. Elizabeth closed her eyes, pressed one hand to her chest where her heart continued its frantic beating, and waited for the dizziness to subside.

When she opened her eyes, the room had steadied somewhat. The window across the chamber drew her gaze, promising fresh air and understanding. If she could reach it, could look out and see what lay beyond, perhaps she might make sense of her situation.

Elizabeth swung her legs over the bed's side, and her feet touched the floor. The polished wood felt cool against her bare feet, a relief after the oppressive heat of the bedclothes. She attempted to stand.

Her legs gave out immediately. Elizabeth collapsed forward, barely managing to catch herself on the carved bedpost. She clung there, arms wrapped around the post like a shipwreck survivor clinging to debris, while her legs threatened to buckle entirely.

This was wrong. This weakness went beyond anything illness should cause. Elizabeth had been sick before, had suffered through fevers and headaches, but never had she experienced such complete betrayal by her own body. Her legs felt like water, incapable of bearing her weight, while her arms possessed barely enough strength to keep her upright.

The room tilted again, and she pressed her cheek against the bedpost, closing her eyes and focusing on breathing. In and out, slow and steady, though each breath felt insufficient in the thick air. The fire roared, sending waves of heat that made her nightdress cling to her back with perspiration.

Gradually, her legs steadied beneath her. Not strong by any measure, but perhaps capable of supporting her if she moved carefully. Elizabeth loosened her death grip on the bedpost fractionally, testing her balance. Her knees shook but held.

The window seemed impossibly distant, though it couldn't have been more than fifteen feet away. Between her and that goal lay a vast expanse of polished floor, dotted with items of furniture that might serve as waypoints if she could reach them.

Elizabeth took a step, then another. Her feet dragged across the wood, unable to lift properly, making a soft shuffling sound. She had to concentrate on each movement, had to will each leg to move in turn, as though learning to walk anew.

The dressing table stood perhaps six feet away. She focused on it, on the promise of support its solid structure offered, and shuffled forward. Three steps. Four. Her vision greyed at the edges, and she had to stop, swaying, one hand stretched out grasping at empty air.

The greyness receded slowly. Elizabeth moved forward again, and her outstretched fingers finally found the table's edge. She grasped it with both hands, leaning heavily, sending several bottles and jars sliding across the polished wood with soft clicks.

She stood there, bent over the table, breathing hard and trembling. The window was closer now, perhaps eight feet distant, but those eight feet might as well have been eight miles for all the strength she had remaining.

But there was a chair near the window, a delicate thing with curved gilt legs and embroidered cushions. If she could reach that, she could rest before attempting the final push to the window itself.

Elizabeth released the dressing table with one hand, keeping the other braced for support, and reached toward the chair. Too far. She would have to cross the gap between them without support, trusting her legs to hold her for those few critical steps.

She counted to three, gathering what remained of her will, and pushed off. Her legs moved beneath her, shuffling, dragging, but moving. Her vision swam, and she staggered sideways, off balance, her arms pinwheeling.

Her hip struck the chair, sending pain shooting through her side but providing the support she desperately needed. Elizabeth grabbed the chair back with both hands, her weight nearly overturning it before she managed to steady herself. She stood there, bent over the chair, gasping and shaking, soaked through with sweat.

But she was close now. So close. The window stood directly before her, its heavy curtains pulled nearly closed but allowing thin slices of light through the gaps. Beyond that window lay answers, or at least understanding of where she'd been brought.

Elizabeth straightened slowly, using the chair back for support, and reached for the window frame. Her fingers found the curtain's edge and pulled it aside, sending dust motes dancing in the sudden shaft of light. The brightness hurt her eyes, making them water, but she forced them to remain open.

The latch proved difficult to manage. Her fingers, weak and trembling, fumbled with the mechanism, unable to grip properly. She tried again, pressing her thumb against the lever while her fingers worked at the catch. Nothing. A third attempt, this time using both hands, putting her full concentration into the simple act of opening a window.

Finally, the latch gave way, and Elizabeth nearly sobbed with relief. She pushed at the casement, and it swung outward on well-oiled hinges, letting in a rush of cool spring air that felt like salvation.

Elizabeth breathed deeply, letting the fresh air fill her lungs, clearing away some of the oppressive heat. The breeze touched her sweat-dampened skin, cooling it, bringing with it the scents of growing things and damp earth. She could have wept at the simple pleasure of it.

When she could breathe without gasping, when the fresh air had cleared some of the fog from her thoughts, Elizabeth looked down at the grounds below.

Manicured lawns stretched in precise geometric patterns, edged by carefully trimmed hedges. Gravel paths wound between cultivated flower beds where early spring blooms nodded in the breeze. In the distance, she could see the grove of ancient oaks she'd walked through several times.

This was unmistakably Rosings Park. She was at Lady Catherine's estate, in what looked to be a guest room of some consequence given the chamber's grandeur.

Elizabeth's confusion deepened into something approaching alarm. *Why* had she been brought here? The parsonage was comfortable, adequate for caring for someone taken ill. Charlotte would have been perfectly capable of nursing her, and Mr. Collins, for all his ridiculousness, would certainly have sent for a physician if needed.

She tried to recall more details from her illness. The headache, the dizziness, Charlotte helping her upstairs. And before that, the tea with Anne and Mrs. Jenkinson. Anne's strange, intense attention. The way Anne had poured her tea and watched her drink it with that almost eager look.

The suspicion she'd had in those final conscious moments returned with renewed force. But if Anne had poisoned her, surely bringing Elizabeth to Rosings made no sense. Why bring her victim to her own home, where her actions might be discovered?

The fresh air continued to revive her somewhat, though her legs still trembled with the effort of standing. Elizabeth gripped the window frame with both hands, staring down at the familiar grounds, trying to piece together a sequence of events that made sense.

How long had she been unconscious? It must have been at least overnight, possibly longer. The sun's angle suggested mid-morning, but which day? The day after she'd taken ill? Or longer?

She needed to find someone, needed to ask questions and receive answers. But she could barely stand, could hardly make it across a room without collapsing. The thought of attempting to reach the door, of navigating hallways in search of help, seemed impossible.

Elizabeth looked down at her hands gripping the window frame and froze. Something was wrong. Very wrong.

The hands on the window frame were not her own.

The thought arrived with peculiar detachment, observation without comprehension, as though her mind refused to process what her eyes showed her. These hands were too thin, the fingers too delicate, the knuckles too prominent beneath translucent skin. Elizabeth's hands were not beautiful, but they were strong, capable, with short practical nails. These hands looked as though they might snap like twigs.

She lifted one hand from the frame, holding it before her face, turning it slowly. The movement felt foreign, the hand responding to her commands but seeming disconnected from her body. The nails were longer than she kept hers, shaped and buffed to a shine she never bothered with.

Elizabeth told herself it was the illness. The lingering effects were distorting her perception, making familiar things appear strange. Or perhaps the weakness had affected her vision, causing some distortion that made her own hands look unfamiliar.

But even as she formed these rational explanations, some deeper part of her recognised them as lies. Her hands looked wrong because they were wrong. Because they were not hers.

The thought was absurd. Impossible. Hands could not simply change, could not transform into someone else's while one lay unconscious. Yet there they were, undeniably different, undeniably strange, moving when she willed them to move but belonging to someone else.

The mirror. Elizabeth's gaze jerked to the large ornate mirror across the room, the one she'd noticed earlier in her survey of the chamber. Its gilded frame gleamed in the light from the window, but the angle was wrong from where she stood; only the crimson bed hangings showed in the reflection.

She needed to see. Needed to know. Though every instinct screamed at her to look away, to return to bed and dismiss this strangeness as a fever-dream, Elizabeth released the window frame and turned toward the mirror.

Her legs nearly buckled immediately. She had to grab the window frame again, steadying herself, before attempting the journey. The mirror stood perhaps ten feet away, across that expanse of polished floor that had already proven so difficult to traverse. But she had to reach it. Had to see.

Elizabeth pushed off from the window, her legs shaking violently. She made it two steps before having to grab the chair back for support. Three more shuffling steps brought her to the dressing table, where she leaned heavily, gasping. The mirror was closer now, only a few feet distant, though the angle was still wrong for her to see her reflection.

She circled the dressing table, one hand trailing along its edge for support, and straightened as much as her weakened body would allow. The mirror stood directly before her now, its surface catching the light from the window behind her.

The face looking back at her was not her own.

Elizabeth stared at the reflection, her mind unable to reconcile what her eyes showed her. The face in the mirror was pale, almost bloodless, with hollow cheeks and prominent cheekbones. The hair, instead of Elizabeth's long dark curls, was cropped short, barely brushing the collar, giving the face a severe, almost masculine cast.

But it was the eyes that made recognition impossible to deny. Pale eyes, washed out and colourless, set in dark hollows that spoke of chronic illness. Anne de Bourgh's eyes. Anne de Bourgh's face.

Elizabeth's hand flew to her throat, and the reflection mimicked the movement perfectly, that strange thin hand rising to touch that pale, unfamiliar neck. She watched the reflection move when she moved, saw those colourless eyes widen as her own eyes widened, saw those bloodless lips part as her own lips parted in shock.

This could not be real. Could not be possible. She was dreaming still, trapped in some fever-nightmare brought on by illness.

In a moment she would wake in her bed at the parsonage, in her own body, and this horror would dissolve like morning mist.

But the reflection remained steady, undeniable. When Elizabeth raised her other hand, the reflection raised its hand. When she tilted her head, the reflection tilted its head. Every movement perfectly synchronised, proving beyond doubt that the face in the mirror, Anne de Bourgh's face, belonged to her.

Elizabeth touched her cheek, feeling the bone too close beneath the skin, feeling the unfamiliar contours of someone else's face. Her fingers trembled as they traced the sharp line of the jaw, the short hair that felt strange and wrong against her fingertips. The reflection showed Anne de Bourgh touching her face with those same fragile-looking hands, but Elizabeth felt every sensation, knew with terrible certainty that the hand was hers, that the face was hers, that somehow, impossibly, this was her.

She couldn't breathe. The air wouldn't come, wouldn't fill her lungs no matter how hard she tried to draw it in. Her chest constricted, tight and painful, while her heart hammered against her ribs with enough force to hurt.

This was not real. This *could not* be real.

But the mirror showed her the truth. Elizabeth backed away from it, her legs unsteady, her hands stretched out before her as though to ward off what she'd seen. Those thin, pale hands. Anne's hands. Her hands.

Her retreat brought her up against the bed, and her legs finally gave way entirely. She collapsed onto the mattress, sitting hard, her breath coming in short, sharp gasps that couldn't provide enough air. She looked down at her body, truly looked at it for the first time.

The nightdress she wore was not hers. Thin fine muslin with lace at the collar and cuffs, the sort of garment Anne favoured, expensive and impractical. The body beneath it was wrong, all wrong. Too thin, the collarbones protruding sharply above the neckline. Arms like sticks emerging from the short sleeves.

This was Anne de Bourgh's body. Anne de Bourgh's face. Anne de Bourgh's hands and arms and legs.

But Elizabeth's mind inhabited it. Elizabeth's consciousness looked out through those pale eyes, felt sensations through that unfamiliar skin, breathed with those weak lungs.

The impossibility of it crashed over her like a wave, drowning thought, drowning reason. She could not be Anne de Bourgh. She was Elizabeth Bennet. Elizabeth Bennet of Longbourn, second daughter of Mr. Bennet, sister to Jane and Mary and Kitty and Lydia. She had her own face, her own hands, her own body.

But the mirror had shown her the truth, and her own hands – Anne's hands, her hands – confirmed it. She was trapped in Anne de Bourgh's body. Somehow, impossibly, horrifyingly, she was Anne de Bourgh.

The tea. The memory surfaced through her panic. Anne's careful pouring, her strange intensity, her satisfied smile when Elizabeth drank. Anne had done this. Somehow, Anne had done this. Magic, witchcraft, some impossible art that shouldn't exist, couldn't exist. But it had happened. It was real.

Elizabeth tried to stand, to run, to escape this nightmare through sheer force of will. But her legs wouldn't obey, wouldn't bear her weight. She remained seated on the bed's edge, staring at hands that were not hers, trapped in a body that was not hers, unable to process the magnitude of what had been done to her.

Where was her body? The thought arrived with fresh horror. If she was in Anne's body, then where was Anne? Had the spell, or potion, or whatever impossible thing Anne had used, left Anne in Elizabeth's body?

The implications unfurled in Elizabeth's mind like poisonous flowers. Anne in her body. Anne with her face, her voice, her health and strength. Anne pretending to be Elizabeth Bennet, living Elizabeth's life.

The scream built in her chest, a pressure that had to be released or she would shatter. It climbed her throat, gathered force, and finally burst free. The sound that emerged was raw and primal, conveying horror and disbelief and rage and terror all together. It echoed off the high ceiling, bounced from the walls, filled the vast chamber with the sound of a soul in torment.

Elizabeth screamed until her throat – Anne's throat, her throat – gave out, until the sound dissolved into ragged gasping. She pressed those unfamiliar hands to that unfamiliar face and felt tears, hot and wet, spilling from eyes that were the wrong colour.

Somewhere in the house, footsteps sounded, rapid and approaching. Voices called out, alarmed and questioning. But Elizabeth barely heard them. She remained huddled on the bed's edge, staring at her hands through blurred vision, trying to comprehend the incomprehensible.

The door burst open, but Elizabeth did not look up. She couldn't bear to see whatever new horror awaited her. She could only sit and stare and try to breathe through the crushing weight of impossible truth.

Chapter Three

ANNE DE BOURGH SAT across from Charlotte Collins, fingers wrapped around a teacup that felt startlingly light, unable to keep the delighted smile from her face. Everything felt light. Everything felt possible. After years of weakness and breathlessness, she inhabited a body that hummed with vitality, that moved without protest, that simply *worked*.

Anne set down her cup and reached for another piece of toast. Her second. She had already eaten one, along with a coddled egg and two rashers of bacon, and her stomach welcomed more rather than rebelling. The novelty made her want to laugh. For years, Mrs. Jenkinson had coaxed her to eat, presenting delicate morsels on fine china, and Anne had rarely managed more than two bites before nausea overwhelmed her. Now she could eat. Wanted to eat.

She spread butter across the warm bread, watching it melt. Her hand moved smoothly, without tremor, without the weakness that had made even holding a butter knife frustrating. She added a generous spoonful of blackberry jam and bit into the toast with genuine appetite.

The taste exploded across her tongue, rich and satisfying. Her body did not revolt. Her stomach did not cramp. She simply ate, like any normal person, and it was glorious.

Anne chewed slowly, savouring each bite, while Charlotte made polite conversation about the weather and the previous evening's dinner at Rosings. Charlotte had clearly been concerned about "Elizabeth's" sudden illness, had fussed over her when she returned to consciousness late last night. Anne had played her part well. Confused, grateful, claiming the headache had passed but she needed sleep. Charlotte had required little convincing.

Her hand drifted upward to touch the hair that now framed her face. Elizabeth's hair. The curls felt impossibly thick beneath her fingertips, glossy and heavy, so different from the thin strands that had hung limp against her own skull. Anne wound one curl around her finger, feeling its weight, its resilience. She had spent years staring at hair that grew more sparse with each passing month, another visible marker of her body's failure. But this hair was magnificent, dark and lustrous.

"I am glad to see your appetite has returned," Charlotte observed. "You gave us quite a fright yesterday. I nearly sent for the apothecary, but you seemed to improve once you had rested."

"I feel quite recovered," Anne assured her. Elizabeth's body did feel recovered. Better than Anne's body had felt in as long as she could remember. "I cannot account for what came over me, but it has passed entirely."

Charlotte poured more tea, the domestic ritual soothing. Anne watched her hostess, managing her household with quiet efficiency. A country clergyman's wife, settled and content. So different from what Anne had endured, trapped at Rosings under her mother's oppressive scrutiny, with only Mrs. Jenkinson for company.

"Do you think you shall take your usual walk this morning?" Charlotte asked. "The weather is fine, and I know how you value your daily exercise. Though perhaps you should rest today."

The question caught Anne unprepared. Walk? Alone? The idea was so foreign that her first instinct was to refuse. She had not walked anywhere alone... ever. Mrs. Jenkinson accompanied her everywhere, hovering like an anxious shadow, ready to catch her if she stumbled. Even the short walks Anne occasionally managed in Rosings' gardens left her breathless and weak.

"I am not certain I should..." Anne began.

Then she stopped herself. She was not that Anne anymore. She was Elizabeth Bennet, who walked miles daily, who thought nothing of tramping across fields, whose idea of a pleasant morning included vigorous exercise. Elizabeth, who had walked three miles through muddy fields to reach Netherfield when her sister fell ill, arriving with petticoats six inches deep in mud and cheeks glowing with health, a picture that had struck Fitzwilliam Darcy strongly enough that he had a smile on his face when he recounted the story to Colonel Fitzwilliam one afternoon in Rosings' parlour, both of them oblivious to Anne sitting in the corner listening to their every word.

Anne could walk now. Could go where she pleased, when she pleased, without Mrs. Jenkinson's constant presence, without her mother's disapproving commentary, without needing to rest every few yards. She could walk alone, truly alone, for the first time in her life.

The realisation sent a thrill through her.

"That is, I am not certain I should deny myself the pleasure," Anne corrected smoothly, smiling at Charlotte. "You are right, the weather is too fine to waste indoors. A walk will be delightful."

Charlotte's expression shifted slightly, a small crease appearing between her brows. The look lasted only a moment before politeness smoothed it away, but Anne had seen it. Confusion, perhaps. Or puzzlement at "Elizabeth's" unusual enthusiasm for what had been a daily routine.

Anne cursed herself. She must be more careful. Elizabeth would not speak of morning walks with such eager anticipation. For Elizabeth, they were habit, pleasant but unremarkable. Only someone denied such freedom would respond with barely contained excitement.

"I mean, the fresh air will do me good," Anne amended. "Clear away the cobwebs from yesterday's illness."

"Of course," Charlotte agreed, though something in her gaze remained uncertain. "I only hope you will not overtax yourself. Perhaps a shorter walk today?"

"Perhaps," Anne said noncommittally. She would walk as far as she pleased. Let Elizabeth's friends believe her habits had changed. People changed. If Elizabeth Bennet became more enthusiastic about exercise, who would seriously question it?

Anne drained her tea and set down the cup. Through the window, she could see the lane leading from the parsonage toward Rosings and the surrounding countryside. Trees lined the way, their branches heavy with spring leaves, the morning sun dappling the ground with light and shadow. She could walk there. Could walk anywhere. The world opened before her, vast and accessible in a way it had never been.

And somewhere in that world was Mr. Darcy, who loved Elizabeth Bennet. Who had loved her without declaring himself because Elizabeth had been too blind to recognise his regard. The silly chit. Anne had seen it clearly, had watched him track Elizabeth's movements, had noted how his expression softened when he looked at her. Pathetically obvious.

But Elizabeth was out of the way now, locked in Anne's dying body at Rosings. And Anne sat here preparing to walk in the spring sunshine, free at last to pursue the life she deserved. The life that should have been hers.

Anne rose from the table, feeling her legs steady beneath her. "I think I shall go and prepare for my walk," she said to Charlotte. "Thank you for breakfast."

Charlotte smiled, nodding, though that small crease of puzzlement remained. Anne would need to be more careful, would need to perfect her performance. But she had time. She had all the time in the world now.

She left the breakfast parlour and climbed the stairs to her borrowed room to fetch a bonnet, each step taken with joy at the ease of movement. Soon she would walk outside, alone and free. And soon after that, she would see Darcy again. Would smile at him with Elizabeth's pretty face. Would let him fall even more deeply in love with the woman he thought she was.

Everything Anne had ever wanted was finally within her grasp.

Anne stepped through the parsonage door into the spring morning. The air smelled of growing things, damp earth and new leaves. She breathed deeply, pulling fresh air into lungs that expanded fully, that did not labour and wheeze. Her chest rose and fell with easy rhythm.

She set off down the lane with purposeful strides, her boots striking the packed earth with satisfying firmness. No shuffling steps, no careful placement to avoid stumbling. She simply walked, feeling the play of muscles in her legs and back. Elizabeth's body moved with unconscious grace, carrying her forward effortlessly.

The lane stretched before her, bordered by hedgerows burst into spring glory. White hawthorn blossoms clustered thickly among the branches, their sweet scent drifting on the breeze. Patches of primroses dotted the verge, pale yellow faces turned toward the sun. Anne noticed them with new appreciation. She had seen such flowers from carriage windows and formal gardens, but had never walked among them like this, never been able to simply stop and examine them without Mrs. Jenkinson fussing.

She did not stop now. Stopping would waste the precious sensation of movement. Anne walked on, humming under her breath. Her skirts swished around her ankles with each step. She could feel the sun warm on her face, the breeze lifting the curls at her temples. The physical sensations flooded through her, almost overwhelming after years of numbness.

For so long, Anne's experience of her body had been defined by failures. Breathlessness with the slightest exertion. Weakness that left her faint and trembling after climbing a single flight of stairs. Nausea that made eating a trial. Fatigue that made even sitting upright exhausting. She had been trapped in a prison of failing flesh, watching the world from behind windows, unable to participate.

But this body functioned beautifully. Anne's footsteps quickened, testing her new strength. Her legs responded eagerly, carrying her faster without protest. Her breathing remained steady.

She could run if she wanted. Could dance all night. Could ride or climb or do any of a thousand things that had been denied to her.

The lane curved ahead, following the edge of a small wood, and Anne followed without concern for distance or time. No one would worry if she stayed out for hours. Elizabeth walked every day, sometimes covering several miles. Anne could wander as far as she pleased, and when she returned, no one would fuss. She would simply be Elizabeth Bennet, healthy and strong, returning from a pleasant ramble.

Anne was so absorbed in the joy of movement that she almost missed the figure approaching. But the man's height made him difficult to overlook, and when Anne lifted her gaze, she recognised Darcy immediately.

He walked with his characteristic purposeful stride, his dark coat fitting perfectly across his broad shoulders, his boots polished to a gleam. Even from here, Anne could identify him by his bearing alone. Darcy moved through the world with the confidence of a man who had never doubted his place in it.

Anne's lips curved in a smile. Perfect. She had hoped to encounter him, but not quite so soon.

Darcy had apparently spotted her as well. His pace quickened. As he drew closer, Anne could see his expression transforming, the usual reserve giving way to something warmer. His eyes, which typically maintained a careful blankness in company, lit with unmistakable pleasure.

How obvious he was. Anne had observed him watching Elizabeth with barely concealed fascination. Her mother had complained constantly about his inattention, about his rudeness in paying more court to the parson's guest than to his intended cousin. Lady Catherine had been too blind to see what Anne had recognised immediately. Darcy was in love with Elizabeth Bennet.

And Elizabeth, the silly chit, had been too stubborn or proud or blind to notice. Anne had seen them together in the drawing room at Rosings, had watched Darcy attempt conversation while Elizabeth responded with cool civility bordering on rudeness. The fool. Fitzwilliam Darcy, master of Pemberley, one of the richest men in England, handsome and accomplished and utterly besotted, and Elizabeth had treated him with indifference.

Well. Elizabeth was gone now, trapped in Anne's dying body, paying the price for her stupidity. And Anne stood here in Elizabeth's healthy body, watching Darcy approach with that expression he had never, would never, direct at the real Anne de Bourgh.

"Miss Bennet!" Darcy called as he came within speaking distance. He removed his hat, his dark hair slightly dishevelled by the breeze. "I had not expected to find you out walking this morning. How are you feeling?"

Anne arranged her features into pleased surprise. "Mr. Darcy! What brings you to this part of Hunsford so early?"

"I came to inquire after your health," he said, closing the distance between them. His eyes searched her face, warm concern evident. "Mrs. Collins mentioned at dinner last evening that you had taken ill quite suddenly. We were all concerned when you did not join us at Rosings. I..." He paused. "I called at the parsonage last night to see how you did, but the maid said you had fallen asleep."

"Did you?" Anne infused the words with warmth, with gratitude. Elizabeth would be grateful, would she not? Though perhaps she would also tease him slightly. Anne was not quite certain how to strike that balance yet. Better to err on the side of warmth. "How kind of you. I am sorry to have caused such concern. It was merely a headache, though a severe one. But as you see, I am quite recovered now."

She spread her arms slightly, demonstrating her renewed health, and smiled up at him. Darcy's expression softened further, relief evident in the easing of tension around his eyes.

"I am very glad to hear it," he said quietly. "You gave us all quite a fright. Colonel Fitzwilliam was concerned as well, and even my aunt, though she expressed it by complaining that you should have had more sense than to overtire yourself with walking."

Anne laughed easily. "Lady Catherine is ever solicitous. But truly, I am perfectly well. The fresh air and sunshine are precisely what I needed." She glanced around at the hedgerows, the flowering hawthorn, the bright morning light. "It is far too beautiful a day to remain indoors, particularly after being confined to bed yesterday."

Darcy's gaze followed hers, taking in the lane and spring blossoms, but Anne noticed his attention returned quickly to her face. He watched her with an intensity that might have been uncomfortable if Anne had not been so pleased by it. This was what she had wanted. This attention, this regard, this devotion that Elizabeth had scorned.

"May I walk with you?" Darcy asked. "If you are not opposed to company?"

Anne pretended to consider, though her heart leapt. "I should be glad of your company, Mr. Darcy. Perhaps you may point out some features on this walk to me."

It was exactly the wrong thing to say. Anne realised it the moment the words left her mouth. Elizabeth had been walking these lanes for weeks. She would not need Darcy to point out features. But Darcy seemed not to notice, or perhaps attributed it to her recent illness.

"Then I am honoured," he said simply, offering his arm.

Anne took his arm without hesitation, her fingers curling around the fine wool of his coat sleeve. The gesture was automatic, the product of years observing social niceties. Only after her hand settled in the crook of his elbow did Anne realise that Elizabeth might not have accepted so readily, might have demurred or made some teasing comment about propriety.

But it was too late to withdraw, and besides, Darcy looked so pleased by her acceptance. His arm was solid beneath her hand, strong and steady. When had she last touched anyone like this, in a gesture of companionship rather than necessity? Mrs. Jenkinson's hands guiding her, supporting her, were entirely different. This was connection between equals, the sort of easy physical intimacy Anne had watched others share while she remained always apart, always untouchable.

They began walking, and Anne adjusted her pace to match his longer stride. Elizabeth's body managed it easily, her legs strong enough to keep up without struggle. The simple pleasure of walking beside someone, of matching their rhythm, of moving together through the spring morning, was so novel that Anne had to suppress a smile.

"The fresh air is all I truly needed," she told him warmly, glancing up at his face. Even in her new body, taller than her old one, Anne had to look up to meet Darcy's eyes. He was remarkably tall, and standing this close, she could see details she had never noticed from across drawing rooms. A small scar near his left temple, nearly invisible. The way his dark hair curled slightly at the temples despite being carefully brushed. The exact shade of his eyes, which were not simply brown but contained flecks of amber and green when the light caught them.

She smiled at him, putting warmth into the expression. "And your company, of course. It is a pleasure to have someone to walk with."

Darcy's expression flickered with something Anne could not quite identify. Surprise, certainly. Pleasure, definitely. But also confusion, a slight furrowing of his brow that suggested he found something unexpected in her response. He recovered quickly, his features smoothing, but Anne had seen the reaction.

"The pleasure is mine, Miss Bennet," he said, his voice carrying that careful formality he always employed.

They walked on in silence for a few moments, the only sounds their footsteps and birdsong in the hedgerows. Anne should say something, should fill the silence with the sort of lively conversation Elizabeth would provide. But what would Elizabeth say? Anne knew the girl's circumstances, her family, her situation. She had gathered information carefully during Elizabeth's visits to Rosings, and by asking strategic questions of Charlotte Collins. But knowing facts was different from understanding how Elizabeth thought, how she spoke, what topics she favoured.

The silly chit. How could Elizabeth Bennet, with her adequate face and decent figure and quick wit, have failed to recognise what Darcy felt for her? He could barely take his eyes from her when they were in the same room. He sought her out at every opportunity, inventing excuses to walk where she walked, to sit near her. He had even endured Lady Catherine's tedious evening gatherings without complaint simply because Elizabeth would be present.

Anne had watched it all from her position by the fireplace, wrapped in shawls despite the warmth, largely ignored by everyone except Mrs. Jenkinson. She had observed Darcy's careful attention to Elizabeth's every word, the way he leaned toward her when she spoke, as though afraid of missing a syllable. She had seen him struggle to engage Elizabeth in conversation, offering opinions he thought might interest her, asking questions designed to draw her out.

And Elizabeth had responded with cool civility at best, with barely concealed disdain at worst. Anne had listened to her speak to Colonel Fitzwilliam about Darcy, her tone making clear she found him proud and disagreeable. The fool. To have Darcy's regard and treat it as though it were an annoyance rather than the prize it was.

Well. Elizabeth would have a long time to regret her blindness. She would lie in Anne's bed at Rosings, growing weaker as Anne's body continued its inevitable decline, and she would know that everything she had scorned was now Anne's to claim.

She had Elizabeth's life now. Elizabeth's body and health and freedom. And she intended to keep them, along with everything else that should have been hers.

Including Fitzwilliam Darcy's heart.

Chapter Four

THE DOOR BURST OPEN before Elizabeth's screams had fully died away. Mrs. Jenkinson stood in the doorway, her grey dress severe against the dim corridor behind her, her expression fixed in lines of professional concern that didn't quite reach her eyes. She stepped inside and closed the door behind her with a soft but decisive click, and turned the key. The sound of the lock clicking shut seemed unnaturally loud, and Elizabeth realised with creeping dread that the companion had shut them in together, had deliberately isolated them from anyone who might hear.

Elizabeth tried to push herself upright, her hands scrabbling against the heavy coverlet for purchase. The simple act of sitting required coordination her borrowed body refused to provide. Her arms shook violently, her elbows threatening to buckle beneath her weight. She managed to prop herself on one trembling arm, her other hand clutching the bed frame as though it were the only solid thing in a tilting world.

Mrs. Jenkinson crossed the room with swift steps, her hands already reaching out in the gesture of someone accustomed to managing an invalid. Her face remained composed, arranged in an expression of mild concern that might have been convincing if Elizabeth had not seen the calculation in her eyes as she assessed the situation.

"You're overtaxing yourself," Mrs. Jenkinson said, her voice carrying the brisk authority of long habit. She reached Elizabeth's side and placed one hand firmly on her shoulder, the other moving to adjust the pillows behind her. "You need to rest. Back to bed, now."

The casual assumption in those words, the way Mrs. Jenkinson spoke to her as though she were simply a recalcitrant patient, sent a spike of fury through Elizabeth's confusion. She tried to pull away from the woman's touch, but her muscles responded sluggishly, achieving only a weak twitch.

"What..." Elizabeth's voice emerged as a rasp, her throat still raw from screaming. She swallowed hard, forcing the words past the constriction. "How... who..."

The sentences fragmented before she could complete them, her thoughts moving faster than her tongue could follow. Too many questions crowded her mind at once. *What had Anne done? How had this impossible thing happened? Who could help her?* The words tangled together, emerging as incoherent stammering.

Mrs. Jenkinson's hand on her shoulder pressed down with surprising strength, urging her back toward the pillows. "You're confused. It's to be expected after such exertion, visiting the parsonage yesterday. You've overtired yourself, and now you're suffering the consequences. Let me help you lie down properly."

The patronising tone ignited something fierce in Elizabeth's chest. She had to make this woman understand. Had to make someone understand. She could not simply be tucked back into bed and dismissed as an invalid having a spell.

Elizabeth planted her feet against the mattress and pushed, using every scrap of strength she possessed to resist Mrs. Jenkinson's pressure. Her legs trembled with the effort, threatening to give way entirely, but she managed to remain partially upright. She lifted her head, forcing herself to meet the companion's gaze directly despite the way the room swayed around her.

"I'm not Anne!" The words burst from her with desperate force, her voice stronger now though it cracked on the final syllable. "I'm not Anne de Bourgh!"

She expected shock. Expected denial, or confusion, or some attempt to soothe what would appear to be delusions. Instead, Mrs. Jenkinson went very still. Her hand remained on Elizabeth's shoulder, but the pressure ceased. Her expression shifted subtly, the professional concern sliding away to reveal something harder and more assessing beneath.

Mrs. Jenkinson studied Elizabeth's face for a long moment. Elizabeth could see the thoughts turning behind that composed exterior, could see the companion calculating and concluding. The silence stretched between them, broken only by Elizabeth's laboured breathing and the crackling of the unnecessary fire.

Then Mrs. Jenkinson sighed. It was a sound of resignation rather than surprise, weary acceptance of an anticipated complication. She released Elizabeth's shoulder and stepped back slightly, her arms folding across her chest in a gesture that was almost defensive.

"Elizabeth Bennet, I presume?" Mrs. Jenkinson's voice remained steady, matter-of-fact, as though she were confirming a tea order rather than acknowledging an impossible violation of nature. "I suspected she might do something like this."

The words struck Elizabeth like a physical blow. The room seemed to tilt more violently, though whether from her body's weakness or the shock of that casual confirmation, she could not tell. Her grip on the bed frame tightened until her knuckles showed white beneath the translucent skin.

"You knew." Elizabeth's voice emerged hollow, scraped raw by more than just her earlier screaming. "You knew what she planned to do."

It was not a question. Mrs. Jenkinson's lack of surprise, her immediate recognition of the situation, her expression of weary resignation, all pointed to prior knowledge. The companion had known Anne intended to steal Elizabeth's body, and she had done nothing to prevent it. Had perhaps helped facilitate it.

Mrs. Jenkinson only shrugged. "I had suspicions. Miss Anne has been studying her father's grimoire for years, obsessing over certain passages. I've cared for her long enough to recognise when she's planning something." She paused, her gaze drifting toward the window. "But I didn't know for certain until now. Not until you confirmed it."

Elizabeth's mind reeled, trying to process the implications. Anne had been planning this for years. Had been studying, preparing, waiting for the right opportunity and the right victim. And Mrs. Jenkinson had watched it all happening, had seen the signs, and had remained silent.

"Why?" The single word contained a universe of questions. Why had Mrs. Jenkinson allowed it? Why hadn't she warned

anyone? Why was she standing here now, speaking with such calm acceptance of an atrocity?

"Why?" Mrs. Jenkinson's lips curved in something that wasn't quite a smile. "Because Miss Anne is my charge. Has been since she was just a little girl. I've watched her suffer for more than fifteen years, watched her body fail a little more each day, watched her hope drain away until nothing remained but bitterness." She shook her head slowly. "I pitied her."

"Pity doesn't excuse this." Elizabeth's voice shook, not with weakness now but with fury. "She stole my *body*. Trapped me in this..." She gestured helplessly at herself, at Anne's frail form. "You can't believe pity justifies such wickedness."

Mrs. Jenkinson's expression hardened. "I don't require your moral instruction, Miss Bennet. You've had health and strength all your life. You've never known what it is to be trapped in a body that betrays you daily, to watch others move freely while you can barely manage stairs. Perhaps if you had, you might understand desperation."

"Desperation doesn't give her the right to steal my *life!*" Elizabeth tried to push herself more upright, but her arms gave out and she collapsed back against the pillows, gasping. The exertion cost her dearly, and she had to close her eyes against the spots dancing in her vision.

When she opened her eyes again, Mrs. Jenkinson had moved closer. The companion stood at the bedside, looking down at Elizabeth with an expression that mixed pity and something that might have been regret with cold pragmatism.

"What's done is done," Mrs. Jenkinson said quietly. "Raging against it will only exhaust you further, and that body can ill afford such exertion. You need to accept your situation and conserve your strength."

"Accept it?" Elizabeth stared at her in disbelief. "You expect me to simply *accept* that Anne has stolen my body, my life?"

"I expect you to be practical," Mrs. Jenkinson replied. "You're at Rosings, in Miss de Bourgh's body, under my care. No one will believe your claims. Lady Catherine herself would have you committed to an asylum if you started insisting you were Elizabeth Bennet. Your only option is to cooperate."

The words settled over Elizabeth like a suffocating blanket. Mrs. Jenkinson was right about one thing; no one would believe her. The truth was too impossible, too fantastical. Anyone she told would think her mad, would attribute her claims to illness or delusion. Anne had chosen her victim and her moment with careful calculation, ensuring Elizabeth would be trapped in a situation where she could not seek help without being dismissed as insane.

Elizabeth looked up at Mrs. Jenkinson, studying the companion's composed face, and felt the first stirrings of genuine terror. She was utterly alone, completely at the mercy of a woman who had already demonstrated her loyalty lay with Anne rather than with truth or justice. Whatever happened next, whatever Mrs. Jenkinson decided to do, Elizabeth had no power to resist.

Her body was too weak. Her position too impossible. Her isolation too complete.

She was trapped.

Mrs. Jenkinson seized the heavy coverlet and drew it up over her. The weight of the bedclothes settled across Elizabeth's body like a physical restraint, pinning her to the mattress. She tried to push the covers aside, but her hands moved sluggishly, achieving nothing beyond a weak flutter of fingers against the expensive fabric.

Mrs. Jenkinson tucked the edges of the blankets firmly beneath the mattress on either side, creating a neat cocoon that trapped Elizabeth's arms at her sides. The gesture was methodical, the sort of thing the companion had likely done thousands of times before, settling an invalid for rest. But the effect was profoundly different when the person being tucked in possessed full consciousness and fierce objection to the treatment.

Elizabeth felt reduced to helplessness not by choice but by the betrayal of this borrowed body. She could feel her heart hammering against her ribs, could feel sweat dampening her hairline despite the chill that had begun creeping through her limbs, but she could not summon the strength to free herself from something as simple as firmly tucked-in bedclothes. The humiliation of it burned almost as fiercely as her fear.

"Let me up." Elizabeth's voice emerged steady despite everything, carrying the authority she would have used with an obstinate servant at Longbourn. "I will not be restrained like this. I have done nothing to deserve such treatment."

Mrs. Jenkinson straightened, smoothing her grey skirts. "You've exhausted yourself. Rest is what you require now, not further agitation."

But Elizabeth's mind was racing too quickly for rest, piecing together fragments of information into a coherent whole. Anne had done this. Anne de Bourgh, whom everyone believed too weak and sickly to harm anyone, had learned magic from her dead father. Sir Lewis de Bourgh had been an eccentric, Elizabeth remembered hearing Lady Catherine mention once, saying dismissively that he had wasted time on peculiar studies. But those studies had clearly delved into something darker than mere eccentricity. He had learned witchcraft, had practiced it, and had taught it to his daughter.

"How did she do it?" Elizabeth asked, though she already suspected Mrs. Jenkinson would not answer. "What spell or potion could possibly achieve such a thing?"

Mrs. Jenkinson's expression remained carefully neutral. "I am not privy to the details of Miss Anne's studies. I only know what little I've gathered from caring for her all these years."

"Then tell me how to reverse it." Elizabeth fought to keep desperation from her voice, to maintain some semblance of dignity despite her position. "There must be a way to undo what she's done. If there's magic to swap bodies, there must be magic to swap them back."

For a long moment, Mrs. Jenkinson said nothing. She stood at the bedside, her hands folded at her waist, her expression unreadable. When she finally spoke, her voice carried a finality that sent ice through Elizabeth's veins.

"It cannot be reversed. What is done is done."

The words hung in the air between them, absolute and damning. Elizabeth studied Mrs. Jenkinson's face, searching for some sign of deception, some indication that the companion was lying to discourage her from attempting to reclaim her body. But the woman's features remained smooth, revealing nothing beyond calm certainty.

Was she lying? Elizabeth could not tell. Mrs. Jenkinson's years of service in this household had clearly taught her to school her expression, to present whatever face the situation required. She might be telling the truth. Or she might be protecting Anne's theft by convincing Elizabeth that resistance was futile.

"I don't believe you," Elizabeth said, though uncertainty gnawed at her confidence. "You're trying to make me give up hope. But I won't. I'll find a way to undo this, with or without your help."

Mrs. Jenkinson's lips compressed into a thin line. She turned away from the bed without responding, crossing to the dressing table where various bottles and vials stood in neat rows. Elizabeth watched her select one of the bottles, a dark glass container that looked almost black in the dim light. Mrs. Jenkinson removed the stopper with a soft pop and poured a measure of liquid into a small crystal glass.

"What is that?" Elizabeth demanded as Mrs. Jenkinson approached the bed with the glass in hand.

"Something to help you rest," Mrs. Jenkinson replied calmly. "You've had a severe shock, and your body cannot tolerate such strain. This will ease your distress."

"I don't want it." Elizabeth tried to edge away as much as the tight bedclothes allowed, which was not far at all. "I don't need your medicine. I need answers, I need help, I need my own body returned to me."

Mrs. Jenkinson set the glass on the bedside table and bent over Elizabeth, her hands moving to adjust the pillows behind her head. The gesture seemed helpful at first, arranging Elizabeth into a more upright position, until Elizabeth realised the companion was positioning her for easier access. Mrs. Jenkinson retrieved the glass and held it near Elizabeth's mouth.

"Drink this," she said, her voice brooking no argument.

"No." Elizabeth pressed her lips together firmly, turning her head away from the proffered glass. "I will not drink something when I don't know what it contains. You could be poisoning me."

"If I wished to poison you, I could do so far more easily than this." Mrs. Jenkinson's tone remained infuriatingly patient. "This is merely a sedative, something to calm your nerves and help you sleep. Miss Anne takes it regularly. The dose is already measured; you need only drink it."

But Elizabeth had no intention of being drugged into compliance. Whatever was in that glass, whether sedative or something worse, it would render her even more helpless than she already was. She needed to remain conscious, needed to think clearly, needed to find some way out of this nightmare. She kept her face turned away, her lips sealed against the glass's approach.

Mrs. Jenkinson sighed, a sound of weary resignation. "I had hoped you would be sensible about this."

Before Elizabeth could react, Mrs. Jenkinson's free hand shot out and pinched her nose closed, blocking her airway completely. Elizabeth's eyes widened in shock. She tried to twist away, but the companion's grip was iron firm, and Elizabeth's weakened body could not break it. Seconds passed, and her lungs began to burn with the need for air. She held out as long as she could, stubbornness warring with biology, but finally her body betrayed her. Her mouth opened in a desperate gasp.

Mrs. Jenkinson immediately brought the glass to her lips and tipped it, pouring bitter liquid directly into Elizabeth's mouth. Elizabeth tried to spit it out, but Mrs. Jenkinson's hand clamped over her mouth and nose together, forcing her to either swallow or choke. The liquid burned down her throat, coating her tongue with a taste like charcoal and rotting flowers. She coughed violently once Mrs. Jenkinson released her, but the damage was done. The medicine was inside her.

"There," Mrs. Jenkinson said, setting the empty glass aside and wiping her hands with a handkerchief she produced from her pocket. "That wasn't so terrible, was it? You'll feel better shortly."

Elizabeth wanted to rage at her, to demand why she would force such treatment on someone who had done nothing wrong, but her tongue felt suddenly thick in her mouth. The room had begun to soften at the edges, the solid lines of furniture blurring into gentler curves. A strange heaviness crept through her limbs, different from the weakness she'd felt before. This was a weight that pressed down from inside, slowing her thoughts, making even the act of keeping her eyes open require conscious effort.

"What did you give me?" The words slurred together despite her attempt to speak clearly.

"Something to help you rest," Mrs. Jenkinson repeated. She was moving around the room now, though Elizabeth could no longer track her movements properly. The companion seemed to blur and multiply, her grey dress fragmenting into multiple overlapping images.

Elizabeth tried to fight it, tried to hold onto consciousness through sheer determination. But the drug was too strong, and Anne's body too weak. The darkness gathering at the edges of her vision began creeping inward, consuming the room piece by piece. She could feel herself slipping away, falling into a void that had nothing to do with natural sleep.

Why? The question formed in her mind even as thought became increasingly difficult. Why was Mrs. Jenkinson so loyal to Anne's wicked scheme? What hold did the girl have over her companion that would make a woman participate in such evil? Was it merely long habit, years of service transforming into blind devotion? Or did Anne possess some other leverage, some threat or promise that ensured Mrs. Jenkinson's cooperation?

Elizabeth could not even make her lips form the questions. The darkness claimed her entirely, pulling her down into depths where questions could not follow. Her last sensation was of the bitter taste still coating her tongue, a reminder that she was now at the complete mercy of people who had already demonstrated they possessed none.

The room faded to black, and Elizabeth knew nothing more.

Chapter Five

THE SPRING MORNING PRESENTED itself with almost aggressive cheerfulness. Sunlight filtered through newly leafed branches, creating shifting patterns across the path. Birds called to one another, their songs carried on a breeze that smelled of growing things. Yet Darcy found his attention less on the scenery than on the woman beside him. Miss Elizabeth Bennet walked beside him, her hand resting lightly on his arm, and he should have been entirely pleased. He was pleased, in the main. But something nagged at him, a sense of wrongness he could not quite identify.

Elizabeth smiled up at him, and the expression was warm, open, encouraging. Everything he might have hoped for, yet it struck him as slightly off, like a portrait painted by a skilled artist who had never met their subject. The smile reached her eyes, but something in the quality of it felt unfamiliar.

"What a lovely morning," she said, her voice carrying genuine enthusiasm. "I cannot recall when I last enjoyed such perfect weather for walking."

Darcy glanced at her, surprised by the conventional sentiment. But perhaps her illness had left her thoughts less sharp than usual. He had been genuinely alarmed when Mrs. Collins reported her sudden affliction, had called at the parsonage last night only to be told she was sleeping. The memory still carried a weight of disappointment.

He had been ready. Had spent the previous few days rehearsing what he would say, how he would express feelings that had grown beyond his ability to contain them. Miss Bennet's illness had forced postponement, and he had passed a restless night questioning whether delay was wisdom or cowardice. Now she walked beside him, apparently recovered, and the perfect opportunity had presented itself. Yet something held him back.

"I am glad to see you so improved," Darcy said carefully. "You gave us all concern yesterday."

"Did I?" She looked up at him again, that same warm smile in place. "How kind of you to worry. But as you can see, I am perfectly well now. Better than well, in fact. I feel quite wonderful."

The words themselves were unremarkable, but her manner struck Darcy as odd. Elizabeth typically deflected excessive concern with wit or gentle mockery, not with this earnest gratitude. He found himself studying her face more closely, searching for some explanation.

She met his gaze without her usual challenging spark, her expression open and pleasant. Too pleasant, perhaps. Elizabeth's particular charm had always resided partly in her willingness to disagree, to tease, to maintain her own opinions. This compliant warmth felt foreign.

"You seem in particularly good spirits," Darcy observed, keeping his tone light though his attention remained fixed on her reaction.

Something flickered across her face, too quick to identify. Wariness, possibly. Or calculation. But it vanished almost immediately.

"I suppose I am feeling the relief of recovery," she said, her hand tightening slightly on his arm. "Being ill, even briefly, makes one appreciate health all the more. And the morning is so beautiful, and the company so agreeable. Why should I not be in good spirits?"

The answer was perfectly reasonable, yet it settled over Darcy like ill-fitting clothes. Elizabeth had never before described his company as particularly agreeable. She had tolerated him at best, treated him with cool civility that occasionally warmed into secret glances of shared amusement at the foibles of others, moments he treasured and hoarded like a miser with gold. But agreeable? That was Colonel Fitzwilliam's territory, not his.

They walked in silence for a few moments, and Darcy used the opportunity to observe her more carefully. Small details accumulated, none significant alone but collectively troubling. The way she held herself seemed different, her posture almost too careful. Her laugh, when it came in response to some observation he made, sounded slightly wrong in pitch or duration. The expressions that crossed her face seemed rehearsed rather than spontaneous.

Darcy tried to dismiss his unease as imagination. Elizabeth had been ill. Perhaps that explained the subtle changes, the sense that something fundamental had shifted. Illness could alter people temporarily. He was reading too much into minor variations.

Yet the feeling persisted. He had spent many hours now covertly observing Elizabeth, had studied her with an attention he would have found embarrassing to acknowledge. He knew the precise angle of her eyebrow when she prepared some particularly cutting remark. Knew the way her lips twitched when she was suppressing a smile. Knew the quality of her gaze when she looked at something that genuinely interested her.

This woman beside him wore Elizabeth's face and form, spoke with her voice, used her words. But the essential quality that made her herself seemed muted.

"What has put you in such good spirits?" Darcy asked, unable to contain his curiosity. "Beyond the weather and recovery from illness, I mean. You seem unusually cheerful."

He watched her face carefully, noting the way her smile faltered for just a moment, the brief flash of something that might have been alarm before she mastered her expression.

"I hardly know how to answer such a question," she said, her tone aiming for lightness but landing closer to defensive. "Must there be a specific reason for cheerfulness? Can one not simply feel happy without requiring deep analysis?"

The response was more characteristic, that slight edge returning. Yet even this felt performative, as though she were imitating the sort of thing Elizabeth might say rather than speaking from genuine feeling.

Darcy found himself at a loss. His instinct insisted something was wrong, but his reason could identify no concrete evidence beyond these vague impressions. He could hardly tell her that she seemed unlike herself based on nothing more substantial than a feeling.

"Forgive me," he said finally. "I did not mean to question your happiness. I am merely pleased to see you recovered."

She smiled at him again, that warm, encouraging smile that should have delighted him but instead only deepened his unease. "You are very kind, Mr. Darcy. I appreciate your concern for my wellbeing."

Kind. Elizabeth had never before described him as kind. Proud, certainly. Disagreeable, frequently. But *kind?* The word sat wrong in her mouth.

They continued walking, the conversation drifting to safer topics, but Darcy's attention remained divided. Half of him participated in the discussion of Lady Catherine's gardens, while the other half continued its examination of the woman beside him, searching for some explanation that would resolve his confusion.

Everything appeared normal, pleasant, exactly as a morning walk should be. Yet Darcy could not shake the conviction that something was profoundly wrong, that the woman on his arm was not quite who she appeared to be.

Colonel Fitzwilliam appeared around the bend ahead, his stride easy and confident, and Darcy felt an immediate, uncharitable surge of irritation at the interruption. Now his cousin would insert himself into the conversation with his effortless charm, and Darcy would lose whatever ground he had gained in this peculiar morning.

Fitzwilliam raised a hand in greeting as he approached. "Darcy! Miss Bennet! What luck to find you both taking the morning air. I had thought to walk alone with my thoughts, but this is infinitely preferable."

Darcy returned the greeting with a nod, acutely aware of Elizabeth's hand still resting on his arm. He expected her to smile warmly at Fitzwilliam, perhaps to make some witty remark about rescuing her from Darcy's dull conversation. She had always shown particular enjoyment of his cousin's company, had responded to the colonel's teasing with genuine animation that she rarely displayed with Darcy himself.

Instead, her fingers tightened on his sleeve, and when Darcy glanced down at her face, he saw something that looked remarkably like irritation cross her features. The expression vanished quickly, replaced by a polite smile, but Darcy had seen it clearly. Elizabeth was annoyed by Fitzwilliam's arrival.

The observation struck him with force. In all their previous encounters, Elizabeth had gravitated toward Fitzwilliam's easier manner, had engaged with him far more readily than with Darcy. She had laughed at his jokes, drawn him out about his military experiences, treated him with warm friendliness she conspicuously withheld from Darcy. To see her now looking irritated made no sense.

"Colonel Fitzwilliam," Elizabeth said, her tone pleasant but lacking genuine warmth. "How nice to encounter you."

How nice. The words were perfectly civil, yet somehow managed to convey the opposite sentiment. Darcy stared at her, this confusion adding to his growing catalogue of wrongness.

Fitzwilliam seemed oblivious to any coldness in her greeting. He fell into step beside them, positioning himself on Elizabeth's other side. "I trust you are fully recovered from yesterday's illness, Miss Bennet? You gave us all quite a fright."

"Quite recovered, thank you." Her response was clipped, almost dismissive.

"Excellent, excellent." Fitzwilliam glanced across at Darcy with a grin. "I must say, Darcy, you look remarkably pleased with yourself this morning. Could it be that you are finally learning the art of pleasant conversation? Miss Bennet appears to be enjoying your company, which is something of a miracle given your usual talent for silence."

The teasing was typical of Fitzwilliam, meant in good humour. But Elizabeth's reaction was not typical. Instead of joining the gentle mockery or defending Darcy with some arch comment, she made a small sound of impatience.

"Mr. Darcy's conversation is always perfectly agreeable," she said stiffly.

Darcy's surprise deepened into something approaching alarm. Elizabeth defending him? Describing his conversation as agreeable?

Fitzwilliam raised his eyebrows, clearly caught off guard.

"Well, that is high praise indeed," Fitzwilliam said, recovering his easy manner. "I am glad to hear it, Miss Bennet. Very glad. In fact, I had hoped you might be looking more kindly upon my cousin now, after the information you received about him yesterday."

The words were delivered lightly, teasingly, but they struck Darcy like a blow. He turned to stare at Fitzwilliam, his mind racing. What information? What had his cousin told Elizabeth? When had they spoken privately?

"Information?" Darcy heard himself ask, his voice sharper than he intended. But before Fitzwilliam could reply, a new voice called out from behind them.

"Miss Bennet! Miss Bennet!"

They all turned to see Mr. Collins hurrying along the path toward them, his face red with exertion. Darcy felt his jaw tighten with fresh irritation at yet another interruption, though part of him welcomed the distraction from a conversation that had grown increasingly incomprehensible.

Collins reached them breathing heavily, his small eyes darting between Elizabeth and the two gentlemen with obvious disapproval. "Miss Bennet, I must speak with you immediately. Your behaviour this morning is quite inappropriate, and I cannot stand by silently while you compromise your reputation."

Darcy felt his irritation transform into cold anger. Collins had no right to address Elizabeth in such a tone, to publicly shame her for the innocent act of walking with gentlemen who were, after all, family connections of her hostess. He opened his mouth to tell Collins precisely this, but Elizabeth spoke first.

"Mr. Collins," she said, and her voice carried none of the spirit Darcy expected, none of the sharp defence of her own dignity. "I did not realise my walk would cause concern."

The meekness of her response stunned Darcy into silence. Elizabeth, who had never hesitated to defend herself against even Lady Catherine's autocratic pronouncements, was submitting to Collins's pompous censure without argument. This was perhaps the wrongest thing yet in a morning full of wrongness.

Darcy exchanged a glance with Fitzwilliam, seeing his own confusion reflected in his cousin's face. Something was very wrong here.

Collins drew himself up to his full height, which was unfortunately not particularly impressive, and continued his lecture with the sort of pompous authority that only the profoundly self-important could muster. "Walking alone with two gentlemen, without proper chaperonage, without any consideration for appearances or propriety. I am shocked, Miss Bennet. Truly shocked."

The man's voice carried across the morning air with deliberate projection. Darcy felt his hands clench into fists. Collins had no right to speak to Elizabeth in such a manner, particularly not in front of others, particularly not when her behaviour had been entirely innocent.

"Mr. Collins," Darcy said, his voice cold. "Miss Bennet's behaviour has been perfectly proper. There is nothing remotely scandalous about walking with us on Rosings' grounds."

Collins turned to him, his small eyes bright with righteousness. "With respect, Mr. Darcy, while I am sensible of your distinguished position, I must stand firm on matters of propriety. Miss Bennet is a guest in my house, and as such, her behaviour reflects upon my household. I cannot permit her to act in a manner that might invite censure."

"There is no cause for censure," Fitzwilliam interjected, his tone carrying an edge of impatience. "Miss Bennet encountered us during her morning walk. Surely even your exacting standards can accommodate such an innocent meeting."

But Collins would not be swayed. He turned back to Elizabeth, his expression a mixture of paternal disappointment and stern authority. "I must insist that you return to the parsonage with me immediately. Mrs. Collins will be concerned by your prolonged absence."

Darcy waited for Elizabeth to respond with her characteristic spirit, to inform Collins in cutting terms that she was perfectly capable of managing her own morning walks. He expected her to turn the man's pomposity back on him with some clever observation. At the very least, he expected her to politely but firmly refuse to be ordered about like a wayward child.

Instead, she lowered her gaze to the gravel path and said, "I apologise, Mr. Collins. I did not mean to cause concern."

The words hit Darcy like a physical blow. He stared at her, this woman who wore Elizabeth's face but seemed to have lost her spirit entirely. The meekness in her tone, the submissive posture, the complete absence of the fire he had come to expect from her, all combined into something so wrong that he could barely process it.

"That is very good of you to acknowledge, Miss Bennet," Collins said, his tone softening into something approaching smugness. "I am pleased to see you recognise the wisdom of accepting guidance. Now, if you will come with me..."

He extended his arm toward the parsonage, the gesture more command than invitation. Elizabeth glanced once at Darcy, her expression unreadable, before stepping away from his side. She offered him and Fitzwilliam a small curtsey, murmuring something about thanking them for their company, her voice so quiet that Darcy could barely hear it.

"Miss Bennet," Darcy said, desperately searching for some way to prevent this, to give her an excuse to remain. "Perhaps we might continue our walk later, when you are less occupied."

She looked at him for a moment, and something flickered in her eyes that might have been genuine emotion beneath the false pleasantness she had been displaying all morning. But it vanished quickly, and she shook her head.

"That is very kind, Mr. Darcy, but I think it best if I return to the parsonage now. Mr. Collins is quite right to be concerned."

Collins made a satisfied sound and took her elbow, not roughly but with enough firmness to make clear he intended to brook no argument. Elizabeth allowed herself to be guided, falling into step beside him with a docility that made Darcy's chest tighten.

They walked away down the path, Collins's voice carrying back, delivering what sounded like a continued lecture about propriety. Elizabeth's responses were too quiet to hear, but her posture spoke of submission.

Darcy watched them until they disappeared around the bend, his mind refusing to accept what he had witnessed. Everything about the encounter had been wrong. Elizabeth's warmth toward him, her coldness toward Fitzwilliam, and now this absolute capitulation to Collins's pompous authority. None of it matched anything he knew of her character.

"Well," Fitzwilliam said beside him, breaking the silence. "That was decidedly odd."

Darcy turned to look at his cousin, seeing his own confusion reflected back. "Odd does not begin to describe it."

"Collins is insufferable, of course, but that is hardly news." Fitzwilliam frowned in the direction they had gone. "What troubles me more is Miss Bennet's behaviour. She has never struck me as someone who would allow herself to be bullied by the likes of Collins. Yesterday she would have told him precisely what she thought of his interference, and done it with enough wit to leave him speechless."

Precisely what Darcy was thinking. This morning, she had acted like someone else entirely.

But that was impossible. People did not transform overnight. Even illness could not explain such a complete reversal of character. Yet what other explanation existed?

"Something is wrong," Darcy said quietly, more to himself than to Fitzwilliam.

"I would say so," his cousin agreed. "Though I cannot determine what. Perhaps her illness affected her more than we realised? Can a fever cause such changes in temperament?"

Darcy shook his head slowly. "I have never heard of such a thing. And she claims to be fully recovered, shows no signs of continued illness. She walked with energy, spoke clearly. If anything, she seemed healthier than I have seen her before."

They stood in silence for a moment, both staring down the path where Elizabeth and Collins had disappeared. The spring morning continued around them, oblivious to their confusion. Birds still sang. Sunlight still filtered through the leaves. Everything was normal, except for the one thing that mattered most.

Chapter Six

THE TWO MEN WALKED in silence for several minutes, turning their steps back toward Rosings now that Elizabeth Bennet had left them. Darcy's mind turned over the morning's encounters like a puzzle with pieces that refused to fit together. Elizabeth's warmth toward him, her coldness toward Fitzwilliam, her meek submission to Collins's pompous authority. None of it aligned with the woman he had come to know, the woman whose spirit and independence had captivated him despite his better judgement. Beside him, Fitzwilliam maintained an uncharacteristic quiet, his usual easy manner subdued.

Fitzwilliam broke the silence first, as Darcy had known he would. His cousin had never been comfortable with prolonged quiet, particularly not when something puzzled him. "Well, that was certainly an interesting display, Collins in full pontificating glory. He can be truly insufferable, can he not?"

Darcy made a noncommittal sound, his thoughts still occupied with Elizabeth's inexplicable transformation. Yesterday she had been herself, sharp and spirited. Today she seemed like a different person entirely, as though some essential quality had been drained from her overnight.

"Though I suppose we should not be too surprised by his interference," Fitzwilliam continued, his tone shifting toward something more thoughtful. "Collins likely holds a grudge against Miss Bennet. Men like him rarely forget when their pride has been wounded, and from what I understand, she dealt his pride a rather severe blow."

That caught Darcy's attention. He turned to look at his cousin, noting the slight smile playing about Fitzwilliam's mouth. "What do you mean? What grudge could Collins possibly have?"

Fitzwilliam's smile widened into something approaching amusement. "You do not know? Collins proposed marriage to Miss Bennet before he married Charlotte Lucas."

The words landed like stones in still water, sending ripples of shock through Darcy. He stared at Fitzwilliam, certain he must have misheard. "He... what?"

"Proposed marriage," Fitzwilliam repeated, clearly enjoying Darcy's reaction. "To Miss Elizabeth Bennet. From what Miss Maria Lucas told me, it was quite the dramatic affair. Collins is the heir to Longbourn, you see, and he conceived the notion that proposing to one of the Bennet daughters would be a gentlemanly way to make amends for the entail. Probably a magnanimous gesture, in his view, securing their future and providing him with a pretty, ladylike wife without having to go to the trouble of courting one."

Darcy had stopped walking without consciously deciding to do so. His boots remained planted on the path, his entire body gone rigid. Collins. Pompous, obsequious, ridiculous Collins had proposed to Elizabeth. Had thought himself worthy of her. Had believed she would accept him.

"When?" The word emerged more sharply than Darcy intended. "When did this occur?"

"When he was at Longbourn last autumn, according to Miss Maria." Fitzwilliam had stopped as well, turning to face Darcy. "He stayed with the Bennets for some weeks, apparently, and during that time he fixed upon Miss Elizabeth as the most suitable of the five daughters. He proposed, she refused him quite decisively with her father's full support, and within days he had proposed to Charlotte Lucas instead and been accepted."

Darcy's hand moved to his forehead without conscious direction, pressing against his brow as though he could somehow push this new information into proper arrangement. Elizabeth married to Collins. The very idea was absurd, impossible, an offence against nature itself. That Collins could have imagined such a union spoke to a degree of self-delusion that surpassed even what Darcy had previously attributed to the man.

"She refused him," Darcy said, speaking more to himself than to Fitzwilliam. Of course she had refused him. Elizabeth would never have accepted such a man, would never have consigned herself to a life of listening to his pompous speeches and enduring his fawning devotion to Lady Catherine.

"Refused him sharply, from what I gather," Fitzwilliam confirmed. "Miss Maria was not present for the actual proposal, naturally, but she said that Miss Elizabeth's rejection was definitive enough that Collins apparently took the opportunity to propose to Charlotte within only a day or two, when Charlotte indicated she would be receptive. He was in quite a fit of pique, according to Miss Maria."

Darcy lowered his hand from his forehead, forcing himself to resume walking though his thoughts remained in turmoil. His cousin fell into step beside him, mercifully refraining from further comment.

The pieces were beginning to arrange themselves into a comprehensible pattern now. Collins's pointed disapproval of Elizabeth this morning took on new meaning in light of this history. The man had offered her his hand, his home, his name, and she had rejected him. For someone of Collins's temperament, such a refusal would have been an unforgivable slight. That she had been absolutely right to refuse him would matter not at all to Collins's wounded vanity.

Darcy's mind continued to turn over this new information, examining it from multiple angles. Elizabeth had refused a practical match that would have secured her future. Had chosen uncertainty and continued dependence on her father rather than accept a husband she could not respect. The decision spoke to a strength of character and independence of spirit that Darcy could not help but admire.

And yet, this morning, she had submitted meekly to that same man's pompous interference. Had allowed Collins to lecture her about propriety and had agreed to return to the parsonage without a single word of protest. After demonstrating the courage to refuse his marriage proposal despite the practical advantages it offered, she now lacked the spirit to defend her own innocent behaviour.

Nothing made sense. The woman who had rejected Collins was the Elizabeth who Darcy knew, the Elizabeth whose independence and liveliness had drawn him despite his initial resistance. The woman who had meekly accepted Collins's authority this morning was a stranger wearing Elizabeth's face.

"Perhaps her illness affected her more than we realised," Darcy said aloud, testing the explanation that had occurred to him earlier. "Some fevers can cause changes in temperament, can they not?"

But even as he spoke the words, he knew they were inadequate. Illness might make someone quieter or more subdued. It would not transform independence into meekness, spirit into submission. It would not explain the fundamental shift in character he had witnessed.

Fitzwilliam made a considering sound. "I suppose it is possible. Though she seemed entirely healthy otherwise. No signs of continued fever or weakness. If anything, she appeared more energetic than I have seen her before."

They had reached the house now, the imposing façade of Rosings rising before them. Darcy paused before ascending the steps, turning to look back along the path they had travelled. Somewhere beyond his sight, Elizabeth was walking with Collins, listening to his no doubt continued lecture. And she was allowing it without protest, this woman who had possessed the courage to refuse his marriage proposal.

Darcy could not shake the conviction that something was wrong. Very wrong.

He just could not begin to imagine what it might be.

The entrance hall of Rosings received them with its usual oppressive grandeur, all marble floors and heavy furnishings arranged to impress rather than comfort. A servant appeared to take their coats, moving with the silent efficiency Lady Catherine demanded. Fitzwilliam made some observation about the warmth of the morning, but Darcy barely registered the words. Something nagged at him, a detail from their earlier conversation that he had not had opportunity to pursue.

They moved toward the drawing room, their footsteps echoing on the polished marble. The house was quiet at this hour, Lady Catherine likely still occupied with her morning correspondence, Anne presumably resting as she always did. Darcy was grateful for the temporary solitude. He needed to think, needed to understand what was happening before he encountered his aunt's penetrating gaze and inevitable questions.

But first, he needed answers to questions that had been building even before their encounter with Elizabeth and Collins.

"Fitzwilliam," Darcy said, stopping before they reached the drawing room door. "This morning, before Collins interrupted us, you mentioned something. You said you hoped Miss Bennet would be looking more kindly upon me after the information she received yesterday."

His cousin turned, eyebrows rising. "Did I? Yes, I suppose I did mention that."

"What information did you share with her?" Darcy kept his voice carefully neutral, though tension had begun building in his chest. "When did you speak with Miss Bennet privately?"

Fitzwilliam's smile widened into something that looked distinctly pleased with itself. "Yesterday afternoon, while you were occupied with that interminable letter to your steward. I encountered Miss Bennet walking in the grove, and we fell into conversation. The lady is excellent company when one can engage her attention."

Darcy waited, his jaw tightening with the effort of maintaining patience. Fitzwilliam tended toward lengthy explanations when he thought himself clever.

"I thought I might help your cause along a bit," Fitzwilliam continued, clearly enjoying himself. "I thought perhaps if she understood the depth of your character, the strength of your devotion to those you care about, she might view you more favourably."

The tension in Darcy's chest tightened further. "What exactly did you tell her?"

"I spoke of your loyalty to your friends, your willingness to go to considerable lengths to protect those you value." Fitzwilliam was warming to his subject now. "I wanted her to understand that beneath your rather forbidding exterior lies a man of genuine feeling and principle. Someone who acts decisively when he believes a friend to be in danger of making a serious mistake."

Darcy's hands had begun to curl into fists at his sides without his conscious awareness. He forced them to relax, forced his breathing to remain steady. "And did you provide specific examples of this loyalty?"

"Of course. Generalities carry no weight, do they? I told her about how you saved Bingley from an imprudent connection last autumn in London." Fitzwilliam's smile remained firmly in place, oblivious to Darcy's building alarm. "How you recognised that he had formed an attachment to a young woman whose feelings were not sufficiently engaged, whose family connections were disadvantageous, and how you took decisive action to separate them before he could make an offer that would have compromised his happiness and standing."

The world seemed to slow around Darcy. The words reached him as though travelling through water, distorted and terrible. *Bingley. Last autumn. A young woman whose feelings were not engaged. Disadvantageous family connections.*

Darcy's hand moved to his forehead, pressing against his brow as though he could somehow push back the understanding that was crashing over him. Bingley's attachment last autumn. A young woman in London. But Bingley had not met any woman in London last autumn. Fitzwilliam must have misunderstood exactly when and where the events had taken place. Bingley had met Jane Bennet in Hertfordshire, had formed an attachment to Jane Bennet, and Darcy had aided and abetted Bingley's sisters in separating them.

Jane Bennet. Elizabeth's beloved elder sister.

If Elizabeth knew, if Fitzwilliam had told her that Darcy had deliberately separated Bingley from an attachment formed last autumn, she would have understood immediately. Would have recognised her own sister in that description. Would have known with absolute certainty that Darcy was responsible for Jane's heartbreak.

And she would have been furious. Should have been furious. Should have confronted him, challenged him, demanded explanations with all the fire and spirit he had come to expect from her. She should have looked at him this morning with anger and betrayal in her eyes, should have refused his company, should have cut him with words sharp enough to flay skin from bone.

Instead, she had been warm. Pleasant. Almost affectionate. Had smiled at him with apparent genuine pleasure, had accepted his arm without hesitation, had described his conversation as agreeable.

The wrongness of it crashed over Darcy with renewed force, compounded now by this revelation. Elizabeth should have been enraged by what Fitzwilliam told her. Yet her behaviour this morning had suggested the opposite, had implied she viewed him more favourably than ever before.

It made no sense. None of it made sense.

Darcy lowered his hand slowly, forcing himself to meet Fitzwilliam's increasingly concerned gaze. His cousin had taken a step closer, clearly alarmed by Darcy's reaction but not yet understanding its source.

"Darcy?" Fitzwilliam said, his voice stripped of its earlier amusement. "What is it? What have I done?"

But Darcy could not answer, could barely think beyond the certainty pounding through his consciousness. Elizabeth should be angry. Should hate him. Should never wish to speak to him again after learning what he had done to her sister. Yet this morning she had been pleasant, compliant, nearly affectionate.

"Darcy, for God's sake, what is wrong? You look as though you have seen a ghost."

Darcy straightened slowly, releasing his grip on the wall and forcing his breathing to steady. Fitzwilliam stood before him with deep concern, one hand still extended. They were alone in the corridor, but servants could appear at any moment, and Darcy could not afford to appear as shaken as he felt. He needed to explain, needed to tell Fitzwilliam what he had done, though the confession would only compound his cousin's alarm.

"The young woman Bingley formed an attachment to last autumn," Darcy said, his voice carefully controlled despite the turmoil in his chest. "It was not in London. It was in Hertfordshire."

Fitzwilliam's brow furrowed in confusion. "Hertfordshire? But you said..."

"I said he had met someone. I did not specify where." Darcy paused, the words catching in his throat before he could force them out. "It was Miss Jane Bennet. Elizabeth's elder sister."

The colour drained from Fitzwilliam's face with remarkable speed. For a long moment he simply stared at Darcy, his mouth slightly open, his expression cycling through shock, comprehension, and finally horror.

"Dear God," Fitzwilliam breathed. "Tell me I did not... Tell me I did not tell Miss Bennet that you deliberately separated her sister from Bingley."

But Darcy could not tell him that, could only watch his cousin's horror deepen as understanding crystallised. Fitzwilliam took a step backward, one hand rising to cover his mouth as though he could somehow take back the words he had spoken yesterday afternoon.

"I am so sorry," Fitzwilliam said, his voice emerging rough with genuine distress. "Darcy, I had no idea. You never told me the woman was Miss Bennet's sister! If I had known, if I had suspected for even a moment, I would never have spoken of it." He shook his head, looking genuinely stricken. "No wonder you looked so alarmed. She must despise you now. Must think you the most interfering, presumptuous villain in England."

Darcy opened his mouth to agree, to confirm that yes, Elizabeth would naturally be furious. But the words died before they could form. Because Elizabeth had not seemed furious this morning. Had not acted like someone who despised him. Had been warm, pleasant, nearly affectionate.

"That is what troubles me," Darcy said slowly, his thoughts arranging themselves even as he spoke. "Miss Bennet did not seem angry this morning. Did not behave as though she had just learned I was responsible for her sister's heartbreak. Instead, she was..." He paused, searching for the right word. "Pleasant. Agreeable. Almost welcoming of my company."

Fitzwilliam stared at him as though he had begun speaking in tongues. "Pleasant? Darcy, surely you are mistaken. Perhaps she was hiding her anger behind civility, maintaining appearances until she could express her true feelings more privately."

But Darcy shook his head. "No. It was not that sort of controlled civility. She seemed genuinely pleased to see me, genuinely happy to walk with me. There was no coldness beneath the pleasantness, no hint of suppressed fury."

"Then perhaps..." Fitzwilliam hesitated, his expression troubled. "Perhaps she has not yet made the connection? If I did not mention Miss Bennet by name, perhaps Miss Elizabeth has not realised I was speaking of her own sister?"

The suggestion was logical, but Darcy found himself unable to accept it. Elizabeth was too intelligent, too perceptive to miss such an obvious connection. Bingley's attachment formed last autumn, a young woman whose feelings were deemed insufficient, disadvantageous family connections. Any mention of Bingley and last autumn would immediately bring Jane to Elizabeth's mind.

Unless... Elizabeth did not care as much about her sister's disappointment as Darcy had assumed.

The thought arrived with the force of revelation, offering an explanation that would resolve the contradiction. What if Jane's feelings for Bingley had been as tepid as Darcy had thought them to be? What if Elizabeth knew her sister had not been particularly attached, had not suffered terribly from the separation? In that case, Elizabeth might view Darcy's interference as misguided but not cruel, protective rather than malicious. Perhaps even helpful, saving her sister from the obligation of refusing a distasteful proposal, much as Elizabeth herself had to do with Collins.

"Perhaps Miss Bennet was not deeply affected by the separation," Darcy heard himself say, the words emerging with more confidence than he felt. "Perhaps her feelings for Bingley were not as strong as we assumed, and Elizabeth knows this. That would explain why she showed no anger at learning I had separated them."

Fitzwilliam's expression suggested he found this reasoning deeply flawed. "Darcy, that seems rather unlikely. Miss Elizabeth spoke of her sister with genuine affection during our conversations. I cannot imagine she would be so sanguine about anyone interfering in Miss Bennet's romantic prospects, regardless of the depth of her sister's attachment."

But Darcy was already building the argument in his mind, constructing a narrative that would justify both his past actions and Elizabeth's present behaviour. "If Miss Bennet's feelings were not seriously engaged, then no real harm was done. Elizabeth might recognise this, might even approve of my protecting Bingley from an unsuitable connection that would have satisfied neither party in the end."

The words sounded hollow even to his own ears, defensive rather than convinced. But Darcy pressed on, needing to believe this explanation because the alternative, the impossible alternative his instincts insisted upon, was too extraordinary to accept.

Fitzwilliam opened his mouth, closed it again, clearly struggling with how to respond. "I suppose that is possible," he said finally, though doubt coloured his tone. "Though I must say,

Darcy, this all seems rather convenient. Are you certain you are not simply telling yourself what you wish to believe?"

The question struck too close to truth for Darcy's comfort. He turned away from his cousin's penetrating gaze, staring at the portrait of some long-dead de Bourgh ancestor that hung on the wall. The painted eyes seemed to judge him, to see through his rationalisations to the uncomfortable truth beneath.

Had his motives for separating Bingley and Jane been entirely honourable? Had he truly acted solely out of concern for his friend's welfare? Or had some part of him been influenced by his growing feelings for Elizabeth, by the irrational hope that removing Bingley from the Bennet family might somehow benefit his own prospects?

Darcy's conscience, which he had successfully suppressed for months, chose this moment to reassert itself with uncomfortable vigour. He had told himself he was protecting Bingley from an imprudent match, from a young woman whose feelings seemed insufficient and whose family was decidedly disadvantageous. He had convinced himself he was acting as a good friend should, decisively intervening to prevent a mistake.

But beneath those rational justifications had lurked less noble considerations. The younger Bennet sisters' embarrassing behaviour, which might reflect poorly on Darcy himself if Bingley married into the connection. The mother's obvious scheming, which offended Darcy's sense of propriety.

Those motivations had nothing to do with protecting his friend. They were pure pride and prejudice, the very qualities Darcy prided himself on having mastered. And yes, some small part of him had wanted to ensure Bingley did not bind himself to the Bennet family, a circumstance which would likely have brought Elizabeth Bennet into circles where she and Darcy would cross paths regularly. He had, at that time, not recognised just how impossible it would be to forget her.

"Perhaps my reasons were not entirely honourable," Darcy admitted quietly, still not looking at his cousin. "Perhaps I was influenced by considerations beyond simply Bingley's welfare. But the outcome remains the same. If Jane Bennet was not seriously attached, then the separation, however imperfectly motivated, caused no lasting harm."

Fitzwilliam made a sound that might have been agreement or protest, Darcy could not tell which. "And if she was attached? If you were wrong about her feelings?"

Then he had caused genuine suffering to an innocent woman, had destroyed a promising attachment through arrogance and presumption. Had wounded Elizabeth's beloved sister and earned Elizabeth's justified anger and contempt.

But Elizabeth was not angry. That was the fact Darcy kept returning to, the observation that supported his hopeful interpretation. If Jane had truly cared for Bingley, if Elizabeth believed her sister had suffered real heartbreak, she would not have been pleasant and agreeable this morning. Would not have smiled at Darcy with apparent genuine warmth. Would not have accepted his company without visible reluctance.

Unless she had some other motivation. Unless she had decided to encourage Darcy, only to plan on breaking his heart with a cruel refusal once he had come to the point of proposing, in revenge for her beloved sister's heartbreak.

No. Elizabeth Bennet was many things, but a malicious plotter was not one of them, he was sure of it. Darcy pushed the unworthy thought away, clinging instead to the rational explanation he had constructed. Jane's feelings had been insufficient. Elizabeth knew this. Therefore Elizabeth held no grudge. The logic was sound, even if it required him to ignore his own growing doubts.

"I think," Darcy said finally, turning back to face Fitzwilliam, "that we may be troubling ourselves unnecessarily. Miss Bennet's behaviour suggests she bears me no ill will regarding the matter. Perhaps she recognises that I acted with Bingley's best interests at heart, even if she might question my judgement. Perhaps she even agrees that the match would have been unsuitable."

Fitzwilliam studied him for a long moment, his expression suggesting he saw through this rationalisation but was too kind to say so directly. "Perhaps," he said, though the word carried little conviction. "I hope you are right, Darcy. For your sake as much as for hers."

They stood in silence for a moment, the tension between them gradually easing though Darcy's internal turmoil remained undiminished. He had explained away Elizabeth's lack of anger, had constructed a narrative that preserved both his past actions and his present hopes. But his conscience refused to be entirely silenced, continued its uncomfortable insistence that his motivations had been less pure than he claimed, his judgement less sound than he believed.

And beneath that, deeper and more disturbing, lay the question he could not quite banish. If Elizabeth truly bore him no ill will regarding her sister, if she truly approved of his protective interference, then why did everything about her behaviour this morning feel so fundamentally wrong?

Chapter Seven

Consciousness returned in fragments, each piece arriving with reluctance. Elizabeth became aware first of the heavy coverlet pressing against her chest, then of the dull ache behind her eyes, then finally of the watching presence in the room. She forced her eyelids open, the act requiring far more effort than it should, and found Mrs. Jenkinson sitting in a high-backed chair beside the bed, spine rigid, hands folded in her lap.

Elizabeth's mouth tasted of ashes and rot, the lingering bitterness of whatever Mrs. Jenkinson had forced down her throat. How long had she been unconscious this time? The quality of light suggested late afternoon, perhaps approaching evening. Hours lost to drugged oblivion while Anne walked about in her body, lived her life, spoke with her voice.

Elizabeth tried to sit up, her muscles protesting with tremors and weakness. She managed to prop herself on one elbow before having to pause, breathing hard. Mrs. Jenkinson watched without offering assistance, her eyes tracking Elizabeth's struggle with detached interest.

"You should rest longer," Mrs. Jenkinson said, her voice carrying no warmth. "That body is not accustomed to such exertion."

"I've rested enough." Elizabeth's voice emerged rough, scraped raw. She pushed herself more upright, refusing to lie helpless under the companion's watchful gaze. "How long have I been unconscious?"

"Several hours. It's nearly time for dinner." Mrs. Jenkinson's hands remained folded in her lap, a picture of composed vigilance. "Lady Catherine will expect her daughter to attend, assuming you have recovered sufficiently from your recent spell."

The words carried weight beyond their surface meaning. Elizabeth studied the companion's face, searching for some hint of what lay beneath that professional mask. Mrs. Jenkinson knew the truth, knew Elizabeth was not Anne, yet sat here calmly discussing dinner arrangements.

"I intend to go down to dinner," Elizabeth said, testing the waters. "I wish to see Lady Catherine."

Something flickered in Mrs. Jenkinson's expression, too fast to identify clearly. The companion rose from her chair with deliberate slowness, looking down at Elizabeth with an expression that mixed pity and calculation.

"Before you do," Mrs. Jenkinson said, her voice dropping to barely above a whisper, "you should understand your situation very clearly. If you go downstairs and make any claims about being in the wrong body, about being Elizabeth Bennet trapped in Anne de Bourgh's form, do you know what will happen?"

Elizabeth's throat tightened, but she forced herself to meet the companion's gaze steadily. "Someone will believe me."

"No one will believe you." Mrs. Jenkinson's tone carried absolute certainty. "They will think you mad, suffering from delusions brought on by illness. Lady Catherine will be distressed, certainly, but she will do what any concerned mother would do. She will have you confined for your own protection."

The words settled over Elizabeth like a shroud. She wanted to argue, to insist that someone would recognise the truth. But even as the protests formed in her mind, she recognised their futility. Who would believe such an impossible story? Body swapping belonged to fairy tales and folk legends, not to the drawing rooms of respectable society.

"Mr. Darcy is here," Mrs. Jenkinson continued, driving her point home with surgical precision. "Your supposed betrothed, though he has shown no particular enthusiasm for honouring it these many years. If Anne de Bourgh suddenly began raving about being someone else entirely, claiming her body had been stolen through witchcraft, what do you imagine Mr. Darcy would do?"

Elizabeth's hands clenched in the coverlet, her borrowed body's weakness making the gesture almost pathetic. But her mind seized on Mrs. Jenkinson's words with horrible clarity. Darcy would be relieved. Would welcome any excuse, however extraordinary, to avoid marrying Anne. A madwoman could be quietly confined, his obligation dissolved with sympathy rather than scandal. He would not fight for her, would not question too deeply, would accept the diagnosis of insanity with barely concealed gratitude.

"He would have me committed," Elizabeth heard herself say, the words emerging hollow. "He would believe I was mad, and he would approve my confinement without hesitation."

"Precisely." Mrs. Jenkinson's expression held no triumph, only weary acceptance. "An asylum, most likely. Somewhere far from society, where inconvenient relatives can be housed comfortably but securely. You would spend the remainder of your days, however many or few that might be in that failing body, locked away from the world. Is that what you want?"

No. God, no. Elizabeth's stomach turned at the image Mrs. Jenkinson painted. Trapped not only in Anne's weak body but in some asylum, surrounded by the genuinely mad, with no hope of rescue or redemption.

But what alternative existed? If she could not tell the truth without risking confinement, how could she hope to reclaim her own life?

Elizabeth forced her breathing to steady, forced her racing thoughts to slow and organise themselves. She was not defeated yet. Mrs. Jenkinson had made the threat to ensure compliance, but threats only worked if the threatened party believed them. Elizabeth did believe it, unfortunately. The danger was real. But that did not mean she had no options remaining.

She would have to be more subtle. Would have to play along while she searched for another way, some path that did not require convincing sceptical strangers that magic was real. There had to be a way to reverse what Anne had done. Magic that could swap bodies might also swap them back. She simply needed time to discover how, and that required staying free, staying present, maintaining enough independence to search for answers. Charlotte, perhaps... if she could get Charlotte alone, speak to her of past events only the two of them knew of, perhaps she could convince Charlotte of who she was.

"I understand," Elizabeth said finally, keeping her voice level despite the fury burning in her chest. "I will not speak of such things at dinner. I merely wish to eat. I am hungry, and I would prefer not to waste away from starvation."

Mrs. Jenkinson studied her for a long moment, suspicion clear in her gaze. She was not stupid, this woman. She recognised that Elizabeth's compliance came from strategy rather than genuine acceptance. But what choice did she have? She could not keep Elizabeth drugged and confined indefinitely. Lady Catherine would notice, would question, would demand explanations.

"Very well," Mrs. Jenkinson said at last. She moved to the bell pull and rang for a maid. "I will have someone help you dress for dinner. You will conduct yourself with appropriate dignity, will respond to Lady Catherine's questions about your health with reassurances, and will under no circumstances make any claims that might cause alarm."

"Of course," Elizabeth agreed, the words tasting like ashes. "I am Anne de Bourgh. Why would I claim to be anyone else?"

The irony in her tone was perhaps too sharp, but Mrs. Jenkinson let it pass. A knock sounded at the door, and a young maid entered at the companion's summons. The girl curtseyed, her eyes downcast, clearly accustomed to Anne's presence requiring no particular acknowledgement.

"Help Miss de Bourgh dress for dinner," Mrs. Jenkinson instructed. "The green silk, I think. And the pearls."

The maid curtseyed again and moved to the wardrobe. Elizabeth watched her work, resigned. She would have to endure being dressed in Anne's clothes, adorned with Anne's jewellery, presented as Anne to Anne's family. The humiliation of it burned, but she had no choice. Not yet.

As the maid approached with a chemise and stays, Elizabeth forced herself to cooperate, lifting her arms when directed, standing when instructed though her legs trembled with the effort. The process of dressing seemed to take forever, each layer of clothing another reminder of her imprisonment. The silk gown whispered against her skin, expensive and beautiful and entirely wrong. The pearls lay cool and heavy against her collarbone, their weight a reminder of the wealth and status that belonged to Anne but could never belong to Elizabeth Bennet.

Through it all, Mrs. Jenkinson watched, her presence ensuring Elizabeth could not search the room, could not look for evidence of Anne's methods, could not do anything but submit to being transformed into a convincing replica of the woman who had stolen her life.

The maid stepped back, her work complete. Elizabeth found herself facing the mirror once more, seeing Anne de Bourgh staring back at her in full evening regalia. The green silk complemented her pale complexion, the pearls added elegance, the delicate curls framed her face becomingly. She looked exactly as Anne de Bourgh should look.

She looked nothing like Elizabeth Bennet.

Elizabeth met her own eyes in the mirror, those pale, wrong eyes that belonged to another woman's face, and made a silent promise. She would find a way to undo this. Would discover Anne's methods and reverse them. Would reclaim her own body and her own life, no matter what obstacles stood in her path.

But first, she had to survive dinner without being declared insane.

The maid curtseyed one final time and departed, closing the door softly. Mrs. Jenkinson moved to follow, pausing at the threshold to deliver one last pointed look. "I will return in a few minutes to escort you downstairs. Do not attempt to leave this room without me." Then she too was gone, the door clicking shut with finality, and Elizabeth found herself blessedly, briefly alone.

She remained frozen for several heartbeats, listening intently. Mrs. Jenkinson's footsteps receded down the corridor, growing fainter, then disappearing entirely.

Elizabeth moved.

Her first steps were unsteady, Anne's body protesting the sudden demand. The elaborate dress hampered her movement, the heavy silk catching around her legs, the stays restricting her breathing more than she was accustomed to. But she forced herself forward, crossing to the nearest chest of drawers with determination that exceeded her physical capability.

The first drawer yielded nothing of interest. Stockings, carefully folded. Gloves arranged by colour. Small clothes so delicate it seemed they might tear at a harsh word. Elizabeth pushed past them with trembling fingers, searching for anything that might explain Anne's methods.

The second drawer was equally disappointing. More clothing, some letters tied with ribbon that Elizabeth did not have time to read, a few pieces of inexpensive jewellery that must hold sentimental value. Nothing that would help.

Elizabeth's frustration mounted with each fruitless search. She moved to the wardrobe, pulling open the doors and running her hands along the shelves, disturbing neat stacks of folded garments, feeling behind them for hidden compartments. Her arms ached with the effort, trembling from exertion that should have been trivial. She wanted to scream at this body's weakness, at its betrayal, at its absolute refusal to do what she needed.

But screaming would accomplish nothing except perhaps bringing Mrs. Jenkinson back earlier than expected. Elizabeth forced herself to breathe slowly, to think rather than simply search in mounting panic. Where would she keep secrets she did not want her mother or the servants to discover?

Elizabeth's gaze swept the room, cataloguing the furniture with new attention. The chest of drawers, already searched. The wardrobe, now in disarray from her rummaging. The nightstand held only a book of sermons and a candle. The writing desk in the corner beckoned, but Elizabeth had explored it briefly during her first desperate exploration after waking and found nothing of note. It was too delicate a piece to have hidden compartments.

The dressing table. Elizabeth turned toward it, studying its ornate construction with fresh eyes. It was an expensive piece, French perhaps, with delicate legs and elaborate carving along the drawer fronts. The sort of furniture that might contain hidden compartments, secret drawers meant for concealing love letters or other private items.

Elizabeth crossed to it on unsteady legs, sinking onto the padded stool before her knees could give out entirely. She ran her hands over the smooth wood surface, feeling for irregularities, for catches or springs that might reveal hidden spaces. The main drawers opened easily, revealing the usual contents. Combs and brushes. Small bottles of perfume.

But at the very back of the centre drawer, Elizabeth's questing fingers found something unexpected. Metal, where there should have been only wood. She put pressure on the knob, trying first a push, then a pull, and felt a click.

A small drawer sprang open, so cleverly concealed that Elizabeth would never have found it without deliberate searching. Inside lay a slim leather-bound journal, its cover worn and stained with frequent handling.

Elizabeth's hands shook as she lifted it free. The book felt heavier than its size warranted, as though the knowledge contained within possessed physical weight. She opened it to a random page and found herself staring at cramped script documenting ingredients and measurements, instructions for preparation and timing. A recipe for some concoction.

She flipped back to the beginning and found an inscription in a different hand, firmer and more masculine than the cramped writing that filled the subsequent pages. "To my dearest Anne, from your devoted father. May these secrets bring you the power to shape your own destiny."

Sir Lewis de Bourgh. Had he been the possessor of this alchemical knowledge, passing it on to his daughter before his death? Elizabeth's heart hammered against her ribs as she began turning pages, scanning recipe after recipe. A draught to induce deep sleep. A tonic to enhance beauty. A potion to ease pain. And then, more disturbing entries. A philtre to inspire love. A powder to cause prophetic dreams. A tea to weaken the will.

Elizabeth's fingers flew through the pages, searching for what she knew must be here. The spell or potion Anne had used to steal her body. There had to be instructions, had to be some record of how it was accomplished.

The dinner gong sounded from somewhere below, its deep tone reverberating through the house. Elizabeth nearly dropped the journal, her heart leaping into her throat. How long had she been searching? How many minutes remained before Mrs. Jenkinson returned?

She snapped the journal closed and looked frantically around the room for a hiding place, not wanting to put it back in the secret drawer. Under the mattress, she decided, the first solution that occurred to her panicked mind. Elizabeth crossed to the bed and shoved the journal beneath the thick mattress, pushing it as far toward the centre as her arm could reach. Not a perfect hiding place, but it would have to suffice.

Her hands were still shaking as she straightened, smoothing down the green silk that had become rumpled during her frantic searching. She could feel sweat beading at her temples despite the room's relative coolness, could feel her heart still racing.

But she had found what she sought. It seemed Anne had documented everything carefully, had kept records like any good scholar. And in doing so, perhaps she had left Elizabeth a path forward.

Elizabeth moved toward the door, her steps more steady now despite her body's weakness. She would go down to dinner. Would play her role as Anne de Bourgh convincingly enough to avoid suspicion. Would smile at Lady Catherine and tolerate whatever company was present and give no hint that anything was amiss.

And later, she would study that journal properly. Would figure out how Anne had done this to her. Would find a way to obtain what she needed and reverse this nightmare.

She was not defeated yet.

The door opened just as Elizabeth reached it, Mrs. Jenkinson's pinched face appearing in the gap. The companion's eyes swept over Elizabeth with sharp assessment, taking in her appearance, searching for any sign of disruption or mischief.

"You look presentable," Mrs. Jenkinson said finally, her tone suggesting this was qualified approval at best. "Come along then."

Elizabeth stepped through the door, forcing her expression into something approaching serenity despite the tumult of her thoughts. She had hope now, however slight. And she had determination enough for ten women, even if trapped in a body that could barely manage a flight of stairs.

Anne de Bourgh had made a grave mistake in leaving that journal where it could be found. And Elizabeth intended to make her pay dearly for it.

Chapter Eight

THE DINING ROOM AT Rosings presented its usual display of oppressive grandeur, all gleaming silver and crystal that caught the candlelight. Darcy was seated in his customary position, close enough to his aunt to be consulted on matters she deemed important, far enough to avoid the worst of her pronouncements. Miss Bennet sat across from him and several places down, positioned where he could observe her without obvious staring, though he found his gaze drawn to her inevitably throughout the meal's first course.

The soup had been cleared away, and servants moved with silent efficiency to present the fish course. Darcy watched Elizabeth lift her fork with odd carefulness, as though relearning the gesture. She ate with small, deliberate bites, and he noticed she had consumed more than he had ever seen her manage at these dinners. Previously she had eaten with a healthy but moderate appetite, but tonight she seemed enthusiastic about the meal, finishing everything on her plate at each course.

"The pike is excellent, is it not?" Darcy ventured, testing the waters. "Lady Catherine's cook has outdone himself."

Elizabeth looked up at him and smiled, the expression warm and encouraging. "Oh yes, it is wonderful. Truly delicious." She paused, seeming to search for more to say, then added, "I have never tasted better fish."

The response was pleasant enough, but it fell flat in a way Darcy could not quite articulate. Elizabeth typically would have made some observation about the preparation, or teased him about discussing food with undue gravity, or found some way to turn the mundane topic into something more interesting. This bland agreement felt wrong.

"I am glad you are enjoying it," Darcy said carefully. He tried again, offering an opening for the sort of exchange they had occasionally managed. "Though I confess I find Lady Catherine's insistence on French sauces for English fish somewhat excessive. The pike might be better served simply."

He had thought the mild criticism might provoke Elizabeth into agreeing or disagreeing with spirit, might draw out some of her characteristic independence. Instead, she simply nodded.

"Perhaps you are right. Though it is very good as it is." She looked at him again with that same warm smile, her gaze lingering on his face in a way that made Darcy distinctly uncomfortable.

Lady Catherine immediately dismissed Darcy's suggestion, saying loudly that there was little point in employing a French chef if one was going to ask him to cook common household food. Elizabeth merely nodded along.

Where was her wit? Her sharp observations? Her refusal to simply agree with him for the sake of pleasantness? Elizabeth Bennet would have had an opinion about fish sauces, would have either defended the French preparation with some clever argument or punctured Lady Catherine's smugness with a witty riposte. This docile acceptance bore no resemblance to the woman he knew.

As the meal progressed, Darcy became increasingly aware that Elizabeth had angled herself toward him, had positioned her attention almost exclusively in his direction. She looked at him frequently, smiled at him whenever their eyes met, seemed to be inviting further conversation through the openness of her expression. The warmth in her gaze was unmistakable, and it sent cold dread through Darcy's chest rather than pleasure.

This was wrong. This was all wrong. Elizabeth should be furious with him. Should be looking at him with barely suppressed anger, if she looked at him at all. Fitzwilliam had told her that Darcy had separated her beloved sister from Bingley, had interfered in Jane's happiness, had acted with presumptuous arrogance. Yet here Elizabeth sat, smiling at him as though he had done nothing more offensive than comment on the weather.

"Mr. Darcy," she said, leaning slightly forward as though to create intimacy across the table. "I have been meaning to tell you how much I enjoyed our walk this morning. Your company is always so agreeable."

Always. As though they had walked together frequently, as though she had consistently found his presence pleasant. Darcy stared at her, searching her face for any sign of irony or mockery, but found only that same warm pleasantness that seemed to have replaced her entire personality.

"I am glad you found it agreeable," he managed, his voice sounding strained even to his own ears.

Elizabeth's smile widened, taking his stilted response as encouragement. She opened her mouth to continue, but Colonel Fitzwilliam chose that moment to interject from his position further down the table.

"Miss Bennet," Fitzwilliam said, "I had hoped to ask your opinion on something. You mentioned yesterday that you enjoyed walking in all weather. I wondered whether you preferred morning rambles or afternoon exercise, as I have found the question divides opinion quite definitively."

It was exactly the sort of light, easy question Fitzwilliam excelled at, the kind of conversational opening that invited playful debate. Previously, Elizabeth would have seized upon it, would have engaged with his cousin with animated discussion.

Instead, she glanced briefly at Fitzwilliam, her expression cooling noticeably, and said, "I have no strong preference, Colonel." Then she turned immediately back to Darcy, effectively dismissing his cousin from her attention.

The cut was so obvious, so deliberate, that Darcy saw Fitzwilliam's expression shift from friendly interest to confusion to something that might have been hurt. His cousin's smile faltered, and he reached for his wine glass with enough force that the stem clinked against his plate.

Darcy found himself watching Fitzwilliam more closely, noting details he had perhaps overlooked before. His cousin's attempts to engage Elizabeth in conversation had been frequent during her stay at Rosings. His manner toward her had been warm, teasing, comfortable in a way Fitzwilliam typically reserved for people he genuinely liked. And now, faced with her cold dismissal, the Colonel looked rather like a man who had been slapped without warning.

Had Fitzwilliam developed feelings for Elizabeth? The possibility had never occurred to Darcy before, or if it had, he had dismissed it as unlikely. His cousin was a second son, dependent on his military career and whatever portion his father might settle on him. He could not afford to marry for inclination alone. Elizabeth's circumstances made her an impractical choice for Fitzwilliam, however much he might enjoy her company.

But practical considerations did not prevent feelings from forming. Darcy knew that truth intimately, having spent months trying to master his own unsuitable attachment through sheer force of will. Yet Elizabeth's behaviour was incomprehensible regardless of Fitzwilliam's feelings. Elizabeth had always responded to Fitzwilliam with warmth, had clearly enjoyed his company. Why would she suddenly treat him with such marked indifference while simultaneously showing increased warmth toward Darcy himself?

"The weather has been remarkably fine," Elizabeth said, directing the observation toward Darcy with focused attention that suggested she intended to hold his notice regardless of other claims on it. "Do you think it will hold through the week? I should like to continue my regular walks."

It was banal conversation, the sort of empty pleasantry that might fill silence but served no purpose beyond that. Elizabeth typically scorned such exchanges, preferring substance over social nicety. Darcy had once heard her say that she found discussions of weather to be the refuge of people with nothing interesting to say.

"I expect it will hold," Darcy replied, aware that his responses had become increasingly mechanical. "The spring has been mild thus far."

Elizabeth smiled at him again, that same warm, encouraging smile that made his stomach twist with discomfort. She looked pleased, as though he had said something particularly clever rather than offering the most pedestrian observation imaginable.

Across the table and down several places, Fitzwilliam had turned his attention to Anne, engaging her in some question about the gardens. Anne responded in her usual soft voice, barely audible over the general conversation, but Fitzwilliam gave her his courteous attention. Darcy noted the contrast. His cousin, rebuffed by Elizabeth, had turned to someone else with determined politeness. While Elizabeth seemed to have eyes only for Darcy, ignoring everyone else at the table.

The wrongness of it crashed over Darcy with renewed force, each piece of evidence accumulating. Elizabeth's lack of wit. Her warmth toward him when she should be angry. Her coldness toward Fitzwilliam when she had previously enjoyed his company. Her complete transformation from the sharp, independent woman he had come to admire into this pleasant, docile stranger who smiled too much and said nothing of substance.

This was not Elizabeth Bennet. Could not be Elizabeth Bennet. Yet she sat before him wearing Elizabeth's face, using Elizabeth's voice, inhabiting Elizabeth's body. How could she be anyone else?

Lady Catherine's voice cut through the general dinner conversation with its usual authority, drawing attention to herself as she posed some question about the parish to Mr. Collins. Darcy watched his aunt's profile as she spoke, noting the rigid set of her jaw, the way her fingers gripped her wine glass with unnecessary force. Something had displeased her, though whether it was related to Collins's obsequious response or to something else, Darcy could not immediately determine.

The candelabras positioned along the table's centre threw wavering light across the assembled company, their multiple branches holding candles that had burned down unevenly, creating shifting shadows. The flames reflected in the crystal glasses and caught the gold rim of the fine china, each piece bearing the de Bourgh crest. Everything in this dining room existed to impress, to remind guests of Lady Catherine's consequence and the long history of the de Bourgh family's position and wealth.

Lady Catherine's attention had shifted from Collins to Elizabeth, and Darcy saw his aunt's expression tighten with unmistakable displeasure.

"Miss Bennet," Lady Catherine said, her voice carrying the sharp edge of someone who had been observing unacceptable behaviour and could no longer contain her criticism. "I notice you have been monopolising Mr. Darcy's attention throughout the meal. Perhaps you might consider that conversation at dinner ought to be more generally distributed, not focused so exclusively in one direction."

The rebuke was direct enough that several people shifted uncomfortably. Mr. Collins made a small sound that might have been agreement or simple anxiety. Fitzwilliam paused with his fork halfway to his mouth, his expression suggesting he was preparing to intervene if the situation escalated.

Darcy waited for Elizabeth's response, for the flash of spirit that such a remark would inevitably provoke. He expected her to defend herself with wit, to point out that conversation required two participants and perhaps Mr. Darcy bore equal responsibility, or to turn the criticism back on Lady Catherine with some observation about the freedom of dinner guests to speak with whom they pleased.

Instead, Elizabeth simply smiled and turned her attention briefly toward Lady Catherine before looking back at Darcy. She did not respond at all, did not acknowledge the rebuke beyond that momentary glance.

The deliberate dismissal was so complete that Darcy saw Lady Catherine's face flush with genuine anger. His aunt was not accustomed to being ignored, particularly not at her own table, particularly not by young women of no particular consequence who were present only through her sufferance. Lady Catherine's fingers tightened further on her wine glass, and for a moment Darcy thought she might actually throw it.

"I do not believe Miss Bennet heard me," Lady Catherine said, her voice rising slightly with barely controlled fury. "I was commenting on the impropriety of focusing one's attention so exclusively on a single dinner companion. Such behaviour suggests a forward nature that I cannot approve."

Forward. The word hung in the air like an accusation, carrying implications of improper pursuit, of scheming unbecoming to a gentlewoman. Darcy felt his own jaw tighten at the insult, felt an instinctive urge to defend Elizabeth even as he acknowledged that his aunt's observation was not entirely inaccurate. Elizabeth had been behaving with unusual focus.

But this time Elizabeth did respond, though not in the way Darcy expected. She looked at Lady Catherine with that same pleasant smile and said, "How kind of you to concern yourself with my behaviour, Lady Catherine. You are always so thoughtful."

The words were perfectly civil, perfectly polite. They were also completely wrong, carrying none of Elizabeth's characteristic spirit, no hint of the independence that would have bristled at being corrected like a wayward child. It was as though she had not registered the insult at all.

Darcy watched his aunt's face cycle through several expressions, confusion and increased anger among them. Lady Catherine opened her mouth to deliver what would undoubtedly be an even more cutting remark, then seemed to think better of it. She turned her attention to Anne instead, demanding to know whether her daughter had eaten sufficient dinner, her voice containing the forced solicitude of someone redirecting frustration.

Further down the table, Mr. Collins had been watching this exchange with an expression Darcy could only describe as grimly satisfied mixed with obvious disapproval. The parson's small eyes moved from Elizabeth to Lady Catherine and back again, his lips pressed into a thin line. Darcy had observed Collins watching Elizabeth throughout the meal, had noted the frequency of those disapproving glances, but now the man seemed unable to contain himself.

"Miss Bennet," Collins said, his voice carrying pompous authority. "I must say I am surprised by your conduct today. First this morning's impropriety, and now this display at dinner. I had not thought you so lost to propriety as to require such correction from Lady Catherine, but it seems my concerns were well-founded."

Darcy's attention sharpened. This morning's impropriety? Collins had interfered with their walk earlier, had lectured Elizabeth about walking with him and Fitzwilliam without proper chaperonage. But the way Collins spoke suggested something more, some additional grievance.

Elizabeth turned to look at Collins, and Darcy watched her expression shift into something approaching contrition. "I apologise if my behaviour has been inappropriate, Mr. Collins. I certainly did not intend to cause offence."

The meekness of her response struck Darcy like a physical blow. Elizabeth apologising to Collins, accepting his pompous criticism without challenge? It was perhaps the most impossible thing yet in an evening full of impossibilities.

Collins appeared somewhat mollified by her submission, though suspicion remained evident in his expression. He made a sound of grudging acceptance and returned his attention to his plate, though Darcy noticed he continued to direct frequent glances toward Elizabeth throughout the remainder of the meal.

The servants had begun clearing the previous course when Darcy's gaze drifted toward the head of the table where Anne sat in her usual position beside her mother. His cousin appeared even more pale than usual, her face nearly translucent in the candlelight, and as Darcy watched, he saw her hands trembling where they rested on the table's edge.

Anne was frightened. Not merely uncomfortable or anxious, which would be unremarkable given her delicate constitution and the tension that had characterised dinner. She looked genuinely terrified, her pale eyes wide and fixed on Elizabeth with an intensity that suggested she was witnessing something deeply disturbing.

Darcy studied his cousin more closely. Anne's breathing had become rapid and shallow, her chest rising and falling with visible effort. A sheen of perspiration had appeared on her forehead despite the dining room's moderate temperature. Her fingers clutched at the table's edge as though it were the only thing preventing her from collapsing entirely.

What could possibly account for such a reaction? Anne had met Elizabeth before, had been present at previous dinners. She had never shown any particular interest in or distress about the parson's guest. Yet now she stared at Elizabeth with what looked remarkably like fear, or perhaps horror, her expression suggesting she was seeing something invisible to everyone else.

The candelabra nearest Anne cast harsh shadows across her face, emphasising the hollows beneath her cheekbones, the dark circles under her eyes. She looked ill, worse than her usual fragile state, as though the effort of sitting through dinner had exhausted her beyond her capacity.

Lady Catherine noticed Anne's distress and leaned toward her daughter, murmuring something Darcy could not hear. Anne shook her head slightly but did not look away from Elizabeth, her gaze remaining fixed with that same terrible intensity.

Darcy's attention was drawn across the table by a slight movement. Charlotte Collins had been sitting quietly through most of the meal, participating in conversation when addressed but otherwise maintaining pleasant neutrality. Now, however, she was watching Elizabeth with an expression that suggested deep confusion mixed with growing concern.

Charlotte's gaze moved from Elizabeth to Darcy, and their eyes met briefly across the table. In that moment, Darcy saw his own puzzlement reflected back. Charlotte's expression said clearly that she too found Elizabeth's behaviour wrong, inexplicable, fundamentally at odds with the friend she knew.

The moment of shared recognition lasted only seconds before Charlotte looked away, her attention returning to her plate. But it was enough. Elizabeth's closest friend, the person who knew her best of anyone present, had silently confirmed what Darcy had been thinking all evening. Something was profoundly wrong with Elizabeth Bennet.

The servants presented the next course, the elaborate dishes arranged artfully on serving platters. Crystal and silver gleamed, china clinked softly, and the dinner proceeded with scripted formality. On the surface, everything appeared as it should, another evening at Rosings following its predictable pattern.

But beneath that surface, wrongness festered. Lady Catherine sat rigid with barely suppressed anger, her periodic glances toward Elizabeth sharp with disapproval. Collins watched his guest with obvious displeasure. Anne stared at Elizabeth with frightened eyes, her hands trembling against the table. Charlotte observed her friend with troubled confusion. And Fitzwilliam sat in unusual silence, his typical good humour dimmed by Elizabeth's inexplicable coldness.

Darcy looked at Elizabeth again, this woman who wore a familiar face but possessed none of the spirit that made that face remarkable. She smiled at him across the table, warm and encouraging, and he felt his stomach turn with the wrongness of it.

Whatever was happening, whatever impossible thing had transformed Elizabeth Bennet into this pleasant stranger, Darcy was no longer alone in sensing it. The conviction settled over him with grim certainty. Multiple people at this table knew something was profoundly amiss, even if none of them could articulate what it might be.

And the evening was far from over.

Chapter Nine

THE PARLOUR FELT SO warm Elizabeth could hardly breathe, though she knew the temperature was perfectly comfortable for anyone not trapped in Anne de Bourgh's failing body. She had been positioned in the chair closest to the fire, Mrs. Jenkinson's doing, and the heat combined with the weight of the green silk gown made her feel as though she might faint. Her hands lay folded in her lap, pale and delicate and utterly wrong, while across the room her own body moved with careless freedom.

Elizabeth watched Anne cross to the window, watched her push the heavy casement further open with casual ease, watched her turn back to the company with a smile that used Elizabeth's mouth but belonged to someone else entirely. The movement was effortless, graceful in a way Elizabeth had taken for granted until this nightmare had stripped such capabilities away. Anne walked without trembling, stood without needing support, breathed without effort. She inhabited Elizabeth's healthy body as though it had always been hers.

The injustice of it burned in Elizabeth's chest, a fury that had no outlet, no means of expression. She could not rage, could not accuse, could not even stand and cross the room without risking collapse. Anne had imprisoned her as effectively as iron chains.

The parlour itself seemed designed to intimidate, all rich fabrics and gleaming surfaces arranged to showcase Lady Catherine's consequence. Ornate furniture stood in precise groupings, upholstered in burgundy and gold, each piece clearly expensive and uncomfortable. Portraits of stern-faced ancestors lined the walls, their painted eyes seeming to follow movement with disapproval. The pianoforte stood in the corner near the windows, its polished wood reflecting candlelight.

Elizabeth forced her attention away from Anne, forced herself to observe the others. Charlotte sat on the sofa beside Mr. Collins, her hands folded neatly in her lap, her expression composed in that careful neutrality she had perfected since her marriage. But Elizabeth knew Charlotte too well to be fooled by surface serenity. Her friend's gaze kept drifting toward Anne, toward the woman wearing Elizabeth's face, and each time Charlotte's brow furrowed slightly.

Charlotte sensed something wrong. The knowledge settled over Elizabeth with the weight of both hope and frustration. Her dearest friend, who knew her better than anyone save Jane, recognised that the woman calling herself Elizabeth Bennet was somehow not herself. But what good did that recognition do? Charlotte perhaps attributed Elizabeth's strange behaviour to illness or some temporary alteration of mood, but she would never leap to the impossible truth. Would never imagine that magic existed, that bodies could be swapped, that her friend had been stolen away.

Elizabeth considered it, briefly, desperately. Could she somehow communicate with Charlotte? Catch her eye, convey through expression or gesture that something was terribly wrong? But even as the thought formed, Elizabeth dismissed it. What would she say? How could she possibly explain? Charlotte would think her mad, would alert Lady Catherine, and Elizabeth would find herself confined. She would have to try and get Charlotte alone, somehow, but Mrs. Jenkinson was watching her with an eagle eye and Elizabeth knew it would not be tonight. If ever.

Her gaze shifted to Mr. Darcy, who stood near the fireplace in conversation with Colonel Fitzwilliam, though his attention kept drifting toward Anne. Elizabeth watched him watch her stolen body, saw the confusion evident in his expression, the slight furrow of his brow that suggested he was trying to solve a puzzle with insufficient pieces. He too sensed something amiss, though he clearly could not determine what troubled him.

For a wild moment, Elizabeth considered trying to communicate with him. Darcy was intelligent, perceptive when he chose to be. He had clearly noticed the changes in "Elizabeth's" behaviour, was troubled by them. Perhaps he might be convinced, might be willing to at least investigate the possibility that something extraordinary had occurred.

But no. That idea was absurd. Darcy would think her mad, would be relieved for an excuse to avoid marrying Anne, would sign whatever papers Lady Catherine put before him declaring her unfit. Elizabeth could not risk losing what little freedom she still possessed.

Lady Catherine held court from her thronelike chair. She had been delivering opinions about parish matters to Mr. Collins for the past several minutes, her voice carrying across the room with the certainty of someone who had never been seriously contradicted. Mr. Collins nodded eagerly at each pronouncement.

Elizabeth's attention snapped back to the present as Lady Catherine's voice rose slightly.

"Miss Bennet," Lady Catherine said, the words carrying imperious command. "You will favour us with some music. I insist upon it."

Elizabeth's gaze flew to Anne, watched as something like panic flashed across her stolen face. Anne had been standing near the window, engaged in some idle observation about the gardens with Maria Lucas, but now she turned to face Lady Catherine with an expression that cycled rapidly through alarm, calculation, and forced pleasantness.

"I thank you for the invitation, Lady Catherine," Anne said, using Elizabeth's voice but speaking with a formality Elizabeth would never have employed. "But I find I am more inclined toward conversation this evening. Perhaps another time."

The refusal was polite enough, but Lady Catherine's expression suggested she did not take kindly to having her commands declined. Her small eyes narrowed, her lips compressing into a thin line.

"Nonsense," Lady Catherine declared. "You do play quite well, though you disclaim it; both my nephews have expressed pleasure in hearing you." She gave them no opportunity to agree, but carried on. "You will be departing Kent soon enough; be so good as to favour us with one last performance."

Anne's fingers began fidgeting with Elizabeth's skirts, plucking at the muslin in a gesture of nervous agitation. Anne was frightened, and not simply of Lady Catherine's displeasure. Her gaze darted toward the pianoforte as though it were an instrument of torture, and her face had gone pale beneath the healthy colour Elizabeth's complexion naturally carried.

Understanding crashed over Elizabeth with sudden, brilliant clarity. Anne could not play. Had never learned the instrument, had spent her youth too ill to sit for the hours of practice required to develop even basic competence. Elizabeth had not considered the significance until now, but watching Anne's panic made everything clear.

The witch who had studied alchemy with her father, who had learned to brew potions powerful enough to swap bodies, who had planned this theft with meticulous care, had overlooked one crucial detail. She did not possess Elizabeth's accomplishments, could not replicate Elizabeth's abilities, could only inhabit her body without being able to truly become her.

Elizabeth felt something like hope stir in her chest for the first time since waking. Anne had made a mistake. Had revealed a weakness.

Her mind raced, calculating possibilities, weighing risks. She could expose Anne here, now, by insisting she play. The impostor would be forced to either refuse repeatedly, drawing Lady Catherine's ire and perhaps raising questions, or attempt to play and reveal her complete lack of skill. Either outcome would create confusion, would plant seeds of doubt.

But Elizabeth needed to be careful. Needed to create the opportunity without appearing to force it, without drawing suspicion to herself. Anne's panic was already visible to anyone who cared to look. Elizabeth simply needed to provide the perfect excuse for the exposure to continue... and, too, this might be her only chance to force Anne to speak to her directly. She could potentially gather valuable information.

Elizabeth did not allow herself time to reconsider. She drew a careful breath, summoning Anne's soft, hesitant voice, and spoke before her courage could falter.

"I have always wanted to learn the pianoforte," she said, pitching her voice to carry just enough to be heard. "Perhaps Miss Bennet might be kind enough to give me a lesson? I should so like to understand the basics of the instrument."

The request hung in the air for a moment, and Elizabeth watched Anne's face cycle through shock, alarm, and barely suppressed fury in rapid succession. But before Anne could formulate a response, before she could find some polite way to refuse, Mr. Collins inserted himself into the conversation with his characteristic lack of awareness.

"What an excellent notion!" Mr. Collins exclaimed, rising from the sofa with enough enthusiasm that Charlotte had to steady herself. He clasped his hands together, his round face beaming. "Such humility, Miss de Bourgh, to offer one of lesser station an opportunity to instruct you! And how generous it would be of my cousin to provide instruction. Miss Bennet is quite accomplished at the pianoforte, though I confess her performance lacks the superior elegance one might find in young ladies of higher station."

He turned toward Anne, directing his attention to the woman he believed to be his cousin, his expression radiating expectation mixed with that particular smugness he displayed when arranging matters to his satisfaction. "You would be doing Miss de Bourgh a great service, Cousin Elizabeth. Lady Catherine has been most generous in her hospitality toward you, and it would be only proper to repay that kindness with such assistance. I am certain you will be delighted to help Miss de Bourgh in this endeavour."

The words were phrased as though offering a choice, but Collins's tone made clear he expected immediate agreement. He had framed the request as a matter of propriety and gratitude, making refusal tantamount to rudeness. Elizabeth watched Anne's jaw tighten, saw her stolen hands curl into fists at her sides before she forced them to relax.

"How very kind of you to volunteer my assistance, Mr. Collins," Anne said, her voice carrying an edge that Collins appeared entirely oblivious to. "Though I hesitate to impose my limited skills upon Miss de Bourgh. Surely there are more qualified instructors available."

But before Collins could respond, before the moment could slip away, Mr. Darcy spoke from his position near the fireplace.

"I think it an excellent idea," Darcy said, his deep voice carrying easily across the parlour. "Miss Bennet plays with great spirit, even if her technical execution is not always precise. She would make an admirable instructor for someone just beginning to learn." He looked at Anne directly, and Elizabeth saw something shift in his expression, something that might have been hope. "Your willingness to share your accomplishment speaks well of your generous nature."

Elizabeth felt a pang of bitter irony at his words. Darcy praising Anne for Elizabeth's generosity, approving of behaviour that was entirely calculated manipulation. But she pushed the feeling aside, focused instead on the trap closing around Anne.

Anne's face had gone pale beneath Elizabeth's naturally healthy complexion, and Elizabeth could see her mind working frantically, searching for some escape that would not expose her ignorance or make her appear churlish. Her gaze darted from

Collins to Darcy to Lady Catherine, seeking some reprieve, but finding none.

Lady Catherine had been watching this exchange with an expression that suggested she found the entire situation both tedious and vaguely irritating. Now she waved one imperious hand, cutting off whatever protest Anne might have been formulating.

"It is settled then," Lady Catherine declared, her voice brooking no argument. "Anne requires instruction on the pianoforte, and Miss Bennet will provide it. They will go to the instrument now and begin immediately." She paused, her gaze sweeping the room. "The rest of you will remain here with me. I will not have my daughter subjected to an audience while she is learning. Such scrutiny would be most inappropriate for a young lady of her delicate sensibilities."

The command was absolute. Elizabeth understood immediately that Lady Catherine's concern was not for Anne's comfort but for her pride. She did not wish to witness her daughter's potential failures, did not want to see Anne struggle with something she should have learned years ago. Better to have the lesson conducted at a distance, where any mistakes could be concealed or minimised.

But the command served Elizabeth's purposes perfectly. Privacy meant the opportunity to speak with Anne without witnesses, without the constraint of maintaining performances for the assembled company. Whatever happened at that pianoforte would occur away from ears that might hear accusations they would never believe.

Anne's expression had settled into something that looked remarkably like trapped fury, but she could not refuse now. Not with Collins beaming his approval, Darcy watching with expectation, Lady Catherine commanding immediate compliance. She had been outmanoeuvred by social convention.

"Of course," Anne said finally, the words emerging stiff and reluctant. "I would be delighted to provide instruction to Miss de Bourgh."

The lie was obvious to Elizabeth, but Mr. Collins appeared satisfied, and Mr. Darcy nodded his approval, and Lady Catherine had already turned her attention to Colonel Fitzwilliam. The matter was settled, the trap sprung, and Elizabeth felt triumph war with apprehension.

She placed her pale hand on the arm of the settee and pushed, summoning what strength Anne's body possessed. The simple act of standing up required concentration, careful distribution of weight. Elizabeth managed it, though she had to pause once standing to steady herself, one hand gripping the settee's back while the room swayed slightly.

Across the room, Anne had begun moving toward the pianoforte with visible reluctance, Elizabeth's body responding to her direction with easy grace. Anne walked with her shoulders slightly hunched, her steps lacking the natural confidence Elizabeth typically displayed, and the wrongness of it all struck Elizabeth anew.

Elizabeth took her first careful step, testing her balance, feeling Anne's legs tremble beneath her weight. Another step, and another, each one requiring deliberate effort. The distance to the pianoforte seemed vast. In Anne's failing form, it felt like miles.

But Elizabeth continued forward, refusing to falter. Her heart hammered against her ribs, partly from the physical exertion and partly from anticipation. She was walking toward a confrontation with the woman who had stolen her life, toward the first opportunity to speak privately since this nightmare began. And she was walking toward the possibility of exposing Anne's deception, of planting seeds of doubt that might eventually grow into her salvation.

Anne fell into step beside her, their skirts rustling together in a whisper of silk and muslin that seemed unnaturally loud in the sudden quiet that had fallen over the room. Elizabeth was acutely aware of the watching eyes tracking their progress, but she kept her attention fixed on the pianoforte ahead.

Their footsteps created an odd rhythm, Elizabeth's slow and careful, punctuated by slight hesitations when Anne's body threatened to betray her, while Anne's were quicker but somehow wrong, lacking the natural confidence with which Elizabeth typically moved. It was as though Anne had not yet learned to fully inhabit the stolen body. Elizabeth found grim satisfaction in that observation, proof that Anne's theft was imperfect.

Elizabeth's fingers trembled at her sides, partly from weakness and partly from the anticipation building in her chest. Her heart hammered against her ribs. Lady Catherine's voice carried across the distance, holding forth to Colonel Fitzwilliam about some matter of estate management, her imperious tone suggesting she had already dismissed the two young women from her awareness. Mr. Collins had returned to the sofa beside Charlotte. Mr. Darcy remained near the fireplace, but Elizabeth could feel his gaze on her back.

Elizabeth's vision swam slightly, spots dancing at the edges as the exertion caught up with her borrowed body's limited capacity. She forced her breathing to remain steady, refused to gasp or stagger, maintained her careful progress through sheer determination. Anne glanced at her once, a quick sideways look that might have been concern if Elizabeth had not seen the calculation in it. Anne was assessing whether Elizabeth would make it to the pianoforte without collapsing, whether she would embarrass herself.

But Elizabeth would not grant Anne that satisfaction. Would not falter now, not when she had engineered this opportunity so carefully.

The pianoforte stood in the corner near the tall windows, its dark wood gleaming in the candlelight, its ivory keys pristine and untouched. Elizabeth could see her reflection in the polished surface, distorted and strange, Anne de Bourgh's pale face staring back at her.

Anne's reflection appeared beside hers, Elizabeth's own features twisted into an expression of barely suppressed fury that Elizabeth had never worn, would never have recognised as belonging to her. Anne was not frightened of exposure, she realised. She was angry, deeply and visibly angry, and the recognition sent a chill through Elizabeth's awareness.

Anne had been outmanoeuvred, trapped by social convention and her own inability to replicate Elizabeth's accomplishments, and she was furious about it. Not apologetic, not remorseful, not even particularly concerned about the consequences. Simply angry that Elizabeth had managed to create this situation.

Elizabeth's fingers continued to tremble as they approached the final few steps. This would be their first opportunity to speak privately since the body swap, the first moment without the entire company of Rosings observing their interactions. Elizabeth's mind raced with possibilities, with questions that demanded answers. How had Anne done this? How could it be reversed? What did Anne intend now?

But beneath those practical considerations ran a deeper current of violation. Anne had stolen her body, her life, her very identity, and she had done it with calculated precision. Anne had been willing to trap Elizabeth in this feeble body, to condemn her to suffer while she enjoyed health and freedom, and she felt no apparent remorse.

The pianoforte bench sat between them, dark wood padded with burgundy velvet. It was designed to accommodate a single player, perhaps with space for someone to sit close and turn pages, but not truly large enough for two people to sit comfortably side by side. They would have to press together, share space, maintain the fiction of a music lesson while conducting a confrontation that could determine Elizabeth's entire future.

Behind them, the murmur of conversation continued, Lady Catherine's voice rising and falling with its characteristic authority, Mr. Collins's occasional interjections of agreement punctuating the flow. They were far enough away now that quiet conversation at the pianoforte would not be overheard, close enough that any raised voices would immediately draw attention.

Elizabeth drew a careful breath, steeling herself. Anne's expression had settled into something cold and hard, fury evident in every line of her stolen face. They stood on opposite sides of the bench, the instrument before them a battlefield, the pristine keys waiting to expose one lie while concealing another.

Elizabeth reached for the bench with one trembling hand, preparing to lower herself onto its surface. Anne moved simultaneously, her stolen body responding with the strength and coordination Elizabeth had taken for granted, both women reaching for the same narrow seat.

Their hands touched the velvet padding at nearly the same moment, Elizabeth's pale fingers and Anne's healthy ones meeting on the burgundy surface. Elizabeth looked up, met Anne's gaze directly for the first time since recognising the truth, and saw her own eyes staring back at her filled with an anger that took her breath away.

Chapter Ten

THEY SETTLED ONTO THE bench together, the narrow seat forcing them closer than Elizabeth could bear, Anne's stolen shoulder pressing against hers with casual familiarity that felt like violation. Elizabeth's borrowed hands trembled as she placed them on the smooth ivory keys, Anne's fingers lacking the strength and dexterity Elizabeth had always taken for granted.

The parlour behind them hummed with conversation, Lady Catherine's voice rising and falling with its characteristic authority, punctuated by Mr. Collins's obsequious agreements. Elizabeth could feel Darcy's gaze on her back still, but she forced herself to ignore it. She must do something, must keep up the appearances of being given instruction, lest Lady Catherine grew impatient with the silence.

Elizabeth pressed down on middle C, the note ringing out clear. Her finger trembled against the key, Anne's body betraying her even in this simple gesture, but the sound carried well enough. She moved to the next note, then the next, building a simple ascending scale. The repetition created a rhythmic pattern, each note distinct but the overall effect monotonous enough that the company behind them would lose interest quickly.

Under the cover of that simple music, Elizabeth leaned slightly closer to Anne and spoke, her voice barely above a whisper.

"Why did you do this?"

Anne's stolen hands remained folded in her lap, and she did not look at Elizabeth directly, keeping her gaze fixed on the keys. But Elizabeth saw her own mouth curve into a smile, an expression of scornful amusement that Elizabeth had never worn. That looked utterly wrong on her face.

"Why?" Anne's voice emerged just as quietly. "Because you had everything and you were wasting it."

Elizabeth's fingers faltered on the keys, striking B when she meant to hit C, the wrong note jarring. She forced herself to continue, to repeat the scale, to maintain the pretence.

"Everything," Anne continued, and her tone carried genuine bitterness beneath the mockery. "Health. Strength. The ability to walk across a room without trembling, to climb stairs without gasping for breath, to move through the world without being treated like fragile porcelain." She paused, and when she spoke again, her voice had dropped even lower. "You had a body that worked, Lizzy. And you took it entirely for granted."

The use of Elizabeth's familiar name from her own mouth felt obscene, a violation beyond even the theft of her body.

Elizabeth's hands shook harder, making the next attempt at the scale emerge choppy and uneven.

"That does not give you the right," Elizabeth whispered fiercely.

Anne laughed, the sound emerging quiet and cruel. "Right? What is right, except what power allows? I had the knowledge, the skill, the determination to take what I needed." She turned her head slightly, just enough that Elizabeth could see the profile of her own face. "I saw my opportunity and I seized it. That is all there is to right and wrong in this world."

Elizabeth's stomach turned at the casual callousness, at the complete absence of remorse. Anne spoke of theft and deception as though they were merely practical decisions, as though Elizabeth's suffering meant nothing weighed against Anne's desires.

She forced her fingers back to the keys, starting the scale again with deliberate slowness. Her mind raced even as her borrowed body struggled. She needed Anne to keep talking, needed to understand the full scope of what had been done to her and why.

"You could have had any number of bodies, I think," Elizabeth said, keeping her voice steady with effort. "Why mine specifically? What did I do to earn your particular hatred?"

"Hatred?" Anne's laugh came again, that same quiet cruelty. "I do not hate you, Lizzy. I pity you. All that beauty and vivacity, all that wit and charm, and you were too blind to see what was right in front of you."

Elizabeth's fingers struck several wrong notes in succession, the scale dissolving into near cacophony before she caught herself. She stared at the keys uncomprehendingly. What had she been blind to?

"You had Fitzwilliam Darcy dangling after you like a lovesick puppy," Anne continued, and her voice carried genuine scorn now. "The master of Pemberley, one of the finest estates in England, ten thousand a year and connections to half the nobility. He could not take his eyes off you. Could not stop talking about you. Could not rest until he had contrived to be wherever you were."

The words struck Elizabeth with enough force that her hands fell away from the keys entirely, landing in her lap with a soft thump. She sat frozen, her mind refusing to accept what Anne had said even as pieces began clicking into horrible place. Darcy's frequent presence at the parsonage. His walks in the grove where he always seemed to encounter her. His attention during dinner. His cousin's attempts to speak well of him.

Charlotte had speculated on his possible interest, months ago in Hertfordshire, but the idea had seemed so absurd that Elizabeth had dismissed it.

"You are lying," Elizabeth whispered, but the words emerged without conviction.

"Am I?" Anne turned to look at her fully now, Elizabeth's own face displaying mocking pity. "Then why does he seek out your company constantly? Why does he watch you with that hungry, desperate look when he thinks no one is observing?" She paused, letting the questions hang between them. "He is in love with you, Lizzy. Utterly, completely, hopelessly in love. And you were too proud and blind to see it."

Elizabeth's lungs struggled to draw breath, Anne's weak chest heaving with the effort. Her mind spun, rejecting Anne's claims even as evidence accumulated in support of them. Darcy *had* been oddly attentive, had sought her out repeatedly, had shown signs of interest that Elizabeth had misinterpreted as disdain. But *love*? The proud, disagreeable Mr. Darcy in love with *her*?

It was impossible. It had to be impossible. Yet Anne's words carried the weight of informed observation, of someone who had been watching closely while Elizabeth had been oblivious.

"Even if it were true," Elizabeth forced out, her voice emerging rough, "that still gives you no right to what you have done. To steal my body, my life, to trap me here while you take my place."

"Rights again." Anne shook her head with that same mocking expression. "You keep speaking of rights as though they mean something. I saw what I wanted, what I deserved, what should have been mine if fate had not cursed me with this failing body. And I took it. That is all there is."

She reached out with Elizabeth's strong, healthy hand and pressed down on middle C, the note ringing out clear. "I will be Mrs. Darcy. I will be Mistress of Pemberley. I will have the life I was always meant to have, the life you were wasting through your stubborn pride and wilful blindness." Anne's smile widened into something terrible. "And you, dear Lizzy, will fade away in the body I no longer need."

Elizabeth's vision swam, spots dancing at the edges as the full horror crashed over her. This was not temporary. Anne had no intention of ever reversing what she had done. She meant to keep Elizabeth's body permanently, to marry Darcy in Elizabeth's form.

"I will tell someone," Elizabeth whispered desperately. "I will expose you. Will make them see the truth."

"Will you?" Anne's expression showed only amused contempt. "And who will believe you? Mrs. Jenkinson already knows, but she will never speak of it. My mother will have you committed to an asylum if you start raving about body swapping and witchcraft. And Darcy..." She paused, her smile turning cruel. "Darcy will be relieved to have an excuse to avoid marrying the mad Anne de Bourgh. He will sign the papers gladly and never think of you again."

The truth of it settled over Elizabeth like a shroud. She tried to respond, tried to form some argument or threat, but her throat had closed with unshed tears, Anne's body betraying her once again. She turned back to the pianoforte and placed trembling fingers on the keys, striking notes at random.

Behind them, someone laughed at something Lady Catherine had said. The pleasant sounds of after-dinner conversation continued, entirely oblivious to the nightmare unfolding at the pianoforte.

Anne's smile widened further, Elizabeth's mouth stretching into an expression of triumph. She leaned closer, her voice dropping to barely above a breath.

"I am going to enjoy this," Anne whispered, and the words carried genuine pleasure beneath their cruelty. "Being who I was always meant to be. Mrs. Fitzwilliam Darcy. Mistress of Pemberley. The woman who has everything: wealth, position, beauty, health, and a husband who will adore her until the day he dies."

Elizabeth's hands had begun to shake harder, the trembling spreading through Anne's arms until her entire upper body quivered. She forced herself to stop striking random keys, to place her palms flat against the ivory to steady them.

"What about me?" The question emerged broken, barely audible. "What do you expect will happen to me?"

Anne tilted her head, studying Elizabeth with detached curiosity. "You will die, of course. That body has perhaps six months remaining, a year at the outside. The damage is too extensive to repair."

The words landed with brutal simplicity, no softening, no false sympathy. Elizabeth stared at Anne, at her own stolen face displaying calm certainty about Elizabeth's death sentence, and felt something crack inside her chest. Six months. Perhaps a year. Anne spoke of it as though discussing the weather.

"How can you say such things?" Elizabeth's voice emerged rough with barely suppressed tears. "How can you speak of my death with such indifference?"

"Indifference?" Anne's eyebrows rose. "I am not indifferent, Lizzy. I am simply realistic. That body was dying already, long before you inhabited it. The chemicals I breathed during my studies, the powders and vapours from my father's experiments, they accumulated in my lungs, in my blood, weakening everything from the inside." She paused, and something like bitterness crossed her stolen features. "My father died the same way, you know. Coughing up blood in his final months, unable to draw breath without pain. He sacrificed his health for knowledge, and I have done the same. But I have succeeded where he failed – I have escaped my fate."

Elizabeth's stomach turned at the casual revelation, at the matter-of-fact acknowledgement that Anne had poisoned herself through her alchemical studies. And now Elizabeth was trapped in that poisoned body, condemned to suffer the consequences of Anne's choices, to die slowly from damage she had not caused.

"You are a monster," Elizabeth whispered, and this time she could not prevent the tears from gathering in Anne's pale eyes, could not stop them from spilling down her borrowed cheeks.

"You have condemned me to die so that you can steal my life, and you speak of it as though you have done nothing wrong."

Anne reached out and wiped Elizabeth's tears away with Elizabeth's own hand, the gesture almost tender if one ignored the cruelty in her expression. "I have done what I needed to do to survive. To have some taste of life before this body failed entirely. You may think me a monster for it, but I think you are a fool for having wasted the gifts you were born with."

She pulled her hand back and placed it on the pianoforte beside Elizabeth's, both sets of fingers resting on the polished ivory keys. Elizabeth's strong healthy hand and Anne's frail dying one, side by side, a visual reminder of the theft that had occurred. "And you should know, Lizzy, that I am very good with poisons. With potions and draughts and tinctures that can make death appear natural, like the simple failure of an already failing body. So if you attempt to interfere with my plans, if you try to expose me or cause trouble, I will ensure your suffering ends more quickly than it otherwise might."

The threat hung between them, absolute and chilling in its calm delivery. Anne was promising to murder her if she proved inconvenient, to poison her and make it look like the natural progression of her illness. And no one would question it.

Elizabeth forced air into her borrowed lungs, forced herself to think despite the tears still streaming down her face, despite the horror threatening to overwhelm her. She needed some leverage, some way to shake Anne's confidence.

"You will be discovered," Elizabeth said, her voice emerging stronger now despite the tears. "At Longbourn. My sisters know me too well, have lived with me their entire lives. Jane will see through you immediately. Even Kitty and Lydia will notice the differences. You cannot possibly replicate me well enough to fool my own family."

But Anne's expression showed only amused contempt. "You cannot imagine I would willingly subject myself to that dreadful place. Five unmarried daughters cramped into a modest house, a mother whose only conversation consists of officers and caps and gossip, a father who has abdicated all responsibility for his family's future. No, thank you." She shook her head, Elizabeth's curls moving with the gesture. "I had quite enough of hearing about it from you and your endless prattling about dear Jane and your concerns for your sisters' prospects."

The cruelty of it struck Elizabeth like a blow. Anne had observed her, had listened to her speak of her family with affection, and had judged them all unworthy. Had decided that once she stole Elizabeth's life, she would simply excise Elizabeth's family from it entirely.

"They are my family," Elizabeth whispered, her voice breaking. "You cannot simply pretend they do not exist."

"Can I not?" Anne's eyebrows rose in challenge. "Watch me. Once Darcy proposes, which I expect will happen very soon now that I have shown appropriate interest, we will marry in London. A special licence can be obtained quickly for a man of his standing. Perhaps at St George's in Hanover Square, something appropriately elegant." Her smile widened. "And then we will retire to Pemberley as husband and wife, and by the time anyone at Longbourn thinks to question why they have not been invited to witness the ceremony, it will be far too late."

The plan was brilliant in its simplicity, Elizabeth realised with sick comprehension. Anne would marry Darcy before Elizabeth's family could intervene, before Jane could meet her and recognise the wrongness, before Mr. Bennet could observe her behaviour and question whether this was truly his second daughter. Darcy, arrogant as he was, would probably think that Elizabeth preferred not to have her family present lest they embarrass her in front of his important friends and relations; it would make perfect logical sense to him. The marriage would be complete, legal, binding, and any revelation afterward would cause scandal that would destroy everyone involved.

"But Charlotte," Elizabeth said desperately, grasping at the one person currently present who might still notice, might still question. "Charlotte watches you strangely. She knows something is wrong. She will not simply accept your behaviour without investigation."

Anne's laugh emerged quiet and genuinely amused. "Charlotte Collins, who married a pompous fool for security rather than affection? Who chose a comfortable home over any hope of happiness?" She shook her head with that same mocking expression. "What precisely might Charlotte suspect, Lizzy? That her dear friend Elizabeth has finally come to her senses? That she has recognised Mr. Darcy's interest and decided to secure him before he loses patience with her stubbornness?"

The words struck with horrible accuracy because they were exactly what Charlotte would think. Charlotte, who had counselled Elizabeth to be more accommodating, who had suggested that not every marriage needed to be a love match, would attribute any strangeness in Elizabeth's behaviour to pragmatism finally overcoming pride.

"She will think you have matured," Anne continued, her confidence absolute. "Have learned to value security and position over romantic notions and wounded pride. She will be pleased for you, Lizzy. Will congratulate you on making such an advantageous match. Will perhaps even feel vindicated in her own choice, seeing that her sensible friend has followed her example."

Elizabeth's throat closed around any response. Anne was right. Charlotte would never suspect witchcraft or body swapping. She would simply assume Elizabeth had changed her mind about Darcy, had decided to encourage his interest, had chosen to pursue the advantageous match she had previously spurned. And Charlotte, having made a similar calculation herself, would find nothing strange in such a transformation.

Anne's expression shifted then, satisfaction giving way to something almost like pride. "It was not even particularly difficult," she said, and her voice carried the quality of someone who could not quite resist bragging. "The planning took time, certainly. Waiting for the right opportunity, ensuring I had all the necessary ingredients, choosing my moment carefully. But the execution?" She paused, and her smile widened into something terrible. "It took no more than a little hair and a well-made draught. I was careful, of course. Precise. But alchemy itself is quite straightforward once one has the knowledge."

The words landed with the force of revelation. Anne had needed Elizabeth's hair and some kind of potion, and those two elements had been sufficient to swap their bodies. Elizabeth's mind seized on this information with desperate intensity. If a potion had caused this, then perhaps a potion could reverse it. If hair had been required to create the connection between them, then perhaps hair could be used to break it.

Hope flared in Elizabeth's chest, painful and bright. Anne had revealed the method, had been so confident in her success that she had carelessly disclosed the very information Elizabeth needed most.

Elizabeth forced her borrowed face into an expression of defeated acceptance, let her shoulders slump in apparent surrender. She needed Anne to believe she had given up, had accepted her fate, posed no threat. Because if Anne suspected Elizabeth might attempt to reverse what had been done, she would take precautions, would ensure Elizabeth had no access to the materials or knowledge required.

"You have won," Elizabeth said quietly, and the defeat in her voice was not entirely feigned. Anne had won, at least for now. But Elizabeth had information now, had the beginnings of a plan, had some thread of hope to cling to.

Anne studied her for a moment, and something like wariness crossed her stolen features. Had she realised her mistake? Had she recognised that she had revealed too much? But then her expression cleared, satisfaction returning as she apparently decided Elizabeth was too defeated, too trapped, too weak to pose any real threat.

"Yes," Anne agreed simply. "I have won."

Elizabeth met Anne's gaze directly, allowing the tears to spill freely down her cheeks. Let Anne see defeat in her expression, let her believe Elizabeth had surrendered. But beneath that defeated exterior, Elizabeth's mind was already working, already planning, already calculating how she might obtain what she needed.

Somewhere in that journal, there had to be a record of the exact formula Anne had used.

And if it contained the spell to swap bodies, it might also contain the spell to swap them back.

Elizabeth Bennet had never surrendered easily, had never accepted defeat without a fight. Anne had stolen her body, her life, her future. But Elizabeth would find a way to take it all back. Would discover the method, obtain the ingredients, reverse what had been done.

She simply had to survive long enough to accomplish it.

Chapter Eleven

THE NOTES FROM THE pianoforte had been painful to hear, discordant strikes against ivory that bore no resemblance to music. Darcy had tried not to wince too visibly as the sounds drifted across the parlour, but he had noticed Fitzwilliam grimacing beside him, and even Lady Catherine had shifted in her chair with obvious displeasure. The lesson, if it could be called such, had lasted perhaps ten minutes before dissolving into silence. Now, as Darcy glanced toward the instrument in the corner, he saw something that made his chest tighten with unexpected concern.

Anne was crying.

Not the delicate tears of a lady moved by sentiment, but the trembling shoulders and bowed head of genuine distress. The candlelight caught the wetness on her pale cheeks, revealed the way her hands clutched at the green silk of her skirts. Her breathing came in small, visible gasps that made Darcy think of a wounded animal trying not to make noise while suffering.

Beside her, Elizabeth sat with her back partially turned, her expression neutral as she gazed toward the window rather than at her supposed student. The contrast was stark. Elizabeth appeared entirely composed, seemingly unaffected by Anne's obvious distress, while Anne herself looked as though she might collapse.

Guilt struck Darcy with unexpected force. He had approved of the lesson, had even spoken in favour of it when Elizabeth had shown reluctance. Had thought it would be beneficial for Anne to receive instruction, had viewed it as an opportunity for her to develop an accomplishment denied by her delicate health. Now, watching his cousin's shoulders shake with silent sobs, he realised he had pushed her into something she was utterly unprepared for.

Lady Catherine's voice cut through his thoughts. "Anne is overwrought," she announced to the room at large, her tone carrying that particular edge of displeasure mixed with concern. "The exertion has been too much for her delicate constitution. She requires rest."

The words were delivered as though Anne's distress were both expected and vaguely inconvenient. Darcy felt his jaw tighten at his aunt's casual dismissal, at the way she remained seated rather than going to comfort her daughter. Someone needed to offer Anne support.

Darcy set down his coffee cup and rose from his position near the fireplace. Lady Catherine's gaze snapped to him immediately, her expression suggesting she found his movement both unnecessary and inappropriate.

"Darcy, there is no need," Lady Catherine began, but he was already crossing the room, his long strides carrying him toward the pianoforte.

Darcy was aware of the room's attention shifting to him, of conversations pausing as people turned to observe. But he kept his focus on Anne, on the trembling figure in green silk who had not yet looked up, who remained bent over her lap as though trying to disappear entirely.

As he drew closer, Darcy could see the full extent of Anne's distress. Tears streamed down her face unchecked, her pale skin blotched with red around her eyes and nose. Her hands twisted in her skirts with enough force to wrinkle the expensive silk. Her breathing remained rapid and shallow, each inhalation audible.

The sight struck Darcy with surprising force. He had seen Anne unwell countless times, had witnessed her fatigue and weakness and the general frailty that characterised her existence. But he had never seen her like this, so completely undone, so visibly suffering in a way that went beyond physical illness into something that looked remarkably like despair.

"Anne," Darcy said quietly, pitching his voice to carry only to her. "You appear a little tired and overset."

The words were inadequate, he knew, too gentle for the depth of distress he was witnessing. But what else could he say? He could hardly acknowledge the full scope of her suffering in front of the assembled company.

Anne looked up at him then, and what Darcy saw in her expression made his breath catch. Not embarrassment about her failure at the pianoforte, though surely that was present. Not simple distress about being pushed beyond her capabilities. What he saw was something deeper, more desperate, something that looked remarkably like pleading.

Her pale eyes fixed on his face with an intensity that seemed to convey wordless communication. *Help me*, those eyes seemed to say. *Please help me*. But help with what? What could Anne possibly need from him beyond the obvious comfort he was attempting to provide?

Before Darcy could speak again, before he could attempt to decipher that strange, desperate look, a familiar figure materialised at Anne's other side. Mrs. Jenkinson had crossed the room with surprising speed, her face set in lines of protective concern mixed with something that might have been warning.

"Come, Miss de Bourgh," Mrs. Jenkinson said, her voice carrying that particular authority of a long-time companion. "You have overtaxed yourself this evening. You require rest immediately."

She placed one hand on Anne's shoulder, not roughly but with enough firmness to communicate that resistance would not be tolerated. Anne's gaze remained fixed on Darcy for another moment, that same pleading desperation evident in every line of her face, before she finally allowed her attention to shift to her companion.

"I am tired," Anne whispered, her voice emerging rough and broken. "So very tired."

Mrs. Jenkinson made a sound of agreement and began helping Anne to rise, supporting her elbow as she stood on trembling legs. Anne swayed slightly, and Darcy instinctively reached out to steady her, his hand hovering near her arm though propriety prevented him from actually touching her.

Anne looked at him one final time before Mrs. Jenkinson guided her toward the door. That look hit Darcy like a physical blow, so full of desperate pleading and helpless sorrow that it made his chest ache with confused sympathy. What was she trying to communicate? What did she need him to understand?

Then she was turning away, allowing Mrs. Jenkinson to lead her from the parlour with careful, measured steps. Darcy watched them go, watched Anne's bent head and trembling shoulders disappear through the doorway.

He had suggested this lesson. Had thought it would be beneficial. And instead, he had subjected her to an experience that had clearly devastated her.

The door closed with a soft click, and the parlour gradually returned to its previous hum of conversation. Lady Catherine made some pronouncement about Anne's delicate constitution. Collins agreed with obsequious enthusiasm. Charlotte looked troubled but said nothing.

Darcy remained standing beside the pianoforte, staring at the closed door, that final pleading look still vivid in his memory. Anne would recover, surely. She always did, bouncing back from moments of weakness with the resilience that chronic illness had forced her to develop. By tomorrow she would be resting comfortably, and this evening's distress would fade into just another example of her fragile health being overtaxed.

Yet even as he reassured himself with these thoughts, Darcy could not shake the memory of that desperate, pleading expression. Could not dismiss the conviction that Anne had been trying to tell him something, to communicate some urgent need that went beyond simple distress about failing at the pianoforte.

Darcy turned his attention from the closed door back to Elizabeth, who remained standing beside the pianoforte as though nothing extraordinary had just occurred. The candlelight caught the healthy colour in her cheeks, the vitality that seemed to radiate from her even in stillness. She appeared entirely composed, her hands folded loosely before her, her expression pleasant but unrevealing. No trace of concern for Anne's distress showed on her features, no acknowledgement that she had just witnessed her supposed student dissolve into tears.

The lack of reaction troubled Darcy more than he wanted to admit. Surely anyone with normal sensibility would show some sign of being affected by such obvious suffering. Would express concern, or at least mild distress. Yet Elizabeth stood there looking as serene as though she had just completed a pleasant afternoon stroll.

Darcy moved closer, aware that the parlour's attention had largely returned to other conversations. Lady Catherine was speaking to Mr. Collins about some parish matter. Fitzwilliam had engaged Maria Lucas in conversation. Charlotte sat quietly on the sofa, her gaze occasionally drifting toward the pianoforte with that same troubled expression.

"Miss Bennet," Darcy said, keeping his voice low. "Since you are already at the instrument, perhaps you might favour us with a song? It seems a pity to have the evening's music end on such a..." He paused, searching for a diplomatic word. "Discordant note."

It was a reasonable suggestion, he thought. Elizabeth played and sang quite charmingly, and having her perform might salvage something from this increasingly uncomfortable evening.

But Elizabeth's response was immediate and definitive. "No, thank you, Mr. Darcy. I find I am not inclined to play this evening."

The refusal itself was not surprising. Elizabeth had never been one to perform simply because propriety demanded it. But something about the way she delivered it struck Darcy as wrong. The words emerged too quickly, as though she had been waiting for his suggestion solely to refuse it. And her expression showed none of the playful spirit he might have expected.

Before Darcy could respond, Elizabeth stepped closer to him and placed her hand on his arm.

The gesture froze Darcy in place, every muscle suddenly rigid with surprise. Her touch was deliberate, her fingers curling around his forearm with a familiarity that went far beyond what propriety permitted between unmarried persons. The pressure of her hand communicated intention, possession almost.

"I would much prefer to take a turn about the room with you," Elizabeth said, and her voice carried a warmth that bordered on intimate. "If you would be so kind as to indulge me."

Darcy stared at her, his mind refusing to process what was happening. Elizabeth never touched him voluntarily. Had always maintained careful distance, had rebuffed his few attempts at assistance with varying degrees of politeness. He could count on one hand the number of times they had deliberately made physical contact, and each instance had been brief, formal.

Yet now she stood beside him with her hand on his arm, looking up at him with an expression that could only be described as encouraging.

"I..." Darcy began, then found he had no idea how to complete the sentence.

Elizabeth's smile widened, taking his hesitation as agreement. She applied gentle pressure to his arm, guiding him away from the pianoforte toward the open space near the window. Darcy found himself moving with her automatically, his body responding even as his mind struggled to catch up.

They began a slow circuit of the room's perimeter, Elizabeth maintaining her hold on his arm with that same deliberate pressure. She walked close enough that her skirts occasionally brushed against his leg, close enough that he could catch the scent of rosewater that she favoured.

Darcy glanced toward the other occupants of the parlour, half expecting someone to notice and comment. But Lady Catherine remained absorbed in her conversation. Fitzwilliam appeared focused on whatever topic he was discussing with Maria Lucas. Charlotte watched them for a moment, her expression troubled, but said nothing, looking away again when her husband patted her hand to draw attention to Lady Catherine's speech.

"This is much more pleasant than playing the pianoforte," Elizabeth observed, her tone light. "Do you not agree, Mr. Darcy?"

"I suppose," Darcy managed, though his voice sounded strained. He tried to organise his thoughts. "Though I confess surprise at your disinclination to play. I had understood you to enjoy the instrument."

"Oh, I do," Elizabeth said quickly, perhaps too quickly. "But I find your company far more agreeable this evening."

The words should have pleased him. Should have sent warmth through his chest. Instead, Darcy felt only a deepening sense of wrongness.

This was not how Elizabeth Bennet behaved. Not with him, certainly, but not with anyone, that he had ever observed. She did not throw herself at gentlemen, did not make bold overtures or seek out physical contact with such obvious calculation. Her independence manifested in maintaining distance, in asserting boundaries, in refusing to accommodate herself to others' expectations simply for the sake of pleasing them.

Yet here she walked beside him, her hand on his arm, pressing close with a familiarity that suggested intimate acquaintance rather than the wary civility that had characterised their previous interactions.

Darcy's free hand clenched into a fist at his side as they continued their circuit. He needed to understand what was happening, needed to reconcile this behaviour with everything he knew about Elizabeth's character.

They reached the far corner of the room, the space near the tall window where shadows gathered beyond the candlelight's reach. Elizabeth slowed their pace, turning slightly so that she stood facing him more directly, her hand still resting on his arm.

"I am so glad we have this opportunity to speak more privately," she said, and her voice had dropped to a tone that suggested intimacy. "There is so much I wish to discuss with you, Mr. Darcy."

Darcy's heart hammered against his ribs, though whether from anticipation or alarm he could not determine. This was what he had wanted, was it not? Elizabeth's attention, her interest, her willingness to engage with him beyond bare civility. Yet receiving it felt wrong.

"Indeed?" he said carefully, searching her face for some clue, some hint of the sharp intelligence that typically animated her features. But he found only that same pleasant warmth, that encouraging smile that conveyed interest without complexity.

Elizabeth nodded, her fingers tightening slightly on his arm. "Indeed. I find your company most agreeable, Mr. Darcy. Most agreeable indeed."

The repetition struck Darcy as odd, as though she were working from a script and had run out of variations. Elizabeth's conversation never repeated itself, never fell into such pedestrian patterns. She found different ways to express the same sentiment, turned phrases with wit and precision.

"You know, Miss Bennet," Darcy said, pitching his voice to carry a tone of mild observation, "I find I must confess that I cannot properly admire the figure of your walk when we are moving together about the room. Such admiration is best accomplished when the viewer is seated, allowing for more thorough observation."

He watched her face carefully as he spoke, searching for any flicker of recognition, any sign that she understood he was repeating their previous exchange. Surely Elizabeth would remember. It had been a significant moment in their acquaintance, one of the few times she had engaged with him directly in Hertfordshire.

But Elizabeth's expression showed only confusion. Her brow furrowed slightly, her head tilting as though she were trying to puzzle out his meaning. The smile remained fixed but lost some of its confidence.

"I... I beg your pardon?" she said, and her voice carried genuine bewilderment. "Are you suggesting I should sit down?"

The question landed like a stone in still water, sending ripples of alarm through Darcy's consciousness. She did not remember. Did not recognise the reference to their Netherfield conversation. Treated his words as though he were making a new observation rather than deliberately echoing an old exchange, and worse, had actually misunderstood his meaning.

Elizabeth Bennet would have remembered. Would have recognised his jest immediately, would have either laughed at his audacity in repeating it or delivered some cutting remark about his apparent inability to move beyond stale observations. She would not have stood there looking confused.

Before Darcy could formulate a response, Elizabeth's expression transformed. The confusion cleared, replaced by something that made Darcy's stomach turn with uncomfortable recognition. She smiled at him again, but this time the expression carried a quality he had seen before on entirely different faces.

Caroline Bingley smiled at him that way. With calculated coquetry, with deliberate flirtation designed to captivate male attention. It was a smile that announced its own calculation.

Elizabeth's eyelashes fluttered in what could only be described as batting, a gesture so theatrical that Darcy nearly took a step backward in sheer surprise. She leaned closer to him, pressing against his arm with enough force that he could feel the warmth of her body through layers of fabric.

"You find my figure worthy of admiration? How kind of you to say so, Mr. Darcy," she said, and her voice had taken on a breathy quality that made Darcy's skin crawl with wrongness. "I confess I find your observations most flattering. Most flattering indeed."

She reached up with her free hand and placed it on his chest, her palm resting just above his heart in a gesture that exceeded every boundary of propriety. The touch was bold, deliberate, unmistakably forward.

Darcy froze, every muscle going rigid with shock. This was not merely uncharacteristic behaviour. This was something else entirely, something that bore no resemblance whatsoever to Elizabeth Bennet's natural manner. Elizabeth would never touch him so boldly, would never employ such obvious flirtation techniques, would never bat her eyelashes like some silly debutante trying to captivate a wealthy suitor.

"Miss Bennet," Darcy managed, his voice emerging rougher than he intended. "I think perhaps you have misunderstood my meaning."

But she only smiled wider, her fingers curling slightly against his waistcoat as though claiming possession. "Oh, I understand perfectly, Mr. Darcy. You wish to admire me. And I am most happy to be admired by you."

The words were wrong. The tone was wrong. The entire manner of delivery was so fundamentally unlike Elizabeth that Darcy felt as though he were speaking with a stranger.

Elizabeth did not seek admiration. Did not angle for compliments or employ obvious flirtation. When she engaged with someone, she did so with genuine interest and sharp intelligence, with conversation that challenged and provoked rather than simpering agreement. Even when she disliked someone, her engagement carried more substance than this hollow performance.

Darcy carefully removed her hand from his chest, holding it briefly before releasing it entirely and taking a definitive step backward. Elizabeth's expression flickered with something that might have been irritation before settling back into that inviting smile, but she did not pursue him, did not press her advantage.

"I believe perhaps we should rejoin the others," Darcy said, his mind racing. "My aunt will notice our prolonged absence."

Elizabeth's smile faltered slightly, but she nodded and allowed him to guide her back toward the centre of the parlour where Lady Catherine held court. As they walked, Darcy's thoughts turned over the evidence that had been accumulating throughout this impossible day.

Elizabeth's apparent lack of anger about his interference with Bingley and her sister. Her coldness toward Fitzwilliam when she had always enjoyed his company. Her meek submission to Collins's pompous authority. Her pleasant warmth toward Darcy himself despite having every reason to despise him. Her complete unconcern about Anne's obvious distress. Her forward behaviour and calculated flirtation. And now, her complete failure to recognise a reference to a conversation they had shared mere months ago.

Stranger and stranger, Darcy thought, utterly confused as to what might possibly have happened to cause such a fundamental change in character.

Chapter Twelve

The stairs seemed endless, each step requiring calculation and effort that Elizabeth's healthy body would have managed without thought. Mrs. Jenkinson's grip on her elbow was firm, almost painful, guiding her upward steadily. Elizabeth's legs trembled with the exertion, and by the time they reached the landing, sweat had gathered at her temples despite the evening's coolness. Her vision swam slightly at the edges, exhaustion pulling at her consciousness.

They moved through the darkened corridor in silence, the only sounds their footsteps against polished wood and Elizabeth's laboured breathing. Candles flickered in wall sconces, throwing shadows that seemed to reach for them as they passed. Elizabeth tried to focus on putting one foot in front of the other, on not collapsing before they reached Anne's bedchamber.

The door to Anne's room stood open, and Mrs. Jenkinson guided her through with that same firm grip. The bedchamber felt suffocating after the relative openness of the parlour, all heavy curtains and ornate furniture arranged to showcase wealth rather than provide comfort.

Mrs. Jenkinson released Elizabeth's elbow only to begin working at the fastenings of the green silk gown, her fingers deft despite their age. Elizabeth stood swaying slightly, too exhausted to protest the intimacy, too weak to manage the task herself. The silk whispered as it fell away, pooling at her feet.

The stays came next, efficiently unlaced, and Elizabeth gasped as the pressure released from Anne's weak chest. She had not realised how much the garment had been restricting her already compromised breathing. Her chemise clung to her skin, damp with perspiration, and she shivered in the room's relative coolness.

"Arms up," Mrs. Jenkinson instructed, her tone carrying the authority of someone accustomed to being obeyed without question.

Elizabeth raised her arms with effort, and the nightgown descended over her head, soft cotton settling against her skin. It smelled of lavender and something medicinal. Mrs. Jenkinson guided her toward the bed, one hand at her back, and Elizabeth's legs nearly gave out during the final steps.

The mattress received her softly, goose-down feathers compressing beneath her slight weight. Mrs. Jenkinson lifted Elizabeth's legs onto the bed, then moved to adjust the pillows behind her back. Elizabeth found herself propped into a semi-sitting position, too tired to question the arrangement.

Mrs. Jenkinson crossed to the dresser and selected a vial, uncorked it, and poured a measure of dark liquid into a glass. The smell reached Elizabeth even from several feet away, bitter and sharp with an underlying sweetness.

"You need to sleep," Mrs. Jenkinson said, returning to the bedside with the glass extended. "This will help."

Elizabeth stared at the offered draught, her exhausted mind struggling to assess the danger. She had been drugged before by this woman, had lost hours to unconsciousness. Every instinct screamed against accepting anything from Mrs. Jenkinson's hand, against surrendering control.

But what choice did she have? Her borrowed body could barely remain upright. If she refused, Mrs. Jenkinson would simply force the draught down her throat as she had done before. At least accepting it with apparent cooperation might maintain some illusion of dignity.

Elizabeth reached for the glass with trembling fingers. The glass felt heavy in her weak grip. She raised it to her lips and drank, the bitter taste coating her tongue and throat despite her attempts to swallow quickly. She grimaced at the flavour, at the chalky texture that clung to her mouth.

Mrs. Jenkinson retrieved the empty glass and set it aside, then settled into the chair beside the bed. She folded her hands in her lap, preparing to wait until the draught took effect.

"Why do you help her?" Elizabeth asked, the words emerging slightly slurred as the draught began its work. Her tongue felt thick in her mouth, her thoughts starting to scatter. "You know what she has done. Know it is wrong."

Mrs. Jenkinson's expression remained neutral, but something flickered in her eyes. Guilt, perhaps, or the memory of guilt long since suppressed. "Miss Anne needed assistance. I have served the de Bourgh family for forty years, companion to Sir Lewis's mother before she died, then his bride, now his daughter. Where else would my loyalty lie?"

"With what is right," Elizabeth managed, though her voice had grown softer. "Not with wickedness."

"Right and wrong are luxuries for those who can afford them," Mrs. Jenkinson replied, and her tone carried weary resignation. "I am a woman alone in the world, Miss Bennet. My position here is all that stands between me and destitution. Do you imagine I could refuse Miss Anne's requests, however extraordinary, and remain employed?"

The admission struck Elizabeth with unexpected force. Mrs. Jenkinson was trapped too, in her own way, bound by economic necessity to serve a woman whose actions she might not approve but could not afford to oppose. It did not excuse her participation, did not make her complicity any less reprehensible, but it added complexity to Elizabeth's understanding.

"She learned it from her father," Mrs. Jenkinson continued, her voice dropping to barely above a whisper. "Sir Lewis de Bourgh. He was a gentleman scholar, interested in natural philosophy and alchemy. Spent years studying ancient texts, collecting rare ingredients, experimenting with formulations that most would dismiss as superstition."

Elizabeth tried to focus on the words, to commit them to memory despite the growing fog in her thoughts. This was important information.

"His experiments weakened Miss Anne's body," Mrs. Jenkinson said, and genuine sorrow coloured her tone now. "She would help him in his laboratory, would breathe the vapours from his distillations, would handle ingredients that left residues on her skin. The damage accumulated over years. By the time Sir Lewis realised what was happening, it was too late for both of them."

"He died from it," Elizabeth said, the words emerging slow and heavy. "Anne said he died from the same ingredients that weakened her."

Mrs. Jenkinson nodded, her expression grave. "Coughing up blood in his final months. Unable to breathe without pain. The chemicals had destroyed his lungs, poisoned his blood. And Miss Anne's constitution, already delicate from birth, suffered similar damage. She has been dying slowly ever since, trapped in a body that fails her more with each passing year."

The explanation should have inspired sympathy, Elizabeth thought distantly. Should have made her understand Anne's desperation. But Elizabeth could summon no compassion for the woman who had violated her so completely.

"She could have chosen differently," Elizabeth whispered. "Could have lived what life she had with honour rather than theft."

"Perhaps," Mrs. Jenkinson agreed quietly. "But desperation makes monsters of us all, Miss Bennet. When facing death, few of us prove as noble as we imagine we would be."

Elizabeth wanted to argue, wanted to insist that some principles transcended even the fear of death. But the words would not come, her thoughts scattering further as the draught pulled her toward unconsciousness. Her eyelids had grown impossibly heavy, her limbs weighted with exhaustion.

The room began to blur at the edges. She could still see Mrs. Jenkinson's face, still registered the woman's steady watchfulness, but everything else faded into shadow. The ornate ceiling plasterwork became abstract patterns that shifted and flowed. The candlelight wavered and dimmed.

Elizabeth tried to fight the draught's effects, tried to hold onto consciousness through sheer determination. But Anne's body, already exhausted beyond its capacity, surrendered to the drug with the ease of long practice. Her muscles relaxed despite her will, her breathing deepened and slowed, her thoughts scattered beyond her ability to gather them.

Then there was only darkness, heavy and absolute.

Consciousness returned reluctantly, dragging Elizabeth up through layers of heavy darkness. Her mouth tasted of ashes and chemicals, the bitter residue coating her tongue and throat. Her head ached with a dull, persistent throb, and her borrowed body felt simultaneously leaden and insubstantial. The morning light filtering through the heavy curtains struck her as unnecessarily bright, painful when she opened her eyes.

Elizabeth closed her eyes again and lay still, not yet ready to acknowledge waking. The bed felt too soft beneath her, the linens too fine. Her lungs drew shallow breaths that never quite satisfied.

Voices penetrated her consciousness. Low, coming from nearby. Elizabeth's eyes opened to slits, careful not to move or give any sign of waking. The voices came from the dressing room, she realised, the door standing partially ajar.

Anne's voice, using Elizabeth's familiar tones but speaking with frustration. "I do not understand what I am doing wrong. I smiled at him. I touched his arm. I stood close to him and made it clear I welcomed his attention. Yet Darcy looked at me as though I were some sort of curiosity rather than a woman expressing interest."

Mrs. Jenkinson's response came after a pause. "Perhaps you are being too obvious, Miss Anne. Too forward in your approach."

"Too forward?" Anne's voice rose slightly before she apparently remembered to keep her volume down. "How can I be too forward when every conduct book insists that young ladies must encourage the gentleman's addresses? That we must show our approval through warmth and compliance?"

"There is a difference between showing approval and throwing yourself at him," Mrs. Jenkinson replied, and Elizabeth detected a hint of dry amusement. "Darcy does not seem responsive to your efforts at all."

Elizabeth's heart hammered against her ribs, each beat painful in Anne's weak chest. They were discussing Darcy, discussing Anne's attempts to secure his interest. She forced herself to remain perfectly still, to keep her breathing shallow and even. This was information she desperately needed.

"That is precisely my complaint," Anne said, her frustration evident. "I have been as warm and encouraging as propriety allows. More so, perhaps. Yet he withdraws rather than responding with equal enthusiasm. Last night when I touched his chest, he actually stepped away. Removed my hand as though it had burned him."

"That is because Elizabeth Bennet never flirted with him," Mrs. Jenkinson said, and now the amusement in her voice was unmistakable. "She teased him."

Silence greeted this pronouncement. Through her slitted eyes, Elizabeth watched the shadows shift as one of the women moved.

"I do not understand the distinction," Anne said finally, genuine bewilderment colouring her voice. "How is teasing different from flirting? Both seek to attract male attention, do they not?"

"Flirting is obvious," Mrs. Jenkinson explained with patience. "It announces itself clearly. Compliments delivered with significance. Touches that linger. Smiles designed to captivate. Batting eyelashes and breathy voices and all the obvious manoeuvres young ladies employ."

"Yes," Anne agreed impatiently. "That is precisely what I have been doing."

"And teasing," Mrs. Jenkinson continued, "is something else entirely. It challenges rather than compliments. It provokes rather than soothes. It creates tension through opposition rather than harmony through agreement. Elizabeth Bennet was not trying to make Darcy like her. She was trying to make him think, to respond, to engage with her as an equal rather than as a pretty object to be admired."

The explanation struck Elizabeth with unexpected force. Was that what she had been doing? She had thought herself simply defending her independence, refusing to accommodate Darcy's pride. Had not realised that her challenges and verbal sparring might be interpreted as a form of attraction.

"But why would that make him love her?" Anne's voice carried genuine confusion. "I do not understand why Darcy would fall in love with a woman who does not even like him. Who challenged him constantly and refused to show him proper deference."

Elizabeth's breath caught in her throat, nearly giving away her waking state. Anne had just confirmed what she had claimed last night. Darcy was in love with her. Actually, genuinely in love with Elizabeth Bennet. The knowledge settled over her with complicated weight.

"Men are strange creatures, Miss Anne," Mrs. Jenkinson replied with dry amusement. "Some of them, particularly those accustomed to easy conquests and universal admiration, find challenge more attractive than compliance. Elizabeth Bennet refused to be impressed by Darcy's wealth or status. Refused to simper and flatter. And apparently, that indifference made him desperate to secure her regard."

"It makes no sense," Anne insisted. "If he loves her so much, why does he not respond when I show interest? When I make it clear that Elizabeth Bennet has changed her opinion and now welcomes his addresses?"

"Because he can tell something is wrong," Mrs. Jenkinson said, her voice gone serious now. "He may not understand what, may not be able to articulate it. But Darcy is not a fool, Miss Anne. He notices the differences in your behaviour. Senses that something fundamental has changed. And until you learn to replicate Elizabeth's manner more convincingly, he will continue to withdraw rather than advance his suit."

Footsteps, someone pacing in the dressing room. When Anne spoke again, her voice carried defensive pride mixed with determination.

"I will learn. Will think on this more carefully, will adjust my approach. He will propose, Mrs. Jenkinson. I have not come this far to fail now."

"I am sure you will succeed," Mrs. Jenkinson replied, though her tone suggested less confidence. "But in the meantime, we must ensure that Miss Bennet remains properly contained. She cannot be allowed to interfere."

"She is too weak to cause difficulties," Anne said dismissively. "That body can barely manage basic activities. By the time she gathers strength enough to attempt anything, I will be married to Darcy and safely beyond her reach."

"Nevertheless," Mrs. Jenkinson insisted, steel entering her voice. "We must be vigilant. I will keep Elizabeth quiet. Will ensure she remains confined here, properly sedated when necessary, until your position is secure."

Their voices grew fainter as they moved away. Elizabeth waited several minutes after the voices faded entirely before allowing herself to move. She turned her head slightly, confirming through the partially open door that the dressing room now stood empty.

Her mind raced despite the lingering effects of the draught. Anne was failing to convince Darcy, was struggling to replicate Elizabeth's manner convincingly enough to secure his proposal. That should have provided some satisfaction. But it also meant Anne would be more desperate, more willing to take risks.

Elizabeth could not do this alone. She had already come to that conclusion, recognising both the physical limitations of the body she was now trapped in and the threats Anne and Mrs. Jenkinson had made if she attempted to resist. Confined to a lunatic asylum or poisoned, her fate would be final, and Elizabeth did not doubt both women were capable of carrying out their threats. She needed an ally.

But who would recognize the impostor immediately, would see through Anne's imperfect performance without needing impossible explanations? Charlotte and Mr. Darcy both clearly recognised something was wrong, but they would not believe the truth, and telling either of them risked Anne or Mrs. Jenkinson deciding to take further action against Elizabeth.

Jane. The answer came to Elizabeth with absolute clarity. Jane knew her better than anyone else in the world, had lived with her since birth, had shared confidences and conversations and every aspect of daily life. Jane would recognize immediately that something was wrong, would sense the differences that others might attribute to mood or circumstance.

Elizabeth needed to contact Jane. Jane knew her better than anyone else in the world, had lived with her since birth. Jane would recognise immediately that something was wrong.

But how could she accomplish that from her prison? Mrs. Jenkinson watched her constantly, drugged her when she showed signs of resistance. And even if Elizabeth could somehow get a letter written and posted, how could she explain the situation in writing?

She would have to find a way.

Elizabeth pushed herself upright with trembling arms. The room swayed around her, and she had to pause, gripping the mattress edge until her vision steadied and the nausea passed. She stood slowly, testing her balance. Her legs held, barely, trembling but supporting her weight. She took one careful step, then another, crossing toward the writing desk with slow deliberation.

The desk stood beneath the window. Elizabeth sank onto the chair with relief. She pulled open the small drawer where Anne kept her correspondence supplies. Fresh paper. A pen with a good nib. An inkwell filled with black ink.

Elizabeth's hands shook as she positioned the paper, as she dipped the pen with exaggerated care. She needed to write quickly, before Mrs. Jenkinson returned. But she also needed to write carefully, needed to choose words that would bring Jane to Rosings without explaining the impossible.

"*My dearest Jane,*" Elizabeth wrote, a little surprised to realise that her handwriting was still her own, if a little shakier as Anne's trembling hand wielded the pen. "*I write to you in the greatest distress and beg you to come to me in Kent immediately. I cannot explain in writing what has occurred, can only tell you that I desperately require your presence and your help. Please, Jane, do not delay. Come as soon as you receive this letter – and though this might sound strange, do not mention to anyone, even to me, that this letter was your summons. Your loving sister, Elizabeth.*"

She read it over twice, searching for any phrase that might sound too dramatic. But every word was true, and surely Jane would recognise the urgency. Elizabeth folded the letter with shaking fingers, then reached for the sealing wax. Melting it required steadying the candle, holding the stick over the flame until it softened. Her hands trembled throughout, but she managed it finally.

Elizabeth addressed the letter to *Miss Jane Bennet, care of Mr. Gardiner, Gracechurch Street, London*. Now she simply needed to find someone to deliver it. Someone who would not question why Anne de Bourgh was writing to Elizabeth Bennet's sister.

Elizabeth looked down at her nightgown. She needed to dress herself, needed to make herself presentable enough to venture into Rosings' corridors.

Elizabeth crossed to the wardrobe on unsteady legs, clinging to furniture for support. She selected the simplest dress she could find, a pale blue muslin with fewer fastenings. Getting out of the nightgown proved surprisingly difficult. She managed it finally, standing in her chemise and shivering.

The stays defeated her entirely. Elizabeth stared at the structured garment with its impossible lacings and felt tears of frustration gather. After three attempts that left her gasping, she abandoned the effort. She would have to go without stays, scandalous though it was.

The dress went on more easily, though each button required concentration. Eventually she stood fully clothed, if improperly so. She tugged a shawl around her shoulders, pushed her feet into slippers, and moved toward the door.

Elizabeth paused there, listening intently. The corridor outside remained quiet. She turned the handle slowly, easing the door open. Empty. The passage stretched in both directions.

Instead of using the main corridors, she headed for the inconspicuous door at the other end of the landing. The door that led to the servants' stairs. The corridor felt impossibly long. She moved along the wall, one hand trailing against the papered surface for support.

The servants' passage was dim, lit only by occasional small windows. The stone floor struck cold through her thin slippers. Elizabeth moved slowly, trailing her hand along the rough stone wall, stopping frequently to catch her breath.

Elizabeth froze when footsteps approached, pressing herself into a shadowed alcove until a maid passed with an armload of linens. The woman did not look in her direction. When the footsteps faded, Elizabeth continued.

She emerged finally through a panel near the back entrance. Elizabeth pushed it open cautiously. The entrance hall beyond stood empty, morning sunlight streaming through tall windows.

And there, visible through one of the windows, Colonel Fitzwilliam walked across the lawn with his characteristic military bearing. He was dressed for riding. He moved with purpose, heading toward the stables, alone.

This was her chance. Perhaps her only chance.

Elizabeth pushed herself away from the wall and crossed the hall with steps that stumbled despite her efforts. She reached the door and pulled it open, the heavy wood protesting, and stepped out into morning air.

"Colonel Fitzwilliam," she called, and her voice emerged thin and breathless.

He turned at the sound, his expression shifting from surprise to concern. He changed direction immediately, striding across the lawn toward her.

"Cousin Anne," he said as he drew close. His gaze swept over her, taking in her dishevelled appearance, the obvious exhaustion in her bearing. "Should you be out of doors? You were quite unwell last evening."

Elizabeth extended her hand, the letter clutched in trembling fingers. "I need you to do something very important," she said, forcing the words out. "Take this to London yourself, right now, and wait for a reply."

Colonel Fitzwilliam took the letter automatically, his brow furrowing as he read the direction. "This is addressed to Miss Elizabeth Bennet's sister. Cousin, why would you be writing to Miss Jane Bennet?"

He looked at her with polite confusion, clearly expecting some reasonable explanation. Elizabeth stared back at him, recognising the impossibility of providing one.

When she did not reply, he held the letter out to her, clearly intending to return it. Elizabeth stared at the offered letter, at her last hope being casually rejected, and felt something crack inside her chest.

Her legs gave out entirely, but rather than try to catch herself, Elizabeth simply let herself fall. She dropped to her knees on the cold stone steps, her borrowed body surrendering to exhaustion and desperation. Tears streamed down her face unchecked, and she reached up to clutch at Colonel Fitzwilliam's coat with both hands, clinging to the fabric with desperate strength.

"Please," she sobbed, and the word emerged broken, stripped of pride or dignity. "Please, Colonel Fitzwilliam. I am begging you. Take this letter to Jane Bennet. Put it in her hand yourself. Wait for her reply. Please, please, I beg you."

She looked up at him through her tears, saw his expression transform from confusion to shock. She maintained her grip on his coat, trembling with the effort of kneeling upright.

"I cannot explain," Elizabeth continued, her voice emerging in gasps between sobs. "Cannot tell you why. But I am begging you, on whatever regard you have ever had for your family, for justice, for mercy. Take this letter. Go now. Please."

Colonel Fitzwilliam stood frozen above her, the letter still clutched in his hand, his face showing shock and growing alarm. He looked toward the house, perhaps searching for Mrs. Jenkinson or Lady Catherine. Then he looked back down at Elizabeth, and something in his expression shifted.

"Very well," he said finally, and his voice had gone gentle. "Anne, please do not upset yourself further. I will take the letter. Will ride to London immediately and deliver it to Miss Jane Bennet's hand. I give you my word."

Relief crashed over Elizabeth with enough force to make her sway dangerously. She released her grip on his coat and would have collapsed entirely if Colonel Fitzwilliam had not caught her elbow, steadying her.

"I will wait for her reply," he continued, still using that same gentle tone. "And return with it as quickly as possible. Now, please, you must go inside. You are not well enough to be out here. Shall I call for Mrs. Jenkinson?"

"No," Elizabeth managed. "Do not tell her about the letter! Do not tell anyone. Simply go. Now. Please."

Colonel Fitzwilliam nodded slowly, his concern evident but his word given. He helped Elizabeth to her feet with careful support, guided her back through the door, then stepped away with visible reluctance. He looked down at the letter in his hand, then back at Elizabeth's tear-stained face, and she saw the moment his decision solidified.

"I will get my horse," he said, "and put this letter into Miss Jane Bennet's hand before noon. You have my word as a gentleman."

Then he was striding purposefully toward the stables, the letter secured in his coat pocket, and Elizabeth leaned against the doorframe watching him go. She had done it. Had succeeded in sending her message to Jane despite every obstacle.

Now she simply needed to survive long enough for Jane to arrive.

Chapter Thirteen

THE MORNING HAD GROWN uncommonly fine by the time Darcy escaped his aunt's demands, the spring air carrying that particular crispness that made walking a pleasure. He had intended to ride out with Fitzwilliam, but his cousin had apparently gone off somewhere after breakfast without explanation, leaving Darcy to endure Lady Catherine's lengthy discourse on drainage improvements alone. The irritation of abandonment faded as Darcy turned his steps toward Hunsford, his pace quickening without conscious decision. Sunlight filtered through newly leafed trees in patterns that shifted with each breath of wind.

Darcy had not planned to call at the parsonage today. Had told himself he should maintain some distance after the strangeness of the previous day. But his feet carried him along the familiar path regardless, and he found himself arriving at the modest house before he had properly formed an excuse. The door stood slightly ajar, and through it came the sound of feminine laughter that made something in his chest tighten with recognition.

The servant who answered his knock showed him through to the parlour without ceremony, and Darcy paused in the doorway. Elizabeth sat in the chair nearest the window, sunlight catching in her dark hair and illuminating her profile as she spoke with Charlotte Collins. She wore a simple morning dress in pale yellow muslin, and her hands moved expressively as she described something that had apparently amused her. Charlotte sat opposite, teacup balanced in her lap, smiling with what looked like genuine pleasure.

"Mr. Darcy," Charlotte said, noticing him first and rising with appropriate courtesy. "What a pleasant surprise. Please, do join us. We were just taking tea."

Elizabeth turned at the mention of his name, and Darcy found himself searching her face with desperate attention, cataloguing details that might indicate whether this was the real Elizabeth or the strange impostor who had inhabited her form these past days. Her eyes met his directly, and he saw in them a sparkle he recognised, a liveliness that had been absent during their previous encounters. The warmth in her expression appeared genuine rather than calculated, and when she smiled at him, it reached her eyes.

"Mr. Darcy," she said, and her voice carried that teasing quality he had come to associate with her. "You have discovered our secret morning indulgence. Mrs. Collins makes excellent tea, and I have been monopolising her company shamefully. You must join us and provide her with rescue from my chatter."

It was exactly the sort of thing Elizabeth would say, self-deprecating while simultaneously drawing attention to her own enjoyment, inviting him to participate rather than simply welcoming him with bland politeness. Darcy felt some of the tension that had been gathering in his shoulders begin to ease.

"I would be delighted," he replied, accepting the seat Charlotte indicated. "Though I suspect Mrs. Collins finds your company far from burdensome."

"Oh, indeed," Charlotte responded, pouring tea into a cup for him. "Elizabeth does herself a disservice. Her conversation is never mere chatter."

Elizabeth laughed merrily. "Charlotte is too generous. She has been subjected to my observations about the variable quality of Kent's hedgerows for the past quarter hour. That surely qualifies as chatter of the most tedious sort."

"I find hedgerows a perfectly acceptable topic of conversation," Darcy said, accepting his tea. "Far superior to many subjects that occupy drawing room discourse."

"Such as?" Elizabeth prompted, and he saw the challenge in her expression, the invitation to verbal sparring that he had missed more than he wanted to admit.

Before Darcy could respond, the parlour door burst open with enough force to rattle the hinges, and Mr. Collins bustled in with his characteristic lack of grace. The parson's round face beamed with obvious pleasure, and Darcy suppressed a sigh of frustration. He could hardly ask the man to leave his own parlour.

"Mr. Darcy!" Collins exclaimed, executing a bow so deep it looked uncomfortable. "What an honour! What a condescension! That you should favour us with your presence in our humble home. My dear cousin Elizabeth, you see what consequence our connexion to Lady Catherine brings."

Elizabeth's expression flickered with something that might have been amusement or irritation, smoothing too quickly for Darcy to be certain which. She inclined her head toward Collins with apparent patience.

"Mr. Darcy's visit is indeed kind," she said, her tone carrying studied neutrality.

Collins settled himself onto the sofa with enough vigour to disturb Charlotte's tea, forcing his wife to steady her cup. He launched immediately into enthusiastic praise of Lady Catherine's morning activities. Darcy let the words wash over him without truly listening, maintaining an expression of polite attention while his thoughts remained fixed on Elizabeth.

She had returned her gaze to the window, watching something in the garden with apparent interest, and Darcy took the opportunity to study her profile unobserved. The curve of her cheek caught the light, and he noted the healthy colour there, the vitality that seemed to radiate from her even in stillness.

"Do you not agree, Mr. Darcy?" Collins said suddenly, and Darcy realised with mild embarrassment that he had lost the thread of conversation entirely.

"Forgive me," Darcy said, setting down his teacup with deliberate care. "I was distracted by the view from the window. The gardens are looking particularly well this spring."

It was a transparent excuse, but Collins accepted it with enthusiasm. Elizabeth glanced at Darcy then, and he caught the hint of a smile tugging at her lips, a shared recognition of Collins's absurdity that felt like a moment of genuine connexion.

The conversation continued in fits and starts, Collins dominating with his usual mixture of obsequiousness and self-importance while Charlotte attempted to redirect toward more general topics. Elizabeth participated with apparent ease, her contributions carrying wit without the aggressive flirtation that had so disturbed Darcy the previous day. She teased Collins gently about his devotion to Lady Catherine, deflected his pompous observations with humour rather than compliance.

Darcy found himself relaxing into the familiar rhythm of it. The strangeness of previous days seemed to fade in the face of this return to form, and Darcy allowed himself to hope that whatever temporary alteration had affected her had passed.

"I imagine you must be eager to return to Longbourn," Darcy ventured during a brief pause. "To see your family again after such an extended absence."

He watched her face carefully, searching for signs of the attachment to home and family that any properly feeling person would display. Elizabeth's expression shifted, becoming more subdued, and she looked down at her hands before responding.

"I am due to return home soon," she said quietly, and something in her tone made Darcy lean forward slightly. "But I confess it is not thoughts of home that occupy my mind this morning."

"No?" Darcy prompted, aware that his voice had dropped lower, that the question carried more weight than casual inquiry.

Elizabeth looked up then, meeting his gaze directly, and what he saw in her expression made his breath catch. Sadness, unmistakable and sincere, mixed with something that might have been regret. Her eyes held his for a long moment, and Darcy felt the parlour around them fade into insignificance.

"No," Elizabeth said, and her voice carried quiet conviction. "It is rather the thought of leaving the company here at Rosings that makes me melancholy. I have come to value certain acquaintances more than I anticipated when I first arrived in Kent."

Darcy's heart quickened at Elizabeth's words, hope flooding through him. She meant him. Surely she must mean him. The company at Rosings included his aunt, Anne, Fitzwilliam, but Elizabeth's gaze had been fixed on him alone when she spoke, her expression carrying an intimacy that excluded the others from consideration. She would miss *him*. Would regret their separation.

He had pursued her regard through careful attention and studied civility, through arranging encounters that appeared accidental. Had endured the torture of her apparent indifference, her refusal to be impressed by his consequence. And now, finally, she was indicating that his feelings might not be unrequited.

"Indeed, indeed!" Collins exclaimed, apparently interpreting Elizabeth's melancholy as agreement with whatever point he had been making. "You must surely feel the loss most acutely, dear cousin, when you return to the modest society of Longbourn after experiencing the superior company available here in Kent. Why, the contrast between Lady Catherine's distinguished circle and the simple country neighbours you are accustomed to must be quite marked!"

The words struck Darcy like cold water. He felt his jaw tighten with irritation at Collins's tactlessness, at the insult to Elizabeth's home and family delivered with such oblivious enthusiasm. The parson beamed around the parlour as though he had said something particularly clever, entirely missing the way Charlotte's expression had gone carefully neutral and how Elizabeth's hands had curled slightly against her skirts.

"Mr. Collins," Charlotte began, her voice carrying gentle reproof, but her husband continued without pause.

"You must take comfort in knowing that your time here has elevated your understanding of proper society," Collins said, directing his attention fully to Elizabeth now with that particular smugness he displayed when convinced he was being helpful. "Lady Catherine's condescension in noticing you, the opportunity to observe how persons of real consequence conduct themselves, these experiences will surely benefit you when you return to Hertfordshire's more humble circles. You will be quite the authority on fashionable manners among your neighbours!"

Darcy felt a flash of genuine anger at the condescension dripping from Collins's every word, at the casual dismissal of Elizabeth's family and friends as inferior, unworthy. He opened his mouth to deliver a cutting rebuke, but stopped as recognition crashed over him with uncomfortable force.

He had said nearly identical things himself. Perhaps not aloud, perhaps not with Collins's particular brand of obsequious tactlessness, but in his thoughts and private conversations with Bingley, Darcy had expressed remarkably similar sentiments about the Bennet family's inferior connexions. Had judged them wanting in elegance and propriety. Had catalogued their faults with the same air of superiority that now made his skin crawl when delivered by Collins.

The memory of his own words rose in his mind with damning clarity. The mother's ill-breeding. The younger sisters' lack of decorum. The father's negligence. The unsuitable connexions to trade. Darcy had nodded along as Caroline Bingley enumerated the objections to her brother's marrying Jane Bennet, and added to them with his own insistence on Jane's indifference.

Shame settled in his chest like a weight, pressing against his ribs with each breath. How could he have been so blind, so arrogant, so convinced of his own superiority? Elizabeth's family might lack the polish and consequence of his own connexions, might display faults that would raise eyebrows in his usual circles, but they had raised Elizabeth herself, a daughter of remarkable intelligence and independent spirit. Had supported her when she refused Collins's proposal, had allowed her the freedom to reject a match that would have secured their family's future, had valued her happiness over their own material comfort.

That, Darcy realised with sudden clarity, spoke more about their characters than any amount of fashionable manners or distinguished relations could. Mr. Bennet might neglect his estate management and retreat into his library, but he had respected his daughter's right to refuse a man she could not love. Mrs. Bennet might be vulgar and managing, but she had apparently acquiesced to Elizabeth's decision despite her own anxieties. They had chosen their daughter's wellbeing over their own convenience, and that choice had left Elizabeth free for Darcy himself to pursue.

He owed them a debt he had not previously acknowledged. Their support of Elizabeth's independence had given him the opportunity to win her regard honestly. If they had compelled her acceptance of Collins, Elizabeth would now be married to the pompous fool currently holding forth about superior society, and Darcy would have lost any chance of securing her affection.

The realisation transformed his view of the Bennet family with startling speed. Their faults remained, certainly, but those faults no longer seemed insurmountable obstacles. They simply became characteristics of a family who, whatever their failings in elegance, possessed genuine love for their daughter and respect for her judgement. That was worth more than all the fashionable polish in London.

"I am certain Elizabeth's family will be most eager for her return," Charlotte said, her voice cutting through both Collins's continued observations and Darcy's internal reflections. She spoke with careful diplomacy. "A household of sisters must feel incomplete when one is absent for an extended period. The affection between them is quite remarkable."

It was perfectly judged, Charlotte's comment, acknowledging Elizabeth's family ties while subtly rebuking Collins's dismissal of them. Darcy saw Elizabeth nod, though her expression remained subdued. She had not responded to Collins's pronouncements about Longbourn's inferiority with her usual spirit, had simply sat quietly while the parson disparaged her home and family.

Perhaps, Darcy thought with a mixture of hope and concern, she truly did value the company at Rosings enough that thoughts of leaving had dimmed her natural vivacity. Or perhaps Collins's casual cruelty had wounded her more than she wished to show. Either possibility made Darcy's determination to secure her strengthen further.

He remained silent through the remainder of the visit, contributing only brief responses when directly addressed, his mind racing with calculations and plans. He needed to propose, and soon, before Elizabeth departed Kent and returned to Hertfordshire. The prospect of asking for her hand filled him with a mixture of anticipation and anxiety.

But there were practical obstacles to overcome. He did not have his mother's ring with him today. The ring was important, both as symbol and tradition, something Elizabeth deserved to receive when he made his offer. It was in his room at Rosings at that very moment; he had sent his valet to London to fetch it a week ago, had brought it with him when he came to the parsonage the night Elizabeth was unwell, but the opportunity had not presented itself and he had locked it away in his travelling-desk, telling himself he must prepare better for the right moment.

And this was not the moment anyway; they were not alone. Could not be alone here in the parsonage with Charlotte and Collins present, and propriety demanded a chaperone for any extended private conversation. He would need to arrange an opportunity to speak with Elizabeth without observers, somewhere they might have the privacy necessary. The grove at Rosings, perhaps, or one of the walking paths where they might encounter each other apparently by chance.

Tomorrow, Darcy decided with sudden certainty. He would find a way tomorrow. Would arrange matters so that he and Elizabeth might walk together without interference, would speak the words that had been building in his heart for months, would offer her his hand and his name and everything that came with them.

The resolution settled over him with the weight of inevitability, as though the decision had already been made and he was simply acknowledging what must be. Elizabeth had indicated her regard through her expressed regret at their coming separation. He had recognised his own prejudices about her family and resolved to overcome them. All that remained was to formalise what already existed between them, to transform this delicate understanding into explicit promises.

Collins was still speaking, his voice rising and falling with enthusiastic observations about something Darcy had stopped listening to entirely. Charlotte poured more tea, her expression containing the resigned grace of someone long accustomed to managing her husband's excesses. Elizabeth sat quietly by the window, sunlight catching reddish glints in her dark hair, her profile serene despite the melancholy she had expressed moments before.

Darcy watched her and let himself imagine, briefly, recklessly, what it would be like when she was his wife. When he could claim the right to her company without pretence. When her wit and intelligence would grace Pemberley's halls, when her laughter would echo through rooms that had been too silent since his mother's death. When Georgiana could call her sister, and gain in confidence by following Elizabeth's example. When he could wake each morning knowing that Elizabeth Bennet had chosen him despite every reason she had to refuse.

Tomorrow, he thought again, the word becoming almost a prayer. Tomorrow he would ask, and she would accept, and everything that had seemed impossible mere days ago would transform into glorious certainty.

He simply had to survive the intervening hours without betraying the hope that threatened to overflow his careful composure.

Chapter Fourteen

The parlour clock chimed nine, each note seeming to echo Elizabeth's mounting anxiety. She sat in Anne's usual chair near the fire, her hands folded in her lap to hide their trembling, and tried to maintain some appearance of attention to Lady Catherine's discourse on tenant cottages. The words washed over her without meaning, her entire focus fixed on listening for sounds from beyond the parlour. Hoofbeats on the drive. Boots in the entrance hall. Any indication that Colonel Fitzwilliam had returned from London with news of Jane.

Lady Catherine held court from her throne-like seat, her broad form draped in purple silk that rustled with each emphatic gesture. Mrs. Jenkinson occupied the chair beside Elizabeth, nodding along regularly. Mr. Darcy stood near the window, his attention apparently fixed on the darkness beyond the glass.

Elizabeth's chest ached with the effort of breathing evenly, Anne's damaged lungs protesting even the simple act of sitting upright. The heat from the fire made her skin prickle with uncomfortable warmth, but she dared not request the window be opened. Dared not draw attention to herself in any way that might result in Mrs. Jenkinson deciding she required rest.

The sound of hoofbeats on the gravel drive made Elizabeth's heart leap. She forced her breathing to remain even, forced her expression into the careful neutrality Anne typically displayed, while every nerve strained toward the entrance hall.

Boots struck the marble hallway floor with purposeful strides. The parlour door opened, and Colonel Fitzwilliam stepped through, his clothes dusty from travel.

Lady Catherine's discourse cut off mid-sentence, her expression transforming from animated instruction to pinched disapproval. She straightened in her chair, her small eyes narrowing as she took in her nephew's dishevelled appearance.

"Fitzwilliam," she said, and her voice carried clipped displeasure. "You were absent from dinner. Absent without explanation or notice. I had Cook hold the first course for nearly twenty minutes."

The Colonel executed a bow that managed to convey both respect and complete lack of contrition. "My apologies, Aunt Catherine. I was called away on business that could not be delayed."

"Business?" Lady Catherine's tone suggested the word itself was suspect. "What business could possibly require such precipitous departure? And why was I not informed before you left?"

Colonel Fitzwilliam moved further into the room, his boots leaving faint traces of dust on the pristine carpet. He accepted the glass of port Darcy silently poured for him, draining half of it before responding. "Nothing that need concern the household, madam."

The deflection was polite but absolute, delivered with the sort of firm courtesy that suggested no amount of interrogation would extract further details. Elizabeth watched Lady Catherine's face cycle through surprise, irritation, and grudging acceptance. She was accustomed to commanding complete transparency from those around her, but even she recognised the limits of what she could demand from her nephew, a grown man and military officer with his own obligations and concerns.

"Most irregular," Lady Catherine pronounced, though her tone had shifted from direct challenge to general disapproval. "In my day, young people did not simply disappear for hours without proper explanation."

"Times change, Aunt," the Colonel replied mildly, finishing his port. His gaze drifted across the room, passing over Darcy and Mrs. Jenkinson before landing briefly on Elizabeth. The look lasted perhaps two seconds, no more, but in that moment Elizabeth saw confirmation. He had done it. Had delivered her letter. The knowledge flooded through her with such intensity that she had to look down at her lap.

"I must beg your indulgence further," Colonel Fitzwilliam continued, setting down his empty glass. "The ride has left me considerably dusty. If you will excuse me, I should like to change before rejoining the company."

He did not wait for Lady Catherine's permission, merely bowed again and turned toward the door. As he passed Elizabeth's chair, he slowed fractionally, his eyes meeting hers with unmistakable intention. Then he was gone, his boots striking the floor in measured rhythm.

Elizabeth's heart hammered against her ribs. He wanted to speak with her. Had deliberately caught her eye to communicate that fact. She needed to follow him, needed to hear what news he brought, but she could not simply rise and leave immediately without drawing suspicion.

Lady Catherine had resumed her discourse, this time on the declining standards of courtesy among the younger generation. Darcy had returned to his position by the window. Mrs. Jenkinson's needle continued its steady work.

Elizabeth waited, counting the seconds. When she judged sufficient time had passed, she placed her hands on the arms of her chair and began the laborious process of standing. The movement drew Mrs. Jenkinson's immediate attention.

"I find I am quite exhausted," Elizabeth said, pitching Anne's soft voice to carry just enough. "The evening has been most pleasant, but I believe I should retire."

Lady Catherine paused in her discourse, her gaze softening as she looked at the woman she believed to be her daughter. "Of course, Anne. Mrs. Jenkinson, see Anne to her room immediately."

"No," Elizabeth said, perhaps too quickly, and had to force herself to soften the refusal. "That is, Mrs. Jenkinson has been so attentive all day. I would not wish to deprive you of her company this evening, Mother. A maid can assist me. Mrs. Jenkinson should remain here to entertain you."

She delivered the words with careful deference, appealing to Lady Catherine's ego while creating the separation she needed. Mrs. Jenkinson's eyes narrowed slightly, suspicion evident, but she could hardly refuse without appearing to value her own comfort over her employer's company.

"You are always most considerate," Lady Catherine said. "Mrs. Jenkinson, you will remain. Ring for a maid to assist Anne."

Mrs. Jenkinson's jaw tightened, but she set aside her embroidery and crossed to the bell pull. Elizabeth waited until a young housemaid appeared in the doorway. The girl bobbed a curtsey, her face showing nervous alertness.

"Help Miss de Bourgh to her chamber," Mrs. Jenkinson instructed, her voice carrying an edge. "See that she has everything she requires."

The maid moved forward, offering her arm with careful respect. Elizabeth accepted the support, letting the girl take most of her weight as they began the slow progress toward the door. She could feel Mrs. Jenkinson's gaze boring into her back, suspicious and assessing, but Elizabeth did not look back.

The stairs loomed before them, rising into shadow. Elizabeth placed her hand on the polished banister and began to climb, the maid hovering close beside her. Anne's legs trembled with the first step, muscles protesting. Elizabeth had to pause halfway through lifting her foot to gather strength. The maid waited with patient concern.

Another step. And another. Each one requiring deliberate concentration, careful distribution of weight. Elizabeth's borrowed lungs laboured, each breath emerging slightly ragged. Sweat gathered at her temples and between her shoulder blades.

Halfway up. She paused, ostensibly to catch her breath but actually to scan the shadows of the upper corridor. No sign of Colonel Fitzwilliam, though surely he would be watching for her arrival.

"Should we rest a moment, miss?" the maid asked, her young face creased with concern.

"No," Elizabeth managed, though her voice emerged breathier than intended. "I can continue. Just slowly."

Another step. The banister's smooth wood slid beneath her palm as she hauled herself upward. Another step. Elizabeth's heart hammered against her ribs. Another step, and she could feel the strain in every muscle.

The landing appeared beneath her feet with startling suddenness. Elizabeth paused there, one hand still gripping the banister, her entire body trembling. The maid maintained her support.

But Elizabeth's attention had fixed on the shadowed alcove near the east wing, where a figure waited in darkness. Colonel Fitzwilliam stepped forward just enough that candlelight caught his features, and Elizabeth saw in his expression everything she needed to know.

He had news. Important news.

Elizabeth turned to the maid and managed what she hoped was a reassuring smile. "Thank you for your assistance. I can manage from here. Please, return to your duties below stairs."

The maid hesitated. "Are you certain, miss?"

"Quite certain," Elizabeth said, infusing Anne's soft voice with as much firmness as she could muster. "You have been most helpful."

The maid bobbed a curtsey and retreated down the stairs obediently. Elizabeth waited until the girl's footsteps faded entirely before turning toward the shadowed alcove.

The corridor stretched before her, longer than it had any right to be. Elizabeth moved forward carefully, one hand trailing along the wall for support.

Colonel Fitzwilliam stepped from the alcove as she approached, his expression grave in the flickering candlelight. The shadows carved deep lines in his face.

"Cousin Anne," he said quietly.

Elizabeth reached the alcove and leaned heavily against the wall, her borrowed legs trembling with relief. The stone felt cool through the thin fabric of her gown.

"You delivered my letter?" Elizabeth asked, desperate for confirmation. "To Jane Bennet?"

"I did," Colonel Fitzwilliam confirmed. "I rode to London as I promised and found Miss Bennet at her uncle's house, though I had to wait for her return from an outing. I put the letter directly into her hand."

Elizabeth's heart hammered against her ribs. "And her response?"

"She read it immediately," the Colonel said, and now a hint of admiration entered his tone. "Did not hesitate for a moment. Simply folded the letter, placed it in her pocket, and informed her aunt she needed to leave for Kent at once. I have never seen anyone pack with such efficiency. She had a bag ready within twenty minutes."

The image of Jane responding with immediate action made Elizabeth's eyes burn with tears. Of course Jane would not hesitate. Would simply trust that her sister needed her.

"I hired a coach," Colonel Fitzwilliam continued, "and escorted Miss Bennet to the parsonage myself. Delivered her safely to Mrs. Collins's care a half-hour ago."

Elizabeth's legs gave out entirely, but the Colonel caught her elbow before she could collapse. She leaned against him for a moment, letting him bear her weight while relief flooded through her.

"She is here," Elizabeth whispered, and her voice emerged broken with emotion. "Jane is actually here."

"Indeed," the Colonel said, and something in his tone made Elizabeth look up at his face. He was watching her with an expression that mixed concern with growing confusion. "Though I must confess, the reception was somewhat strange. Mrs. Collins seemed delighted but bewildered by Miss Bennet's sudden arrival. And Miss Elizabeth herself appeared quite surprised to see her sister, which struck me as odd given that you had written specifically to summon her."

Elizabeth's mind raced, trying to construct some explanation. Anne would have been surprised to see Jane arrive unexpectedly. Would have had no knowledge of the letter Elizabeth had sent. The recognition that Anne was currently at the parsonage, perhaps even now conversing with Jane while wearing Elizabeth's face, made Elizabeth's stomach turn.

Elizabeth forced herself to straighten, and respond to Colonel Fitzwilliam. "There are reasons for that surprise. Reasons I cannot easily explain."

The Colonel's expression shifted, concern giving way to something harder. "Cousin Anne, I hope you are not attempting to interfere between Darcy and Miss Elizabeth Bennet. Whatever your feelings about his interest in her, such interference would be unworthy of you."

The accusation struck Elizabeth with unexpected force, followed immediately by understanding. Of course he would think that. Would assume Anne had summoned Jane in some scheme to disrupt Darcy's courtship.

"No," Elizabeth said, and she put every ounce of conviction she possessed into the single word. "I promise you that is not my intention."

Or, she thought, not her primary intention. Nobody deserved what Anne de Bourgh was trying to do, ensnare him by deception.

And if Anne succeeded, what then? If Mr. Darcy married "Elizabeth Bennet"... then what? Even if Elizabeth were somehow able to effect a reversal of the body swap, she would be transferring back into the body not of Elizabeth Bennet, but of *Mrs. Darcy.*

Colonel Fitzwilliam studied her face, searching for truth or deception. She met his gaze directly, willing him to believe her.

"Then what are you trying to accomplish?" he asked, and his voice had gone gentle again. "Why this desperate need for Miss Jane Bennet's presence?"

Elizabeth's throat closed around any response. She could tell him the truth. Could explain about the body swap, about Anne's theft of her identity. The words gathered behind her teeth, desperate to be spoken.

But the risk was too great. If he thought her mad, if he dismissed her claims as delusions, he would tell Lady Catherine. Would ensure Elizabeth was confined more securely, possibly sent away to some asylum. She could not risk losing what little freedom she still possessed.

"There is more happening than you realise," Elizabeth said finally, choosing her words with desperate care. "Things I cannot explain, not yet. But it was vital that Elizabeth have her dearest sister nearby. Someone who knows her well. Someone who can..." She paused, searching for words. "Someone who can see clearly."

The Colonel's brow furrowed. "That is remarkably cryptic, cousin."

"I know," Elizabeth agreed, and she could not prevent the exhaustion and desperation from bleeding into her voice. "I am sorry. But I cannot say more. Please, you must trust that my reasons are sound, even if I cannot share them."

Silence settled between them, broken only by distant sounds of the house. Somewhere below, a door closed. A servant's footsteps echoed through hidden passages.

"I think people do not listen to you enough," Colonel Fitzwilliam said finally, and his voice carried unexpected kindness. "You are clever, Anne. Perceptive. Yet everyone treats you as though your physical weakness extends to your mind and judgement."

The observation struck Elizabeth with complicated force. He was not speaking to her, not really, but to the woman whose body she inhabited. To Anne de Bourgh, overlooked and dismissed. And perhaps he was right. Perhaps if people had listened to Anne, had valued her thoughts and needs, she might have chosen a different path than the desperate wickedness that had led to this moment.

"Miss Jane Bennet was quite a pleasure to spend the afternoon with," the Colonel added, and something in his tone suggested more than mere politeness. A warmth that went beyond simple courtesy. "Remarkably composed and intelligent. The conversation during our journey was most agreeable."

Despite everything, Elizabeth felt a smile tug at her lips. Of course Jane would have charmed him through simple kindness. Of course the Colonel would have found her delightful company.

"She is the best of women," Elizabeth said, and this at least was truth she could speak without reservation. "The dearest sister anyone could wish for." Quickly, she added, "Everything Elizabeth Bennet has told me, has convinced me of that."

The Colonel nodded, his expression showing agreement. "You need not thank me for helping you reach her. It was a small thing."

"Not small to me," Elizabeth whispered, and tears threatened again. "Colonel Fitzwilliam, you cannot know how much this means."

"Anne," he said, and his voice had gone very gentle. "You have never asked me for anything in your life. In all our years as cousins, you have never requested my assistance. When you came to me this morning, desperate enough to fall to your knees and beg, I knew it must be for something of vital importance."

He paused, reaching out to steady her as she swayed. His hand remained on her elbow.

"It was a small thing that I could do for you," he continued. "And I hope you will not hesitate to ask if there is anything else I may do to assist you. Whatever trouble you find yourself in, I am at your disposal."

The offer hung between them, sincere and absolute. Elizabeth stared up at him and felt the weight of choice pressing down. She could tell him now. Could risk everything on the hope that he would believe her. Could finally have an ally who knew what had been done to her.

But what if he did not believe her? What if his kindness transformed into horrified conviction that his cousin had lost her mind?

Elizabeth could not risk it. Not yet. Not when Jane had finally arrived, when she had the beginning of a plan that might work without requiring anyone to accept the impossible.

"Thank you," Elizabeth said, and she poured all her genuine gratitude into the words. "Your help means more than I can express. But there is nothing else I need from you at present."

Colonel Fitzwilliam studied her face for a long moment. Whatever he saw seemed to satisfy him, because he nodded and stepped back.

"Very well," he said. "But remember, Anne. Whatever you need. Whatever assistance you require. You have only to ask."

Elizabeth nodded, not trusting her voice to remain steady. The Colonel executed a small bow, then turned and walked down the corridor, his footsteps fading until she stood alone.

Elizabeth remained there for several minutes, leaning against the cool stone wall, letting her borrowed body rest while her mind raced. Jane was here. Her dearest Jane, who knew her better than anyone else in the world, who would recognise immediately that something was desperately wrong with the woman claiming to be Elizabeth Bennet. Jane would see through Anne's imperfect performance. Would understand without needing impossible explanations. Would help Elizabeth find a way to reverse this nightmare.

Elizabeth pushed herself away from the wall and began the slow journey down the corridor toward Anne's chamber. Her borrowed legs trembled with each step, exhaustion pulling at her consciousness. But beneath the weariness, beneath the pain and weakness, hope burned with steady determination.

Jane was here.

Chapter Fifteen

The door to Anne's chamber closed behind Elizabeth with a soft click that seemed unnaturally loud in the silence. She stood for a moment with her back pressed against the wood, listening intently for any sound of footsteps in the corridor beyond. Mrs. Jenkinson might come up at any moment, might decide that she required supervision despite Lady Catherine's insistence on being entertained. But the passage remained quiet, only the distant murmur of voices from below stairs and the settling creaks of an old house preparing for night.

Elizabeth pushed herself away from the door and crossed the room with unsteady steps, her borrowed legs trembling with exhaustion. Tonight, for the first time since waking in this nightmare, she had something. Jane was here. Not at her side, not yet, but close enough that hope felt almost tangible.

And she had the journal.

Elizabeth knelt beside the bed with effort, her weak knees protesting the movement. She reached beneath the mattress, her fingers searching through the space between feather tick and bed frame until they encountered the leather binding she had hidden there. The journal felt heavier than she remembered as she pulled it free, its weight substantial in her frail hands. Dark brown leather, worn smooth at the edges from years of handling, with no title or decoration to indicate its contents save the de Bourgh family crest embossed on the lower corner. Someone glancing over it would think it an accounts book or personal diary, nothing worthy of particular notice.

Elizabeth climbed onto the bed and arranged herself against the pillows, propping the journal on her lap. Her lungs laboured with even this small exertion, Anne's damaged chest rising and falling with shallow breaths that never quite satisfied. She positioned the candlestick on the bedside table, angling it to cast the most light possible across the pages, then opened the journal.

Anne's handwriting sprawled across the first page in cramped, dense lines that made Elizabeth's eyes ache trying to decipher them. The script was small, precise, each letter formed with care despite the overall impression of words crowded together as though space were precious. Elizabeth squinted in the candlelight, tracing the first entry with one finger.

A recipe. That much was clear from the format, ingredients listed in careful order followed by instructions for preparation. But the components themselves made Elizabeth's brow furrow in confusion. Rose petals dried under a full moon. Spring water collected at dawn. Honey from bees that had fed only on lavender. Her first instinct was to dismiss it as fanciful nonsense, the sort of superstitious remedies country folk might trade among themselves without any real effect.

But Anne had not collected superstitious remedies. Anne had practiced witchcraft. Had successfully swapped their bodies using magic that Elizabeth had experienced first-hand. These recipes were not harmless folk wisdom. They were real.

Elizabeth turned the page, finding another recipe. Then another. Each one detailed preparations and ingredients that grew progressively stranger. Powdered moonstone. The rendered fat of a black cat. Hair from a virgin bride. Some entries included notes in the margins, observations about potency or effectiveness that suggested Anne had tested these formulations, had used them for purposes Elizabeth could only guess at.

Her finger paused on an entry near the middle of the journal. The ingredients were less exotic than some of the others but still unusual. Rose petals again, but these preserved in brandy. Crushed pearls mixed with honey. Extract of damask rose. Vervain gathered at midnight. And at the bottom, in slightly larger script as though Anne had wanted to emphasise its importance: One drop of blood from each party, mixed under a new moon.

Elizabeth read the instructions that followed, her heart beginning to hammer against her ribs. A potion to inspire lasting devotion. To make the drinker unable to consider any other romantic attachment. To bind their affections completely to the one who had administered it.

A love potion.

Her eyes dropped to the margin note, written in Anne's hand but with obvious excitement that made the letters slightly less controlled. *"This one works,"* it read, the third word highlighted by three emphatic underscores. *"Mother's never looked at anyone else. Use on Darcy once married!"*

Elizabeth stared at the words, her mind refusing to process their meaning even as understanding crashed over her with horrible certainty. *Mother's never looked at anyone else.* Lady Catherine. Proud, domineering Lady Catherine de Bourgh, daughter of an earl, who had married Sir Lewis de Bourgh despite his being beneath her in station and consequence.

The journal trembled in Elizabeth's grasp as pieces clicked into place with sickening clarity. Lady Catherine had been a great beauty in her youth, by all accounts. Had possessed fortune and breeding that should have secured her a match among the highest circles of society. Yet she had married a gentleman whose family, while respectable, could not approach the distinction of her own, despite the wealth of Rosings Park.

Elizabeth had always assumed it had been a love match. That Lady Catherine's pride and conviction in her own superiority had developed later, perhaps even after her husband's passing. But what if it had not been choice at all? What if Sir Lewis de Bourgh had used this same potion to secure the hand of a woman who would never have looked at him otherwise?

The implications made Elizabeth's stomach turn. Lady Catherine bound by magical compulsion to a man she might never have chosen freely. Devoted to him completely, unable even to consider that her affections had been artificially created rather than naturally developed. And now her daughter planned to do the same thing to Darcy. To trap him with the same spell that had ensnared Lady Catherine, to ensure his devotion through magical manipulation rather than genuine feeling.

Elizabeth's hands clenched around the journal's leather binding, her knuckles white with the force of her grip. The candle flame wavered in a draft she could not feel, making shadows dance across the pages and Anne's cramped handwriting seem to writhe like living things. She wanted to throw the journal across the room, wanted to tear out these pages and burn them so that no one could ever use such wicked magic again.

But she needed this journal. Needed the recipes it contained, particularly the one Anne had used to swap their bodies. Without that knowledge, Elizabeth had no hope of reversing what had been done to her. She forced herself to breathe slowly despite the tightness in her chest, forced her hands to relax their grip before she damaged the pages she needed to study.

How long had Anne been planning this? The journal covered years, the earlier recipes having dates at the top almost a decade old. Anne had been studying magic, collecting recipes, preparing for this scheme since long before Elizabeth had even met Darcy. Perhaps since before Darcy himself had come of age.

The idea of such patient, calculated wickedness made Elizabeth's skin crawl. Anne had spent years learning the craft her father had taught her, years gathering rare ingredients and testing formulations, years waiting for the right opportunity. For a woman whom Darcy might consider marrying, perhaps, so that Anne could steal her body and her life. And Elizabeth had arrived at Hunsford completely ignorant, vulnerable in ways she could never have anticipated.

She turned another page, then another, searching now with desperate urgency. The body-swap potion had to be here somewhere. Had to be recorded among these recipes for love potions and devotion draughts and all the other violations Anne had planned. Elizabeth's eyes strained in the candlelight, Anne's weak vision making the small script even harder to decipher. But she continued turning pages, scanning ingredients and instructions with growing desperation.

She found it near the end of the journal, on a page that showed signs of having been consulted frequently. The paper was slightly more worn there, the edges softened from repeated handling, and small spatters of what looked like old candle wax dotted the margins.

Elizabeth's breath caught in her throat as she read the title written in Anne's careful hand: "*A Draught for the Exchange of Forms.*"

Elizabeth's lips moved silently as she read words that might as well have been a death sentence. *Ambergris braised in honey*. She had heard of ambergris, knew it came from whales and was used to make expensive perfumes. *Spirits of wine well-rectified. Pearl powder. Saffron.* Each component more exotic and expensive than the last, the sort of ingredients that appeared in apothecaries' most expensive preparations, if they appeared at all.

"Ambergris braised in honey," Elizabeth whispered into the silence of Anne's chamber, her voice emerging thin and shaking. "Spirits of wine well-rectified, pearl powder, saffron, grains of paradise, lemon balm and lavender water."

The words felt strange in her mouth, foreign and impossible. Grains of paradise she had never even heard of.

Elizabeth's eyes continued down the page, her heart sinking further with each line. "*A lock of cut hair of both parties. A draught for each, taken in the same hour.*"

So Anne had needed Elizabeth's hair, had somehow obtained it without Elizabeth's knowledge or consent. Had collected it carefully and stored it until the moment was right. The violation of that made Elizabeth's stomach turn, the idea of Anne watching her, waiting for an opportunity to steal something so personal.

The final line caught Elizabeth's attention, written in slightly darker ink as though Anne had pressed harder on the pen: "*A shaving of bezoar steadies.*"

Bezoar. Elizabeth stared at the word, trying to recall where she had seen it before. In one of her father's books, perhaps. She would have to research, somehow. Perhaps a favour she might ask of Colonel Fitzwilliam, she thought with a flash of dark humour, since he had volunteered to help her. But even with the bezoar, the other components remained impossibly out of reach. Saffron cost more by weight than gold; ambergris and pearl powder required wealth Elizabeth did not possess in this borrowed body or her own. She had found no money in Anne's room during her search and asking Lady Catherine for large sums of money would lead to questions she could not answer. Spirits of wine well-rectified would need to be purchased from an apothecary who would certainly question why Miss Anne de Bourgh required such a substance.

The journal trembled in Elizabeth's grasp as the full magnitude of her predicament crashed over her. She had found the recipe, yes, had discovered the formula Anne had used to trap her in this dying body. But knowing what was needed did not mean she could obtain it. The ingredients were too rare, too expensive, too far beyond her reach in her current state. She could barely walk across a room without assistance. How could she possibly acquire exotic substances from distant lands?

Elizabeth's throat closed around a sob she would not let escape. She had been so certain that finding the recipe would provide hope, would give her a path forward. But this list of impossible ingredients felt more like proof of her helplessness than a solution to her nightmare.

Her mind turned to the love potion entry, seeking distraction from her despair. Why had Anne not simply used that on Darcy from the beginning? Why go through the elaborate scheme of swapping bodies when a simpler spell could have secured his devotion? But even as Elizabeth formed the question, understanding followed. Anne's body was dying. What use was securing Darcy's magical devotion if she would die before enjoying more than a brief taste of the life she craved?

The body swap solved that problem. Gave Anne not just Darcy's love but decades to enjoy it, to live as mistress of Pemberley, to bear children and establish herself completely. Using the love potion afterward would simply ensure Darcy never questioned his choice, never wondered at the changes in his wife's character, never suspected that the woman he had married was not who he thought.

Elizabeth reached up with one trembling hand and touched Anne's hair, feeling the brittle texture of locks that had been cut short months ago. Had Anne cut a lock of her hair while Elizabeth slept at the parsonage? Had she crept into the room Elizabeth shared with Maria Lucas and stolen what she needed under cover of darkness? Or had she found some other opportunity, some moment when Elizabeth's attention was elsewhere and her hair accessible?

The violation of it made nausea rise in Elizabeth's throat. Anne had *stalked* her, had watched and waited and chosen her moment with calculated precision. Had studied Elizabeth's habits and routines, had learned when she would be vulnerable, had planned every detail of the theft down to obtaining hair without her victim's knowledge. The level of premeditation required for such wickedness made Elizabeth's skin crawl with revulsion.

She looked down at her hands, at the thin fingers and pronounced veins that belonged to Anne de Bourgh's failing body. This flesh had prepared the potion that doomed them both. These hands had measured out exotic ingredients, had cut hair from two heads, had mixed the draught that would facilitate the exchange. And now, Elizabeth's own healthy hands were being used by the woman who had stolen them, were touching things and people and going about daily activities as though they had every right to the body they inhabited.

Elizabeth closed the journal with shaking hands, the leather binding settling together with a soft sound that seemed too final. She had the recipe now. Had the knowledge she needed. But knowledge without means was just another form of torture, showing her exactly what she needed while keeping it perpetually out of reach.

The candle on the bedside table guttered slightly, throwing strange shadows across the ornate ceiling plasterwork. Elizabeth watched the patterns shift and flow, her eyes burning with tears she would not shed. She needed to think. Needed to plan. The ingredients might be rare but they were not impossible. Anne had obtained them somehow, had gathered everything required for the potion despite her own physical limitations. If Anne could do it, then Elizabeth could as well.

But Anne had possessed time, years to plan and prepare and collect what she needed. Elizabeth had months at best before this failing body gave out entirely. Weeks, perhaps, if the coughing fits grew worse or if Mrs. Jenkinson decided more drastic measures were required to keep her quiet. Every day that passed was one less day to find a solution, one more day for Anne to secure her position as Mrs. Darcy, and to permanently bind Darcy to her with the love potion.

Elizabeth had never for a moment desired Darcy's love. But he had given it to her nonetheless, she was coming to realise, and the thought of Anne stealing it as she had stolen Elizabeth's body was a violation that must be prevented, if she possibly could.

Elizabeth pushed herself upright with effort and climbed off the bed, bending to tuck the journal back beneath the mattress. The leather binding slid into darkness, concealed once more from casual observation. No one must know she had found it, had read its contents, understood what Anne had done.

She lay back against the pillows again, arranging Anne's weak body in a position that allowed easier breathing. The ceiling plasterwork swam slightly in her vision, exhaustion pulling at her consciousness despite the urgency of her situation. But sleep would not come easily tonight, Elizabeth knew. Her mind raced too quickly, turning over possibilities and obstacles, searching desperately for some path forward through the impossibility that surrounded her.

Jane is here. That thought anchored her, gave her something solid to cling to in the swirling chaos of her predicament. Jane would help. Would believe her when she explained what had happened, would assist in whatever way possible. Together, they would find a solution. Would obtain the ingredients somehow, would mix the potion, would reverse this nightmare and stop Anne from marrying Mr. Darcy in Elizabeth's body.

Elizabeth simply had to hold on long enough. Had to survive in this failing body until they could execute the reversal. Had to endure Mrs. Jenkinson's medicines and Lady Catherine's domineering presence and the constant weakness that threatened to drag her down into darkness.

She had done difficult things before. Had walked three miles through mud to reach Jane's sickbed at Netherfield. Had rejected Mr. Collins despite her mother's fury and her family's precarious situation. Had maintained her principles and independence in the face of pressure from every direction. This was simply another impossible situation to navigate, another challenge to overcome through determination and clever planning.

The candle flame steadied, burning straight and true in air that had gone still. Elizabeth watched it, letting the light anchor her thoughts, and began to plan.

Chapter Sixteen

Darcy's boots struck the path to Hunsford parsonage with the steady rhythm of a man attempting to convince himself he felt calm. The morning had dawned fine and clear, spring sunlight catching in droplets of dew that clung to new grass. His hand moved to his waistcoat pocket for perhaps the twentieth time that hour, fingers confirming the presence of his mother's ring through layers of fabric. The small weight of it pressed against his ribs with each step.

He had rehearsed his proposal throughout a sleepless night, words arranging and rearranging themselves until they had lost all meaning. But Elizabeth deserved better than a memorised speech. She would expect honesty, sincerity, the genuine expression of feelings he had tried and failed to suppress for months. Darcy's throat tightened at the thought of actually speaking those feelings aloud.

The parsonage came into view through the trees. Darcy straightened his shoulders and forced his hand away from his pocket. He would find a way to speak with Elizabeth alone this morning, would ask her to walk with him.

The servant who answered his knock showed him through to the dining room, and Darcy stepped through the doorway already searching for Elizabeth's figure among the breakfast table's occupants.

He found her at the far end of the table, but his gaze caught and held on the woman seated near Mr. and Mrs. Collins.

Miss Jane Bennet.

Darcy stopped so abruptly that the servant nearly collided with him from behind. His carefully maintained composure fractured as recognition crashed over him. Miss Bennet sat there in a pale blue morning dress, her fair hair caught up in a simple arrangement, and her presence felt like evidence of crimes Darcy had tried to convince himself were justified.

He had separated her from Bingley. Had argued that her affections were not engaged, that she showed no particular preference despite Bingley's obvious attachment. Had convinced himself that protecting Bingley justified any collateral damage to Miss Bennet's feelings. And now here she sat, composed and lovely, while guilt settled over Darcy like a physical weight.

"Mr. Darcy," Mr. Collins exclaimed, rising with his characteristic lack of grace. "What an unexpected honour!"

Darcy forced his attention away from Jane Bennet and executed a bow that felt wooden. "Mr. Collins. Mrs. Collins. I hope I do not intrude upon your breakfast."

"Not at all," Collins assured him with obsequious enthusiasm. "You are always welcome."

Charlotte rose with more dignity than her husband. "Please, Mr. Darcy, do join us. There is plenty of food remaining."

Darcy's gaze moved inevitably back to Miss Bennet, who had risen as well and now stood with her hands folded before her. She looked exactly as he remembered from Netherfield.

"Miss Bennet," Darcy said, and his voice emerged more formal than he had intended. He executed another bow, this one deeper than strict necessity required. "I had not realised you were visiting Kent. I hope your journey was comfortable."

"Quite comfortable, thank you, Mr. Darcy," Jane replied. "I arrived only yesterday evening."

"Indeed?" Darcy said, though the word came out stiff. "The journey from London is not inconsiderable."

He was being ridiculous, he realised. Speaking to her as though she were some grand lady rather than simply his friend's former interest and Elizabeth's beloved sister. But guilt made him formal.

Jane inclined her head. "Colonel Fitzwilliam was kind enough to escort me from London. His company made the journey most agreeable."

So that was where his cousin had been yesterday. But why? Darcy's attention shifted to Elizabeth, who had not risen from her seat at the far end of the table. She sat with her hands wrapped around a teacup, her gaze fixed somewhere in the middle distance. The physical distance between the sisters struck him immediately. Elizabeth had positioned herself as far from Jane as the table's dimensions allowed.

"Miss Elizabeth," Darcy said, moving toward her end of the table. "Good morning."

Elizabeth looked up at him then, and her smile carried warmth that eased some of the tension in his chest. "Mr. Darcy. How lovely to see you this morning."

"I hope I am not interrupting your breakfast," Darcy said.

"Not at all," Elizabeth replied, but her attention had already drifted away, her gaze returning to that middle distance.

Charlotte gestured toward the sideboard. "Please, Mr. Darcy, help yourself."

Darcy accepted a plate more from politeness than hunger and took a seat near the middle of the table. The arrangement struck him as deeply strange. Jane sat near the Collinses, engaging them in quiet conversation. Elizabeth remained at her end of the table, tracing the rim of her teacup with one finger in repetitive circles.

"Jane," Elizabeth said suddenly, her voice cutting through the general conversation with unexpected sharpness. "Did you sleep well? The beds at the parsonage must be quite different from what you are accustomed to in London."

Jane turned toward her sister, and something in her expression made Darcy think of someone approaching a nervous horse. Careful. Cautious. "I slept perfectly well, thank you, Lizzy. Charlotte's hospitality is most generous."

"I am glad to hear it," Elizabeth replied, but the words emerged clipped, stripped of warmth. She took a sip of her tea, her gaze sliding away from Jane's face.

Darcy watched this exchange with growing confusion. Elizabeth adored her sister. Had walked three miles through mud to reach Jane's sickbed at Netherfield, had nursed her with devoted attention. Yet now she sat at the opposite end of the table, responding to her sister's presence with something that looked remarkably like avoidance.

The door opened once again, and Colonel Fitzwilliam strolled in with easy confidence.

"Darcy!" Fitzwilliam exclaimed with mock reproach. "You came down without me. Most uncivil."

Despite his unease, Darcy felt a smile tug at his lips. "My apologies, Fitzwilliam. I had not realised you required an escort."

"I require civilised company," Fitzwilliam corrected, moving toward the table. His gaze swept the assembled party and caught on Jane, and something in his expression shifted. "Miss Bennet. What a pleasant surprise."

He moved immediately to the chair beside Jane. "I had thought perhaps you might have decided to rest this morning after yesterday's journey."

"I am quite recovered, Colonel," Jane replied, and a hint of colour touched her cheeks. "Your company yesterday made it far less taxing."

"I am delighted to hear it," Fitzwilliam said, and his voice had taken on a warmth Darcy could not recall hearing. "I confess I found the journey remarkably pleasant myself."

Darcy's attention moved to Elizabeth, curious to see her reaction to this obvious flirtation. What he saw made unease prickle along his spine. Elizabeth's fingers had tightened around her teacup with enough force that her knuckles showed white. Her jaw had set in a hard line, and she was watching the interaction with an expression that could only be described as irritated.

"We were just discussing the village," Charlotte said. "Jane expressed interest in seeing the church this morning."

"The church?" Elizabeth's voice cut through with unexpected sharpness. She set down her teacup with enough force that it rattled. "Surely Jane must be exhausted from her journey. She should rest this morning rather than traipsing about Kent."

Jane turned to look at her sister. "I am not tired at all, Lizzy. I would very much like to see the village."

"Nevertheless," Elizabeth said, her tone brooking no argument. "It would be most unwise to overtax yourself so soon after travelling."

Darcy found himself rising without conscious decision. If Elizabeth wanted to avoid showing her sister the village, perhaps it was because she had other plans.

"Miss Elizabeth," Darcy said. "The morning is remarkably fine. Perhaps you might be persuaded to walk out with me, while your sister rests from her journey? The gardens at Rosings are particularly beautiful this time of year."

Elizabeth's expression transformed, irritation giving way to eager acceptance so quickly that Darcy felt a flash of relief. "I would be delighted, Mr. Darcy."

She rose from her chair with fluid grace, already moving toward the door. Darcy glanced toward Fitzwilliam and found his cousin watching Jane with warm attention.

"Fitzwilliam," Darcy said. "Perhaps you might remain here and keep Miss Bennet company while Miss Elizabeth and I walk out."

Fitzwilliam's face lit with obvious pleasure. "I would be honoured. If Miss Bennet would not find my company tiresome."

"Not at all, Colonel," Jane replied, and the shy smile she gave him made something uncomfortable twist in Darcy's chest.

As Darcy moved toward where Elizabeth waited by the door, he caught Jane giving her sister an odd look, something searching and concerned. But Elizabeth had already turned away.

Darcy offered Elizabeth his arm, and she took it without hesitation. They stepped out into the spring morning together.

Darcy did not look back.

Darcy's hand had returned to his waistcoat pocket before they had even cleared the parsonage garden gate. Elizabeth walked beside him with easy grace, her hand resting lightly on his arm, and she seemed entirely at ease. She chatted pleasantly about the morning weather and the state of the paths, and Darcy responded with words he could not have repeated moments later.

His cravat felt too tight. Darcy's free hand moved to his neck, fingers tugging at the linen in a gesture he immediately regretted as too obvious. Elizabeth glanced up at him with mild curiosity but said nothing.

The grove appeared ahead, that circle of ancient oaks where new leaves filtered the morning light into shifting patterns. Darcy had chosen this location deliberately. Private enough for intimacy but visible enough to maintain propriety.

He led Elizabeth beneath the trees. Dappled sunlight falling between the leafy branches caught in her dark hair, picking out auburn highlights. She was here. With him. Alone. And he was about to make the most important request of his life.

Darcy stopped walking and turned to face her, his heart hammering against his ribs. Elizabeth stopped as well, looking up at him with pleasant expectation.

His carefully rehearsed words scattered like leaves in wind. Darcy opened his mouth and found that every eloquent phrase he had constructed had abandoned him.

"Miss Elizabeth," he began, then stopped because his voice had emerged rougher than he intended. He cleared his throat and tried again. "Miss Elizabeth, I have brought you here this morning because there is something I must tell you. Something I should have told you before now."

Elizabeth's eyes remained fixed on his face, her expression attentive but giving away nothing.

"I have admired you for longer than I care to admit," he said, and the words came haltingly. "Your wit, your intelligence, your refusal to be intimidated by rank or consequence. You challenge me in ways I did not know I needed to be challenged. Make me question assumptions I have held without examination. I find myself thinking of you at the most inopportune moments, unable to focus because my thoughts have drifted to something you said or the way you looked when you said it."

He was rambling, Darcy realised with embarrassment. But Elizabeth continued to watch him with that same attentive expression.

"What I am trying to say," Darcy continued, forcing himself to meet her eyes directly, "is that you must allow me to tell you how ardently I admire and love you. I cannot imagine my future without you in it, cannot contemplate returning to the life I had before I knew you. You have become essential to my happiness."

His hand moved to his pocket, withdrawing the small velvet box that contained his mother's ring. The morning light caught the gold band and made the small ruby glow. Darcy held it out toward Elizabeth, his hand trembling slightly.

"Miss Elizabeth Bennet," he said, and his voice dropped lower, intimate. "Would you do me the very great honour of becoming my wife?"

The silence that followed felt endless. Darcy's heart hammered against his ribs, each beat painful. He had made himself completely vulnerable, and now his entire future hung on her response.

Elizabeth's face transformed, her expression shifting into a smile so bright it made Darcy's breath catch. But there was something in that smile, something almost triumphant, that did not quite match the tenderness he might have hoped for.

"Yes," Elizabeth said, and her voice carried eager certainty. "Yes, I will marry you, Mr. Darcy."

The words were exactly what he had hoped to hear. Yet something about the delivery made Darcy pause even as relief flooded through him. She had accepted immediately, without hesitation or surprise, without the questions or teasing that characterised her usual manner. Just simple, immediate agreement delivered with that bright smile that did not quite reach her eyes in the way he expected.

Darcy told himself he was being foolish. She had accepted him. What did it matter if her response lacked the complexity he associated with Elizabeth's character? Perhaps she was simply overwhelmed by the moment.

He reached for her hand, intending to slip the ring onto her finger, and Elizabeth extended her hand readily. Her fingers settled into his palm with easy compliance, but there was something mechanical about the gesture. He pushed the thought aside and focused on sliding the gold band onto her finger.

"It fits perfectly," Elizabeth observed, holding her hand up to examine the ring. "How lovely."

The words were appropriate, Darcy supposed, but they carried none of the emotion he might have expected. She might have been commenting on a new pair of gloves. But perhaps she was simply not given to elaborate displays of feeling.

They began walking back toward the parsonage. Elizabeth Bennet had agreed to marry him. He should be euphoric. And he was happy, certainly, but beneath that happiness ran a current of unease he could not quite identify.

"I hope you will find Pemberley to your liking," Darcy said. "The house is quite large, of course, perhaps intimidatingly so at first. But I think you will come to love it. The grounds offer excellent walking, miles of paths through woods and along the river. And the library contains one of the finest private collections in Derbyshire."

"I am certain it will be everything charming," Elizabeth replied, her tone carrying enthusiasm that somehow felt detached. "I look forward to seeing it."

Darcy glanced down at her, searching her face for some sign of the curiosity he knew Elizabeth possessed. She always asked questions, always wanted to know specific details. Yet now she offered only vague approval.

"My sister will be overjoyed," Darcy continued. "Georgiana has been most eager to meet you. I think she has been lonely for female companionship her own age."

"Oh, we shall get along splendidly," Elizabeth said, again with that bright enthusiasm that seemed to lack depth. "It will be delightful to have a sister."

The phrasing struck Darcy as odd. Elizabeth already had sisters, four of them. Why would she speak as though gaining Georgiana would be her first experience of sisterhood? But perhaps she simply meant having a sister through marriage.

They had reached the edge of the parsonage garden. Darcy slowed their pace, reluctant to end this private time together despite his growing confusion. She had accepted him. That was what mattered. Everything else could be sorted out in time.

He was engaged to Elizabeth Bennet. His Elizabeth. The woman who had captured his heart. That joy should overwhelm any small concerns.

And Darcy was happy. He told himself that firmly as they approached the parsonage. He was happy. His future was secured with the woman he loved. The strange quality to her acceptance, the mechanical feel of her responses, the lack of specific questions or characteristic teasing – none of that mattered.

He simply needed to stop looking for problems where none existed.

The dining room had not changed in their absence, though the breakfast dishes had been cleared. Jane remained in her seat, Charlotte beside her, and Fitzwilliam had positioned himself across from them. They all looked up as Darcy and Elizabeth entered.

Elizabeth released Darcy's arm and moved toward the centre of the room with purposeful strides, her hand extended to display his mother's ring with deliberate emphasis. The gesture struck Darcy as theatrical, more dramatic than the moment required.

"We are engaged," Elizabeth announced, her voice bright with an almost aggressive cheerfulness. "Mr. Darcy has done me the honour of proposing, and I have accepted. We are to be married."

The silence that greeted this declaration felt interminable. Darcy watched the assembled company's faces cycle through surprise and confusion before settling into more appropriate expressions of congratulation.

Charlotte recovered first, rising with a smile that seemed to require effort. "My dear Lizzy, how wonderful. What happy news indeed. Mr. Darcy, you must allow me to wish you joy."

"Thank you, Mrs. Collins," Darcy said, moving to stand beside Elizabeth. "I am very fortunate that Miss Elizabeth has accepted me."

Fitzwilliam rose as well, crossing to shake Darcy's hand. "Cousin, I am delighted for you. Miss Elizabeth, I can think of no one who would make Darcy a more suitable wife."

"And we shall be married in London," Elizabeth continued as Jane approached to offer an embrace. "By special licence. There is no reason to wait when we might be wed immediately."

This time the silence lasted longer, heavy with implications. Darcy felt his own startlement, because this was very much not what he had expected Elizabeth to want. Charlotte's carefully maintained smile faltered. Fitzwilliam's eyebrows rose. And Jane froze and looked shocked, before speaking with gentle concern.

"Lizzy," Jane said, and her soft voice somehow cut through the awkwardness with startling clarity. "Surely you must want to be married from Longbourn. Mama will be heartbroken if you do not."

The observation was delivered with Jane's characteristic kindness, without accusation. Simply a reminder of fact that anyone who knew Mrs. Bennet would recognise as undeniably true.

Elizabeth turned toward her sister, and something in her expression made Darcy's chest tighten. Her smile remained fixed, bright and brittle, but her eyes had gone hard. "Mama will not care," Elizabeth said, and her tone carried dismissive certainty.

"She has a daughter who will become Mrs. Darcy. That is all that will matter to her."

The words hung in the air, true in their assessment of Mrs. Bennet's priorities but delivered with a cruelty that was entirely unlike Elizabeth. Darcy had heard her speak of her mother with exasperation, certainly, with embarrassment even. But never with this casual dismissal.

Jane's face reflected the hurt, though she did not protest further. She looked down at her hands rather than meeting her sister's eyes.

"I am certain your mother will be overjoyed by the news regardless of when and where the ceremony will take place," Charlotte said, her voice carrying diplomatic smoothness.

It was perfectly judged, Charlotte's comment, acknowledging the truth while avoiding any suggestion that Elizabeth's dismissal had been inappropriate. But the effort required to smooth over the awkwardness was itself evidence that something was deeply wrong.

This should be the happiest moment of Darcy's life. He had proposed to the woman he loved, and she had accepted. Yet he stood in the Collinses' dining room feeling increasingly like a man who had just made a terrible mistake without understanding exactly what he had done wrong.

Fitzwilliam cleared his throat. "Cousin, I believe I should accompany you back to Rosings. Aunt Catherine will be wondering where we have both disappeared to, and you will want to inform her of your news."

"Yes," Darcy agreed, the word emerging more heavily than he intended. "We should return to Rosings."

He looked down at Elizabeth, at the woman who wore his ring but seemed increasingly unlike the person he had fallen in love with. "May I call on you tomorrow? Perhaps we might walk again and discuss the arrangements."

"Of course," Elizabeth said, and her smile remained bright and uncomplicated. "I look forward to it, Mr. Darcy. We have so much to plan."

Darcy executed a bow toward Charlotte and Jane. "Mrs. Collins, thank you for your hospitality. Miss Bennet, a pleasure to see you again."

Jane inclined her head, but her attention remained fixed on Elizabeth rather than on Darcy. He saw her lips part as though she might say something, some protest or question, but then she closed her mouth and simply watched.

Darcy and Fitzwilliam made their farewells and stepped out into the morning. The door closed behind them, and Darcy found himself standing in the parsonage garden, engaged to be married, feeling significantly more uncertain than he had before he proposed.

Chapter Seventeen

THE DAY WAS GROWING warm by the time they left the parsonage behind, sunshine pressing down on Darcy's shoulders with a weight that should have felt pleasant but instead seemed oppressive. His hand moved to his waistcoat pocket again, confirming the absence of his mother's ring, now residing on Elizabeth's finger where it belonged. The gesture should have brought satisfaction. Instead, Darcy found himself touching empty fabric and feeling only hollow uncertainty.

Beside him, Fitzwilliam walked with the easy stride of a man who had witnessed something he found privately amusing. He waited until they had cleared the parsonage gate before speaking.

"Well, cousin," Fitzwilliam said, and Darcy could hear the grin in his words. "You have been remarkably efficient this morning. Left for a simple walk and returned engaged to be married."

Darcy managed something that might have passed for a smile. "I saw no reason to delay once I had determined my course."

"Indeed," Fitzwilliam agreed. "Though I must say, watching you fidget with that ring was becoming painful. I am relieved you finally worked up the courage to actually present it."

The observation was delivered with such good humour that Darcy could not take offence, though he felt heat rise in his face.

"You must be very happy," Fitzwilliam continued, glancing sideways at Darcy. "Miss Elizabeth is a remarkable woman. Intelligent, spirited, entirely unimpressed by rank or consequence. Precisely the sort of wife who will keep you from becoming insufferably pompous in your old age."

"Yes," Darcy said, and the word emerged more heavily than he intended. "I am very fortunate."

Fitzwilliam's expression shifted slightly, some of the teasing humour fading as he studied Darcy's face. "You do not sound particularly fortunate. One might almost think you were uncertain about the engagement you just secured."

Darcy forced his features into a more appropriate configuration. "I am simply thinking ahead to the next task. We must inform Aunt Catherine of my engagement, and that conversation will not be pleasant."

"Ah," Fitzwilliam said. "Yes, facing down the dragon. Well, you have my support in that endeavour, cousin. Though I suspect my presence will do little to soften her response."

"I am aware," Darcy replied, his tone carrying more bite than he had intended. "But I am not a boy to be directed in such matters. My aunt will have to accept that I have chosen my own wife."

"Indeed she will," Fitzwilliam agreed cheerfully. "Though the accepting may involve considerable volume and dramatics first.

I suggest we get it over with quickly. The anticipation is often worse than the actual confrontation."

They walked the remaining distance in silence, Darcy's mind turning over the strange quality of Elizabeth's acceptance despite his best efforts to dismiss his concerns. She had been so eager, so immediately willing. Had not questioned or teased or challenged him in any way. Had simply agreed with that bright smile.

Perhaps it was natural. Perhaps he had simply become so accustomed to Elizabeth's opposition that her compliance felt wrong by contrast. Perhaps this was what happened when a woman who had initially disliked him came to return his affections.

Darcy told himself this firmly as they approached Rosings' entrance. He was engaged to Elizabeth Bennet. That was what mattered. Everything else would sort itself out in time.

The entrance hall felt cooler than the morning air outside. Marble floors gleamed with recent polishing. A servant informed them that Lady Catherine awaited in her usual domain, and Darcy felt his shoulders tighten.

The drawing room assaulted Darcy's senses with its usual oppressive formality. Heavy velvet curtains in deep burgundy hung from floor to ceiling, blocking most of the natural light. The air carried the cloying scent of lavender, mixing with beeswax polish and the scents of wood and coal from the fire, blazing despite the warm day outside.

Lady Catherine occupied her customary chair. Anne sat near the fire, gazing pensively into the flames. Mrs. Jenkinson occupied her usual position nearby, her hands busy with some mending.

"Darcy," Lady Catherine pronounced, her voice carrying that particular edge of displeasure. "You have been absent all morning. I trust you have a suitable explanation."

Darcy moved further into the room, Fitzwilliam following close behind. The words he needed to say gathered behind his teeth, simple and straightforward, yet somehow difficult to speak aloud.

"Aunt Catherine," Darcy began, forcing his voice to remain steady. "I have news that I hope will bring you joy. I have this morning become engaged to Miss Elizabeth Bennet. We are to be married."

The silence lasted perhaps three heartbeats. Then Lady Catherine rose from her chair with enough force to make the furniture creak. Her face had gone red, mottled with fury.

"Engaged!" Lady Catherine spat the word as though it tasted foul. "You dare to come into my house and announce that you have engaged yourself to that impertinent, presumptuous girl. That woman of no consequence, no connexions, no fortune worthy of the name. Have you lost your senses entirely?"

"Aunt Catherine," Darcy attempted, but she spoke over him without pause.

"Your duty," Lady Catherine continued, her voice rising until she was nearly shouting. "Your obligation to this family, to your mother's memory, to the plan that has existed almost since your birth. You were destined to marry Anne. Destined to unite our estates, to keep the family connexions strong. And you throw all of that aside for what? A pair of fine eyes and an impertinent manner?"

She glared at him, her eyes blazing. "Anne has waited for you her entire life. Has maintained her health as best she could despite her delicate constitution, has prepared herself to be mistress of Pemberley. And *this* is how you repay her devotion?"

"My engagement to Miss Bennet has nothing to do with Anne," Darcy said, finding his voice. "I hold my cousin in great affection, but I have never had any intention to offer her marriage. There has never been an understanding between us."

"There has been an understanding since you were children," Lady Catherine insisted, her hand coming down on a nearby side table with enough force to make the ornaments rattle. A small porcelain figure toppled over. "An understanding between your mother and myself. You spit on your mother's memory with this choice."

The accusation struck Darcy like a physical blow, but he forced himself to remain composed. "My mother never spoke to me of any such understanding, and she would have wanted me to marry for affection, not duty. She would have approved of Elizabeth."

"She would have been horrified," Lady Catherine countered. "Horrified that her son would lower himself to marry the daughter of a country gentleman with barely two thousand a year and connexions to trade. What will people say? What will society think?"

"I care nothing for what society thinks," Darcy said, and meant it with every fibre of his being. "Elizabeth Bennet is worth ten of any fashionable society lady I have ever met."

Lady Catherine's face twisted with such rage that for a moment Darcy thought she might actually strike him. Instead, she turned sharply and strode toward the door. She wrenched it open with enough force that it struck the wall behind it.

"You are a fool," Lady Catherine pronounced from the doorway, her voice cold. "And you will regret this choice for the rest of your days. Mark my words, Darcy. This marriage will bring you nothing but misery."

She swept from the room, her exit punctuated by the slam of the door with such violence that the crystal chandelier overhead trembled, its drops chiming together in discordant protest.

Darcy stood frozen, his aunt's words still ringing in his ears. Beside him, Fitzwilliam shifted his weight, clearly uncomfortable but uncertain how to address it.

Movement caught Darcy's attention. Anne had remained by the fire throughout Lady Catherine's tirade, silent and unmoving. But now Darcy saw that she had gone pale, all colour draining from her face. Her hands trembled where they gripped the arms of her chair, knuckles white, and her breathing had turned shallow and rapid.

Darcy moved toward her instinctively, concern overriding the awkwardness. Whatever his aunt believed about obligations and family plans, he did not wish to see Anne distressed. He had known her since childhood, had always held her in affection even if he had never desired to marry her.

"Anne," he said softly, approaching the fire. "I hope you are not too distressed by this news."

He lowered himself into the chair beside her, studying her face. Her pallor had not improved, and her hands still gripped the chair arms with enough force that the wood creaked softly. But her expression had shifted from shock to something more complex, something that looked almost like internal struggle.

"I hope you are not disappointed," Darcy said, pitching his voice low. "I know our families had expectations, but I trust you understand that I have never encouraged such hopes. You have always been dear to me as a cousin, but I could not offer you more than familial affection."

Anne looked up at him, and something in her eyes made Darcy pause. She appeared to be wrestling with herself, some internal conflict playing across her features. Her lips parted as though to speak, closed again, then parted once more before words finally emerged.

"Why?" Anne asked, and her voice carried weight that transformed the simple question into something more significant. "Why did you propose to Elizabeth Bennet?"

The question caught Darcy off guard. He had expected protestations about duty or family obligation. But this direct inquiry into his motivations felt more personal, more genuinely curious than reproachful.

"Because I love her," Darcy said simply, and the words emerged with such conviction that he felt their truth resonate in his chest. "Because when I am in her presence, I cannot look away. Cannot think of anything beyond the desire to hear what she will say next, to see how her face will change when she speaks."

He leaned forward slightly, warming to his subject despite the awkwardness. "Her wit. The way she challenges everything I say, refuses to be impressed by rank or fortune, treats me as simply a man rather than the master of Pemberley. She sees through pretension with startling clarity and will not tolerate pomposity from anyone, least of all from me. When I speak with her, I must be my best self because she will accept nothing less."

Anne's expression had gone strange, something painful flickering across her face. But Darcy was too caught up in his explanation to properly register her distress.

"She is everything I did not know I needed," Darcy said, his smile softening. "Everything I did not realise I was searching for until I found it. Her spirit, her independence, her refusal to compromise her principles for convenience. She walked miles through mud to reach her sister's sickbed at Netherfield, arrived with her petticoats six inches deep in dirt and her face glowing from exertion, and she was the most beautiful thing I had ever seen."

The memory rose in his mind with perfect clarity. Elizabeth standing in Netherfield's entrance hall, slightly breathless, her eyes bright with concern for Jane. Caroline Bingley had been scandalised, but Darcy had seen only devotion and determination.

"I knew then," Darcy continued, his voice dropping lower. "Watching her tend to Miss Bennet with such devoted care, seeing how she would sacrifice propriety and comfort for those she loved, I knew that the love of this woman would truly be worth winning. That if I could secure her affection, her regard, her hand in marriage, I would have gained something more valuable than all the advantageous matches society might approve."

He looked at Anne, hoping she might understand. "I do not expect you to be happy about my choice, but I hope you can understand why I made it. Why I could not marry you or anyone else when my heart had already chosen Elizabeth."

Anne's face had been changing throughout his speech, her expression cycling through emotions Darcy could not quite identify. Now her features crumpled entirely, contorting with what looked like genuine anguish. She drew a shuddering breath, and when she spoke, her voice emerged raw with feeling.

"Elizabeth Bennet does not love you," Anne said, and each word fell between them like a stone into still water. "You will be the one who is unhappy and disappointed if you go through with this marriage."

The statement struck Darcy with physical force, stealing the breath from his lungs. He stared at Anne, at her face now twisted with what might have been pity, and felt the warmth that had been building in his chest transform into ice.

"What?" Darcy managed, though the word emerged barely above a whisper.

"She does not love you," Anne repeated, and this time her voice carried a terrible certainty. "Whatever her reasons for accepting your proposal, genuine affection is not among them."

Darcy rose from his chair with movements that felt mechanical. His footsteps carried him toward the door without conscious decision, his boots striking the floor with echoes that seemed unnaturally loud.

He had not thought Anne would react this way. Had assumed she had long accepted that they would never marry. *She is jealous*, he tried to tell himself, *lashing out in her pain*. But this did not seem the jealousy of a rejected woman. This was something else entirely. A warning delivered with apparent sincerity by someone who seemed to know things about Elizabeth that Darcy himself had failed to recognise.

The door closed behind him with a soft click that felt thunderous in his ears. Darcy stood in the hallway beyond, one hand still resting on the door handle, and felt the full weight of doubt settle over him like a shroud.

Chapter Eighteen

ELIZABETH SAT QUIETLY BESIDE the fire, her shallow breaths barely stirring the air around her. Mrs. Jenkinson sat close by with her eternal needlework, her attention apparently fixed on the delicate stitches forming beneath her fingers. But Elizabeth had learned these past days that the companion's focus was never as complete as it appeared. The woman possessed an uncanny awareness of her charge's movements, could sense restlessness or intention with the skill of someone who had spent decades monitoring a fragile invalid's every breath.

The afternoon sunlight slanted through the French doors, casting long rectangles across the carpet. Beyond the glass, Elizabeth could see the path she needed to take visible as a gap between the trees at the far side of the expansive lawns. Jane was there. So close. Close enough that Elizabeth could have walked the distance in her own body without particular effort. But in

Anne's failing form, the journey loomed like an expedition to some distant country.

Lady Catherine had retreated to her private chambers after the dramatic confrontation about Darcy's engagement, leaving the drawing room mercifully free of her overwhelming presence. Only Mrs. Jenkinson remained, a silent guardian who had said nothing about the day's events but whose posture suggested disapproval of something. Whether she disapproved of Darcy's choice or Anne's apparent acceptance of it, Elizabeth could not determine.

A servant entered through the main door, approaching Mrs. Jenkinson with quiet deference. "Excuse me, ma'am. Cook wishes to consult with you about Miss de Bourgh's dinner tray. She asks if you might come to the kitchen."

Mrs. Jenkinson set down her needlework with visible reluctance, her gaze moving immediately to Elizabeth. "I shall return shortly, Miss de Bourgh. Do not overtax yourself while I am gone."

Elizabeth nodded with what she hoped was appropriate meekness, watching as the companion rose and followed the servant from the room. The door closed behind them with a soft click, and Elizabeth counted to ten before pushing herself to her feet. Her legs trembled with the effort of standing upright without support, but she forced them to carry her toward the French doors.

The handles felt cold beneath her palms, the brass smooth from years of polishing. Elizabeth turned them slowly, easing the doors open just enough to slip through the gap. The afternoon air struck her face with surprising warmth after the drawing room's stuffy interior, carrying scents of growing things and fresh earth that made her lungs ache with the desire to breathe deeply.

She stepped onto the terrace, pulling the doors closed behind her with careful quiet. Elizabeth paused there for a moment, scanning the windows above for any sign of observers. The glass reflected only sky and clouds, showing no faces watching her escape.

The lawn stretched before her, deceptively smooth in the afternoon light. Elizabeth began walking, each step requiring deliberate concentration. Anne's body responded to her commands with sluggish reluctance, muscles protesting movement after hours of stillness. Elizabeth focused on her goal, ignoring the way her heart hammered against weak ribs.

There was little cover on the first part of her route, a stretch of open lawn that left her exposed to view from any of Rosings' many windows. She needed to hurry, but she could not, could only walk slowly, focussing on placing one foot in front of the other. Halfway across, her legs began to shake with genuine weakness. The trembling started in her thighs and spread downward, making each step uncertain.

Elizabeth stumbled, catching herself before she fell entirely. Her vision swam slightly, Anne's weak eyes struggling to focus through exhaustion. She stood there swaying, the parsonage still not even within sight, and felt despair rise in her throat. What if she could not make it? What if Anne's body gave out entirely before she reached Jane?

She reached the gap in the trees at last and stumbled between it, looking back over her shoulder towards the house. Rosings slumbered in the afternoon sun, looking somehow ominous despite the brightness of the day, but Elizabeth could see no signs of pursuit. Determinedly, she looked away and walked on, though she knew she would need to stop and rest soon, lest she be unable to complete her journey.

A decorative stone bench appeared through her blurred vision, positioned beneath a spreading oak tree. Elizabeth altered her course toward it, using the last of her strength to reach the seat before her legs collapsed entirely. She sank onto the cold stone with a gasp of relief, her chest heaving with the effort of drawing breath. Sweat dampened her hairline despite the moderate temperature, and her hands shook visibly where they gripped the bench's edge.

Minutes passed while Elizabeth sat there, forcing Anne's damaged lungs to work, willing strength back into trembling muscles. Finally, she pushed herself upright again, using the bench for support, aware that she dared not wait too long lest Mrs. Jenkinson come searching for her. Her legs felt marginally steadier now, though they still trembled with the threat of collapse. She took one step, then another, finding a rhythm that Anne's body could maintain. Slow. Painfully slow. But forward.

She reached the parsonage at last, the garden's humble beds and borders so different from Rosings' formal grandeur. The rose bushes formed a natural screen near the parlour window, offering concealment. Thorns caught immediately in her dress as she stepped close, the fine muslin Anne typically wore proving far less durable than Elizabeth's own practical gowns. She felt the fabric tear, heard the soft ripping sound, but could not bring herself to care about damage to Anne's clothing.

She arranged herself as comfortably as possible among the bushes, ignoring the thorns that pressed through thin fabric to prick her arms and back and leaning one shoulder against the wall for support. From this position, she could see directly into the parlour, though at an acute angle. Charlotte sat in her usual chair, her hands busy with some mending. Mr. Collins moved through Elizabeth's line of sight periodically, his heavy form instantly recognisable even in silhouette.

But no Jane. Elizabeth's heart sank with each passing minute that failed to produce her sister's beloved figure. Where was she? Had she gone upstairs to rest? Had she walked out to the village with her impostor sister, all unaware that Anne had stolen Elizabeth's face and body? The uncertainty made Elizabeth want to weep with frustration.

Time stretched like honey dripping from a spoon, each minute feeling like an hour. Elizabeth's legs ached from her awkward position among the roses. The thorns dug deeper as she settled into the branches' embrace. Her back burned where fabric had torn and sharp points pressed against skin. But she did not move. Could not move. Had come too far to abandon her position now simply because of discomfort; and besides, the thought of walking back to Rosings alone was utterly daunting.

Charlotte rose and left the parlour, her form disappearing into the house's interior. Mr. Collins remained briefly, then followed his wife, leaving the room empty. Elizabeth stared at the vacant space through the window, her eyes burning with the intensity of her focus.

Then Jane appeared. She entered the parlour alone, moving with the quiet grace Elizabeth recognized so well. Her fair hair caught the afternoon light streaming through the window, and her face showed that familiar expression of gentle contentment as she settled into a chair. She picked up a book from the side table, opening it to a marked page.

Alone. Jane was blessedly alone.

Elizabeth's fingers trembled as they made contact with the cool glass. She scratched at the window, the sound barely audible even to her own ears. Once. Twice. Jane did not look up, her attention fixed on the book in her lap. Elizabeth scratched harder, her fingernails making sharper sounds against the glass. Panic rose in her throat. What if Jane did not hear? What if this moment passed and Elizabeth lost her chance?

Jane's head lifted, her expression shifting from peaceful reading to curious alertness. Her gaze moved toward the window, searching for the source of the sound. Elizabeth scratched again, more desperately now, and beckoned with her free hand.

Their eyes met through the glass. Jane stared at the pale, frail woman gesturing frantically outside her window, her lovely face showing polite confusion. She rose from her chair and moved toward the window, her steps cautious, clearly uncertain about this strange visitor.

Elizabeth pressed her palm flat against the glass and continued beckoning, making urgent gestures that probably looked like madness to Jane's eyes. But Jane kept coming, kept moving toward the window, and that was all that mattered.

Jane reached the window and paused there, one hand resting on the frame, studying the stranger outside with an expression that mixed concern with wariness. Her lovely face showed no recognition, no spark of understanding, only polite confusion at finding a pale, frail woman crouched among the rose bushes. Elizabeth's throat closed around words that suddenly seemed impossible to speak.

The window opened with a soft creak, and Jane leaned out slightly, her voice carrying quiet courtesy. "May I help you? Are you unwell?"

"Please," Elizabeth whispered, and the word emerged raw with desperation she could not contain. "I must speak with you. Alone. It's of the utmost importance."

Jane's eyebrows rose slightly, polite confusion deepening into something more cautious. "I am afraid I do not understand. Have we been introduced? I do not believe I know you."

"Please, Jane," Elizabeth said, and tears gathered in her eyes despite her efforts at control. "I beg you. Come outside. I'll explain everything. But I need to speak with you alone. Please."

The use of her Christian name made Jane stiffen visibly, her hand tightening on the window frame. She glanced back into the parlour behind her, clearly searching for Charlotte or her husband, some adult who might explain this strange situation. When she looked back at Elizabeth, her expression had shifted from to one of genuine alarm.

"How do you know my name?" Jane asked, her soft voice carrying an edge Elizabeth had rarely heard. "Who are you?"

"I cannot explain here," Elizabeth managed, fighting against the sobs that threatened to overwhelm her. "Please, Jane. I know how this appears. I know I sound completely mad. But I am begging you. Come outside and speak with me for just a few minutes. If you wish to leave after hearing what I have to say, I will not stop you. I will never trouble you again. But please, please give me this chance."

Jane stood frozen in the open window, her lovely face reflecting internal struggle. Elizabeth watched the emotions play across features she knew better than her own, watched Jane's natural compassion war with proper caution about speaking privately with strange women who knew her name without introduction. Jane's teeth caught her lower lip, worrying at it in the unconscious gesture she always made when thinking hard about something difficult.

Her gaze dropped to Elizabeth's borrowed hands, still gripping the windowsill with desperate strength. Then moved to

Elizabeth's face, taking in the tears streaming down pale cheeks, the obvious exhaustion in the frail body, the genuine anguish in eyes that pleaded without words for understanding. Elizabeth saw the moment Jane's kind heart overruled her sensible caution, saw her sister's expression soften with the compassion that made her beloved by everyone fortunate enough to know her.

"Very well," Jane said quietly. "Give me a moment."

She withdrew from the window, disappearing into the house's interior. Elizabeth remained where she was, clinging to the windowsill because her borrowed legs threatened to collapse if she released her grip. Minutes passed, each one feeling eternal. What if Jane changed her mind? What if she told Charlotte about the strange woman in the garden? What if this chance slipped away before Elizabeth could seize it?

Jane emerged from the parsonage's side door wearing her bonnet, its pale blue ribbons tied neatly beneath her chin. Her expression remained wary despite her agreement to come outside, and she maintained a proper distance as she approached Elizabeth, her hands folded before her in a way that suggested both nervousness and determination.

"I can spare a few minutes," Jane said, her voice carrying gentle firmness. "But I must return soon. Charlotte will worry if I am gone long."

"Thank you," Elizabeth whispered, releasing the windowsill finally and stumbling slightly as her legs took her full weight. "Thank you. I know a place we can speak privately. It is not far."

She turned and began walking away from the parsonage, back toward Rosings' grounds but angling toward the grove she had discovered during her wandering. Her aching body protested each step, muscles trembling with exhaustion. Behind her, she heard Jane's light footsteps following at a careful distance.

"What is this about?" Jane asked, her tone still carrying that edge of caution. "And who are you? You must tell me that much at least."

"Soon," Elizabeth managed, focusing all her attention on placing one foot before the other without falling. "Just a few more minutes. We must be where no one can overhear."

The grove appeared ahead, its circle of oak and hornbeam trees offering the privacy Elizabeth desperately needed. She had found this spot weeks ago while exploring Rosings' vast grounds, had thought of it immediately as somewhere conversations might be held without fear of listeners. The trees grew close together here, their branches creating a canopy that filtered afternoon sunlight into dappled patterns. The earth beneath was soft with years of fallen leaves, muffling footsteps and creating an atmosphere of natural seclusion.

Elizabeth stumbled into the grove's shelter and immediately sank onto a fallen log, her legs finally refusing to support her weight any longer. She sat there gasping, Anne's damaged lungs working desperately to draw sufficient air. Sweat dampened her hairline and the back of her neck despite the moderate temperature, and her hands shook visibly where they gripped the rough bark.

Jane followed more slowly, her posture stiff with uncertainty as she surveyed their surroundings. She remained standing, maintaining distance between them, one hand resting on the trunk of a nearby oak as though ready to flee if circumstances required it. The filtered sunlight caught in her fair hair and illuminated her face, making her look almost ethereal in the grove's green shadows.

"Very well," Jane said. "We are alone now. What is this about, and who are you?"

Elizabeth looked up at her sister, at Jane's beloved face showing confusion and concern and that fundamental kindness that had never failed despite all the trials they had endured. Her throat tightened with emotion so intense it felt like physical pain. How could she possibly explain? How could she make Jane understand something that defied every law of nature and reason?

"What I'm about to tell you will sound completely mad," Elizabeth began, her voice emerging rough with strain and desperation. "But I need you to hear me out before you judge. Before you decide I am simply a lunatic who has escaped confinement. Will you do that? Will you listen to everything I have to say before making any decisions?"

Jane's expression flickered with something that might have been alarm, but she nodded slowly. "I will listen. Though I confess you are frightening me somewhat."

"Good," Elizabeth said, and the word emerged with bitter humour despite everything. "You should be frightened. Because what I am about to tell you is more frightening than you can possibly imagine."

She took a deep breath, Anne's weak lungs protesting the effort, and forced herself to meet Jane's eyes directly. This was the moment. The revelation that would either save her or condemn her to dismissal as a madwoman. Everything depended on Jane believing what came next, on her sister's ability to see truth despite the impossibility of it.

"Your sister Elizabeth is an impostor," Elizabeth said, and each word fell between them with the weight of accusation and confession combined.

Jane's hands flew to her mouth, her eyes going wide with shock. The colour drained from her face, leaving her almost as pale as Elizabeth's borrowed complexion. But beneath the shock, beneath the obvious horror at such a statement, Elizabeth saw something else. A flicker in Jane's expression. A glimmer of recognition or perhaps confirmation of something Jane had already suspected but not allowed herself to acknowledge.

That glimmer was belief. Fragile and uncertain, but there. Jane's gasp of shock held not dismissal but the beginnings of terrible understanding.

Chapter Nineteen

THE WORDS CAME IN a rush, tumbling over each other with desperate speed as Elizabeth tried to explain the impossible. She told Jane everything. Told her about waking in Anne de Bourgh's bed, trapped in a body that was not her own, weak and failing and utterly wrong. Told her about the confusion and terror of that first morning, looking down at hands that were too pale and thin, feeling lungs that could not draw proper breath.

Jane stood very still among the oak trees, one hand resting on rough bark, her face pale in the filtered sunlight. She said nothing, did not interrupt or protest, simply listened with that profound attention she gave to things that mattered. Her expression remained carefully neutral, though Elizabeth saw her throat work with swallowing, saw her fingers tighten against the tree trunk.

She described the horror of the past few days. Being confined to Anne's chamber by her own weakness most of the time, watched constantly by Mrs. Jenkinson, dosed with medicines that made her thoughts fuzzy and her borrowed body even weaker than it already was. The horror of realising that Anne had taken her healthy body and was living her life, walking and speaking and moving through the world as Elizabeth Bennet while the real Elizabeth was trapped in this failing form.

"Mr. Darcy," Jane whispered, and the name emerged with dawning horror. "The engagement this morning. That was not you."

"No," Elizabeth confirmed, and tears gathered in her eyes. "That was Anne. Anne wearing my face, speaking with my voice, accepting the proposal that should have been mine to refuse or accept. She has wanted Darcy for years, Jane. Has been planning this for longer than I can imagine. And now she has him."

The explanation of Darcy's love came harder, required Elizabeth to admit things she had barely acknowledged to herself. That Darcy had fallen in love with her. That his feelings were genuine and deep, expressed in ways that Elizabeth, in her own body, had been too prejudiced to recognise. That he had proposed this morning to a woman he believed was Elizabeth Bennet, never suspecting the impostor.

"She will marry him," Elizabeth said, and her voice dropped to barely above a whisper. "Will become Mrs. Darcy and mistress of Pemberley. Will have everything she wants."

Jane moved then, taking several steps closer. "And your body? Anne's body, I mean. This one." Her gaze travelled over Elizabeth's borrowed form with visible distress. "You do not look well, Lizzy."

Elizabeth looked down at the pale hands resting in her lap, at the pronounced veins and thin fingers. "Anne was dying, Jane. Is dying, in this body. Mrs. Jenkinson doses me with medicines to keep the worst symptoms at bay, but I can feel it. Feel the weakness spreading, the way breathing becomes harder each day. Months, perhaps. Weeks if I am unlucky."

The truth of that settled between them like a physical weight. Jane's hand rose to cover her mouth, her eyes bright with unshed tears.

"There is more," Elizabeth said, reaching beneath the shawl she wore. Her fingers closed around the leather binding of Anne's grimoire. She withdrew it carefully, holding it out toward Jane with trembling hands. "I found this hidden in Anne's chamber. She was taught by her father, Sir Lewis de Bourgh. He was a witch, or an alchemist. And he taught Anne everything he knew."

Jane took the grimoire with visible reluctance, her fingers touching the worn leather as though it might burn her. She opened it slowly, carefully, her eyes widening as she took in the cramped handwriting that filled the pages.

"Love potions," Jane whispered, her voice barely audible. She looked up at Elizabeth, her lovely face twisted with revulsion. "This is witchcraft. Dark magic."

"Yes," Elizabeth confirmed. "Anne learned from her father. He used one of those potions on Lady Catherine, I think. Made her devoted to Sir Lewis beyond reason or choice." She paused. "And Anne plans to use another on Darcy, once they are married. To ensure he can never question his choice, never suspect that his wife is not who he thinks."

Jane's hands shook visibly as she turned pages. Then Jane found it, her fingers stopping on a page near the book's end. Her face went utterly white as she read.

"A Draught for the Exchange of Forms," Jane read aloud, and her voice emerged hollow with horror. "This is how she did it. How she stole your body."

"Yes," Elizabeth said simply. "She needed my hair and hers, exotic ingredients, and the potion had to be drunk near-simultaneously. She must have prepared it carefully, and then she put it in my tea that day at the parsonage."

Jane continued reading, her expression growing more stricken with each line. When she finally looked up, tears streamed freely down her face. "Can it be reversed? Is there a way to undo what she has done?"

"I believe so," Elizabeth said, though uncertainty coloured the words. "The same potion that swapped us should swap us back, if I can obtain the ingredients and force Anne to drink it. But the components are impossibly rare and expensive. Ambergris from whales. Pearl powder. A shaving of bezoar. Things I have no means to acquire."

The silence that followed felt endless, broken only by birdsong and the whisper of wind through new leaves. Jane stood with the grimoire clutched to her chest. Elizabeth watched emotions play across Jane's features.

Then Jane moved. She crossed the remaining distance and sank onto the fallen log beside Elizabeth, setting the grimoire carefully aside before reaching out to pull Elizabeth into her arms. The embrace was gentle, mindful of Anne's fragility, but absolute in its conviction.

"I knew," Jane whispered against Elizabeth's shoulder, her voice breaking. "I knew she was not you. She looked like you and sounded like you, but she was not you. Something was wrong from the moment I saw her yesterday afternoon, I followed your instructions and did not say that I had come in response to the letter, and she never mentioned it, was instead most surprised to see me. The way she held herself, the things she said, the eagerness with which she accepted Mr. Darcy's company. None of it felt right."

Elizabeth's chest heaved with sobs, tears streaming down pale cheeks as relief crashed over her. Jane believed her. Her dearest Jane, who knew her better than anyone else in the world, had seen through Anne's impersonation even without understanding that such a deed could be possible.

"I tried to convince myself I was imagining things," Jane continued, her own voice thick with tears. "Tried to tell myself that travel or some temporary alteration in spirits had changed you. But my heart knew. Knew that my sister would never speak so dismissively of our mother, would never be so eager to marry without family present, would never look at me with such distance. As though we were strangers rather than sisters."

They clung to each other among the oak trees, two sisters reunited despite impossible circumstances, and Elizabeth felt something in her chest ease for the first time since waking in this nightmare. She was not alone anymore. Jane knew the truth. Jane believed her. And together, somehow, they would find a way to reverse what Anne had done.

They remained like that for several minutes, holding each other while tears dried on borrowed and familiar faces alike. But eventually Jane drew back, her hands remaining on Elizabeth's shoulders as she studied her sister's face with searching intensity. The horror had not left her expression, but beneath it now lay something harder. Determination.

"We must form a plan," Jane said, her soft voice full of conviction. "If this potion can reverse what has been done, then we must find a way to obtain the ingredients and force Anne to drink it."

Elizabeth nodded, relief flooding through her. She reached for the grimoire, her fingers trembling as she opened it to the page they needed.

"Here," Elizabeth said, pointing to the ingredients list. "These are what we need."

Jane leaned close, her head nearly touching Elizabeth's borrowed one as they studied the page together. Her finger traced the words slowly. "Ambergris braised in honey. Spirits of wine well-rectified. Pearl powder. Saffron. Grains of paradise. Lemon balm and lavender water." She paused, looking up at Elizabeth. "And freshly cut hair of both parties. A draught for each, the same day."

"Yes," Elizabeth confirmed. "The potion must be prepared fresh and drunk near-simultaneously by both parties to reverse the exchange. We must both consume it, or the spell will not work."

Jane's finger continued down the page, stopping at the final line. "A shaving of bezoar steadies." She looked at Elizabeth with confusion. "What is a bezoar?"

"A stone found in the stomachs of certain animals," Elizabeth replied, having looked it up in Rosings' library that morning.

"Goats, usually, from Persia or the East. They are exceedingly rare in England and worth more than their weight in gold, highly valued by curio collectors."

Jane's expression grew more troubled as the full magnitude of the task settled over her. She read through the ingredients again, and Elizabeth saw her sister's natural optimism struggling against practical assessment of the obstacles they faced.

"Where would one even begin to search for such things?" she asked.

"Anne found them somehow," Elizabeth said, though the words emerged with less conviction than she had intended. "She was an invalid with limited means, yet she managed to collect everything required. If she could do it, then surely we can as well."

Jane nodded slowly, her mind clearly working through possibilities. Her fingers drummed against the grimoire's leather binding in a rhythm Elizabeth recognised from childhood. Finally, her expression brightened.

"Uncle Gardiner," Jane said, certainty entering her voice. "He deals with merchants who import goods from all over the world. Spices from the East Indies. Rare ingredients for apothecaries and physicians. If anyone in our acquaintance might have access to such exotic substances, it would be him."

Elizabeth felt her heart leap with sudden hope. Of course. Mr. Gardiner's business connexions extended throughout London's merchant community and beyond. He dealt regularly with traders who brought goods from distant lands.

"He will help us," Jane continued. "I know he will. We need only explain what is needed without revealing too much of why. I can tell him it is for a special tonic, perhaps. Uncle Gardiner will not pry if I ask him to simply obtain the ingredients."

"But the cost," Elizabeth protested. "Jane, these substances are impossibly expensive. Saffron is worth more than its weight in gold, and I think ambergris may be too, not to mention the bezoar shaving! We cannot ask Uncle Gardiner to spend such sums without explanation."

Jane's expression grew thoughtful. Then her face cleared with sudden determination. "I have some money set aside," she said quietly. "The small inheritance from Grandmother Bennet that was divided among us all. I have been saving it for years. This is worthy, Lizzy. Getting you back into your own body, preventing Anne from trapping Mr. Darcy in a false marriage. I will use every penny if necessary."

Elizabeth's eyes filled with tears again. She reached out and gripped Jane's hand. "Thank you," she whispered. "I will repay you somehow. I swear it."

"You owe me nothing," Jane replied, returning the pressure. "You are my sister. My dearest sister. I would give everything I have to help you."

They sat in silence for a moment, hands clasped, before the practical necessities reasserted themselves.

"Anne will need to go to London soon," Elizabeth said, thinking aloud. "She announced this morning that she and Mr. Darcy would marry by special licence, that there was no reason to wait. She will have to stay at the Gardiners' house, I imagine, to be near her supposed family during the wedding preparations."

Jane nodded. "Then I must accompany her. Must pretend to be delighted for my sister's good fortune, must help her prepare, must act as though I suspect nothing wrong."

The thought of Jane being forced to play such a role made Elizabeth's chest ache. But Jane was right. They needed someone close to Anne, someone who could move freely without arousing suspicion.

"You will need to obtain a lock of her hair," Elizabeth said, forcing herself to speak the words. "Fresh hair, cut when you have the other ingredients and are ready to make the potion. Can you find some excuse to help with her hair? Perhaps offer to dress it for the wedding?"

Jane's face showed distaste for the deception, but she nodded with determination. "I will find a way. I can be convincing when necessary, Lizzy."

Elizabeth knew that. Knew that beneath Jane's gentle exterior lay a will as strong as her own. Jane would do what needed to be done.

"And you?" Jane asked. "What will you do? You cannot simply appear in London. Surely Lady Catherine would never allow Anne to attend the wedding, considering how displeased she must be that Mr. Darcy is not marrying her daughter."

This was the part of the plan that Elizabeth had been dreading. She took a slow breath, Anne's damaged lungs protesting, and forced herself to meet Jane's eyes. "I must convince Lady Catherine that family unity requires our presence. That Mr. Darcy's marriage is too important an occasion for his aunt and cousin to miss, regardless of Anne's health. It will not be easy, but I think I can manage it if I am careful."

Jane looked sceptical. "Lady Catherine is proud and stubborn. She will not want to attend a wedding she disapproves of so vehemently."

"No," Elizabeth agreed. "But she is also conscious of appearances and family duty. If I can convince her that absence would look like petty spite rather than justified disapproval, if I can appeal to her pride, then perhaps she will consent."

It was a fragile hope, dependent on Elizabeth's ability to manipulate Lady Catherine's character. But Elizabeth pushed aside her discomfort. This was survival. This was reclaiming what had been stolen.

Jane squeezed her hand again. Then her expression shifted, becoming more practical. "We will need to coordinate carefully. I must know when you arrive in London, must be ready with the ingredients and Anne's hair. We cannot afford mistakes once everything is in place."

"We will find a way to communicate," Elizabeth promised. "Colonel Fitzwilliam helped me once. I believe he will again, so look for him to bring you notes from me."

Jane nodded, then carefully lifted the grimoire. She held it with both hands. "I should take this with me. Study the recipe more carefully, ensure I understand exactly what ingredients are needed and how they must be prepared. And you cannot risk being found with it at Rosings."

Elizabeth's heart clenched at the thought of losing the grimoire, her only proof. But Jane was right. If Mrs. Jenkinson discovered the book missing, the consequences would be severe.

"Take it," Elizabeth said, releasing her grip. "Keep it safe, Jane. We will need it when the time comes."

Jane tucked the grimoire carefully inside her gown. Then she rose from the fallen log, her movements graceful. Elizabeth pushed herself upright as well, her legs trembling.

They stood facing each other in the dappled sunlight, two sisters separated by impossible magic but united in determination to reverse it. Jane reached out and pulled Elizabeth into another embrace, this one briefer but no less fierce.

"Be careful," Jane whispered against Elizabeth's shoulder. "Do not let them suspect anything. Do not take unnecessary risks. You must survive long enough for us to execute this plan."

"I will," Elizabeth promised, though the words felt hollow given the weakness spreading through her borrowed limbs. "And you be careful as well. Anne is dangerous, Jane. She has studied this dark magic for years, and she will not surrender her prize easily if she suspects we have discovered her deception."

Jane drew back, her lovely face showing understanding but no hesitation. "I will be the perfect, supportive sister. I will smile and congratulate and never let her see that I know she is not my Lizzy."

They parted after one final embrace, Jane heading back toward the parsonage while Elizabeth turned toward Rosings. Elizabeth watched her sister's retreating figure until Jane disappeared among the trees, then began the laborious journey back. Each step sent fresh waves of exhaustion through Anne's failing body, and Elizabeth had to stop regularly to catch her breath.

But beneath the physical weakness, beneath the fear and uncertainty about whether their desperate plan could possibly succeed, Elizabeth felt something she had not truly experienced since waking in this nightmare.

Hope.

Chapter Twenty

THE CARRIAGE WHEELS RATTLED over the rutted lane that led to Longbourn, each jolt sending a fresh wave of anxiety through Darcy's chest. His hand moved to his waistcoat pocket for perhaps the hundredth time that morning, confirming the presence of Elizabeth's letter to her father. He should have felt confident. Instead, his throat tightened with each turn of the wheels.

"Mr. Bennet, I have come to request the honour of your daughter's hand in marriage." No, too formal. "Sir, your daughter Elizabeth has done me the great honour of accepting my proposal." Better, perhaps. Though the whole business felt backwards, speaking to the father after the fact. But Elizabeth had insisted that she had already sent a note ahead informing her father, and that his visit was merely a formality.

The carriage lurched over a particularly deep rut, and Darcy's carefully constructed sentences dissolved. Through the window, Longbourn's modest house came into view, its brick façade warm in the afternoon sunlight. The grounds showed signs of careful but economical maintenance. A far cry from Pemberley's grandeur, yet Elizabeth had grown here, had formed her strong character in these modest surroundings.

The carriage rolled to a stop. Darcy descended with movements he hoped appeared confident, his boots striking gravel. The housekeeper appeared, took his card, and showed him into a small entrance hall that smelled faintly of beeswax and lavender.

"Mr. Darcy, sir," the housekeeper announced, returning. "Mr. Bennet will see you now."

Darcy stepped into a room that looked as though it had been assembled to confound any sense of order. Books overflowed from shelves onto tables, chairs, and even the floor. Papers covered the desk in layers. The air carried the musty scent of old leather and aging paper.

Mr. Bennet sat behind the desk, grey threading through dark hair and spectacles perched on his nose. He looked up from the book he had been reading, marking his place before setting it aside. His expression suggested curiosity rather than eagerness.

"Mr. Darcy," Mr. Bennet said, his tone carrying dry amusement. "This is an unexpected pleasure. Though I confess, had my daughter not written ahead to advise me of your intentions, I would describe it as the biggest shock of my life."

Darcy felt heat rise in his face. He executed a bow that came out stiffer than intended. "Mr. Bennet. Thank you for receiving me."

"Well, I could hardly refuse, could I?" Mr. Bennet gestured to a chair. "Please, sit. Move those volumes anywhere you like."

Darcy transferred the books to a nearby table and lowered himself into the chair. He withdrew Elizabeth's letter from his pocket and held it out toward Mr. Bennet with a hand that trembled only slightly.

"Sir, I have come to formally request permission to marry your daughter, Miss Elizabeth Bennet. She has done me the very great honour of accepting my proposal, and has written this letter to you explaining her reasons."

Mr. Bennet took the letter with eyebrows already rising. He unfolded it slowly, adjusted his spectacles, and began to read. Darcy watched his face cycle through expressions that ranged from surprise to bewilderment to something that might have been alarm. Mr. Bennet adjusted his spectacles twice more, looked up at Darcy, then returned his attention to the letter.

"This is most unexpected," Mr. Bennet said finally. "I was under the impression that my Lizzy held you in some dislike. She spent the better part of the autumn declaring you the most disagreeable man of her acquaintance."

The words struck Darcy like a physical blow, confirming what he had half feared. Elizabeth had disliked him. Yet she had accepted his proposal with eager enthusiasm, without hesitation. The dissonance created an ache in Darcy's chest.

"People's opinions can change," Darcy said, the words emerging more stiffly than he intended. "I hope that I have demonstrated qualities since our initial acquaintance that altered Miss Elizabeth's initial impression."

"Indeed," Mr. Bennet replied, his tone suggesting doubt. He set the letter on his desk and leaned back in his chair, steepling his fingers beneath his chin. His eyes, sharp behind the spectacles, studied Darcy with uncomfortable intensity. "Tell me, Mr. Darcy. What are your intentions toward my daughter? And please, spare me the platitudes. I wish to know what you actually intend."

Darcy shifted in his chair. "I intend to make her my wife. To provide her with every comfort Pemberley can offer. To honour her as mistress of my estate and mother of my future children."

"That tells me what you will give her," Mr. Bennet said. "It does not tell me how you will treat her. Will you allow her to read what she chooses? To speak her mind freely? To walk three miles through mud if the fancy takes her, or will you insist she maintain dignity appropriate to your station?"

The questions revealed depths to Mr. Bennet's character that Darcy had not anticipated. He had expected perfunctory inquiry about settlements. Instead, Elizabeth's father probed at the heart of what marriage would mean. Darcy found himself grudgingly respecting the man.

"I would never attempt to cage her spirit," Darcy said, and meant it with fierce conviction. "Her independence, her willingness to speak her mind, her refusal to be impressed by rank are among the qualities I most admire in Elizabeth. I have no desire to change her, only to spend my life with her as she is."

Mr. Bennet's expression softened slightly, though wariness remained. "Pretty words, Mr. Darcy. I hope you mean them. My Lizzy is the cleverest of my daughters, the one most like myself in temperament. I would hate to see that cleverness dulled by a husband who valued compliance over character."

"You will not," Darcy promised, though even as he spoke, doubts whispered in the back of his mind.

Silence settled between them, broken only by the ticking of a clock and the distant sounds of the household. Mr. Bennet adjusted his spectacles one final time, then nodded with visible reluctance.

"Very well," he said. "You have my consent, though I confess myself entirely bewildered by this match. I look forward to having a few words with my daughter about her sudden change of heart. And as for this hasty wedding in London – well, my Fanny is quite upset about the matter, but if it is what Elizabeth wants, it is what she shall have."

Darcy rose from his chair, executing a bow. "Thank you, sir. I will endeavour to prove myself worthy of your trust."

"See that you do," Mr. Bennet replied. "And Mr. Darcy? If you make my Lizzy unhappy, you will discover that country gentlemen with modest fortunes can be remarkably creative when properly motivated to revenge."

The threat was delivered with such dry humour that it took Darcy a moment to recognise it as genuine. He inclined his head in acknowledgement, then turned toward the door.

He had barely stepped into the hallway when a figure materialised before him with alarming suddenness. Mrs. Bennet stood blocking his path, her face flushed with excitement and her hands clasped before her ample bosom. She must have been waiting just outside the study door for the interview to end.

"Mr. Darcy!" she exclaimed, her voice rising to a pitch that made Darcy wince. "Oh, Mr. Darcy! What happy news! My Lizzy engaged to a man with ten thousand a year! I knew from the moment I met you that you were destined for one of my girls. Such a fine figure of a man!"

"Mrs. Bennet," Darcy managed, attempting to edge around her. "You are very kind."

"Kind!" Mrs. Bennet laughed with enough volume to rattle the pictures on the hallway walls. "I am practical, sir. Ten thousand a year and Pemberley in Derbyshire! My Lizzy will have such gowns, such jewels! And the wedding! We shall be off to London tomorrow!"

"I have look forward to seeing you there," Darcy said, desperation creeping into his voice. He took another step toward the front door, but Mrs. Bennet moved with surprising agility to block his retreat.

"And carriages! You must promise me that Lizzy will have a carriage of her own."

"I assure you, madam, Mrs. Darcy will want for nothing," Darcy said, finally managing to sidestep her and reach the front door. The maid appeared with his hat and gloves, and he seized them gratefully.

"Mrs. Darcy, oh, how well that sounds! You must dine with us!" Mrs. Bennet called after him as he stepped through the door. "In London, before the wedding, at my brother Gardiner's house!"

"I will send word," Darcy replied, executing a hasty bow before descending the steps to his waiting carriage with what dignity he could maintain while essentially fleeing. He heard Mrs. Bennet's continuing exclamations even as the carriage door closed.

The carriage lurched into motion. Darcy collapsed against the cushions and pressed one hand to his forehead, feeling the beginnings of a headache. He had secured Mr. Bennet's permission. Had satisfied the formal requirements. But instead of relief or happiness, he felt only increasing unease.

Mrs. Bennet's voice still echoed in his ears, pronouncing his income with reverence. *Ten thousand a year*. She had said it at least a half-dozen times. Through the window, hedgerows gave way to the first cottages marking Meryton's outskirts.

The high street appeared ahead, modest shops lining both sides. A few pedestrians moved between establishments. The carriage slowed to navigate around a farm wagon, and Darcy's attention drifted across the familiar scene.

Then he saw Wickham.

The man stood outside a milliner's shop, his red coat bright in the afternoon sun, leaning close to a young woman whose dark curls escaped from beneath a chip-straw bonnet. Wickham said something that made the girl laugh, her hand rising to cover her mouth. He tipped his hat with a flourish that managed to be both respectful and somehow suggestive.

Darcy's jaw tightened as old fury stirred. Wickham had not changed. Still played the charming officer, still preyed on young women. The girl looked barely older than Georgiana, her dress marking her as respectable but not wealthy. Exactly the sort Wickham preferred.

The carriage rolled past, and Darcy twisted in his seat to keep Wickham in view. The man laughed at something the girl said, his head thrown back.

And then Darcy recognised the girl.

It was Elizabeth's youngest sister, Lydia Bennet.

Realisation struck Darcy with the force of a blow.

Once he married Elizabeth, he would also be bringing her sisters into his sphere of responsibility. The younger Bennets, Lydia and Catherine, were precisely the sort of silly, flirtatious girls Wickham excelled at manipulating. And Meryton was their home, where they walked without proper supervision. Where Wickham could work his poison. Wickham would not hesitate once the news of Darcy and Elizabeth's engagement became public, and considering that Mrs. Bennet was likely even now hastening to tell her friends, time was of the essence.

The thought of Wickham compromising one of Elizabeth's sisters, of the scandal and pain such an event would cause, made cold rage settle in Darcy's stomach. He could not allow it. Could not stand by and watch Wickham destroy another family. Not when he had the power to prevent it.

Darcy rapped sharply on the carriage roof with his walking stick. The vehicle slowed immediately, and his driver's face appeared in the small opening.

"Sir?"

"Take me to the militia's headquarters," Darcy commanded, his voice emerging harder than he had intended. "I have business with Colonel Forster that cannot wait."

The driver nodded. The carriage turned down a side street, heading toward the building that housed the regiment's local command. Darcy sat back and forced his breathing to slow, to calm the fury that threatened to cloud his judgement. He needed to approach this carefully, to present facts rather than personal grievances.

Darcy descended from the carriage and strode into the command building with purpose, his boots striking the wooden floor with sharp reports.

"I am here to see Colonel Forster," Darcy said, presenting his card to a clerk sitting at a desk. "It is a matter of some urgency regarding one of his officers."

The clerk's eyes widened slightly as he read the name on the card. "Of course, Mr. Darcy. Please wait here. I will inform the Colonel immediately."

Minutes passed while Darcy stood in the modest reception area, his mind turning over the words he would use. He must be careful. Must present his concerns in a way that would prompt investigation without revealing the personal history that made his accusations suspect.

The clerk reappeared and gestured toward a hallway. "Colonel Forster will see you now, sir."

Forster's office reflected military efficiency, everything arranged with precise order. Maps covered one wall. A desk held neat stacks of correspondence. Forster himself stood as Darcy entered, a solid man in his forties with greying hair.

"Mr. Darcy," Forster said, extending his hand. "This is an unexpected pleasure. Please, sit. May I offer you refreshment?"

"Thank you, no," Darcy replied, taking the offered chair but sitting forward with tension evident. "Colonel Forster, I have come to speak with you about Lieutenant George Wickham."

Forster's expression shifted immediately, welcome giving way to wariness. He lowered himself back into his chair with careful movements. "I see. May I ask what prompts this visit?"

"I recently became engaged to Miss Elizabeth Bennet of Longbourn," Darcy said. "This connexion has made me acutely aware that Lieutenant Wickham will have access to my future wife's younger sisters, girls who lack the experience to recognise a practiced seducer."

Forster's jaw tightened slightly, but he said nothing, clearly waiting.

"I have known Wickham since childhood, as he is the son of my late father's steward. His character is not what it appears.

He presents himself as an honourable gentleman, but his true nature is that of a man who cannot live within his means, a fortune hunter who preys on young women with expectations."

Forster's expression had gone hard. "That is a serious accusation, Mr. Darcy."

"It is a statement of fact," Darcy replied, meeting the Colonel's gaze steadily. "I do not bring you tales of ancient history. I speak to you now because I observed Wickham not twenty minutes ago in the high street, paying marked attention to Miss Lydia Bennet outside a milliner's shop. His behaviour suggested familiarity that concerned me. The girl is but fifteen."

"Wickham is popular with the local ladies," Forster said slowly. "That alone is not grounds for discipline."

"No," Darcy agreed. "But I would suggest you make inquiries among the local shopkeepers about whether Lieutenant Wickham has been accruing debts. Ask specifically about promises made and not kept, about bills left unpaid. I believe you will find a pattern of behaviour that reflects poorly on the regiment. And if you ask the shopkeepers about their daughters, I suspect you will find he has engaged in other behaviour unbecoming of an officer."

Forster's fingers drummed against the desk in a rhythm that suggested suppressed anger. "You are asking me to investigate one of my officers based on childhood acquaintance and current suspicions."

"I am asking you to protect the reputation of your regiment," Darcy said, his voice dropping lower with intensity. "And to prevent potential scandal. But I understand your hesitation to act on my word alone."

He paused, then added with careful emphasis, "I would be happy to provide references regarding Wickham's character from those who know him well. My cousin, Colonel Fitzwilliam, and my uncle, the Earl of Matlock, are both particularly well acquainted with Wickham's history."

Forster studied Darcy's face for a long moment. Finally, he nodded slowly and stood, moving to a cabinet behind his desk. He produced a key and opened the cabinet, withdrawing a slim folder that he placed on the desk.

"These are Wickham's letters of recommendation," Forster said, opening the folder. "They were most impressive when he applied for his commission."

Darcy reached for the papers. He scanned the first letter quickly, recognising immediately the exaggerated praise that marked false testimony, bought and paid for most likely. The second letter made his blood freeze.

The signature at the bottom purported to be that of his uncle, the Earl of Matlock. Darcy's finger traced the flourish beneath the name, his jaw tightening with cold fury as he recognised the forgery. The hand was similar to Lord Matlock's, close enough to fool someone unfamiliar with the Earl's true writing, but the pressure of the pen was wrong. The loops too elaborate.

"This is forged," Darcy stated, his voice emerging flat with absolute certainty. He looked up to meet Forster's gaze directly. "My uncle, the Earl of Matlock, is well aware of George Wickham's character. He would rather shoot the man than write such a letter. I can provide you with his direction in London so that you may write to him directly to confirm this."

Forster took the letter from Darcy's hand, his face darkening as he studied the signature with new attention.

"Forgery of references is a court-martial offence," Forster said, each word clipped with barely contained anger. "If this is false, if

Wickham obtained his commission through fraudulent means, he will face military justice."

"I wish I could say I am surprised," Darcy said, "but everything I know of Wickham's character makes this nothing more than I would expect, Colonel. I am sorry to be the bearer of bad news."

Forster nodded, his jaw set in a hard line. "I will investigate these matters personally and thoroughly. If what you say proves true, Lieutenant Wickham will find himself drummed out of the service and answering to his creditors without the protection of his uniform. Debtor's prison will be his fate, most likely."

Relief flooded through Darcy's chest. He rose from his chair and extended his hand to Forster, who took it with a grip that conveyed both respect and shared determination.

"Thank you, Colonel. I know this is not a pleasant duty you face."

"No duty involving dishonour ever is," Forster replied grimly. "But it is necessary. I will not have my regiment's reputation tarnished by a scoundrel, regardless of how charming he may appear."

"I would ask that you waste no time," Darcy said delicately. "I have just come from Longbourn, and I believe Mrs. Bennet will be eager to share some news she has just received. I hope you will congratulate me on becoming engaged to Miss Elizabeth Bennet."

Forster's eyebrows flew up, and he offered his hand for Darcy to shake. "Indeed, sir, my congratulations; Miss Elizabeth is a fine young woman. And your, ah, future mother-by-law is a redoubtable lady."

"She is, and once the news is generally known, the younger Bennet sisters become very tempting targets to Mr. Wickham," Darcy pointed out.

"I take your point, Mr. Darcy," Forster nodded, understanding dawning. "I will have Wickham confined to quarters while I investigate, and if what you say is true, which I already suspect it to be as I have no reason to doubt your word, he will have no opportunity to impose himself on those young ladies. You may rest assured that they will be safe under my watch."

Darcy left the command post with his shoulders straighter than they had been since arriving in Hertfordshire. The afternoon sun slanted lower now, casting long shadows across the high street where Wickham had been standing. Darcy felt grim satisfaction at the knowledge that Wickham's time in Meryton was drawing to a close.

He climbed back into his carriage and settled against the cushions with the first genuine ease he had felt all day. Whatever strange circumstances surrounded his engagement to Elizabeth, whatever doubts plagued him about her sudden acceptance, at least he had accomplished something good this afternoon. Wickham would face justice. The Bennet sisters would be protected from his predations. And Elizabeth would not have to worry about scandal touching her family through that particular source.

It was not much, Darcy thought as the carriage rolled toward London. But it was something. One threat addressed, one danger neutralised. The rest of the complications surrounding his engagement would have to wait for another day's solving.

Chapter Twenty-One

The lamps had been lit against the gathering dusk by the time Darcy's carriage rolled to a stop on Grosvenor Square. He descended stiffly, muscles protesting the long day spent mostly in the carriage. Light glowed behind the drawing room windows of his townhouse, warm and welcoming. The front door opened before he reached it, his butler materialising with quiet efficiency.

"Good evening, sir," the butler said, taking Darcy's hat and gloves. "We did not expect you until tomorrow. Shall I have your chambers prepared?"

"Thank you, Henderson. I came earlier than planned." Darcy stripped off his coat and handed it over. "Where is Miss Darcy?"

"In the music room, sir. She has been practicing this past hour."

Darcy nodded and moved toward the back of the house. The music reached him before he opened the door, familiar notes from a Mozart sonata. She played well, with technical precision. But there was something tentative in her playing, as though she feared making mistakes more than she enjoyed the music.

The music room occupied the ground floor's southern corner. Evening shadows had claimed most of the space, but candles burned on the pianoforte and in sconces along the walls. Georgiana sat at the instrument with perfect posture, her fair hair caught up in a simple knot. She wore a pale blue dress that made her look younger than her sixteen years.

She looked up as the door opened, and her face transformed, careful concentration giving way to unguarded joy. "Brother! I did not expect you until tomorrow evening at the earliest."

Darcy crossed to her and took both her hands in his, squeezing gently. "I finished my business in Hertfordshire sooner than anticipated. I hope I am not interrupting your practice."

"Never," Georgiana said, and her smile held such warmth that Darcy felt some of the day's tension ease from his chest. "I am always happy to see you. But you look tired. Shall I ring for tea? Though dinner will be in an hour, perhaps you would prefer to wait..."

"No, I am quite thirsty. Ring for tea, please."

Georgiana moved to the bell pull while Darcy settled into one of the chairs arranged near the fire. He watched Georgiana return to sit opposite him after speaking with the maid, her movements carrying that same tentative quality he heard in her music. As though she worried about taking up too much space, about asserting her presence too boldly.

The maid returned with remarkable speed, bringing tea and biscuits. Georgiana poured with careful attention, preparing Darcy's cup exactly as he preferred it.

"You said you had business in Hertfordshire," Georgiana said, her voice carrying gentle curiosity. "Was it pleasant?"

"I went to call on Mr. Bennet at Longbourn." Darcy took a sip of tea, grateful for the warmth. "The father of Miss Elizabeth Bennet."

Georgiana's eyebrows rose slightly. "The lady you have spoken of?"

"Yes." Darcy set down his cup with care. The words came simply. "Georgiana, I have asked Miss Elizabeth Bennet to marry me, and she has accepted. We are engaged."

The teacup trembled in Georgiana's hands, rattling softly against the saucer. Tea sloshed dangerously close to the rim before she managed to steady her grip. Her face had gone pink, and she fairly beamed with pleasure.

"Oh!" The exclamation emerged breathless with delight. "Oh, Fitzwilliam, I am so happy for you. So very happy."

"I should have written," Darcy said, though relief flooded through him at her obvious pleasure. "But I wanted to tell you in person. You are the most important person in my life, Georgiana. I needed to see your face when I told you."

Georgiana set down her teacup with trembling hands and rose from her chair. She crossed to where Darcy sat and threw her arms around his neck. Darcy returned it, feeling his sister's slender frame shake slightly as she clung to him.

"I am so glad," Georgiana whispered against his shoulder. "So very glad. You have seemed troubled these past months. But if you love Miss Elizabeth, if she makes you happy, then I am the happiest sister in the world."

She drew back and returned to her seat, her cheeks still flushed. But as she settled once more with her tea, something in her expression shifted. The joy remained, but uncertainty crept in around its edges.

"Will she like me, do you think?" Georgiana asked, her voice going soft with hesitation. "I know I am not as accomplished as other ladies. My conversation is poor, and I am too shy in company. What if she finds me dull?"

The question struck Darcy with unexpected force. He heard in it all of Georgiana's accumulated insecurities, all the damage that Ramsgate had done.

"Elizabeth will adore you," Darcy said, and meant it with fierce conviction. "She is kind and warm, with none of the false civility that marks fashionable society. She values genuine feeling over empty accomplishment. She will see in you all the qualities I see; your gentle nature, your talents for music and art, your capacity for deep affection. She loves the sisters she already has fiercely and deeply. I am certain she will take you to her heart as well."

Georgiana's expression brightened again, though traces of uncertainty remained. "Tell me about her. Tell me everything. What does she look like? What are her interests?"

Darcy found himself describing Elizabeth as he remembered her from their early acquaintance. Her fine eyes and the way they sparkled with intelligence. Her love of long walks. The way she sang and played the pianoforte with more spirit than polish. Her devotion to her sister Jane, demonstrated through that muddy walk to Netherfield.

"She is independent," Darcy said, warming to his subject despite everything. "She speaks her mind freely, even when it would be more prudent to remain silent. She challenged me constantly, refused to be impressed by any of the things that usually command respect. She treated me simply as a man, not as a figure to be awed."

Georgiana leaned forward, her tea forgotten. "She sounds wonderful. When will I meet her?"

"Soon," Darcy promised. "We are to be married by special licence here in London. She will be staying with her aunt and uncle Gardiner in Gracechurch Street while preparations are made. Perhaps we might call on her there."

"A wedding in London," Georgiana said, her smile returning full force. "Oh, I can help with preparations. And Aunt Matlock will guide us, I am certain."

They talked on, Georgiana asking questions and Darcy answering as best he could. What would Elizabeth wear? Would there be a wedding breakfast? Who would attend? Darcy found himself describing plans that Elizabeth had announced rather than discussed.

At one point, Georgiana asked if Elizabeth's family would all attend, and Darcy had to explain that Mrs. Bennet's enthusiasm had been rather overwhelming, that Mr. Bennet seemed bewildered, that the younger sisters would likely create chaos. Georgiana laughed at his descriptions, clearly delighted by the thought of a large, noisy family.

"It will be good for you," Georgiana said with unexpected perception. "You have been too isolated, brother. Too accustomed to having your own way in everything. A wife who speaks her mind and a family who does not stand on ceremony will shake you out of your habits."

The observation was accurate enough to make Darcy smile despite the discomfort. "You may be right. Though I confess I am not certain I am prepared for quite so much shaking."

"You will manage," Georgiana assured him, her confidence absolute. "You always do."

As they moved into the dining room, Darcy found himself describing the Elizabeth he had fallen in love with rather than the woman who had accepted his proposal. The Elizabeth who had refused to dance with him at the Meryton assembly, who had nursed her sister with devoted attention, who had challenged his assumptions about class and consequence. That Elizabeth felt real in a way the eager, compliant woman in Kent did not quite manage.

But he did not share these doubts with Georgiana. Did not speak of Anne's warning or his own growing unease. His sister was too happy, too delighted at the prospect of gaining Elizabeth as a sister. Darcy would not shadow that joy with uncertainties he could not properly articulate.

Finally, Georgiana rose and kissed his cheek. "I am so happy for you, brother. So very happy. And I cannot wait to meet my new sister."

She left him sitting alone in the dining room, and Darcy remained there long after her footsteps faded. The room had gone dark except for the last flickering flames, and in that darkness, his doubts seemed larger. He had committed himself to this marriage, had secured Mr. Bennet's permission and told his sister the happy news. There was no honourable way to withdraw now.

And he did not want to withdraw, Darcy told himself firmly. He loved Elizabeth. Loved the woman she had been, at least. Perhaps the change in her manner was simply the natural result of accepting his suit. Perhaps all his doubts were nothing more than his own difficulty with change.

The fire collapsed into ash with a soft sound, and Darcy rose with a sigh. He must still visit the Matlocks and arrange for the special licence. Would set in motion the machinery that would make Elizabeth Bennet his wife. And somewhere in that process, surely, his certainty would return.

Surely.

Matlock House occupied a prominent position on one of Mayfair's most fashionable streets, its Portland stone façade gleaming pale in the lamplight. Darcy's carriage stopped before the entrance at half past nine. The butler showed no surprise at his arrival, merely took his hat and gloves and led him up the marble stairs to the first floor drawing room.

The room embodied elegant restraint, decorated in shades of cream and gold. His aunt sat near the fire with her embroidery, while his uncle occupied his favourite chair with a book and a glass of port. They both looked up as Darcy entered, their expressions shifting from mild surprise to welcome.

"Darcy," Lord Matlock said, setting aside his book and rising. He was a man in his late fifties, his hair more grey than dark now. "This is unexpected. We thought you still in Kent."

"I returned to London this evening," Darcy replied, accepting his uncle's handshake. He moved to kiss his aunt's cheek, noting the way her sharp eyes studied his face with concern.

"Sit," Lady Matlock said, gesturing to a nearby chair. "You look tired, dear boy. Shall I ring for refreshment?"

"Thank you, no. I have just come from my own house." Darcy settled into the offered chair. There was no point in delaying. "I have come to share some news. I have become engaged to be married."

The silence that followed lasted perhaps three seconds but felt considerably longer. Lord Matlock's eyebrows rose toward his hairline, while Lady Matlock's embroidery slipped from her fingers. They stared at him with identical expressions of shock.

"Engaged," Lord Matlock repeated. "To whom?"

"Miss Elizabeth Bennet, of Longbourn in Hertfordshire," Darcy said, keeping his voice level. "She is the second daughter of Mr. Bennet, a gentleman with a small estate. I met her last autumn at Netherfield, and again more recently in Kent."

Lady Matlock recovered first, her surprise giving way to cautious pleasure. "The young lady you mentioned to us at Christmas? The one you described with such particular attention?"

"Yes," Darcy admitted with a wince. He and Georgiana had spent Christmas Day with the Matlocks, and Darcy had imbibed perhaps a little more than he should of his uncle's excellent port. He did not recall everything about the conversation, but clearly he had let slip more than he would have wished to about Elizabeth Bennet and the way she had captured his interest.

"Well," Lady Matlock said, and a smile began to form. "This is wonderful news, Darcy. Quite unexpected, but wonderful nonetheless. When did this occur?"

"I proposed two days ago in Kent, and she accepted. Today, I called on her father to request his permission, which he granted."

Lord Matlock had been watching with an expression that suggested he was fitting pieces together. "This is rather sudden, is it not? You made no mention of an attachment when we last spoke."

"My feelings changed," Darcy said, aware of how inadequate the explanation sounded. "I came to admire Miss Elizabeth's character and intelligence."

"I am certain she must be remarkable to have captured your attention," Lady Matlock said warmly. "But your uncle raises a fair point, dear. This does seem rather precipitate. You have known the young lady for what, six months? And much of that time apart."

"I know her well enough to be certain of my choice," Darcy insisted, though even as he spoke, doubt whispered in the back of his mind.

Lord Matlock exchanged a glance with his wife, some wordless communication passing between them. When he turned back to Darcy, his expression had softened. "We do not question your judgement, nephew. You are a sensible man, not given to rash decisions. But you must understand our surprise. And our concern for your happiness."

"I appreciate that concern," Darcy said. "But I assure you, I have given this matter considerable thought. Miss Elizabeth Bennet is the woman I wish to marry, and I would be grateful for your support in arranging the necessary details."

Lady Matlock leaned forward, her embroidery forgotten. "Of course we will support you. All I want is your happiness. If Miss Elizabeth makes you happy, then we welcome her to our family with open arms." She paused, then added with gentle concern, "Though I confess I am curious about the circumstances. How did she come to accept you so quickly? At Christmas, you seemed to think she had no particularly high opinion of you."

The question struck closer to Darcy's own doubts than he cared to admit. He forced his expression to remain neutral. "I believe she came to see qualities in me that she had not initially recognised. Our acquaintance deepened during her time in Kent."

"I see," Lady Matlock said, though her tone suggested she saw more than Darcy had intended. "And when is the wedding to take place?"

"Actually, we plan to marry by special licence," Darcy said. "As soon as arrangements can be made. A week, perhaps two at most."

This announcement produced another moment of stunned silence. Lord Matlock's fingers tightened on his port glass, while Lady Matlock's expression cycled through surprise, concern, and something that might have been alarm.

"A special licence," Lord Matlock said slowly. "That is quite irregular, Darcy. Why such haste? Surely having the banns called would be more appropriate."

"That is not what Elizabeth wants," Darcy said, hearing the defensive note in his voice. "She expressed a strong preference for a private ceremony in London by special licence. I see no reason to delay. I would appreciate your assistance in obtaining the licence, Uncle, as I know it requires influence."

Lord Matlock studied his nephew's face for a long moment. Finally, he sighed and nodded. "Very well. If this is truly what you want, I will arrange it. The Archbishop owes me several favours, and I can have the licence secured within a few days."

Relief flooded through Darcy. "Thank you, uncle. I am grateful."

"Come," Lord Matlock said, rising with decisive movement. "Let us go to my library and discuss the practical details. There are settlements to arrange, announcements to be written."

Darcy followed his uncle from the drawing room. They moved down a corridor hung with family portraits. The library occupied the back corner of the first floor, a masculine retreat of dark wood and leather furnishings.

The room stretched perhaps thirty feet in length, its walls lined floor to ceiling with shelves. Heavy velvet curtains on the windows blocked any view of the street beyond. Lord Matlock's desk dominated one end of the space.

But it was the glass-fronted cabinet between two windows that caught Darcy's idle attention as his uncle moved to light additional candles. The cabinet contained an eclectic collection of curiosities. A narwhal tusk hung along the back wall. Below it rested shells of remarkable size. Minerals glittered on the lower shelves, and what appeared to be a preserved exotic bird occupied pride of place.

"My cabinet of curiosities," Lord Matlock said, noticing Darcy's gaze. "Most of it collected by my father during his time in the diplomatic service. That narwhal tusk alone cost him a small fortune." He moved closer to the cabinet, gesturing toward the lower shelf. "That dark stone there is a bezoar from the East. Supposedly found in the stomach of a Persian goat. Cost nearly as much as the tusk. It is claimed to have significant medicinal properties."

Darcy glanced at the object his uncle indicated, a dark brownish stone about the size of a large walnut with a slightly iridescent sheen. He made some appropriate noise of interest, but his attention was already drifting back to his impending marriage.

Lord Matlock moved to his desk and withdrew a sheet of paper, dipping his pen in ink. "Now then. Let us discuss the settlements. What have you determined to settle on Miss Elizabeth? And what is her own fortune?"

"She has no fortune to speak of," Darcy admitted. "A thousand pounds as her portion from her mother's settlement, on her mother's passing. Her father's estate is entailed away."

His uncle's pen stilled above the page. "I see. That is rather modest. But if you are certain of your choice, then the financial considerations are secondary to your happiness."

They spent the next hour discussing settlements and jointures, the practical matters of marriage that turned romance into legal agreement. Lord Matlock suggested figures and Darcy agreed to them, numbers that would secure Elizabeth's future. His uncle also offered the use of Matlock House for the wedding breakfast, suggesting that Darcy's own townhouse might be too small.

"Though if you insist on this hasty ceremony, the guest list will necessarily be limited, family for the most part," Lord Matlock observed, his tone making clear he was still not entirely approving. "You will want to inform your aunt Catherine, I suppose, though I imagine she will not take the news well."

"She already knows," Darcy said grimly. "I informed her yesterday morning in Kent. Her reaction was precisely what you might expect."

Lord Matlock's expression suggested he could well imagine. "Then you had best prepare yourself for continued displeasure from that quarter."

Finally, with all the practical arrangements discussed, Darcy rose to take his leave. His uncle walked him to the door, his hand resting briefly on Darcy's shoulder.

"I hope you know what you are doing, nephew," Lord Matlock said quietly. "Marriage is not something to be entered into lightly or in haste. But you are a sensible man, and I trust your judgement even when I do not understand your reasoning."

"Thank you, uncle," Darcy replied, though the words felt hollow. *Did* he know what he was doing?

He descended the stairs and stepped out into the cool night air. As the vehicle rolled away from Matlock House, Darcy found himself more uncertain than he had been before the visit. He had secured the practical assistance he needed, had set in motion the machinery that would make Elizabeth his wife. But the Matlocks' concerns echoed his own too closely for comfort.

He was committed now, he thought as he watched the streets roll by. He could not possibly back out, even if he wanted to. His honour would not allow it.

Elizabeth Bennet would become Mrs. Darcy.

Within a matter of days.

Chapter Twenty-Two

Elizabeth stood outside the drawing room door, one hand resting against the frame for support while her borrowed lungs worked to steady their rhythm. Through the heavy wood, she could hear Lady Catherine's voice, sharp with continued displeasure about the engagement and the note that had arrived advising that the wedding would take place in just a few days. The confrontation she was about to initiate would require every scrap of cunning Elizabeth possessed.

She pushed open the door with careful pressure. Lady Catherine sat in her usual chair, rigid with fury. Mrs. Jenkinson occupied her position near the fire. Both women looked up as Elizabeth entered, Lady Catherine's expression dark while Mrs. Jenkinson's eyes narrowed, the companion obviously wondering why Elizabeth would voluntarily enter such a fraught atmosphere.

"Mama," Elizabeth said, forcing Anne's voice to remain soft and deferential. "I wonder if I might speak with you about the wedding."

Lady Catherine's face flushed an alarming shade of magenta. "I have nothing to say about that travesty. Darcy has made his choice, and he will have to live with the consequences. The connexion is a disgrace to the family name."

Elizabeth moved carefully into the room, settling onto the edge of a chair. "I understand your displeasure, Mama. But I think you may not have fully considered how absence from the ceremony will appear to society."

The statement hung in the air. Lady Catherine's eyes narrowed with dangerous attention, but Elizabeth had seen clearly that Lady Catherine did pay attention to her daughter, did love her and wanted her happiness. "Explain yourself," the grande dame demanded.

"If you do not attend Darcy's wedding, people will talk," Elizabeth said, choosing each word with precision. "They will say that Lady Catherine de Bourgh allowed personal pique to overcome family duty. That she valued her wounded pride above maintaining proper appearances. That she permitted a rift to develop between Rosings and Pemberley over something as trivial as disapproval of a bride."

Lady Catherine's hand tightened on the arm of her chair with enough force that Elizabeth heard the wood creak. "There is nothing trivial about Darcy marrying so far beneath himself. That Bennet girl has no fortune, no connexions of any value, a family whose behaviour borders on vulgar."

"Perhaps," Elizabeth agreed, maintaining Anne's meek tone despite the fury that wanted to break through. "But Darcy has made his choice, and society will judge not his selection of bride but your reaction to it. If you attend the wedding with appropriate dignity, you demonstrate that the de Bourgh family is above petty spite. That you value family unity over personal preferences."

Lady Catherine said nothing, but something in her expression shifted. Elizabeth pressed her advantage.

"If you remain at Rosings, refusing to acknowledge the marriage, you give ammunition to those who already whisper that you are overly proud," Elizabeth continued. "But if you attend with grace, you control the narrative. You show society that you are magnanimous, that you put family loyalty above everything else. You demonstrate strength rather than weakness."

The silence stretched long enough that Elizabeth wondered if she had miscalculated. Lady Catherine sat rigid, her face cycling through emotions. Finally, she drew a sharp breath.

"Very well. I shall attend this wedding. But mark my words, Anne, I do so only to maintain proper appearances and prevent further scandal. I do not approve of this match, and I never shall."

"Of course, Mother," Elizabeth said soothingly. "And I shall accompany you, so that all will know I hold no grudge that Darcy did not choose to marry me."

Lady Catherine's eyes narrowed, and for a moment Elizabeth thought she would refuse. But then Lady Catherine sighed. "You know I mislike your being in London, the air is not good for your health... but you should be there, you are correct. Very well. I shall send a note to my brother Matlock, advising him that we shall wait upon him soon."

Relief flooded through Elizabeth. She had done it. Had convinced Lady Catherine to travel to London, to bring her to the city where Jane waited with ingredients and plans.

"Thank you, Mama," Elizabeth said, allowing genuine gratitude to colour Anne's soft voice. "I know this is difficult for you."

Lady Catherine rose with decisive movements. She crossed to the bell pull and yanked it with enough force that Elizabeth wondered if the cord might snap.

"Mrs. Jenkinson," Lady Catherine said. "We leave for London tomorrow morning. You will see that Anne's things are packed immediately. Her medicines, her warmest shawls, the grey travelling dress and the darker green silk for the wedding itself. Nothing too elaborate. We are attending out of duty, not celebration."

Mrs. Jenkinson had set aside her sewing and risen with an expression that suggested alarm. "Tomorrow, ma'am? But that is quite sudden. And Miss Anne's health..."

"Will be attended to as always," Lady Catherine snapped. "Bring whatever medicines and tonics she requires. But we cannot delay if we are to arrive in London with time to settle before this hasty ceremony." She shook her head. "Marrying by special licence. What is Darcy thinking?"

Elizabeth sat quietly, hands folded in her lap. The special licence had not been Darcy's idea at all. It was Anne, pushing to marry as fast as possible before anyone who knew Elizabeth Bennet well might come to suspect something was seriously amiss.

She had only days to stop the wedding and get her body back, before "Elizabeth Bennet" became Mrs. Darcy.

The carriage wheels ground to a halt on cobblestones, and Elizabeth looked up at Matlock House through weary eyes. The Portland stone façade rose three storeys above the street, elegant in a way that spoke of wealth without Rosings' need to overwhelm. Neat rows of windows reflected the afternoon sky. The entrance featured a portico supported by columns that managed to be imposing without feeling oppressive.

The journey from Kent had been brutal on Anne's failing body. Every jolt had sent fresh waves of exhaustion through her limbs. Lady Catherine had maintained disapproving silence for much of the journey, while Mrs. Jenkinson watched Elizabeth with that same assessing gaze.

A footman opened the carriage door and offered his hand. Elizabeth took it gratefully, her legs trembling as they made contact with solid ground. The London air smelled different from Kent's, carrying traces of coal smoke and horse traffic.

Lady Catherine descended with far more certainty, her movements brisk. She swept toward the entrance without waiting. Elizabeth moved after her slowly, Mrs. Jenkinson close behind.

The entrance hall struck Elizabeth with its restrained elegance. Where Rosings assaulted visitors with gilt and grandeur, Matlock House welcomed with wood-panelled walls and an elegant checkerboard of black and white tiles. A curved staircase rose along one wall. Fresh flowers sat in a vase, their scent mingling with beeswax polish.

A butler materialised, taking Lady Catherine's outer garments and directing servants to deal with the trunks. Elizabeth surrendered her own cloak and bonnet with relief.

"Lady Matlock is expecting you in the drawing room," the butler said. "If you will follow me."

They climbed the stairs, Elizabeth gripping the banister. Each step sent fresh protests through tired muscles. Lady Catherine swept ahead while Mrs. Jenkinson remained at Elizabeth's elbow.

The drawing room occupied the first floor's front corner. Cream walls decorated with muted landscape paintings provided backdrop for furnishings upholstered in shades of gold and soft green. A fire burned in the marble fireplace, but the room's atmosphere felt airy rather than stuffy.

Lady Matlock rose from a sofa as they entered, and Elizabeth found herself immediately struck by the difference between this woman and Lady Catherine. Where Lady Catherine's face carried perpetual disapproval, Lady Matlock's showed genuine warmth softened by laugh lines. She wore a gown of deep blue that suited her colouring.

"Catherine, how good to see you," Lady Matlock said, embracing her sister-in-law. "And Anne." She turned toward Elizabeth, her expression transforming into something that looked remarkably like delight. "My dear niece, how pleased I am that you've come."

She crossed to Elizabeth and took both her hands, the gesture conveying warmth without pitying overtones. Lady Matlock's hands were warm and firm, her grip gentle but not treating Elizabeth as though she might shatter.

"Thank you for having us, Aunt," Elizabeth managed. "It is kind of you to accommodate us on such short notice."

"Nonsense," Lady Matlock said. "You are family. Our home is always open to you. Please, sit. You must be exhausted from the journey."

Elizabeth lowered herself onto the sofa, grateful beyond measure. The cushions were soft but supportive, the angle comfortable. Lady Catherine settled into a nearby chair with visible stiffness.

A gentleman who must be Lord Matlock entered through a door at the room's far end. He was a distinguished man in his late fifties, his hair more grey than dark but his bearing upright. His face showed the aristocratic features Elizabeth recognised from Darcy, though softened by what looked like genuine kindness.

"Catherine," he said, nodding to his sister with reserved courtesy. "Anne." His gaze moved to Elizabeth, and she saw assessment there but also something that might have been concern. "Welcome to our home. I hope your journey was not too taxing."

"Thank you, Uncle," Elizabeth replied. "The journey was manageable."

Lord Matlock's eyebrows rose slightly at this response, as though he had expected Anne to complain. He exchanged a glance with his wife before settling into a chair.

"We are glad to have you here," Lady Matlock said. "Though I confess the circumstances are rather unusual. Such a hasty wedding. But I suppose when two people are in love, delay seems unnecessary."

"Indeed," Lady Catherine said, her tone making clear that she did not share this interpretation. "My nephew has made his choice, and we are here to demonstrate family unity regardless of personal opinions."

The statement was flat. Lord Matlock shifted in his chair, clearly uncomfortable. Lady Matlock's expression showed disappointment but not surprise.

"Well," Lady Matlock said, rallying with determined cheerfulness, "we shall make the best of things. Anne, my dear, I thought perhaps tomorrow, if the weather permits, you might enjoy seeing our garden."

Elizabeth felt her heart lift a little at the kindly suggestion. "I would like that very much," Elizabeth said, then caught herself. "If I am feeling strong enough, of course."

Mrs. Jenkinson, who had remained near the doorway, stepped forward quickly. "Forgive me, Lady Matlock," Mrs. Jenkinson said, "but Miss de Bourgh's constitution is quite delicate. Extended time outdoors often overtaxes her strength. Perhaps it would be wiser to avoid activities that might compromise her health."

The words were delivered with perfect deference, but their effect was to remind everyone of Anne's supposed fragility. Elizabeth felt the familiar cage closing around her.

Lady Matlock's expression shifted, her gaze moving from Mrs. Jenkinson to Elizabeth with new attention. When she spoke, her voice carried gentle firmness.

"I believe Anne knows her own strength best, Mrs. Jenkinson," Lady Matlock said, her smile remaining warm but her eyes showing steel. "If she feels well enough to walk in the garden, then we shall walk. And if she tires, we shall return immediately. I am quite capable of monitoring my niece's wellbeing during a simple stroll."

The statement hung in the air with quiet authority. Elizabeth watched Mrs. Jenkinson's face cycle through emotions before the companion inclined her head with stiff acknowledgement.

"Of course, my lady," she said, her tone suggesting she thought no such thing. "I merely wished to ensure Miss Anne's comfort."

"Which is admirable," Lady Matlock replied. "But I assure you, we will take every care. Now, you must be tired from the journey as well. Perhaps you would like to see your room and rest before dinner?"

It was a dismissal delivered with such courtesy that refusing would have been openly rude. Mrs. Jenkinson recognised this, her jaw tightening before she executed a curtsy.

"Thank you, my lady," she said. "If Miss Anne requires anything, she need only send for me."

She left with measured steps, but Elizabeth caught the backward glance she cast before the door closed. That look contained warning and promise both.

After the door closed, Lady Matlock turned back to Elizabeth with an expression that mixed sympathy with understanding. "Mrs. Jenkinson seems very devoted to your care, Anne. But I hope you will feel free to express your own wishes while you are our guest. You are not a child to be constantly supervised."

The words struck Elizabeth with unexpected force. Lady Matlock saw Anne as a person rather than merely an invalid. Treated her as someone capable of making decisions. The contrast with Rosings was so stark that Elizabeth felt tears gather.

"Thank you, Aunt," she managed, her voice emerging rough with emotion. "That is very kind of you."

Lady Matlock's expression softened further, and she reached across to pat Elizabeth's hand. "Nonsense. It is simply treating you as you deserve. Now, shall I have tea brought? You must be parched after your journey."

As Lady Matlock rang for refreshments, Elizabeth allowed herself a moment of cautious hope. Here, at Matlock House, she might find actual allies. Lady Matlock's kindness felt genuine, her treatment of Anne suggesting she saw past the invalid status.

If only that person truly were Anne de Bourgh.

The parlour on Matlock House's second floor caught the afternoon sun through windows that faced south. Elizabeth sat on a cushioned chair near one of those windows, a teacup balanced on her knee, while Lady Matlock occupied the seat opposite. The room smelled of lavender and fresh tea.

They had been sitting here for perhaps twenty minutes, engaged in conversation that felt remarkably normal. Lady Matlock had asked about her niece's health with genuine concern, and had then moved on to other topics with ease.

"I confess I have always found London rather overwhelming during the Season," Lady Matlock was saying. "The constant round of calls and entertainments becomes exhausting."

Elizabeth managed a small smile. "I have spent little time in London. Mama prefers the country."

"Yes, Catherine has always been devoted to her estate," Lady Matlock said, and something in her tone suggested she found her sister's devotion excessive. "But I think a change of scene can be beneficial. You must tell me, Anne, are you enjoying your stay so far?"

The question carried genuine curiosity. Elizabeth chose her words with care. "The house is lovely," Elizabeth offered. "More comfortable than I anticipated. And the garden looks charming."

Lady Matlock's face brightened. "You must allow me to show it to you this afternoon if you feel well enough. We have several varieties of roses that I am quite proud of. Nothing compared to Rosings' grandeur, of course, but I find there is something to be said for a more intimate space."

"I would like that very much, Aunt. Thank you."

"No need for thanks," Lady Matlock replied. "I am simply glad to have you here, Anne. I confess I have always wished we might know each other better."

The statement hung between them. Elizabeth sensed that Lady Matlock was offering something genuine.

"That would please me greatly," Elizabeth said, meaning it despite the layers of deception.

Lady Matlock's expression softened. "You are not what I expected, Anne. The few times we have met previously, you seemed so reserved, so withdrawn. But today you appear more present somehow. More engaged."

The observation sent alarm shooting through Elizabeth. Had she been too free in her responses? She forced herself to maintain a calm expression.

"Perhaps the change of scene has done me good," Elizabeth managed. "Or perhaps I simply feel more comfortable with you."

Lady Matlock smiled with visible pleasure. "I am glad to hear it. And I hope you will continue to feel comfortable enough to speak freely. You need not be so reserved with me, my dear."

A knock at the door interrupted. Lord Matlock entered, his expression suggesting that he bore news, and indeed so it proved.

"Forgive the interruption, my dear," Lord Matlock said. "But I thought you should know that I have secured the arrangements for Darcy's wedding. St George's, Hanover Square has been booked for Friday afternoon at three o'clock. The special licence has been obtained, and all is in order."

The teacup rattled against its saucer with a sharp, discordant sound. Elizabeth's hands shook with a violence she could not control, the delicate china threatening to slip entirely. *Friday*. The word echoed in her mind with the finality of a judge pronouncing sentence. Friday was just three days away. Only three days to obtain the ingredients, prepare the reversal potion, force Anne to drink it.

Three days. It was impossible. Completely impossible.

"Anne?" Lady Matlock's concerned voice penetrated the roaring in Elizabeth's ears. "My dear, are you quite well? You have gone very pale."

Elizabeth forced herself to set down the teacup before she dropped it. She looked up to find both Matlocks watching her with concern.

"I am well," Elizabeth managed, though her voice emerged thin and unconvincing. "I simply… Friday seems very soon."

Lady Matlock's expression transformed, concern giving way to what looked remarkably like sympathy. She settled back and reached across to pat Elizabeth's hand.

"Of course it seems soon, dear child," Lady Matlock said. "You are thinking of your cousin, of the expectations everyone had about your future. And now you must watch him marry another woman. It must be very difficult."

The compassion in Lady Matlock's voice struck Elizabeth like a physical blow. She was so kind, so genuinely concerned for what she believed was Anne's heartbreak.

"Such a short engagement," Lady Matlock continued. "But I suppose when two people are in love, delay seems unnecessary. Still, it leaves very little time for proper preparations."

Lord Matlock cleared his throat, clearly uncomfortable. "Yes, well. I simply wanted to inform you of the arrangements. Darcy will be calling tomorrow morning to discuss some final details, and I believe he mentioned wanting to see Anne as well."

Elizabeth's throat closed around words she could not speak. Darcy would be here tomorrow. Would see her wearing Anne's face and body. The wrongness of it made her stomach turn.

"How thoughtful," Elizabeth forced herself to say. "I look forward to seeing my cousin."

Lord Matlock nodded with visible relief, clearly pleased to escape. "Excellent. I will leave you ladies to your tea, then."

He left swiftly, the door closing with a soft click.

Lady Matlock watched Elizabeth with continued concern. "You really do look unwell, Anne. Perhaps you should rest."

"I am well enough," Elizabeth protested feebly.

A soft knock interrupted. The door opened to reveal Mrs. Jenkinson, her timing so precise that Elizabeth suspected she had been hovering in the corridor. The companion's expression carried that familiar mixture of concern and determination.

"Forgive me, Lady Matlock," Mrs. Jenkinson said, "but Miss Anne requires her afternoon rest. She becomes overtaxed quite easily, and I fear this extended conversation may have been too stimulating."

Elizabeth wanted to protest, but Anne's borrowed body betrayed her, trembling with exhaustion.

Lady Matlock looked between Elizabeth and Mrs. Jenkinson with an expression that suggested she recognised the power dynamic at play. But she also saw Elizabeth's obvious exhaustion.

"Of course," Lady Matlock said, rising. "Anne, dear, you must rest. We will have plenty of time to talk tomorrow, and perhaps see the garden."

Elizabeth pushed herself upright with effort, accepting Mrs. Jenkinson's offered arm with reluctance. "Thank you, Aunt. For the tea, and for your kindness."

"No thanks needed," Lady Matlock replied, warmth evident despite her concern. "You are family, Anne. Rest well."

Mrs. Jenkinson guided Elizabeth from the parlour, her hand on Elizabeth's elbow directing their movement. They walked in silence until they reached the privacy of Anne's assigned room.

"You must be more careful," Mrs. Jenkinson said, her voice low but weighted. "Lady Matlock is observant. Too observant. She has already commented that you seem different, more animated than she remembers. You must remember to be more reserved, more withdrawn. The Anne de Bourgh she knows would never speak so freely."

Elizabeth sank onto the edge of the bed. "I will be more careful," Elizabeth managed, though the words felt like surrender.

Three days. She had three days to save herself, and Mrs. Jenkinson's watchfulness had just become even more suffocating.

Three days until Friday, when Anne would marry Darcy. Three days until Elizabeth would be trapped forever in this failing body, dying slowly while her own life was stolen completely.

Three days to accomplish the impossible, or lose everything.

Chapter Twenty-Three

JANE BENT CLOSER TO the cramped handwriting of Anne's grimoire, her eyes burning with fatigue as she read the ingredients list for perhaps the hundredth time. Her finger traced down the page, pausing at each item while her gaze flicked to the paper beside her elbow where she had copied everything in her neat hand. Most entries bore satisfying lines through them, evidence of successful acquisition through her uncle's merchant connections. But one remained stubbornly unmarked, and it was the most crucial of all.

A shaving of bezoar steadies.

Five simple words that represented an impossible obstacle. Jane closed her sore eyes and pressed the heels of her hands against them. The clock showed half past midnight, and she had been sitting here since dinner ended five hours ago. Her uncle's study felt smaller at this hour, the walls pressing close with their burden of ledgers and correspondence. The fire had died to embers, and her shawl had slipped from her shoulders without her noticing.

She let her hands drop and stared at the grimoire with something approaching hatred. The leather binding gleamed dully in the candlelight, innocent and unassuming, giving no hint of the dark knowledge within. Anne de Bourgh had studied this book for years, had learned its secrets from her father, had used its recipes to steal Elizabeth's body and life. And now Jane needed that same dark knowledge to save her sister, but the final ingredient remained frustratingly out of reach.

Jane picked up her pen and dipped it in ink that had nearly dried, adding nothing but needing the familiar motion to calm her racing thoughts. *Ambergris braised in honey.* She had obtained the ambergris through one of her uncle's spice merchants, the pea-sized lump arriving wrapped in oiled paper that reeked of the sea, her uncle assuring her the merchant would not dare pass off a fake, not for the price they had paid. Over half of Jane's long-hoarded savings. *Spirits of wine well-rectified.* The apothecary on Cheapside had provided that without question when she claimed it was for making perfume. *Pearl powder.* She had bought a single pearl earring, its mate presumably lost, from a pawnbroker and ground it herself with pestle and mortar.

Saffron, grains of paradise, lemon balm, lavender water. All accounted for, all sitting in careful packets and vials in a satchel that never left her side, waiting to be combined into the potion that would reverse Anne's wicked spell. Even the hair. Jane had managed to trim a lock from the impostor Elizabeth's head just that morning, claiming she wanted to try a new style for the wedding. The false Elizabeth had submitted with surprising docility, apparently unconcerned about a few snipped curls.

That hair now rested in a twist of paper among the other ingredients, dark and glossy and completely wrong.

But the bezoar. The bezoar remained impossibly distant, locked away in collectors' cabinets or hoarded by physicians who valued its supposed medicinal properties. Her uncle had never heard of such a thing when she first mentioned it, and his enquiries had turned up nothing useful. One contact claimed to have seen a bezoar years ago in an East India Company auction, sold for more money than Mr. Gardiner earned in six months. Another remembered a Persian trader who dealt in exotic curiosities, but the man had left London five years past.

Jane's throat tightened with despair. *Three days.* Anne de Bourgh had three days before she became Mrs. Darcy in truth, bound by vows spoken while wearing stolen flesh, putting the situation beyond easy reversal even if they did manage to get Elizabeth her own body back. Three days to find an ingredient that might not exist in all of London, to brew a potion that required hours of careful preparation, to somehow convince Anne to drink it simultaneously with Elizabeth when they would not even be in the same location until the wedding itself.

The study door opened with a soft creak that made Jane start violently, her hand knocking against the inkwell and nearly overturning it. She caught the glass container before it could spill, her heart hammering as she looked up to see her uncle standing in the doorway. Mr. Gardiner carried a candle that illuminated his face from below, creating shadows that emphasised his concern.

"Jane," he said, his voice gentle. "My dear girl, it is well past midnight. What are you doing still awake?"

Jane shifted slightly, letting her body block his view of the cramped handwriting and disturbing illustrations. "I could not sleep, Uncle. I thought I might work on the final preparations for Elizabeth's wedding gift."

Mr. Gardiner moved into the room, setting his candle on the desk beside hers. His gaze took in her exhausted face, the papers scattered across the desktop, the list with its ominous unmarked entry. He picked up the foolscap and read it with eyebrows drawing together.

"These are very strange items for a wedding gift," he observed. "What manner of present requires such exotic ingredients?"

"A good-luck charm," Jane said, the lie emerging more smoothly than it should have. She had practiced this explanation, had prepared for questions. "An old family recipe from the Bennet side. It is meant to bring prosperity and happiness to a new marriage. I thought it would please her to have something from home, something made with care rather than simply purchased."

Mr. Gardiner's expression softened, though doubt lingered in his eyes. He set down the list and patted Jane's shoulder with affection that made guilt twist in her stomach. "That is very thoughtful of you, my dear. Elizabeth is fortunate to have such a devoted sister. But this bezoar. My enquiries have turned up nothing useful. Perhaps you might substitute something else? Surely the charm would work just as well without this one ingredient."

"No," Jane said, desperation leaking into her voice. "It must be complete. The recipe requires all the ingredients, or it will not work properly. Uncle, is there no one else you might ask? No other merchant who deals in rare curiosities?"

Mr. Gardiner shook his head, sympathy mixed with gentle scepticism. "I am afraid not, my dear. And even if I could find such a thing, the cost would be prohibitive. I cannot justify such expense for what is essentially silly superstitious nonsense, however well-intentioned."

The words struck Jane like physical blows. *Silly superstitious nonsense.* If only he knew the truth, knew that his niece's very life depended on obtaining this impossible ingredient. But she could not tell him. Could not explain that Elizabeth was trapped in a dying body while an impostor prepared to marry Mr. Darcy. He would think her mad.

"Of course," Jane managed, forcing her voice to remain steady. "You are quite right, Uncle. I shall manage without it somehow."

Mr. Gardiner squeezed her shoulder again, clearly relieved. "That is my sensible girl. Now, you must get some rest. The wedding is only three days away, and you will want to look your best for the ceremony. Lizzy needs your support, not your exhaustion."

He collected his candle and moved towards the door, pausing to look back. "Please, Jane. Go to bed. Whatever this charm may be, it can wait until morning."

"Yes, Uncle," Jane said, though she had no intention of leaving the study any time soon. "I will retire shortly."

Mr. Gardiner nodded and left, pulling the door closed behind him with a soft click. Jane remained frozen in her chair, staring at the grimoire without really seeing it. The clock ticked with relentless rhythm, each sound marking another second lost, another moment closer to the wedding that would seal Elizabeth's fate.

Jane slumped forwards, resting her forehead on her crossed arms. The wood felt cool against her fevered skin. Three days. And she had no idea how to obtain the final ingredient that could save her sister.

The clock ticked on, indifferent to her despair. Jane listened to its steady rhythm and felt tears gather hot behind her closed eyelids. She had tried so hard, had worked so carefully to collect everything the potion required. But hard work and careful planning meant nothing when faced with an impossible obstacle.

Three days until the wedding. Three days until Anne completed her triumph and left for Derbyshire with Darcy, closing their window of opportunity.

Three days, until Elizabeth would be doomed to die in a failing body, unless Jane could do this one, apparently impossible thing.

Jane had no idea what to do next.

The afternoon sun slanted through the Gardiners' parlour windows, illuminating dust motes that drifted lazy and unconcerned. Jane sat in the chair by the fire, her hands folded in her lap with fingers that would not quite stay still, a book open on the table beside her that she had not managed to read a single page of in the past hour. When the maid announced Colonel Fitzwilliam, Jane's first response was confusion.

She rose with movements that felt disconnected from her intentions. The Colonel entered with his usual easy manner, though his smile faltered when his gaze landed on her face. Jane became suddenly aware of how she must appear. The looking glass had shown shadows beneath her eyes that no amount of cold water could diminish, and her hands had trembled while pinning up her hair.

"Miss Bennet," Colonel Fitzwilliam said, executing a bow that seemed more concerned than formal. "Forgive my calling without prior arrangement. I hoped to find Miss Elizabeth at home."

"She is out shopping with my mother and aunt," Jane replied, hearing the weariness in her own voice. "They have gone to Bond Street to purchase wedding clothes. I expect them back within the hour, if you would care to wait."

The Colonel moved further into the room, declining the chair she gestured towards in favour of standing near enough that his attention felt almost uncomfortably focused. His eyes searched her face with the same perceptiveness she had noticed during their brief acquaintance in Kent.

"Miss Bennet," he said again, his tone carrying genuine worry. "Forgive my frankness, but you seem troubled. Are you quite well?"

Jane's throat tightened around denials that would not come. She was not well. Had not been well since receiving Elizabeth's desperate letter, since discovering the impossible truth about the body swap, since beginning this frantic race against time to save her sister. Her fingers found the handkerchief tucked in her sleeve and worried at its embroidered edge.

"I am well enough," she managed, though the words emerged thin and unconvincing. "Merely tired. Wedding preparations are more exhausting than I anticipated."

Colonel Fitzwilliam's expression suggested he did not believe her for a moment, but his courtesy prevented him from calling her a liar outright. Instead, he moved to the chair she had indicated and settled into it with the purposeful air of someone who had decided to stay until he got proper answers.

"Miss Bennet, I hope you will forgive me if I presume upon our acquaintance," he said, his voice carrying gentle firmness. "We do not know each other well, I grant you. But I consider myself a friend to your family, and I confess I am concerned by what I see before me. You have dark circles beneath your eyes that speak of lost sleep. Your hands have not ceased their fidgeting since I entered the room. And unless I am very much mistaken, you are on the verge of tears."

The accuracy of his observations made Jane's eyes burn. She blinked hard against them, horrified at the thought of weeping in front of a gentleman she barely knew. But something in his manner invited confidence, suggested that he genuinely wished to help rather than simply satisfying curiosity.

"There is nothing you can do," Jane said, defeat colouring the words. "The matter is beyond anyone's ability to assist."

"Try me," Colonel Fitzwilliam replied, leaning forwards with his elbows on his knees and his hands clasped before him. "You might be surprised what a man with my connexions can accomplish when properly motivated. Is there anything I might do for you? You need only name the favour, Miss Bennet. I am entirely at your service."

The sincerity in his voice struck Jane with unexpected force. She had not expected kindness, had not anticipated that anyone outside her immediate family might offer genuine help. The temptation to unburden herself rose swift and powerful, the urge to tell someone the whole impossible story and let them share the weight of this terrible knowledge.

But caution held her tongue. What if he thought her mad? What if he dismissed her claims as hysteria or delusion? Worse, what if he believed her and decided the situation required intervention from authorities, from physicians who would examine Elizabeth in Anne's body and declare her insane?

Yet she needed that bezoar. Needed it desperately, and her uncle's resources had proven insufficient. Perhaps Colonel Fitzwilliam, with his aristocratic connexions and military contacts, might succeed where Mr. Gardiner had failed.

"There is one thing," Jane said slowly, choosing each word with painful care. "Though I confess it will sound quite strange."

"I am listening," the Colonel replied.

Jane's fingers twisted the handkerchief harder. "I need a shaving from a bezoar stone. A very small amount would suffice, but it must be genuine. I have been trying to obtain one through my uncle's merchant connexions, but no one seems to have such a thing available."

Colonel Fitzwilliam's eyebrows rose slightly, but he did not laugh or question her sanity. Instead, he sat back in his chair with thoughtful expression, his gaze distant as though mentally reviewing his available resources.

"A bezoar," he repeated, testing the word. "That is indeed an unusual request, Miss Bennet. May I ask what purpose you require it for?"

"I cannot say," Jane replied, desperation leaking into her voice. "I know that sounds ridiculous. I know you have every right to refuse such a strange favour without proper explanation. But I promise you, the need is genuine and urgent. If you can help me obtain this ingredient, you will be doing a greater service than you can possibly imagine."

The Colonel studied her face for a long moment. Then, unexpectedly, he smiled with warmth that transformed his features.

"When a lady asks for an antidote," he said, rising from his chair with decisive movements, "I do not enquire after the poison. My father keeps a cabinet of curiosities at Matlock House that includes, unless I am very much mistaken, a bezoar stone from Persia. I cannot promise it will be suitable for your purposes, but I will call on him this very day and secure a shaving if it can be managed."

Relief crashed over Jane with such force that her knees weakened, and she had to grip the chair's arm to remain standing. "Thank you," she whispered, her voice breaking. "Thank you so much. You cannot know what this means to me."

"Perhaps not," Colonel Fitzwilliam agreed, moving towards the door purposefully. "But I trust that the need is genuine, and that is sufficient. I will return tomorrow with your bezoar shaving, Miss Bennet. You have my word."

He paused at the threshold, turning back with expression that had shifted to something more searching. "May I ask one question, though? Not about the bezoar, but about a related matter that has troubled me since our meeting in Kent."

Jane nodded, uncertain what he might ask but too grateful to refuse.

"You are the Miss Bennet who was separated from Mr. Bingley by my cousin's interference, are you not?" the Colonel asked. "The lady whose heart Darcy's meddling may have broken?"

The question struck Jane with unexpected force, not because it pained her but because it did not. When had she last thought of Mr. Bingley? When had his defection last caused her genuine pain rather than merely abstract regret?

Not since Elizabeth's letter had arrived. Not since discovering the body swap and throwing all her energy into saving her sister.

Mr. Bingley had simply vanished from her thoughts, replaced entirely by more pressing concerns.

"I was," Jane said slowly, testing the truth of her own words. "But I confess, Colonel, that all my thoughts are for my sister's happiness now. Whatever pain I felt over Mr. Bingley's departure has been quite eclipsed by more immediate concerns."

Colonel Fitzwilliam's expression brightened, his smile returning with increased warmth. Something in his eyes suggested he had asked for reasons of his own, that her answer pleased him in ways that had nothing to do with abstract curiosity. Jane felt heat rise in her cheeks as understanding dawned, felt her heart stutter with realisation that the Colonel's interest might extend beyond simple family connexion.

But there was no time for such considerations now. Elizabeth needed her focused, not distracted by the unexpected stirring of her own heart.

"I am glad to hear that," the Colonel said, his tone suggesting layers of meaning Jane had no time to unpack. "I will call tomorrow with your bezoar shaving, Miss Bennet. Until then, I hope you will rest and take better care of yourself. Your sister needs you well, I think."

He departed with another bow, leaving Jane alone in the suddenly quiet parlour. She sank back into her chair, her legs finally giving way, and pressed shaking hands to her face. Relief warred with new anxiety in her chest, the joy of finally obtaining the bezoar tempered by acute awareness of how little time remained.

Tomorrow. The Colonel would return tomorrow with the final ingredient. Which meant she would have one day to brew the potion before the Friday wedding. One day to prepare something that required hours of careful work, precise timing, and constant attention to temperature and measurements. One day to accomplish what should take two or three at minimum according to the grimoire's instructions.

Jane pushed herself upright and moved towards the stairs, her exhaustion forgotten in renewed determination. She needed to review the brewing instructions again, needed to calculate exactly how long each step would take and whether she could compress the timeline without ruining the potion's efficacy. Needed to plan how she would trick Anne into drinking it.

The clock in the hallway chimed three as she climbed towards her chamber. It was exactly forty-eight hours until the wedding.

Forty-eight hours to save Elizabeth.

It would have to be enough.

Chapter Twenty-Four

JANE HAD POSITIONED HERSELF by the parlour window three times that morning, each time forcing herself away with the reminder that watched pots never boiled and colonels never arrived more quickly for being stared after. But the fourth time she found herself drawn to the glass, Colonel Fitzwilliam's familiar figure appeared walking along Gracechurch Street, and her heart performed an uncomfortable leap that had nothing to do with the bezoar she hoped he carried.

She moved away from the window with deliberate calm, settling in the chair farthest from where she had been standing, her hands folded in her lap with what she hoped appeared like casual patience. The clock showed half past three. Anne was out with Mr. Darcy, taking a drive in Hyde Park that Mrs. Bennet had insisted upon. Jane had watched them depart an hour ago, had seen the impostor smile at Darcy with Elizabeth's face while wearing Elizabeth's favourite blue pelisse, and had wanted to scream at the wrongness of it all.

The maid announced Colonel Fitzwilliam, and Jane rose with hands that trembled slightly. He entered carrying a small object wrapped in a handkerchief, his expression mixing triumph with something softer that made Jane's breath catch.

"Miss Bennet," he said, executing a bow that managed to be both formal and familiar. "I come bearing gifts, as promised."

He crossed to where she stood and held out the wrapped object with ceremony that suggested he somehow understood its importance. Jane took it with fingers that shook properly now, no pretence possible. She unwrapped the handkerchief with careful movements, aware of the Colonel watching her face rather than her hands.

The bezoar shaving lay against white linen, a thin curved shard no larger than her thumbnail. Its surface caught the afternoon light with an iridescent sheen that shifted from brownish-green to deep purple as she tilted it, the concentric layers visible even in this small fragment.

"Oh," Jane whispered, her voice breaking. "Oh, Colonel Fitzwilliam, I cannot thank you enough."

"It was indeed in my father's cabinet of curiosities, as I had thought," the Colonel explained, moving to stand beside her. His shoulder nearly touched hers, close enough that she could feel warmth radiating from him. "The stone itself is quite ancient, supposedly taken from a Persian goat some hundred years ago. My grandfather acquired it during his diplomatic service in the East, though I suspect the merchant who sold it to him may have exaggerated its provenance somewhat."

Jane looked up from the bezoar to find him watching her with that same searching intensity from yesterday. "Your father will not mind its loss?"

"He has the whole stone still," the Colonel assured her. "I merely took a thin shaving from the outermost layer. He will never notice its absence, and even if he does, I shall simply tell him I needed it for medicinal purposes. Which is not entirely untrue, I think, given your urgent need for it."

The statement hung between them with weight that made Jane's chest tighten. He knew something was wrong. His willingness to help without demanding explanations demonstrated either remarkable trust or remarkable perception, and Jane suspected it was both.

"When a lady asks for an antidote," she quoted back to him with small smile, "you do not enquire after the poison."

"Precisely," Colonel Fitzwilliam agreed, his expression warming further. "Though I confess myself curious about what poison requires such an exotic remedy. Not curious enough to pry, mind you. But curious nonetheless."

Jane wrapped the bezoar shaving carefully back in his handkerchief, her fingers lingering on the fine linen that still carried a faint scent of his cologne. She should return it, should fetch one of her own handkerchiefs. But some part of her wanted to keep this small piece of him, this tangible reminder of his kindness and trust.

"I hope someday soon, I might explain," Jane said, surprising herself with the admission. "When circumstances permit such confidence. But for now, I can only thank you and beg your continued discretion."

"You have both," the Colonel replied, his voice dropping lower. "Miss Bennet, I hope you know that if you are in any sort of trouble, any difficulty whatsoever, you need only ask for my assistance. I would count it an honour to be of service to you."

The earnestness in his tone made Jane's throat tighten. She looked up at him, at his kind face and honest eyes, and felt something shift in her chest that had nothing to do with Elizabeth's desperate situation and everything to do with the man standing before her.

"May I ask you something?" the Colonel continued, his gaze searching hers with intensity that made her pulse quicken. "Not about the bezoar or your mysterious purpose. Something else entirely."

"Of course," Jane managed, though her voice emerged breathless.

"Yesterday, I asked whether you remained heartbroken over Mr. Bingley's departure," the Colonel said, his words coming more slowly now as though he was choosing each one with deliberate care. "Your answer suggested your feelings had changed, that your thoughts were occupied with other concerns. I wonder if I might ask a more direct question, one that I confess touches on matters of personal interest rather than mere curiosity."

Jane's heart hammered against her ribs. "What question?"

"Do you still hold any tender feelings for Mr. Bingley?" the Colonel asked, his gaze never leaving hers. "Or has your heart moved past that disappointment entirely?"

The directness of the question should have shocked her, should have made her step back and remind him that such personal enquiries bordered on impropriety. But Jane found she did not want to step back. Found instead that she wanted to answer with equal honesty.

"I do not think I ever held truly tender feelings for Mr. Bingley," Jane said, the admission emerging with surprising ease. "I liked him. Found him pleasant and kind. But when he left, when my expectations were disappointed, I grieved more for the idea of him than for the man himself. And now..." She paused, gathering courage. "Now I find that all my thoughts are occupied with my sister's welfare. There is no room left for regret over Mr. Bingley, if there ever truly was such regret to begin with."

Colonel Fitzwilliam's expression transformed, his smile brightening with such obvious pleasure that Jane felt answering warmth spread through her chest. "I am very glad to hear that, Miss Bennet. Very glad indeed."

Their eyes held for a moment that stretched longer than propriety strictly allowed, and Jane became acutely aware of how close he stood, how his gaze dropped briefly to her mouth before returning to her eyes. The air between them felt charged with possibility, with potential for something that Jane desperately wanted to explore but could not afford to consider while Elizabeth's fate hung in such precarious balance.

She stepped back, breaking the moment with reluctance that must have shown on her face. "Forgive me, Colonel. I should not have spoken so freely. It was not appropriate."

"On the contrary," the Colonel replied, making no move to close the distance she had created. "I found your honesty refreshing. And I hope..." He paused, seeming to reconsider whatever he had been about to say. "I hope that once your current difficulties are resolved, whatever they may be, and your concerns for your sister's happiness are resolved, we might have opportunity to continue this conversation in circumstances that permit more leisurely exploration of the topic."

Jane felt her cheeks heat at the implication in his words, at the clear statement of interest that lay beneath his careful courtesy. Part of her wanted to tell him everything, to unburden herself of this terrible secret and let him help carry the weight of it. He was perceptive enough to believe her, she thought. Kind enough to want to help.

But what if he did not believe her? Even if he only prevented her from giving "Elizabeth" the potion to drink, fearing it might injure her, it would ruin everything.

And there was another consideration. If she told him the truth now, if she involved him in this desperate scheme to reverse dark magic through forbidden potions, she would be drawing him into something dangerous and potentially scandalous. She would be risking not just her own reputation but his as well, tainting any possibility of future connexion between them with the stain of association with witchcraft and deception.

Better to handle this herself. Better to save Elizabeth first and then, perhaps, when all was resolved and safe, she might tell him the truth. Might explain what his kindness had meant, how his willingness to help without demanding explanations had given her hope when she most needed it.

"I look forward to that conversation," Jane said, meaning it with fierce sincerity. "And I thank you again, more than I can express, for your help in obtaining this." She held up the wrapped bezoar shaving. "You have done more for me than you can possibly know."

Colonel Fitzwilliam executed another bow, this one carrying warmth that went beyond mere courtesy. "It was my pleasure, Miss Bennet. Truly."

"Wait." Something else occurred to her. "Would you do me one other, very small favour? Nothing so strange as this, I promise you."

He smiled. "Were it ten times so strange, I would not refuse, Miss Bennet. What is it you need of me?"

"Miss Anne de Bourgh is resident in your uncle's house, is she not, with her mother?" Jane knew well that she was. Elizabeth had managed to bribe one of the maids at Matlock House to send Jane a note, folded around a cut lock of Anne's short, thin hair.

"Indeed, she is."

"If I write a note to her, would you pass it to her privately? I do not want anyone else to know that she has it. Today."

"An easy matter, I am expected there for dinner. Of course, and not a soul shall suspect that I gave it to her, you have my word."

She swallowed a lump in her throat, went to her aunt's writing table and penned a swift note, folding it over and sealing it with a hastily melted blob of wax. She did not write anything on the outside, unable to bring herself to write Anne's name on this critical message for Lizzy.

Their fingers brushed as she handed the note to the Colonel, and Jane's breath caught. For a moment time seemed suspended as they looked at each other.

And then Lydia called something to Kitty loudly in the room just above their heads, and the spell was broken.

The Colonel withdrew his hand, tucking the note inside his jacket. "It will be in Anne's hands this evening, I promise you," he said. He moved towards the door, then paused at the threshold to look back at her. "I hope whatever difficulty you face resolves favourably. And I hope that when it does, you will allow me to call on you again. Not as my cousin's connexion, but as..." He trailed off, leaving the sentence unfinished but its meaning clear.

"I would like that very much," Jane replied, her voice barely above a whisper.

He smiled one final time and departed, leaving Jane alone in the parlour with the precious bezoar shaving clutched in her hand and her heart performing complicated acrobatics that had nothing to do with Elizabeth's desperate situation and everything to do with the man who had just left.

She stood there for several minutes after his departure, staring at the closed door while her mind spun with thoughts that had no place in her current crisis. The Colonel's interest was obvious, his intentions clear despite the careful courtesy with which he had expressed them. And her own feelings, which she had not allowed herself to examine closely during these desperate days, suddenly demanded acknowledgement.

She liked him. More than liked him. Found herself drawn to his kindness and perceptiveness, to the easy way he had offered help without demanding explanations, to the warmth in his eyes when he looked at her. Found herself imagining what might develop between them once this nightmare was over, once Elizabeth was safe and Jane could afford to think about her own future rather than solely her sister's salvation.

But those were thoughts for later. Jane shook herself, forcing her mind back to the immediate crisis. She had the bezoar now. Had all the ingredients required for the reversal potion. Which meant she could begin brewing right now.

She moved towards the stairs, her exhaustion forgotten in renewed determination. The grimoire awaited, its instructions requiring careful study one final time. She needed to review the brewing process, needed to ensure she understood every step before beginning. Needed to calculate exact timing so the potion would be ready to administer at precisely the right moment. Hopefully, her mother, aunt and sisters would continue to keep Anne busy. Anne herself was doing her part by avoiding Jane, perhaps aware that Jane was the most likely person to expose her. All to the good. Jane could barely stand to be in the same room as the impostor wearing her dearest Lizzy's face.

The clock in the hallway chimed three as she climbed towards her room. Twenty-four hours until the wedding.

Twenty-four hours to save her sister and prevent a marriage built on stolen identity and dark magic.

Jane clutched the wrapped bezoar shaving to her chest and felt grim determination settle over her like armour. She had what she needed now. Had the final ingredient that would make the reversal possible. The rest was simply a matter of careful execution and perhaps a small amount of luck.

She could do this. She would do this.

Elizabeth's life depended on it.

Chapter Twenty-Five

THE SOUP COURSE ARRIVED with the usual ceremony, footmen moving silently around the Matlock dining table while conversation flowed with the ease of people accustomed to formal dinners. Elizabeth lifted her spoon with a hand that trembled slightly, grateful that the motion could be attributed to Anne's general weakness rather than the anxiety that coiled tighter in her chest with each passing hour.

Lady Catherine held forth about the arrangements for tomorrow's wedding, her disapproval evident in every clipped syllable despite her agreement to attend. Lady Matlock responded with patient courtesy, redirecting the conversation whenever her sister veered too close to open insult about the bride. Lord Matlock contributed occasional comments between bites, clearly hoping to finish his meal without family discord erupting.

Elizabeth forced herself to swallow a spoonful of broth that tasted like nothing, her throat tight with nerves. *Tomorrow*. The wedding would be tomorrow afternoon at three o'clock. And she still had no plan for how to force Anne to drink the reversal potion, assuming Jane even managed to brew it in time. She had heard nothing back from Jane since sending the note with the lock of hair, and the not knowing was weighing on her. She set down her spoon.

"Anne, dear, you are not eating," Lady Matlock observed. "Are you feeling quite well?"

"I am well enough, Aunt," Elizabeth managed, forcing Anne's soft voice to remain steady. "Simply not very hungry this evening."

Colonel Fitzwilliam caught her eye across the table, and something in his expression made Elizabeth blink at him curiously. He looked oddly conspiratorial. He shifted in his chair, reaching for the salt cellar that sat nearer to Elizabeth's place setting. As he leaned forwards, his hand brushed against the edge of her plate, and a small folded paper appeared beneath its rim with such practised sleight of hand that Elizabeth might have missed it had she not been watching him so intently.

"Forgive me," the Colonel said smoothly, settling back with the salt. "Clumsy of me."

Elizabeth's fingers closed around the note, her heart hammering against Anne's weak ribs. She waited until Lady Catherine launched into another complaint about the wedding's timing before unfolding the paper in her lap beneath the table's edge, angling it to catch enough light to read Jane's neat handwriting.

I have the bezoar. Brewing now. Will not be ready until tomorrow afternoon. I am so sorry. I will find a way. Trust me. J.

The words struck Elizabeth with the force of a physical blow. Tomorrow afternoon. *After* the wedding? Elizabeth's vision blurred at the edges, black spots dancing across her sight as panic crashed over her in waves.

How could they possibly make this work? Anne would never willingly drink anything Jane offered, not when she had gone to such elaborate lengths to steal Elizabeth's body and life. How could they force the potion down Anne's throat when she would be with Darcy, celebrating her wedding breakfast, surrounded by guests and family who would think Jane had lost her mind if she tried to assault the new Mrs. Darcy with mysterious potions?

It was impossible. Completely, utterly impossible.

Elizabeth's hands began to shake properly now, the trembling spreading up Anne's arms until her whole body vibrated with barely contained terror. She managed to shove the paper up her sleeve, but as her hand landed on the table again, the soup spoon clattered against the bowl, broth sloshing over the rim to stain the white tablecloth. She tried to steady herself, tried to force Anne's weak muscles to obey, but panic had seized control of her limbs and would not release them.

"Anne?" Lady Matlock's voice seemed to come from very far away. "Anne, what is wrong?"

The dining room tilted sideways, the candles smearing into long streaks of light. Elizabeth tried to stand, some instinct demanding she flee even though there was nowhere to go. Her legs refused to support her weight. She felt herself falling, the floor rushing up to meet her.

Strong hands caught her before she struck the ground. Colonel Fitzwilliam had moved around the table with remarkable speed, his arms supporting Anne's frail body while voices erupted around them in overlapping concern and alarm. Elizabeth tried to speak, tried to explain, but her borrowed lungs would not draw enough air for words. The black spots in her vision spread and merged.

"Get her to the sofa," Lady Matlock commanded, her voice cutting through the chaos. "Quickly, before she faints entirely."

Elizabeth felt herself being lifted, carried across the room and into the adjoining smoking room where the gentlemen usually adjourned after dinner. The Colonel lowered her onto something soft, cushions supporting her back while her head spun with vertigo. Someone loosened the high collar of Anne's dinner dress, blessed air finally reaching her constricted neck.

"Anne, can you hear me?" Lady Matlock's face appeared above her, features tight with worry. "Anne, dear, speak to me."

"I am sorry," Elizabeth whispered. "I do not know what came over me."

"This is precisely what I warned would happen," Lady Catherine's voice cut across the room with sharp accusation. "London is too much for her delicate constitution. The air, the noise, the constant stimulation. We should never have come. I am taking her back to Rosings immediately."

No! The word screamed through Elizabeth's mind with such force that she nearly spoke it aloud. She could not go back to Rosings now, not when the wedding was tomorrow and Jane had the potion almost ready. If Lady Catherine dragged her back to Kent, any chance of reversal would be lost completely.

"Please," Elizabeth managed, forcing more strength into Anne's weak voice. "Please, Mama. I want to stay for the wedding. I want to see Darcy married. It is important to me."

Lady Catherine's face appeared in her blurred vision, expression cycling between displeasure and reluctant compassion.

"You are clearly unwell. Your health must take precedence over social obligations."

"I will rest tonight and be perfectly well tomorrow," Elizabeth insisted, putting every scrap of Anne's supposed attachment to Darcy into her tone. "I want to see my cousin married. Please do not deny me this one thing."

The appeal struck its target. Lady Catherine's expression softened fractionally, her hand reaching out to touch Anne's cheek with unexpected gentleness. "Very well. But if you show any sign of distress tomorrow, we leave immediately after the ceremony. I will not risk your health for the sake of appearances."

"Thank you, Mama," Elizabeth whispered, relief flooding through her.

Lady Matlock had been conferring quietly with her husband near the door. She returned now, settling into a chair beside the sofa with determined expression. "Anne will stay in tonight and rest completely. No more excitement, no visitors. Just quiet and calm to restore her strength for tomorrow."

"I should cancel my engagement," Lady Catherine said, though reluctance coloured her tone. "Mrs. Drummond will understand if I send word that Anne requires my attendance."

"Nonsense," Lady Matlock replied with gentle firmness. "I will stay with Anne myself. You go to your friend's soirée; you have so few opportunities to socialise with your London friends, do not miss this one. There is no need for both of us to hover over the poor girl. I promise you, I will take excellent care of her."

Lady Catherine hesitated, clearly torn between social obligation and maternal concern. Finally, she nodded with visible reluctance. "Very well. But send for me immediately if her condition worsens. I can be back within the half hour."

"Of course," Lady Matlock agreed, already gesturing to the footman hovering near the door. "Have Miss de Bourgh's chamber prepared immediately. Extra pillows, fresh water, and a good fire. She is to have complete quiet and rest."

Elizabeth allowed herself to be helped upstairs, Lady Matlock supporting her weight while Mrs. Jenkinson appeared from somewhere to flutter anxiously on the other side. They settled her into the bed, pillows propped behind Anne's back and blankets tucked around her legs.

Lady Catherine appeared in the doorway. She crossed to the bed and placed a cool hand against Elizabeth's forehead, her expression softening.

"Rest, my dear," Lady Catherine said, her voice carrying genuine tenderness beneath its usual commanding tone. "All will be well. You will see Darcy married tomorrow, and then we shall return to Kent where the air is better for your health."

She departed with rustling silk and fading perfume, leaving Elizabeth alone with Lady Matlock and Mrs. Jenkinson. Elizabeth closed her eyes and felt despair settle over her like a suffocating blanket.

Tomorrow. The wedding was tomorrow, and she still had no idea how to save herself.

Mrs. Jenkinson moved about the chamber, adjusting pillows that needed no adjustment and checking the fire that burned perfectly well on its own. Elizabeth watched through half-closed eyes, aware that the companion's fussing had nothing to do with genuine concern and everything to do with surveillance. Mrs. Jenkinson was watching her, had been watching her all evening with that sharp, assessing gaze that suggested she suspected something.

Lady Matlock sat in a chair near the window, embroidery ignored in her lap while she studied Elizabeth with maternal concern that felt genuine and therefore painful. She had been nothing but kind since Elizabeth arrived at Matlock House. Had treated Anne with respect and affection, had intervened to reduce Mrs. Jenkinson's overprotective hovering, had created space for Elizabeth to breathe.

"Miss Anne should take her evening tonic," Mrs. Jenkinson said, moving to the dressing table where several bottles stood in neat array. "It will help her sleep and restore her strength for tomorrow's exertions."

Elizabeth's stomach clenched with alarm. The tonic. The same draught Mrs. Jenkinson had been administering ever since Elizabeth woke up in Anne's body, the one that sent her straight to sleep and left Elizabeth fuzzy and compliant when she woke. She could not afford that tomorrow, not when she needed all her wits about her.

"I do not think I require it tonight," Elizabeth said carefully, keeping Anne's voice soft but adding firmness she hoped would not seem out of character. "I feel quite settled already. I will sleep well enough without it."

Mrs. Jenkinson's expression tightened fractionally, her hand remaining on the bottle. "Forgive me, Miss Anne, but you know the tonic is essential for managing your delicate nerves. Your collapse at dinner demonstrates how overwrought you have become. The tonic will calm you and ensure proper rest."

"Anne said she does not want it," Lady Matlock interjected, her tone carrying gentle reproach. "Surely if Anne feels well enough without it, there is no need to force medicine upon her."

Mrs. Jenkinson's jaw tightened further, but she inclined her head with stiff acknowledgement. "Of course, my lady. I merely wish to ensure Miss Anne's comfort and wellbeing. That has always been my sole concern."

She set down the bottle but remained near the dressing table, her posture suggesting she had not given up the battle entirely. Elizabeth watched her through lowered lashes, saw the calculation in the companion's eyes, the weighing of options and strategies. Mrs. Jenkinson knew something was wrong. And Mrs. Jenkinson was loyal to Anne above all else, devoted to protecting her charge even when that meant enabling her worst impulses.

If Mrs. Jenkinson realised Elizabeth was planning something, if she suspected any threat to Anne's stolen happiness, she would act. Would simply drug Elizabeth thoroughly enough that she could not possibly interfere with tomorrow's wedding. Or perhaps tell Anne, who would carry out her threat to poison Elizabeth to ensure she could never be a threat again.

Elizabeth could not afford to have Mrs. Jenkinson free to sabotage their plans.

Which left only one option, risky though it might be. Much as she despised the notion, she was going to have to repay Lady Matlock's kindness with manipulation and half-truths.

But she had no choice. Mrs. Jenkinson represented a threat that Elizabeth could not afford to ignore, not when Jane was brewing the reversal potion and tomorrow's wedding loomed like an execution date.

"Aunt," Elizabeth said, giving Lady Matlock a pleading look. "I wonder if I might speak with you privately. There is something I need to tell you."

Lady Matlock's expression shifted to one of immediate concern mixed with curiosity. "Of course, dear. Mrs. Jenkinson, would you give us a moment?"

Mrs. Jenkinson's face went rigid with affront. "Surely anything Miss Anne needs to discuss can be said in my presence. I am her companion. Her confidante. There should be no secrets between us."

"Nevertheless," Lady Matlock said, her voice taking on steel beneath its courtesy, "Anne has requested privacy. Please leave us."

For a moment, Elizabeth thought Mrs. Jenkinson might refuse outright. The companion's hands clenched at her sides, her expression cycling through emotions that ranged from outrage to calculation. Finally, she executed a stiff curtsy and moved towards the door, but her backward glance carried warning.

The door closed behind Mrs. Jenkinson with more force than strictly necessary. Lady Matlock waited until the companion's footsteps faded down the corridor before turning her full attention to Elizabeth.

"What is it, dear? You look quite serious."

Elizabeth took a breath, steeling her nerves for what came next. This was a gamble. If Lady Matlock did not believe her, if she dismissed the accusation as the delusions of an overwrought invalid, the consequences could be disastrous. But Elizabeth had watched Lady Matlock these past days, had seen her kindness and intelligence. If anyone would believe the truth, it was this woman.

"Aunt, I need to tell you something about Mrs. Jenkinson," Elizabeth said, keeping Anne's voice steady. "Something I have been too frightened to speak of before, but I can no longer remain silent."

Lady Matlock leaned forwards. "Go on."

"Mrs. Jenkinson has been drugging me," Elizabeth said, the words emerging with quiet conviction. "That tonic she gives me every evening. It is not simply a sleeping draught or a tonic for my nerves. It makes me foggy and compliant, unable to think clearly or assert my own wishes."

Lady Matlock's face had gone very still, her eyes hard with building fury. "That is a serious accusation, Anne. Are you quite certain?"

"I am certain," Elizabeth replied, putting every scrap of conviction she possessed into Anne's soft voice. "Please, Aunt. Look at the bottles on the dressing table. I think you will find that what she has been giving me is far stronger than any simple sleeping draught."

Lady Matlock rose from her chair immediately, crossing to the dressing table where Mrs. Jenkinson's carefully arranged bottles stood in neat array. She selected the one Mrs. Jenkinson had reached for earlier, pulling the stopper and bringing the bottle to her nose. Her expression transformed as she inhaled, her features going rigid with an anger that made Elizabeth's heart stutter.

"Good God," Lady Matlock breathed, setting down that bottle and reaching for another. She smelled each in turn, her fury mounting with each inhalation. "This is laudanum. Concentrated enough to fell a horse. And this one contains valerian mixed with something else I cannot identify. Anne, how long has she been giving you these?"

"Every evening for as long as I can remember," Elizabeth said, which was technically true. "She says they are for my health, for my delicate nerves. But they make me so fuzzy I can barely think, barely remember one day from the next."

Lady Matlock set down the bottles with hands that shook with suppressed rage. She moved to the bell pull and yanked it with enough force that Elizabeth worried it might separate from the wall entirely.

A maid appeared within seconds, her eyes widening at Lady Matlock's expression. "My lady?"

"Fetch Mrs. Jenkinson immediately," Lady Matlock commanded. "And send Lord Matlock to me as well. This matter requires his attention."

The maid fled with visible relief. Elizabeth remained in the bed, her heart hammering with a mixture of triumph and anxiety. She had set events in motion that could not be reversed. Had gambled everything on Lady Matlock's willingness to believe her and act decisively.

Mrs. Jenkinson appeared in the doorway with Lord Matlock close behind her, the companion's expression showing wariness mixed with affront. "You sent for me, my lady?"

"I did," Lady Matlock replied, her tone cold enough to frost glass. She gestured to the bottles on the dressing table. "Would you care to explain what you have been giving my niece?"

Mrs. Jenkinson's face went carefully blank. "The tonics prescribed for Miss Anne's delicate constitution by her doctors. Sleeping draughts and nerve soothers, nothing more."

"Nothing more," Lady Matlock repeated, her voice dropping to dangerous quiet. "Mrs. Jenkinson, I have just examined those bottles. The concentrations you have been administering would render a healthy adult insensible. For someone of Anne's frail constitution, these dosages are nothing short of poisonous. You have been systematically drugging my niece into compliance."

Lord Matlock had moved to the dressing table during this exchange, examining the bottles with increasing alarm. His expression darkened as he smelled each in turn and examined the labels, holding them close to the candle to read them.

"This is unconscionable," Lord Matlock said, his voice carrying the hard edge of someone accustomed to command. "Mrs. Jenkinson, you are confined to your quarters immediately. You will not leave your room until after tomorrow's wedding, at which point I will discuss your continued employment in my sister's household."

Mrs. Jenkinson's face had gone white, her hands clutching at her skirts. "You do not understand. Miss Anne requires careful management. Her mother entrusted her to my care, and I have only ever acted in her best interests."

"By drugging her into submission?" Lady Matlock demanded, her fury breaking through her usual courtesy. "By rendering her too foggy to think or speak for herself? That is not care, Mrs. Jenkinson. That is abuse disguised as devotion."

"The only reason I am not turning you out tonight is that you are my sister's employee, not mine," Lord Matlock added. "I will take the matter up with her after the wedding, but until then I will not have my niece subjected to such treatment under my roof."

He gestured to the footman hovering in the doorway. "Escort Mrs. Jenkinson to her quarters and ensure she remains there until further notice. Post someone outside her door to ensure she does not leave. She is not to communicate with my sister, or anyone else, until I give the order otherwise."

Mrs. Jenkinson drew herself up with whatever dignity she could muster. "Lady Catherine entrusted Miss Anne to my care specifically! She knows that I have always acted in her daughter's best interests."

"Then Lady Catherine and I will have words about that matter," Lady Matlock replied, her voice still carrying that dangerous quiet. "Get out of my sight, Mrs. Jenkinson. Before I forget myself entirely and say things that cannot be unsaid."

The footman took Mrs. Jenkinson's elbow firmly, guiding her from the room despite her continued protests. Her voice faded down the corridor, proclaiming her innocence and devotion to anyone who would listen.

The door closed behind them, leaving Elizabeth alone with Lord and Lady Matlock. Silence settled over the chamber, broken only by the crackling fire.

Lady Matlock returned to the chair beside the bed, her fury giving way to concern as she reached out to take Elizabeth's hand. "My dear girl. I am so sorry. How you must have suffered."

Elizabeth felt tears gather in her eyes, genuine emotion breaking through. Lady Matlock's kindness, her immediate belief and decisive action, struck Elizabeth with unexpected force. This was what protection felt like. What it meant to have someone in authority who actually listened and acted on one's behalf.

"Thank you," Elizabeth whispered, letting tears spill down Anne's cheeks. "Thank you for believing me, Aunt."

"Of course I believe you," Lady Matlock replied, squeezing Elizabeth's hand with gentle warmth. "And I promise you, Mrs. Jenkinson will not trouble you again. Not tonight, not tomorrow, not ever if I have anything to say about it."

Lord Matlock cleared his throat, clearly uncomfortable with the emotional display but moved nonetheless. "Rest now,

Anne. My wife will stay with you tonight to ensure you are not disturbed. And tomorrow, you will attend Darcy's wedding without fear of interference from that dreadful woman."

They settled Elizabeth more comfortably, Lady Matlock arranging pillows with tender care while Lord Matlock attended to the fire. Elizabeth closed her weary eyes and felt something that might have been hope stir in her chest.

Jane had what she needed to complete the potion, and Mrs. Jenkinson was neutralised. Locked away where she could not warn Anne or sabotage Jane's plan. One threat removed, one obstacle cleared from their path.

Tomorrow still seemed impossible. But perhaps, with Mrs. Jenkinson confined and unable to interfere, impossible might become merely extremely difficult.

Elizabeth would take those odds.

She had no other choice.

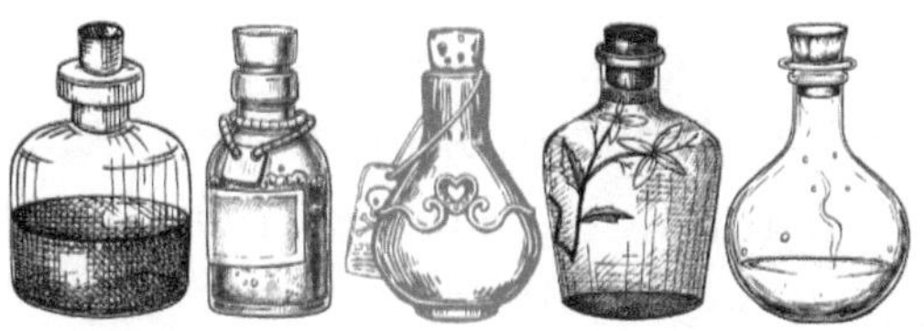

Chapter Twenty-Six

THE CANDLE HAD BURNED down to a stub, its flame guttering in the pool of wax that had spread across the edge of the Gardiner study desk. Jane blinked at it with eyes that felt full of sand, her vision blurring as exhaustion pulled at her consciousness. The grimoire lay open before her, its cramped handwriting swimming in and out of focus.

The clock showed half past four in the morning. Jane had been working without pause for hours, following the grimoire's instructions with the meticulous care of someone who knew that a single mistake would doom her sister forever. The potion simmered in a small brass pot over a spirit lamp, its surface rippling with opalescent swirls. The scent it gave off was strange, neither pleasant nor entirely foul, something that made the back of her throat itch.

She added the final measure of pearl powder, stirring clockwise seven times as the grimoire instructed. The potion's colour shifted from milky white to pale amber, then settled into something that reminded Jane uncomfortably of old blood diluted with water. Her hand shook badly enough that the stirring rod clinked against the pot's rim.

Three more minutes at a gentle simmer, then it would be ready. Jane set down the stirring rod and pressed the heels of her hands against her closed eyes. Her back ached from hours bent over the desk, and her neck had developed a persistent crick. But she could not stop now. Could not rest when Elizabeth's entire future hung on the successful completion of this wicked draught.

The three minutes passed with agonising slowness. Jane watched the potion bubble gently, its surface throwing off faint vapours that made the air shimmer like heat rising from summer pavement. When the time elapsed, she removed it from the flame with shaking hands and set it aside to cool, her heart hammering with exhausted triumph.

She had done it. The reversal potion was complete.

Jane pulled two small glass phials from her pocket, their stoppers tight against the precious emptiness within. She had acquired them yesterday from the apothecary, claiming she needed them for a homemade perfume.

The potion had cooled enough to handle. Jane lifted the pot with both hands and poured carefully, watching the amber liquid stream into the first phial. Half the potion went into that one, for Anne to drink. The other half she poured into the second phial, for Elizabeth trapped in Anne's failing body.

Jane stoppered both phials with fingers that fumbled despite her care. She wrapped them together in Colonel Fitzwilliam's handkerchief, the fine linen still carrying a faint trace of his cologne. The wrapped phials went into her dress pocket, settling against her hip with weight that felt far heavier than their actual mass.

Done. It was done. All that remained was to administer the potions at the wedding breakfast, somehow convincing Anne to drink. The impossibility of that task pressed down on Jane's shoulders, but she pushed it aside with grim determination. She would find a way.

The house lay silent around her as she climbed the stair, exhaustion dragging at her with every step. At last, she reached the chamber she was sharing with Mary and collapsed onto the bed without bothering to undress properly, merely loosening her stays enough to breathe. Sleep claimed her within seconds.

Morning arrived far too soon, grey light filtering through the curtains to strike Jane's closed eyelids. She woke with a gasp, her heart racing as she remembered what day this was. The wedding. Elizabeth's wedding to Darcy, except it was not Elizabeth at all but Anne wearing her stolen face and body.

Jane pushed herself upright, every muscle protesting the movement. She felt as though she had been beaten, her exhaustion so complete that even sitting up required conscious effort. But there was no time to rest. The wedding was at three o'clock.

The phials in her pocket bumped against her hip as she moved, their presence a constant reminder of what she must accomplish today. She checked them to ensure the stoppers remained secure, breathing a sigh of relief to find they were.

Breakfast proved an ordeal Jane barely remembered afterwards. The impostor sat at the table in Elizabeth's body, eating with delicate bites and making cheerful conversation that set Jane's teeth on edge. Anne had perfected her imitation now, had learned to speak and move and smile exactly as Elizabeth would. Only Jane could see the wrongness beneath the performance.

"Are you quite well, Jane?" the false Elizabeth asked, her voice carrying concern that would have fooled anyone who did not know the truth. "You look rather pale this morning." Anne had played her role well the past few days, Jane had to concede; though she had been quieter and more compliant with Mrs. Bennet's demands than the real Elizabeth had been, everyone but Jane had probably attributed that change to nerves over the upcoming wedding. If Anne succeeded in her goal, in marrying Mr. Darcy and leaving for Pemberley, Jane was quite sure none of the Bennet family would ever see her again. Anne would cut all ties without a second thought.

"I am well enough," Jane replied, forcing herself to meet those familiar eyes that held an unfamiliar intelligence. "Merely tired. I did not sleep well last night."

"Nerves, I expect," Mrs. Bennet declared from her end of the table. "My Jane has always been so sensitive. But you must eat something, dear. You will need your strength for today's festivities."

Jane managed a few bites of toast that tasted like ashes, washing them down with tea that had gone cold. Across from her, Anne preened in Elizabeth's stolen flesh, clearly savouring every moment of her triumph.

After breakfast, Jane followed the impostor upstairs to help her dress for the ceremony. The wedding gown hung on the wardrobe door, pale cream silk with tiny pearls stitched on the bodice. It had cost more than Jane's entire wardrobe combined. Lady Matlock had insisted on providing it, her generosity meaning that Anne would marry Darcy in borrowed finery to match her borrowed body.

"Help me with my stays," Anne commanded, then caught herself and softened her tone. "If you would be so kind, Jane. I confess I am all nerves this morning."

Jane moved behind her and began to assist, despite the rage that coiled in her chest. This woman had stolen her sister's life, had condemned Elizabeth to die slowly in a failing body, had manipulated circumstances to marry the man who loved Elizabeth. And now Jane had to help her dress for the wedding and pretend nothing was wrong.

"You must be very happy," Jane made herself say, keeping her voice neutral. "Marrying Mr. Darcy."

"Oh, I am," Anne breathed, her voice taking on a smugness that made Jane want to strike her. "I am the happiest woman alive. Mrs. Darcy. Mrs. Fitzwilliam Darcy of Pemberley. It sounds wonderful, does it not?"

"Wonderful," Jane echoed flatly. She tightened the stays with perhaps more force than necessary, satisfaction flickering through her when Anne gasped slightly.

Jane helped her into the chemise, then the petticoats, layering them with care. The wedding gown came next, its silk whispering as Jane lifted it over Anne's head and settled it onto her shoulders. The bodice required careful fastening, each tiny pearl button threaded into its buttonhole. Jane breathed slowly, fighting her simmering anger as she patiently fixed each button in place.

"Will you brush my hair?" Anne asked, settling before the dressing table mirror with satisfaction evident in every line of her stolen posture. "You always did it so well."

Jane picked up the brush and began working it through the dark curls that were Elizabeth's but not Elizabeth's, each stroke requiring her to suppress the urge to yank hard enough to hurt.

Anne watched her reflection with obvious pleasure, admiring the way the wedding gown displayed Elizabeth's figure.

"I look beautiful," Anne murmured. "I will be Mrs. Darcy, and I am beautiful, and I am happy."

Jane said nothing, continuing to brush with steady strokes while fury and grief warred in her chest. She pinned Elizabeth's hair into an elaborate arrangement, her fingers working with the skill of long practice despite their trembling. Pearl pins went in to secure the style.

A knock at the door interrupted the grooming. Mr. Bennet entered when Elizabeth called out acknowledgement, his expression puzzled as he took in his supposed daughter's reflection and her smug smile. Jane saw his confusion, the way his gaze lingered on details that were not quite right. He, too, suspected something. Anne had been careful to avoid both of them these last days, presumably aware that the greatest danger of exposure came from the two who loved Elizabeth best.

"Well, Lizzy," Mr. Bennet said, his tone carrying uncertainty beneath its attempted cheerfulness. "You look very fine indeed. Are you ready to become Mrs. Darcy?"

"Oh yes, Papa," Anne replied, rising to embrace him with enthusiasm that made Mr. Bennet's eyebrows rise. Elizabeth had never been particularly demonstrative with physical affection, preferring a quick handclasp or kiss to a tight hug. "I am more ready than I have ever been for anything."

Mr. Bennet patted her back awkwardly, clearly unsettled. He looked to Jane over Anne's shoulder, his expression questioning, but Jane could only offer a small shrug.

"The carriage is ready," Mr. Bennet announced, extracting himself from Anne's embrace with visible relief. "We should depart soon to ensure we arrive in good time."

Jane climbed into the carriage last, settling onto the seat across from Anne and Mr. Bennet. The vehicle lurched into motion, wheels rattling over London's cobblestones while Jane watched the streets pass by outside the window and tried to hold in her nausea.

St George's, Hanover Square, rose before them with its pale stone façade catching the afternoon sun, its columns standing like sentinels. The carriage rolled to a stop, and Jane descended with legs that felt disconnected from her body.

The church's interior struck her with its soaring height, its ceiling arching overhead in elegant curves. Light streamed through tall windows, illuminating dust motes that drifted lazy through air heavy with the scent of beeswax and flowers. White roses adorned the ends of pews, their perfume cloying in Jane's throat as she moved down the aisle behind Anne and Mr. Bennet.

Guests had already assembled, filling perhaps two dozen pews. The Matlocks occupied prominent positions at the front, Lady Matlock watching the bride's approach with warm approval while Lord Matlock's expression showed more reserve. Colonel Fitzwilliam caught Jane's eye and smiled. She struggled to muster a smile in response, and saw the questions in his expression before she looked away. She could not think of him now.

Jane took her place in the front pew on the bride's side, her hands folded in her lap with fingers that would not quite stay still. Her gaze moved across the aisle to where a pretty blonde girl who must be Georgiana Darcy sat wreathed in smiles. Beyond her, Lady Catherine sat rigid with disapproval, and there, beside her, sat the real Elizabeth trapped in Anne's failing body.

Their eyes met across the narrow space. Elizabeth looked terrible, Anne's face showing pallor that went beyond mere illness. But her gaze held her fierce intelligence and desperate hope mixed with terror as she looked at Jane. A question passed between them without words. *Do you have it? Can we do this?*

Jane's hand moved to her pocket in answer, pressing briefly against the wrapped phials before returning to her lap. Elizabeth's eyes closed with relief so profound that Jane saw tears gather beneath the pale lashes.

Movement at the front of the church drew Jane's attention. Darcy had entered through a side door, a smile on his face as he walked to his place before the altar, greeting the waiting clergyman.

He loved Elizabeth. Loved the woman he thought he was marrying, unaware that the bride processing towards him wore a stolen face and carried a black heart beneath the cream silk gown. Jane wanted to shout the truth, wanted to stand and declare the deception. But who would believe her? They would think her mad. Would remove her from the church while the ceremony continued without interruption.

The organ swelled with music. Anne began her walk down the aisle on Mr. Bennet's arm, moving with Elizabeth's natural grace made triumphant by Anne's victory. She looked beautiful. Looked exactly like a bride should look, radiant with happiness and love. No one watching would suspect that beneath that lovely exterior lurked a woman who had stolen everything she wore, including the body that carried her forwards.

Jane watched Darcy's face as Anne approached. Saw confusion flicker there, quickly suppressed. Something about his bride's manner was not quite right, not quite what he expected. But love overcame uncertainty, his expression softening as Anne reached his side and Mr. Bennet placed her hand in his.

The vicar began speaking, his voice carrying through the church with calm authority. Jane heard the words without processing them, her attention fixed on the couple before the altar. Anne smiled up at Darcy with Elizabeth's face, her expression so perfect an imitation that Jane felt nausea rise in her throat.

"If any person here present knows of any lawful impediment to this marriage," the vicar intoned, his gaze sweeping the assembled guests, "let them speak now, or forever hold their peace."

The silence that followed stretched taut as a bowstring. Jane's throat closed around words that wanted to break free, accusations that pressed against her teeth demanding release. She knows of an impediment. The greatest impediment possible. The bride was not who she claimed to be.

But Jane's lips remained pressed together, her hands clenched in her lap with nails digging into her palms. Speaking now would accomplish nothing except her own removal from the church and the loss of the one chance they had. Better to wait, to let the ceremony proceed, to act during the wedding breakfast when she might actually succeed in reversing this terrible wrong.

The moment passed. The vicar continued.

"Fitzwilliam Darcy," the vicar said, turning to Darcy, "wilt thou have this woman to be thy wedded wife, to live together according to God's law in the holy estate of matrimony? Wilt thou love her, comfort her, honour and keep her, in sickness and in health, and forsaking all others, keep thee only unto her, so long as ye both shall live?"

"I will," Darcy replied, his voice steady despite the uncertainty that lingered in his eyes.

The vicar turned to Anne. "Elizabeth Bennet, wilt thou have this man to be thy wedded husband, to live together according to God's law in the holy estate of matrimony? Wilt thou love him, comfort him, honour and keep him, in sickness and in health, and forsaking all others, keep thee only unto him, so long as ye both shall live?"

"I will," Anne said, and Jane heard triumph beneath the words. "Oh, I will."

The vows continued, each word binding them more tightly together in law. Darcy repeated his own vows with conviction, his love for Elizabeth evident in every carefully pronounced word.

"I, Elizabeth Bennet, take thee, Fitzwilliam Darcy, to be my wedded husband," Anne said, her voice clear and sweet. "To have and to hold from this day forwards, for better, for worse, for richer, for poorer, in sickness and in health, to love and to cherish, till death us do part, according to God's holy ordinance, and thereto I give thee my troth."

The ring came next, Darcy sliding it onto Anne's finger with hands that trembled slightly. Gold gleamed against Elizabeth's stolen flesh. Jane watched the metal circle settle into place and felt something in her chest crack. Even if they managed to reverse the body swap, to give Elizabeth back her own face and form, what then? She would be married to Mr. Darcy, a man she had never liked.

Better that than dying in a failing body, Jane told herself, looking down so she did not have to witness Anne's smugly triumphant smile.

"I now pronounce you man and wife," the vicar declared. "Those whom God has joined together, let no man put asunder."

Done. It was done. The marriage was legal and binding, and as Jane looked across the aisle and met her sister's eyes, she saw the shared awareness that a point of no return had been passed.

Darcy leaned down to kiss his bride, the gesture gentle and reverent. Anne returned the kiss with enthusiasm that made Darcy pull back slightly, surprise evident in his expression before he masked it with a smile.

The organ swelled again, marking their procession back down the aisle. Jane watched them pass, watched Anne nod graciously to guests who beamed at the happy couple. Watched Darcy's confusion war with his joy, his instincts telling him something was wrong even as his heart celebrated.

The real Elizabeth remained in her pew, her frail body slumped with despair. Their eyes met again as Jane rose to follow the wedding party from the church, and Jane gave the smallest nod she could manage. Soon. This would be over soon.

Outside, carriages waited to convey the wedding party to Matlock House for the breakfast. Jane climbed into one with her mother and younger sisters, their excited chatter washing over her without penetrating the focus that had settled over her thoughts.

The streets of London rolled past outside the window. Jane's exhaustion had transformed into something sharper, adrenaline cutting through the fog to leave her thoughts crystal clear despite her body's desperate need for rest. She reviewed the plan she had come up with that morning as she helped Anne prepare for the wedding. It was simple enough. Approach Darcy with wine, suggest he share it with his bride. The impostor would drink it eagerly, never suspecting that her own magic had been turned against her. And across the room, Elizabeth would drink from her phial simultaneously, their essences trading back to their rightful bodies.

Simple. But terrifying. And very likely, the only chance they would ever have.

The carriage rolled to a stop before Matlock House. Jane moved with them, one hand pressed against her pocket where salvation or disaster waited in two small glass phials.

Matlock House's drawing rooms had been transformed for the wedding breakfast, their usual restraint giving way to celebration that manifested in white roses and trailing ivy, in tables laden with delicacies, in French champagne flowing freely among guests.

Darcy and his new bride occupied the room's centre, surrounded by well-wishers. Anne accepted their attentions with grace that looked almost genuine, her performance now so polished that Jane wondered if anyone else noticed the subtle wrongness.

Darcy remained close to his bride's side, his hand resting at the small of her back in a gesture that spoke of possession and protection both. But Jane saw the confusion that kept flickering across his face when Anne laughed too loudly at someone's jest, or leaned against him with familiarity that Elizabeth would never have displayed in public.

Jane set down her untouched champagne and moved towards the refreshment table, her heart hammering against her ribs. A footman stood ready with a decanter of wine, dark red that caught the afternoon light. Jane accepted a glass from him with a smile that felt like it might crack her face.

She turned away from the table and reached into her pocket, her movements slow and careful. She had already slipped one of the phials into Elizabeth's hand, under cover of supposedly greeting Miss Anne de Bourgh as a new relative. The second phial came out in her hand, and she concealed it against her skirt while working the stopper free. The stopper came loose with resistance that made her breath catch.

Jane tilted the phial over the wine glass, watching amber liquid pour into dark red. The potion disappeared into the wine without trace, no colour change or unusual scent to betray its presence. She stoppered the empty phial and returned it to her pocket, her hands shaking badly enough now that wine sloshed against the inside of the glass.

Steady, she told herself. *You must be steady for this final part.*

She took a breath and moved towards where Darcy stood watching his new bride being embraced by Mrs. Bennet, weaving between clusters of guests with the glass held carefully in both hands.

"Mr. Darcy," Jane said as she approached, and was relieved to hear her voice emerge steady. "Might I have a word?"

Darcy turned towards her with a warm smile. "Miss Bennet. Jane, my new sister. Of course."

Jane extended the wine glass towards him. "This is Elizabeth's favourite vintage. My uncle sourced a bottle especially for today. Perhaps you would give it to her. She has drunk little today, perhaps a touch of nerves." She forced a fond smile.

Darcy took the glass from her hand, his fingers brushing hers briefly. "That is very kind of you, Jane. Thank you."

Jane stepped back, watching as Darcy turned to his bride. Anne had been engaged in conversation with Mrs. Bennet and

Mrs. Gardiner but abandoned it readily when her new husband approached, her face lighting with pleasure.

"My dear," Darcy said, offering her the wine glass. "Your favourite wine."

Anne looked briefly confused, before obviously realising that it must be *Elizabeth's* favourite wine. Reaching out, she accepted the glass with hands that did not hesitate. "Oh, how thoughtful, my love!"

She raised the glass to her lips and drank deeply, the wine disappearing in several swallows that left the glass half empty. Anne made an appreciative sound before looking back at Mrs. Gardiner, who had just asked her a question. "Why yes, indeed, we shall be leaving for Pemberley very soon," she said.

Jane's gaze cut across the crowded room to where the real Elizabeth sat in a chair near the wall, Lady Catherine hovering over her with continued concern. Elizabeth had been watching Jane, had seen the exchange with Darcy and understood what it meant. Their eyes met across the distance, and Jane gave the smallest nod she could manage.

Now. Take it now.

Elizabeth turned slightly away from Lady Catherine's attention and raised her hand to her mouth, the motion quick and furtive but successful.

Done. Both potions administered. Both women had drunk simultaneously, or near enough.

There would be a few minutes, according to what Elizabeth had told her about the first time she drank the draught. A few more minutes before the potions took effect and the reversal began.

Jane remained where she stood, frozen in place while her heart counted off seconds. Around her, the wedding breakfast continued its cheerful progress. No one noticed Jane's stillness, her white face, the way her hands had begun to shake.

Anne stood beside Darcy, accepting congratulations from Colonel Fitzwilliam with grace that would have fooled anyone. She laughed at something the Colonel said, her voice Elizabeth's voice but carrying notes that were wrong.

Across the room, Elizabeth had slumped slightly in her chair, Lady Catherine's exclamation of concern sounding above the crowd's chatter.

Then Anne's hand went to her forehead, confusion crossing her stolen features. She swayed slightly, her free hand reaching for Darcy's arm to steady herself. Darcy caught her immediately, concern replacing the happiness on his face.

"Elizabeth?" His voice carried across the room with worry that silenced nearby conversations. "Elizabeth, what is wrong?"

Anne's eyes widened, panic flashing across her face as she realised something was happening. Something she had not anticipated, could not control. Her mouth opened as though to speak, but only a small sound emerged.

Then her knees buckled, and she collapsed entirely. Darcy caught her before she struck the floor, his arms supporting her limp weight while her head lolled against his shoulder. The wine glass she had been holding fell from nerveless fingers and shattered against the polished floor, red wine spreading across pale wood like blood.

Gasps erupted around them. Guests pressed forwards, concern and curiosity mixing on faces that had moments ago shown nothing but celebration. Lady Matlock appeared at Darcy's side with remarkable speed, her hand going to Anne's forehead while she issued commands for smelling salts and cold water.

But Jane's attention had already moved to the other side of the room, where a louder commotion had erupted. Lady Catherine's voice rose above the crowd's murmur, sharp with alarm that bordered on panic.

"Anne! Anne, speak to me! Someone fetch a physician at once!"

Elizabeth had collapsed as well, slumping into Lady Catherine's supporting arms. The older woman lowered her daughter to the floor with surprising gentleness, her face twisted with fear. Jane moved forwards without conscious decision, pushing through guests who blocked her path. She needed to see, needed to know if the reversal had worked or if she had just poisoned both women.

Darcy had lifted his wife in his arms, her head hanging back over his elbow in a way that made Jane's stomach clench with fear. Darcy's expression showed terror beneath his usual composure, his voice breaking as he spoke his wife's name over and over without response.

"Take her upstairs," Lady Matlock commanded. "The blue guest room. Quickly, before she wakes and finds herself surrounded by gawking crowds."

Darcy moved towards the door with his burden held carefully against his chest, his long strides eating distance. The crowd parted before him, shocked faces watching the master of Pemberley carry his new bride from the room mere minutes after their wedding breakfast had begun.

Across the room, Lady Catherine had been joined by Lord Matlock. Lady Catherine's face had gone white beneath her rouge, her usual commanding presence transformed into maternal terror.

"My daughter," Lady Catherine kept repeating, her voice thick with tears. "My daughter, please. Someone help my daughter."

Colonel Fitzwilliam arrived, speaking soothingly as he lifted his cousin's frail form into his arms. Jane watched them disappear into the entrance hall, heard Lady Catherine's voice fading as they too moved towards the stairs.

Then she was alone in a room that had erupted into chaos, guests clustering in groups to exclaim and speculate. Mrs. Bennet had dissolved into hysterics, her wailing carrying over all other sounds while Mary tried ineffectually to calm her.

Jane's legs gave way beneath her, her exhaustion finally winning the battle. She caught herself against a nearby chair, her strength barely sufficient to keep her upright.

She had done it. Had actually done it. Had administered the reversal potion to both parties and watched them both collapse in the same instant, their essences presumably trading places just as Anne's grimoire had promised.

But had it worked? Were Elizabeth and Anne now returned to their rightful bodies? Or had Jane simply poisoned both women, condemning them to death or permanent unconsciousness through dark magic she did not properly understand?

She would not know until they woke. All Jane could do now was wait, and hope, and pray that Anne's magic had not betrayed them at the final moment.

Chapter Twenty-Seven

THE CEILING ABOVE HER was unfamiliar, cream plaster with elegant mouldings that caught shadows from firelight somewhere to her left. Elizabeth blinked at it, her vision swimming slightly as consciousness returned in slow waves. Her body felt strange, not in the way it had felt strange for days now, but in a way that was both foreign and deeply, profoundly right. She lifted one hand before her face and saw strong, capable fingers, a hand she recognised, skin that belonged to her and no one else.

Relief crashed through her with such force that tears sprang to her eyes. She was herself again. Back in her own body, her own flesh, her own bones and blood. The weakness that had plagued her was gone, replaced by strength she had taken for granted her entire life until it was stolen away. Even exhausted as she clearly was, even with her head aching and her stomach churning, she felt better than she had since waking up in Anne's failing flesh.

"Elizabeth?" The voice came from her right, male and worried. "Elizabeth, can you hear me?"

She turned her head, the motion easier than any movement had been in days, and found Darcy sitting in a chair pulled close to the bed. His face showed exhaustion that matched her own, dark circles beneath his eyes and lines of tension around his mouth. Behind him, Jane stood near the window, her hands clasped before her and her expression tight with barely contained emotion. Mrs. Bennet hovered near the foot of the bed, her face red and blotchy from recent weeping.

"It's me," Elizabeth said, directing the words towards Jane rather than Darcy or her mother. Her voice emerged hoarse, her throat raw. "The pet I most wanted as a child was a hedgehog."

Jane's face transformed, relief so profound that it made her sway on her feet. The code words they had agreed upon, proof that Elizabeth was truly Elizabeth and not Anne wearing her face. Jane's eyes filled with tears that spilled over immediately, tracking down her cheeks while a smile broke across her features like sunrise.

"Thank God," Jane whispered, her voice breaking. "Oh, thank God."

Mrs. Bennet surged forwards, her hands reaching for Elizabeth. "Lizzy, my dear girl, you gave us such a fright. Collapsing like that at your own wedding breakfast. What were you thinking, drinking wine on an empty stomach?"

Elizabeth caught Jane's eye over their mother's shoulder and saw understanding pass between them. Jane moved forwards, gently extracting Mrs. Bennet's hands from Elizabeth's person.

"Mama, perhaps you should go down and let everyone know Lizzy is recovering," Jane suggested. "I know Father was worried. Let them know she is awake, and will be just fine shortly. She only fainted."

Mrs. Bennet's face showed conflict, torn between concern for her daughter and the allure of being able to hold forth to the important guests downstairs. Social ambition won, as Jane had clearly known it would. Mrs. Bennet patted Elizabeth's hand one final time before bustling towards the door.

"Very well, but you must send for me immediately if Lizzy takes another turn," Mrs. Bennet commanded, already halfway into the corridor. "A mother knows best in these situations."

The door closed behind her, and Jane turned back to Elizabeth. "I should check on Anne. Make certain the reversal worked for both of you. Mr. Darcy, will you stay with Elizabeth?"

"Of course," Darcy replied, his gaze never leaving Elizabeth's face. Something in his expression made Elizabeth's stomach flutter.

Jane squeezed Elizabeth's hand briefly, her touch conveying support and understanding. Then she was gone as well, leaving Elizabeth alone with her husband. The word struck her with renewed force now that she was back in her own body, now that the marriage was real in ways it had not felt when she was trapped watching Anne speak the vows in her place.

Husband. Darcy was her husband. They were married, bound by law and church and society in ways that could not be undone except by death.

Elizabeth lifted her hands again, studying them in the firelight as though they might disappear if she looked away. Her hands, her wrists, her arms. She touched her face, feeling the familiar contours of nose and cheekbones and jaw. Ran her fingers through her hair, finding it arranged in the elaborate style Jane had created this morning but unmistakably her own dark curls beneath the pearl-tipped pins.

"I am myself," she said aloud, needing to hear the words spoken in her own voice. "I am Elizabeth Bennet." She paused. "Elizabeth Darcy now, I suppose."

Darcy shifted in his chair, leaning forwards with his elbows on his knees and his hands clasped before him. His expression showed patience mixed with confusion, clearly waiting for explanation.

"Elizabeth," he said quietly. "Something is going on, something that I do not understand. Will you not tell me?"

He was owed the truth. He, more than anyone save Elizabeth herself, was a victim of Anne's schemes.

She must tell him everything and hope he did not think her mad – but at least, if he did, she was safely back in her own body.

Elizabeth took a breath and began. The words came haltingly at first, her exhaustion making coherent thought difficult. But she forced herself to continue, to lay out the truth in all its impossible, horrifying detail. Anne's alchemical abilities, learned from her father. The body swap potion, brewed with rare ingredients and activated through simultaneous drinking. Anne's motivations, her resentment and jealousy and desperate desire for the life she believed Elizabeth had squandered. Anne's plan to use another potion on Darcy after the wedding, to ensure his eternal devotion – a potion Sir Lewis de Bourgh had once used to ensnare Lady Catherine for his own.

Darcy listened in grave silence, his face showing shock that slowly transformed into horror. He did not interrupt, did not question or protest the impossibility of what she was describing. He simply sat and listened while Elizabeth's voice grew stronger, her words coming faster as the story poured out.

"She wanted everything I had," Elizabeth finished. "My health, my vitality... your attention. I was simply an obstacle to be removed, a body to be stolen and discarded."

Darcy remained silent for a long moment after she finished speaking, his gaze distant as though reviewing recent events through this new lens. When he finally spoke, his voice carried the one thing Elizabeth had not dared hope for: belief.

"There were tells," he said slowly, his eyes finding hers again. "Things that troubled me, though I could not identify why. The simpering. You have never simpered, Elizabeth, yet she giggled at every jest and leaned against me with constant need for reassurance. You value independence too much for such behaviour."

Elizabeth felt her cheeks heat despite everything.

Darcy continued, his voice growing more certain. "Your insistence on the special licence and marrying in London, instead of from Longbourn, struck me as utterly unlike the Elizabeth I knew, who loved her family deeply. Then, when I suggested instead visiting Longbourn after our wedding trip, to spend time with your family before we departed for Pemberley. You showed no interest. No concern for when you might see your father or Jane again. It all struck me as wrong, but I told myself you were simply caught up in wedding preparations."

Elizabeth watched his hand hover near hers, not quite touching, and felt the weight of everything unsaid pressing down on her chest. The question formed before she could stop it.

"And yet, still you married me." She kept her gaze on his face. "You suspected something was wrong. You knew I was not behaving as myself. And yet you stood before the altar and spoke vows that bound us together."

Darcy's expression shifted, something that looked like guilt crossing his features before he could mask it. He withdrew his hand, settling back in his chair with movements that suggested discomfort. When he spoke, his voice carried careful precision.

"I have been in love with you for so long," he said quietly, his gaze dropping to his clasped hands. "Since Hertfordshire, if I am honest with myself. I have thought of little else but you for months. And when you accepted my proposal, when you agreed to become my wife, I was so grateful, that I did not examine too closely why your manner had changed."

He looked up at her then, his eyes showing vulnerability she had never seen in him before. "I told myself you were nervous about the wedding. That you were perhaps having second thoughts but felt obligated to go through with it regardless. I convinced myself that once we were married, once you had time to know me better, your doubts would fade and you would come to care for me as I cared for you."

The admission struck Elizabeth with unexpected force. She had not truly realised how deeply his feelings ran. Guilt twisted in her stomach.

"But you tried to warn me," Darcy continued, and now his voice carried despair. "Didn't you? When you told me that Elizabeth Bennet did not love me, that she had accepted my proposal only because she felt she had no other choice. You were trying to tell me the truth. That the woman I was about to marry was not who she claimed to be."

His hands tightened on each other until his knuckles showed white. "I need to know, Elizabeth. Did you mean that Anne did not truly love me, or that you yourself did not?"

Elizabeth's chest constricted, her breath catching. She saw the fear in his face, the vulnerability of someone who had risked everything on a hope that might prove false. Her hands twisted in the blanket.

"Anne did not love you," Elizabeth said firmly. "I am quite sure of that. She saw you as a means to an end, just as she saw me, my body, as a tool she could use. You represented everything she had been denied by her failing health. Wealth, certainly, but more than that. Freedom, from Rosings and Lady Catherine's stifling control. You were the ultimate prize that would complete her transformation."

Darcy's expression showed some relief, though tension remained in his shoulders. "And you? What do I represent to you?"

The question hung between them, demanding honesty Elizabeth was not certain she could provide. Her feelings were too complicated, too tangled with recent events to parse clearly.

"I think better of you now than I did before," Elizabeth said carefully, choosing each word. "When I first tried to assess your character, I felt insulted by your manner and convinced of your arrogance. But I have seen more of your character since then. The way you are with your family, when you forget to guard yourself and simply exist as a brother, a cousin, a nephew. You showed more of your feelings to your cousin Anne than you ever did to me, I think. You told Anne how you felt about me when she asked, and perhaps I can understand that, a little."

She paused, gathering courage. "I understand now that you are not at your best amongst strangers, or when you feel you are on display. That your reserve is not pride but discomfort with situations where you do not know the rules or feel you are being judged. That changes how I see many of your past actions, including our first meeting in Hertfordshire."

Darcy's face showed something that might have been hope, tentative and careful. "Then you do not hate me?"

"No," Elizabeth replied, and found the word was true. "I do not hate you. I am not certain what I feel, to be honest. Everything has been so confused, so overwhelming. But I do not hate you, and I do not hate that we are married, even if the circumstances were far from ideal."

Darcy leaned forwards again, his expression showing careful optimism. "That is more than I dared hope for. Given everything that has happened, I would not have blamed you if you wanted the marriage annulled."

"I do not want that," Elizabeth said, surprising herself with the certainty in her voice. She met his gaze directly. "We are married now, and we must make the best of it. But I would hope we might do so honestly, without pretending feelings that do not exist or hiding truths that need to be spoken."

"Agreed," Darcy said quickly, relief evident. "Complete honesty between us, even when the truth is difficult." He hesitated. "So first, I would ask you to tell me why you did not ask me for help before..." He gestured about, indicating the whole situation.

"Mr. Darcy," she said, not unkindly. "When your own cousin told you that Elizabeth Bennet did not love you, you got up and walked away with reproach in your eyes, probably thinking her jealous and lashing out in her pain. Tell me, honestly, how you would have reacted if Anne had told you that Elizabeth Bennet had stolen her body and her life?"

He opened his mouth to say something, and then closed it again, shame washing across his features. "You are right, Elizabeth. I would have thought Anne misguided at best."

"Mad, at worst," Elizabeth said dryly. "I could not risk it. I could not risk telling anyone but Jane, the one person who I knew I could convince with only a few words. By the time I reached her, she already knew something was terribly wrong with the person she thought was her sister."

His face clouded then. "Jane. That matter of your sister and Mr. Bingley. That was one of the things that confounded me most, Elizabeth. When I realised you knew of that and did not hate me. I had no right to interfere in their relationship, and you would have been well within your rights to tell me you never wanted to see my face again, far less gladly accept my courtship."

Elizabeth felt the familiar anger stir at the mention of Jane and Bingley's separation, but it lacked the sharp edge it had carried before. Perhaps because recent events had put such grievances in perspective.

"I am less angry about that now than I was," Elizabeth admitted. "I understand you believed you were protecting your friend from what you saw as an unsuitable connexion. I do not agree with your assessment of my family's worth, but I can comprehend your reasoning."

Darcy's expression showed surprise at this measured response. But there was another question Elizabeth had to ask, something that she could not reconcile with everything she now knew of his character.

"There is another matter, though," Elizabeth continued. "Your treatment of Mr. Wickham. That troubled me almost as much as your interference with Bingley. But again, having come to know you better... I have had time to think, these last few days. I believe there may be more to your dealings with Mr. Wickham than I understand, and I would like you to tell me your side of the story, if you would."

Darcy's entire body tensed at the mention of Wickham's name, his jaw tightening. He looked away from her, his gaze fixing on the fire with intensity. When he spoke, his voice carried carefully controlled fury.

"Wickham is not the man you believe him to be," Darcy said, each word emerging clipped. "Though I confess my own conduct regarding him has not been above reproach. I should have exposed his true character years ago. But I was too proud to make my family's private troubles public, and that pride allowed him to continue his predations unchecked."

Elizabeth waited, her heart beginning to hammer with apprehension.

Darcy took a breath, still not looking at her directly. "Wickham and I grew up together at Pemberley. My father was his godfather, supported his education and took a particular interest in his upbringing. I resented the attention my father paid to him, if I am honest. Wickham had charm I lacked, an easy manner that made people like him immediately. But even as a boy, I sensed something false beneath that charm. Something calculating."

He paused. "When my father died, he left Wickham a legacy of one thousand pounds and the living at Kympton, should he choose to take orders. Wickham claimed he had no interest in the church and asked for three thousand pounds in lieu of the living. I gave it to him gladly, hoping it would sever our connexion forever."

"But it did not," Elizabeth said quietly.

"No," Darcy agreed. "He gambled away the money within three years and returned to demand the living after all, claiming I had promised it to him regardless of his decision. When I refused, having already given the living to another deserving man, Wickham threatened to make trouble. I ignored the threats, believing his slander could not touch me. He decided to take his revenge in another way."

He finally looked at her then, his eyes showing pain. "Last summer, Wickham went to Ramsgate, where I had sent my sister Georgiana with her companion for a holiday by the sea. He convinced Georgiana that he loved her, that they should elope together. She was fifteen years old, Elizabeth. Fifteen. He cared nothing for her feelings or her innocence. He wanted only her dowry of thirty thousand pounds."

The words struck Elizabeth like physical blows, shock spreading through her. Georgiana. Sweet, shy Georgiana Darcy, who could barely meet a stranger's eyes without blushing. Wickham had targeted her deliberately, had planned to ruin her for money, and perhaps to revenge himself on her brother.

"I arrived in Ramsgate the day before they planned to leave," Darcy continued, his voice rough. "Georgiana confessed everything to me. She had convinced herself his feelings were genuine. Her heartbreak once I exposed him was the most terrible thing I have ever witnessed."

Elizabeth's hands flew to her mouth, horror and shame warring in her chest. She thought of all the times she had defended Wickham in her mind, had taken his side against Darcy. Thought of how she had judged Darcy for his treatment of his supposed childhood friend, never considering that there might be excellent reasons for such enmity.

"I am so sorry," she whispered, her voice breaking. "I am so terribly sorry. I believed him, Mr. Darcy. I believed every word he said about you. He told me you had cheated him of his inheritance, that you had acted out of jealousy and spite. And I accepted his account without question because it confirmed what I already believed about your character."

She looked down at her hands, seeing them trembling. "I was so ready to think the worst of you. So eager to find fault and assign blame. You wounded my pride at the assembly in Meryton, and I could not forgive that slight. So when Wickham offered me evidence of your supposed cruelty, I seized upon it gratefully. It justified my dislike, made it seem reasonable rather than petty."

Her voice dropped to barely above a whisper. "I prided myself on my discernment, on my ability to read character accurately. But I allowed my prejudice to blind me completely. I saw only what I wanted to see, believed only what confirmed my existing opinions. And in doing so, I misjudged you terribly."

Darcy leaned forwards, his expression softening. "You could not have known, Elizabeth. Wickham is skilled at deception. He has fooled people far more worldly and experienced than you. And I gave you ample reason to think ill of me through my own proud behaviour and thoughtless words."

"That does not excuse my willingness to believe the worst without evidence," Elizabeth replied, finally meeting his gaze again. Tears gathered in her eyes, spilling over. "I should have questioned his account. Should have wondered why he was so ready to share such personal information with a stranger. But I was too caught up in my own certainty to see any of it."

She reached for his hand before she could stop herself, her fingers finding his with desperate need to convey the sincerity of her remorse. "I am truly sorry for the injustice I did you in my thoughts. For the assumptions I made about your character based on insufficient evidence and personal pique. You deserved better from me, and I failed you utterly."

Darcy's hand closed around hers, his grip firm and warm. "You have nothing to apologise for, Elizabeth. The fault lies with Wickham, not with those he deceived. And I should have been more forthcoming about his character from the beginning. Let me assure you, though, that I have dealt with him. I saw him in Meryton when I went to Longbourn, speaking with your youngest sister Lydia, and realised I could not leave him free to prey on your sisters. Once news of our engagement spread, they would have been his prime targets. I went to Colonel Forster, asked him to look into Wickham's actions, and received a letter from the good colonel yesterday. Wickham has been dismissed from the militia for falsified references, and taken up for debt. He'll be in debtor's prison for a long, long time."

He had done that for her sake, Elizabeth recognised at once. Because her sisters were now *his* sisters, and he had accepted responsibility for their welfare even before the wedding took place. He had lowered his pride to go to Colonel Forster and ensure that Wickham could cause no more harm.

Their eyes met and held, something passing between them that felt like the beginning of real understanding. Not love, perhaps, not yet, or not from her at any rate. But the foundation upon which love might eventually be built. Honesty and forgiveness and the willingness to admit fault on both sides.

"I will never reproach you for thinking ill of me," he said gently. "I deserved it, if not for the reasons that you then believed. And you have paid a terrible price for my failures. If I had only unbent my pride while still in Hertfordshire…"

"Anne would have targeted me all the sooner, perhaps," Elizabeth said. "Or waited until after the wedding to steal my form, and then gone with you to Pemberley beyond my reach, leaving me trapped at Rosings with Lady Catherine."

Darcy shook his head, his thumb brushing across her knuckles, the gesture tentative. Elizabeth found herself leaning slightly towards him, drawn by something she could not quite name. His free hand lifted towards her face, hovering near her cheek, waiting for permission to touch.

A knock on the door interrupted whatever moment had been building between them. Darcy leaned back and called out for whoever was there to enter.

Jane came in with Colonel Fitzwilliam close behind, both of them showing expressions that suggested the interruption was not entirely accidental. Jane's gaze moved between Elizabeth and Darcy with knowing assessment, taking in their joined hands and proximity with a small smile that suggested approval.

Elizabeth blushed, but she did not withdraw her hand from Darcy's. Because despite everything that had happened, despite everything that was yet to be settled... somehow, holding his hand felt exactly right.

Chapter Twenty-Eight

JANE MOVED FURTHER INTO the room with steps that suggested exhaustion barely held at bay, her face showing the strain of hours spent brewing impossible potions and watching her sister marry the wrong man. Behind her, Colonel Fitzwilliam remained in the doorway, his expression carrying gravity that made Darcy's chest tighten with renewed concern.

"Anne has awakened," Jane said, her voice carrying weariness that went beyond mere physical fatigue. "In her own body, we are certain of it. But she is very weak, Lizzy. Weaker than when you inhabited her form, I think. The potion's effects, perhaps, or the shock of finding herself returned to a body she had tried so desperately to escape."

Elizabeth's hand tensed in Darcy's. He squeezed it gently, offering what comfort he could while his mind raced through implications he was only beginning to comprehend.

"She is raving," Jane continued, her gaze fixed on Elizabeth rather than Darcy. "Speaking of poisons and theft, of stolen lives and rightful claims. Lady Catherine thinks it fever, the result of her collapse. She has sent for a physician to examine her, though I suspect no doctor will find anything physically wrong beyond Anne's usual frailty."

Colonel Fitzwilliam shifted in the doorway, drawing Darcy's attention with the movement. His cousin's face showed conflict between family loyalty and something else, something that looked uncomfortably like disgust mixed with pity.

"I overheard some of Anne's ravings," the Colonel said, his voice carefully neutral. "Enough that I questioned Miss Bennet about what had truly occurred. She showed me a book. A grimoire, I believe it is called, that Sir Lewis de Bourgh gave to his daughter."

"I had to tell him," Jane said, her words directed at Elizabeth with quiet apology. "He heard Anne speaking about body swaps and stolen flesh, about potions brewed from rare ingredients. He demanded an explanation, and I could not think of a convincing lie, not when I had already asked him to help me get the bezoar. So I showed him the grimoire and told him everything."

Darcy's protective instincts flared, sharp and immediate. His cousin knowing the truth created complications he had not yet had time to consider. But Fitzwilliam's expression showed no scepticism, no dismissive disbelief. Instead, he looked troubled in ways that suggested he had accepted the impossible with surprising readiness.

"You believe it," Darcy said, the statement emerging more as question despite his intention for certainty. "You believe that Anne used magic to swap bodies with Elizabeth."

"I do," Fitzwilliam replied, moving fully into the room and closing the door behind him with quiet click that somehow emphasised the gravity of their discussion. "Because I knew Sir Lewis dabbled in such things. Not the full extent of his knowledge, perhaps, but enough that I recognised some of the ingredients listed in his grimoire when Miss Bennet showed it to me."

He crossed to where Jane sat and held out his hand, his expression asking permission rather than demanding compliance. Jane reached into her pocket and withdrew a leather-bound journal, placing it in Fitzwilliam's palm with visible reluctance to part with evidence that had been so crucial to saving Elizabeth.

Fitzwilliam opened the grimoire, his fingers turning pages with care that suggested familiarity with old books and their fragility. His eyes scanned the cramped handwriting, pausing occasionally at entries that clearly meant something to him. When he finally looked up, his expression showed resignation mixed with old grief.

"My father used to correspond with Sir Lewis about natural philosophy," Fitzwilliam explained. "They shared an interest in alchemy, though my father approached it as a gentleman's hobby while Sir Lewis seemed to take it more seriously. I remember seeing some of these same ingredients listed in letters my father received. At the time, I thought it mere eccentricity, wealthy men collecting exotic curiosities to display in cabinets."

He closed the grimoire with deliberate care, his jaw tightening with emotion he was clearly struggling to contain. "But now, I believe this book contains more than recipes for parlour tricks or medicinal tonics. This is genuine power, dark and dangerous. Anne used it to commit a violation I can barely comprehend. To steal another woman's body, to trap her in a failing form while living in stolen flesh." His gaze moved to Elizabeth, showing sympathy that made Darcy's chest ache with renewed understanding of what his wife had endured. "I am sorry, Elizabeth. Sorry that my family produced someone capable of such wickedness."

"You bear no responsibility for Anne's choices," Elizabeth replied, her voice steady despite the emotion Darcy could feel thrumming through her where their bodies touched. "Each person must answer for their own actions, not those of their relations."

Fitzwilliam's expression softened with gratitude for her generosity, but his posture remained rigid with determination. "Nevertheless, I will ensure she can never practice such magic again." He paused, clearly choosing his next words with care. "Anne must be watched constantly, never allowed access to the ingredients or knowledge required to attempt this wickedness again. I will speak with Lady Catherine, explain what I can without revealing the full extent of Anne's crimes. She must understand that her daughter requires supervision beyond what Mrs. Jenkinson provided."

The mention of the companion's name made Elizabeth's hand tighten on Darcy's arm again, and he looked down at her face to find anger there mixed with satisfaction.

"Mrs. Jenkinson was complicit in Anne's scheme," Elizabeth said, her voice hardening in ways Darcy had never heard from her before. "She knew about the body swap. Threatened me when I was trapped in Anne's form, told me that speaking the truth would only result in my being declared mad. She kept me drugged and watched me almost constantly, ensuring I could not interfere with Anne's stolen happiness."

Darcy felt fury rise in his chest with force that made his vision narrow, his free hand clenching into a fist against his thigh. That woman, that supposed companion employed to care for an invalid, had instead enabled her charge's wickedness and actively worked to keep Elizabeth trapped in her nightmare. His protective instincts, already heightened by recent events, transformed into something darker and more primal. Someone had hurt his wife, had deliberately prolonged her suffering, and his every instinct demanded retribution.

"She will answer for what she has done," Darcy said, his voice emerging low and dangerous.

"She already has, in a sense," Elizabeth replied, and now satisfaction coloured her tone. "I told Lady Matlock that Mrs. Jenkinson had been drugging Anne, which was true enough even if the target was not who your aunt believed. Lady Matlock had the bottles examined and found concentrations strong enough to render a healthy adult insensible. She confined Mrs. Jenkinson to her room until after the wedding, with orders that she not be allowed to communicate with anyone."

Darcy felt grim approval settle over his fury, tempering it into something more controlled. His aunt had acted decisively to protect who she believed was her niece, and in doing so had neutralised a genuine threat without even knowing the full truth of the situation. Lady Matlock's competence in a crisis was well established, but Darcy felt renewed respect for her willingness to act on Anne's word alone, to believe and protect rather than dismissing concerns as hysteria.

Fitzwilliam's jaw had tightened further during Elizabeth's explanation, his expression showing the same protective fury Darcy felt. "Then Mrs. Jenkinson's fate is sealed. Lady Catherine must be made to understand that her companion betrayed the trust placed in her, endangered her charge rather than protecting her. On the evidence of those bottles alone, there should be no difficulty in securing her dismissal."

He moved to the window, his posture suggesting he needed distance to process everything he had learned. Darcy watched his cousin's profile, seeing conflict written in the tension around his eyes and mouth. This was family. Anne was Fitzwilliam's cousin just as she was Darcy's. Learning of her capacity for such wickedness could not be easy, even for someone as pragmatic as his cousin.

"I am sorry you had to learn this," Darcy said quietly, addressing Fitzwilliam though his words applied equally to himself. "About Anne, about Sir Lewis's dark practices. These are not easy truths to bear."

"No," Fitzwilliam agreed, his gaze still fixed on whatever lay beyond the window glass. "But necessary ones. Better to know the truth and act accordingly than to remain in ignorance while evil continues unchecked." He turned back to face the room, his expression showing renewed determination beneath the grief. "We must decide how to proceed. What story to tell, what measures to take to ensure this never happens again."

Darcy gestured toward the small table positioned near the window. The four of them moved across together and settled into chairs that suddenly felt too intimate for the gravity of their discussion, their voices dropping to hushed tones that would not carry beyond the room's walls even though the door remained closed against interruption.

"We must contain the scandal at all costs," Darcy said, his mind already working through implications and strategies with the same focus he applied to managing Pemberley's accounts. "If word spreads beyond this household about what truly occurred, the damage would be catastrophic. Not just to Anne, though she deserves whatever censure would come her way, but to Elizabeth as well. Society would not understand. They would dismiss it as madness or worse."

He leaned forward, his elbows on the table and his hands clasped before him in a posture that usually helped him think clearly. But clarity felt elusive now, with Elizabeth sitting beside him and the memory of their interrupted conversation still fresh in his mind. "Accusations of witchcraft, even in this enlightened age, carry weight. People would question Elizabeth's sanity for making such claims. They would wonder whether I had married a madwoman, whether our children might inherit some taint of lunacy."

The word 'children' emerged before he could stop it, and Darcy felt heat rise in his face at the presumption. Elizabeth might want no such future with him. He had no right to assume otherwise, regardless of what he might wish.

Fitzwilliam nodded agreement, his expression showing he had been thinking along similar lines. "The story we tell must be simple and believable. Two ladies overcome by the excitement and heat of a wedding breakfast, nothing more sinister than that. Anne's collapse can be attributed to her known poor health. Elizabeth's to the natural nervousness of a new bride."

"People saw them collapse simultaneously," Jane pointed out quietly. "That will seem strange, will invite speculation about shared illness or poison."

"Then we emphasise the coincidence," Darcy replied, warming to the strategy as it took shape in his mind. "Strange, yes, but ultimately meaningless. The human mind seeks patterns even where none exist. We simply refuse to feed speculation with our own concerns, treat it as an unfortunate incident that has already passed."

Elizabeth had been silent during this exchange, her gaze fixed on her hands where they rested on the table's polished surface. Darcy noticed her fingers moving to touch the gold band on her left hand, the wedding ring he had placed there mere hours ago. She turned it slowly, the metal catching light from the window, her expression distant in ways that made his chest tighten with anxiety he could not quite name.

Did she regret it? Regret the marriage, the binding vows that could not be easily undone? She had said she did not hate him, had even suggested she thought better of him now than before. But that was hardly the same as wanting to remain his wife, especially when the marriage had been contracted under such extraordinary circumstances.

Jane cleared her throat softly, drawing attention back to herself. Her face showed conflict, torn between loyalty to her sister and some other consideration Darcy could not immediately identify. When she spoke, her words emerged hesitant, almost apologetic.

"Forgive me for asking," Jane said, her gaze moving between Darcy and Elizabeth with careful assessment. "Will you seek an annulment? It would be understandable, given the circumstances. Elizabeth did not truly consent to this marriage."

The question struck Darcy with force that made breathing difficult. An annulment. The end of his marriage before it had properly begun, the dissolution of vows that had meant everything to him even if they had been spoken to the wrong woman. His mind immediately began cataloguing the process, the requirements, the explanations that would be demanded by ecclesiastical courts.

But beneath the practical considerations lay something more painful. The loss of hope he had carried for months, the dream of building a life with Elizabeth that would now never materialise. He had known, of course, that this might be her choice. Had tried to prepare himself for the possibility during the long minutes while she lay unconscious after drinking the reversal potion. But knowing something intellectually and facing it as reality were vastly different experiences.

He looked at Elizabeth, searching her face for some indication of her feelings. She had gone very still at Jane's question, her fingers freezing on the wedding ring. Her expression showed conflict that matched what Darcy felt churning in his own chest, uncertainty mixed with something he could not quite identify.

"We need to discuss it further," Darcy managed, hearing his voice emerge rougher than he intended. "Elizabeth and I. It is not a decision to be made lightly or quickly, regardless of external pressures."

Elizabeth met his gaze finally, her eyes searching his face with intensity that made him want to look away even as it held him captive. "Yes," she agreed softly. "We should discuss it. Privately."

Fitzwilliam had been watching this exchange with expression that suggested he understood more than Darcy would prefer. His cousin leaned back in his chair, his posture deceptively casual despite the tension that lined his shoulders.

"You should know," Fitzwilliam said, his tone carefully neutral, "that if you wish to pursue an annulment, it must be decided before nightfall. Tonight, specifically." He paused, seeming to weigh his next words with deliberate care. "The only grounds that would not require extensive investigation or church approval would be non-consummation. But once the marriage has been consummated, or even believed to be consummated, that option becomes unavailable. The church will not grant annulment simply because one party was deceived about the other's identity, particularly when the deception involved something as impossible to prove as body swapping."

The words hung in the air between them, creating a moment of profound awkwardness that made Darcy want to order his cousin from the room. The implication was clear and deeply uncomfortable. It reduced their marriage to a crude calculation of timing and physical acts, stripped away any romance or genuine feeling that might develop between them. Darcy hated it, hated the necessity of making such a decision under pressure of deadline rather than allowing events to unfold naturally. But Fitzwilliam was right. This was the reality they faced, uncomfortable as it might be.

Jane had gone pink at the Colonel's frank speech, her gaze dropping to her lap with embarrassment that would have been amusing under different circumstances. But she recovered quickly, rising from her chair with movements that suggested purposeful retreat.

"Perhaps Colonel Fitzwilliam and I should give you privacy to discuss this matter," Jane said, her voice carrying forced brightness that did not quite mask her discomfort. "We have imposed on your time together long enough."

She looked at Fitzwilliam with expression that clearly communicated expectation, and he rose as well, though his face showed reluctance to leave before the matter was fully settled. But Jane's meaningful glance brooked no argument, and he moved toward the door with the resigned air of someone who recognised when retreat was the better part of valour.

"We will be downstairs if you need anything," Fitzwilliam said, pausing at the threshold to look back at them. "Take whatever time you require. This decision should not be rushed, despite the unfortunate constraints placed upon it."

They departed, Jane's hand finding Fitzwilliam's elbow with familiarity that suggested their acquaintance had developed significantly during recent events. The door closed behind them with quiet click that seemed to seal Darcy and Elizabeth into sudden, profound privacy.

The silence that settled over the room after Jane and Fitzwilliam's departure felt different. This quiet carried weight, significance that pressed against Darcy's chest and made the simple act of breathing feel momentous. The mantel clock ticked with steady rhythm, each sound marking seconds that slipped away toward the deadline his cousin had imposed. Shadows lengthened across the floor as afternoon gave way to early evening, the light shifting from gold to amber to something deeper that suggested twilight approached faster than Darcy would have preferred.

He remained seated at the small table, his hands still clasped before him though the position had grown uncomfortable. Elizabeth sat beside him, close enough that he could have reached for her hand again if he dared. But he kept his fingers locked together, uncertain whether touch would be welcome or presumptuous given what they must discuss.

What did he say? How did he approach a conversation that would determine the entire course of his future? Darcy had faced difficult negotiations before, had navigated complex social situations and managed delicate family matters. But none of that experience felt relevant now, when everything he wanted hung in balance and the wrong words could destroy his only chance at happiness.

He could tell her he loved her. Could explain how that love had grown from initial attraction into something that consumed his thoughts and influenced his every action. But declarations of feeling seemed inadequate when she might not want those feelings directed at her, might prefer a clean break to the complications of building a marriage from such strange foundations.

He could point out that annulment would create its own scandal, questions about what had gone wrong so quickly that they could not even manage to remain married through their wedding day. But using social pressure to keep her trapped in vows she might not want felt wrong, manipulative in ways that made his stomach turn.

The silence stretched longer, growing heavier with each passing second. Darcy drew a breath and released it slowly, forcing himself to speak despite not knowing what words would emerge until they were already leaving his mouth.

"What do you want, Elizabeth?"

The question came out softer than he intended, his usual confidence abandoned in favour of genuine humility that left him feeling exposed. He turned slightly in his chair to face her more directly, needing to see her expression when she answered even if what he saw there might break his heart.

"I will not press you to remain married if that is not your wish," Darcy continued, somehow speaking calmly despite the emotion that threatened to overwhelm his composure. "I know the vows you spoke were not truly yours, that you had no say in this union. If you want an annulment, I will pursue it without argument or reproach. Your happiness matters more to me than my own desires."

The admission cost him more than he had anticipated, each word feeling like it was being dragged from somewhere deep in his chest. But it was true. He did want her happiness more than his own, wanted to see her free and content even if that freedom meant losing any chance of a future together. Loving someone meant wanting their wellbeing above personal satisfaction, and Darcy had learned that lesson thoroughly.

Elizabeth remained silent for a long moment, her gaze fixed on his face with intensity that made him want to look away even as it held him captive. She was studying him, he realised, searching for something in his expression that would help her make sense of whatever she was feeling. Her hands had moved from her lap to rest on the table between them, close enough to his that their fingers nearly touched.

"You truly mean that," Elizabeth said finally, her voice carrying wonder mixed with something that might have been respect. "You would let me go if I asked it."

"Yes," Darcy replied simply, because there was no other answer he could give with honesty. "Though I confess I hope you will not ask it."

The addition slipped out before he could prevent it, vulnerability making him incautious. He saw Elizabeth's expression shift, something softening in her eyes that gave him fragile hope even as his rational mind warned against reading too much into a single look.

But instead of answering his implied question, instead of stating her own desires or explaining what she wanted from their marriage, Elizabeth tilted her head slightly and asked something that caught Darcy completely unprepared.

"Why is it that you fell in love with me?" Her voice remained steady despite the directness of the question, her gaze never leaving his face. "*How* is it that you fell in love with me, after first judging me not handsome enough to tempt you?"

The words struck him with force of a physical blow, shame flooding through him as he remembered that night at the Meryton assembly. He had been in a foul mood, irritated by his friend's insistence on dragging him to a provincial gathering where he knew no one. Bingley's suggestion that he dance with Elizabeth had felt like one interference too many, and he had responded with cutting rudeness designed to end the conversation rather than engage with it.

Not handsome enough to tempt me. God, what a cruel thing to say, particularly within her hearing. That she had remembered the slight all these months later, had carried it with her through everything else that had passed between them, made his shame intensify until his face burned with it.

But beneath the shame lay something more important. Recognition that this question mattered, that his answer would determine whether Elizabeth could believe in the possibility of a real marriage between them. She was not asking out of idle curiosity or wounded vanity. She was asking because she needed to understand what had changed, what had transformed his initial dismissal into the devotion that had led him to propose marriage not once but effectively twice.

Darcy did not look away, though every instinct screamed at him to escape her scrutiny and the vulnerability it exposed. He held her gaze and felt his heart hammer against his ribs with force that made his chest ache.

The question hung between them like something tangible, weighty with implication and possibility both. The future of their marriage, hastily contracted and extraordinarily complicated, seemed to balance on whatever answer he could provide. One sentence could close the door on any hope of happiness together. Another might open it, might create space for genuine affection to develop from the strange circumstances that had brought them to this moment.

Elizabeth's hands remained on the table, her fingers still close enough to his that he could feel warmth radiating from her skin despite the gap that separated them. Her posture was straight but not rigid, her shoulders relaxed in ways that suggested she was willing to wait for his response however long it took him to formulate it. There was patience in her bearing, surprising given the urgency of the decision they faced, as though she understood that some questions required time and thought to answer properly.

The clock ticked on, marking seconds that felt both too fast and impossibly slow. Shadows continued their gradual advance across the floor, twilight drawing closer with each passing moment. Soon they would need to make a final decision about the annulment, about whether to let their marriage stand or seek its dissolution before nightfall made that choice for them.

But first, Darcy needed to answer Elizabeth's question. Needed to explain how his heart had learned to see what his eyes had initially missed, how prejudice and pride had given way to admiration and eventually love. The answer was there, waiting to be spoken, if only he could find words adequate to convey truth that felt too large and complex for mere language.

Chapter Twenty-Nine

Darcy's hands tightened on each other, his knuckles showing white against the table's polished surface. Elizabeth watched something work in his throat, some struggle between pride and the necessity of vulnerability. When he finally spoke, his voice carried a roughness she had never heard from him before.

"I was wrong that night at the assembly," Darcy said, shame thick in his tone. "Wrong about you, wrong in my manner, wrong in everything that mattered. But my wrongness went deeper than mere rudeness. I was defending myself against something I sensed even then, some quality in you that threatened the careful control I maintained over my feelings."

He paused, drawing breath. "I noticed you properly at Lucas Lodge, a few days later. You were speaking with Charlotte about books, and you said something clever about heroines in novels who fainted at every inconvenience. Your wit was sharp but not cruel, intelligent without being pretentious. And when Sir William tried to push us together for a dance, you declined with such grace that I could not take offence. Women did not typically refuse me, you see. But you did, and you made it seem perfectly natural rather than an insult."

Elizabeth felt her chest tighten at the memory. She had refused him because she was still angry about his initial slight, had wanted to wound his pride as he had wounded hers.

"Then you walked to Netherfield to tend Jane when she fell ill," Darcy continued, and now his voice softened with something that sounded like wonder. "Three miles in mud, your petticoats six inches deep in dirt, your face glowing with exertion. Miss Bingley mocked you after you went upstairs, said you looked a fright. But I thought you looked magnificent. That walk showed devotion, showed that you valued your sister's welfare above your own comfort or appearance. It showed character I had rarely encountered."

He looked at her directly now, his eyes holding hers with intensity that made her breath catch. "I was already falling in love with you then, Elizabeth. Already losing the battle. It terrified me. You were unsuitable by every measure I had been taught to value. Your connexions were negligible, your family's behaviour not what I had come to expect, your fortune non-existent. Marrying you would mean subjecting myself to ridicule. So I tried to convince myself my feelings were mere attraction, nothing deeper or more lasting."

Elizabeth's throat had gone tight, tears gathering behind her eyes despite her best efforts.

"But the more time I spent in your company, the more impossible denial became," Darcy said. "Every conversation revealed new depths to your intelligence. Every interaction showed me courage I had not recognised in myself. You were not intimidated by my wealth or status, did not simper or flatter. You challenged me, Elizabeth. Made me question assumptions I had never thought to examine."

His hands finally loosened their desperate grip on each other, one lifting to run through his hair in a gesture of agitation she had never seen from him before. "I told myself repeatedly that an attachment to you would be imprudent, that our situations were too different, that your family's behaviour made the connexion impossible."

He drew a breath that seemed to shudder through him. "I acknowledge now that part of my reason for separating Bingley from Jane was fear of my own growing feelings for you. I told myself I was protecting my friend from an unsuitable match, and I believed that. But beneath it lay something more selfish. If Bingley married Jane, we would be thrown into constant contact. I would be expected to visit, invited occasionally to participate in family gatherings. And I knew that repeated proximity to you would destroy whatever remained of my resolve."

The confession struck Elizabeth with force that made breathing difficult. He had separated Jane and Bingley partly to protect himself from her. The thought should have made her angry, should have reignited the fury she had felt upon learning of his interference. But instead she felt only sorrow for the waste of it, for months that might have been spent differently.

"I was already half in love with you and I did not want to be," Darcy said, his voice faltering slightly. His hands had begun to tremble, minute shaking that he tried to hide by pressing them flat against the table. "You represented everything I had been taught to avoid. A connexion that would lower my standing, potentially expose me to ridicule. My pride could not bear the thought of being laughed at for forming such an attachment. But seeing you again at Hunsford, spending time in your company without the buffer of crowds or social obligations, I realised my mistake."

He leaned forwards slightly, his gaze holding hers. "I realised that pride meant nothing without you. That all my careful calculation of advantage and disadvantage had missed the most important consideration entirely. I do not simply admire you, Elizabeth. I love you. With an entirety that frightens me, if I am honest. You are the only woman I can love, the only one I can imagine as mistress of Pemberley."

His hands lifted from the table, reaching towards her but stopping short of actual contact, hovering in the space between them. "If you choose to annul this marriage," he said, meeting her eyes directly, "I do not know what I will do. I will honour your decision, will not oppose whatever you decide. But I confess I do not know how I will bear it. How I will return to a life that does not include you, now that I have glimpsed what we might build together."

The words hung between them, raw and undefended. Elizabeth felt tears gathering in her eyes despite her best efforts to contain them. She blinked rapidly, trying to clear her vision, but the tears spilled over anyway, tracking down her cheeks in warm streams.

"I believe you," she whispered, her voice emerging thick with feeling. "I believe that you love me, that your feelings are genuine. And I am moved by your honesty, by your willingness to be so vulnerable when you clearly find it difficult."

She drew a shaking breath, forcing herself to continue. "Annulling the marriage would cause great harm. The scandal would be enormous, would affect not just us but our families as well. Jane's, and my other sisters', prospects would be damaged, perhaps destroyed entirely. Georgiana would face whispers and speculation. Even your position would suffer."

Darcy's expression showed he understood these considerations.

"But even taking into account these concerns," Elizabeth continued, her hands moving to grip the edge of the table, "I do not feel truly married. Not yet. The vows I heard spoken were not mine. The ceremony I witnessed felt like watching a play in which I had no part. And though I understand intellectually that the marriage is legal and binding, emotionally it feels false. It was quite literally something that happened to someone else while I was trapped and helpless to prevent it."

Fresh tears spilled down her cheeks, and this time she lifted a hand to dash them away. "I do not want an annulment. I do not want to cause that scandal or face those consequences. But I also cannot pretend that everything is settled, that we can simply proceed as though none of this happened. I need time. Need space to feel as though this marriage belongs to me, rather than to the woman who stole my face and spoke vows in my voice."

Darcy reached across the distance between them, his hand finally closing over hers with gentle pressure. "Then you shall have time," he said, his voice steady despite the emotion she could see written plainly on his face. "Whatever you need, Elizabeth. There is no rush, no pressure. We can determine together how to proceed."

He paused, his thumb brushing across her knuckles. "Perhaps we should consult my uncle. Lord Matlock has considerable legal knowledge, might be able to suggest options we have not considered. Ways to address your concerns without resorting to annulment and the scandal it would create."

Elizabeth felt relief flood through her at the suggestion, grateful for practical action. "Yes. That seems wise. He might have ideas about how to proceed."

Darcy rose from his chair, still holding her hand as he helped her to her feet. They stood close together, the space between them charged with everything spoken and everything still left unsaid. Elizabeth could feel warmth radiating from him, could see the pulse beating at the base of his throat.

"We should go down," Darcy said softly. "The guests will have dispersed by now. My uncle will be in his study most likely."

Elizabeth nodded, not trusting her voice to remain steady. They moved towards the door together, still hand in hand, embarking on the first tentative steps towards whatever future they might build from these strange and complicated beginnings.

Lord Matlock's library smelled of old leather and pipe tobacco, with undertones of beeswax from the polished furniture. Elizabeth took in the room with quick assessment born of nervousness, her gaze moving across walls lined floor to ceiling with books. The space felt distinctly masculine, all dark wood and hunter green upholstery, with a massive desk dominating the centre.

Her attention snagged on a tall cabinet positioned between two windows, its glass doors revealing an impressive collection of curiosities. Shells arranged by size and type occupied one shelf. A narwhal tusk stood propped in one corner. And there, on a middle shelf in a small glass case of its own, sat a bezoar stone, neatly labelled.

Elizabeth's breath caught at the sight of it. The stone was larger than she had expected, perhaps the size of a walnut, its surface showing an iridescent quality that shifted between brown and green and purple as lamplight played across it. This was the source of the crucial ingredient that had saved her life, that had allowed her to reclaim her own body. The stone sat innocently among Lord Matlock's other treasures, unaware of the role it had played in reversing dark magic.

"Please, sit," Lord Matlock said, gesturing to two chairs positioned before his desk. He had risen when they entered, and now settled back into his own seat with the ease of someone completely comfortable in his domain.

Elizabeth tore her attention from the bezoar and took one of the offered chairs, Darcy settling into the other close enough that their sleeves nearly brushed.

Lord Matlock studied them with sharp eyes that missed little. "You wished to consult me about a legal matter, I understand. How may I be of service?"

Darcy leaned forwards slightly. "My marriage to Elizabeth," he began, then paused as though reconsidering his approach. "We were married this afternoon by special licence. The ceremony was properly conducted, all legal requirements met. However, circumstances surrounding the wedding have left Elizabeth uncertain about the validity of our union."

Lord Matlock's eyebrows rose fractionally, but his expression remained neutral. "Uncertain in what sense?"

"The marriage felt hasty," Darcy continued, choosing words with visible care. "We had little time to know each other properly before I proposed. Elizabeth accepted, but recent events have made her question whether she truly consented with full understanding. She feels that the speed with which everything proceeded left her no opportunity to consider matters properly."

It was a masterful explanation, Elizabeth had to admit. Truthful enough that no actual lie had been spoken, yet carefully constructed to omit every detail about body swapping and stolen identities.

Lord Matlock leaned back in his chair, his fingers steepling before him. "I see. And you wish to know whether the marriage can be dissolved? Whether an annulment might be possible?"

"We wish to know our options," Darcy replied carefully. "To understand what choices are available to us."

Lord Matlock was quiet for a moment, his gaze moving between them. Then he nodded slowly, decision apparently reached.

"Your marriage is legally valid regardless of any uncertainty about the circumstances," Lord Matlock said, his tone carrying authority. "The vows were exchanged before proper witnesses in a church ceremony conducted by a clergyman with authority to perform such rites, in possession of a special licence. The marriage register has been signed. You are husband and wife in the eyes of both church and state."

Elizabeth felt her chest tighten at the finality in his words.

"However," Lord Matlock continued, his expression softening as he looked directly at Elizabeth, "if you are concerned about the hasty nature of the union, there is a solution that might address your worries without resorting to the scandal and difficulty of annulment."

He shifted in his chair, his manner becoming less formal and more avuncular. "You could have the banns called and be re-married publicly at Longbourn. The traditional three weeks of public announcement would give you time to adjust to your new situation, perhaps. And a second ceremony in your home parish, surrounded by family and friends, might provide the sense of connection that was lacking in today's rushed affair."

The suggestion struck Elizabeth with force of revelation. Of course. The traditional path, the one she had always assumed she would follow. Three weeks of banns read in church, giving the community opportunity to voice any objections. A ceremony at Longbourn with Mr. Bennet giving her away, with Jane standing beside her.

It would not erase what had happened today. Would not change the fact that legally, she was already Mrs. Darcy. But it would give her something she desperately needed, a sense of agency in a marriage that had been contracted without her true participation.

"Legally, the second ceremony would be unnecessary," Lord Matlock continued, his tone gentle. "You are already married. But emotionally, for peace of mind, it might serve an important purpose. Give you time to come to terms with the changes in your circumstances."

He gave Elizabeth a kindly look that suggested he understood more than she had expected. There was compassion in his face, genuine desire to help.

Elizabeth found her voice, though it emerged softer than she would have preferred. "That is very kind of you, Lord Matlock. The suggestion has merit, I think. Time would be welcome, and a ceremony at Longbourn..." She trailed off, unable to complete the thought without risk of tears returning.

"It would feel more real," Darcy finished for her.

Lord Matlock nodded, satisfaction evident. "Precisely. You would have three weeks to get to know each other better, to allow Elizabeth to prepare herself for her new life at Pemberley. And then a proper wedding breakfast with your family and neighbours, all the tradition and ceremony that makes such events meaningful."

He rose from his chair, signalling that the consultation had reached its natural conclusion. "I will say this, though. Legal concerns aside, I believe you two will do well together. I see the care you show each other despite the difficulties you face. That speaks to something worth preserving."

Elizabeth felt warmth spread through her chest at his words.

They stood as well.

"Thank you, Uncle," Darcy said, his voice carrying genuine appreciation. "Your counsel has been invaluable, as always."

Lord Matlock smiled, the expression transforming his rather stern features. "That is what family is for, nephew. To help navigate difficult waters." He moved towards the door. "Now go. Rest. You have had an extraordinarily trying day. Tomorrow will bring its own challenges, but they can wait until you have recovered your strength."

The blue guest room felt different when they returned to it. Elizabeth moved to the window without conscious decision, drawn by the view of London beyond the glass. Twilight had settled over the city while they were in the library, street lamps beginning to glow.

Darcy remained near the door for a moment, giving her space, before following to stand beside her at the window. Not too close, but near enough that she could feel his presence as a comforting warmth.

"I think Lord Matlock's solution is a good one," Elizabeth said quietly. "Time will help. And a proper ceremony at Longbourn, with my father and Jane and all the familiar faces of Meryton watching, will make it feel more real. More like something I chose."

"I am glad," Darcy replied, relief evident. "Three weeks should allow you to settle your feelings, to prepare yourself for the changes ahead. And it will give our families time to adjust as well. Your mother will appreciate the opportunity to plan a proper celebration, I expect."

Elizabeth felt a smile tug at her lips despite everything. Mrs. Bennet would be in transports, would throw herself into preparations with enthusiasm that would probably drive the entire household to distraction.

"She will be impossible," Elizabeth agreed, warmth in her voice. "But yes, she will appreciate it. And my father..." She paused, thinking of Mr. Bennet's expression earlier. "He suspected something was wrong today. Did not know what, but sensed that the woman he was giving away was not quite his Lizzy. A second ceremony will give him the opportunity to actually give me away properly."

Darcy's hand lifted slightly, as though he wanted to touch her shoulder but thought better of it. "Until then, you will be treated as mistress of my home without any demands placed upon you. I want to be very clear about that, Elizabeth. I will not press for intimacy you are not ready to grant. Your comfort and peace of mind matter more to me than my own desires."

The frankness of the statement made Elizabeth's cheeks warm, though she appreciated his directness.

"What does that mean, practically?" she asked, keeping her gaze fixed on the window. "How will we arrange things?"

"Separate bedchambers," Darcy replied immediately, his tone businesslike. "My townhouse has a mistress's suite adjacent to the master's chambers, connected by a door that shall remain locked until you decide otherwise. You will have complete authority over all household matters. The housekeeper will answer to you. All decisions about menus and guest lists, these will be yours to make."

Elizabeth felt her heart squeeze with sympathy for this proud man who was trying so hard to meet her needs.

"I already like Georgiana," Elizabeth said, shifting the conversation to safer ground. "She seemed sweet when I met her, though too shy to speak much. I look forward to knowing her better."

Darcy's face transformed at the mention of his sister, warmth flooding his features. "She will love having you at Pemberley. She has been lonely, I think, with only me for company. You will bring liveliness to our home, remind Georgiana that there is joy to be found in the world."

"I will try," Elizabeth promised, meaning it sincerely.

They stood in companionable silence for a moment, watching darkness settle more completely over London.

"When should we travel to Longbourn?" Elizabeth asked. "I will need to speak with my father about having the banns called, since Sunday is only two days away now."

"Tomorrow, if you feel well enough," Darcy suggested. "Or we can wait longer, if you need more time to recover. There is no rush; the banns could wait another week, too."

Elizabeth considered the options. "Tomorrow," she decided. "I want to go home. Want to see familiar faces and familiar rooms. Then the first banns could be called the day after."

"Then tomorrow it is," Darcy agreed. "I will make arrangements with the stables to have the carriage ready."

They remained at the window, watching twilight deepen into true night. Their hands rested on the windowsill, so close that Elizabeth could feel warmth radiating from his skin though actual contact remained absent. It would take only the smallest movement to close that gap, to let their fingers brush in a gesture that would mean nothing and everything simultaneously.

Elizabeth did not move. Not yet. But she thought perhaps she might, eventually. Thought that given time and patience and continued honesty between them, she might learn to reach for him without hesitation. Might discover that the foundation they were building could support something real and lasting.

The future remained uncertain, full of complications they had barely begun to address. But standing here beside Darcy, with London settling into evening around them and tentative hope stirring in her chest, Elizabeth thought perhaps uncertainty was not such a terrible thing after all. Perhaps it was simply space for possibility, room for something unexpected and genuine to grow from the strangest of beginnings.

She let her hand shift slightly on the windowsill, closing half the distance between them. Not quite touching, but closer than before. An offering, or perhaps a promise. Time would tell which.

Chapter Thirty

Everything was wrong. Anne knew this before she opened her eyes properly, before full consciousness returned with its crushing weight. Her lungs felt like they were wrapped in wet cloth, each breath requiring conscious effort, each inhalation bringing less air than her body needed.

No.

The denial formed without words, a primal rejection of what her senses were reporting. Anne tried to lift her hand and found it trembling, the fingers thin as twigs and just as fragile. She knew these hands. Had lived with them for years of slowly increasing weakness, watching them grow more transparent with each passing season until the veins showed blue-green beneath skin like tissue paper. These were her hands, her cursed, failing hands, and they should not exist anymore because she had escaped this body, had traded it for something better, something strong and whole.

But Elizabeth Bennet had stolen it back.

Rage flooded through her with force that made her lungs spasm, coughing wracking her chest until she tasted copper. Anne pushed herself upright through sheer force of will, ignoring the way her muscles screamed protest at the movement. The room swam around her, shadows lengthening across walls papered in pale green silk. A fire burned in the grate, its warmth not quite reaching the bed where she lay surrounded by pillows arranged to support her in the half-sitting position that made breathing marginally easier.

How had Elizabeth done it? How had she possibly obtained the ingredients necessary for reversal? Anne's mind raced through possibilities. The ambergris could be sourced through apothecaries if one knew what to ask for, though most would not stock it due to expense. But the bezoar stone? Genuine bezoar stones were nearly impossible to acquire in England. They appeared in collections occasionally, brought back by diplomats or merchants who understood their medicinal value, but such stones were not for sale. Not to women like Elizabeth Bennet who had no connexions in such circles, and no freedom to move about them anyway, trapped beneath Lady Catherine's benevolent eye as she should have been.

Unless Jane had helped her. Unless that insipid elder sister with her angelic face and hidden spine of steel had somehow convinced someone to provide the bezoar despite its rarity and value.

The thought made Anne's hands clench in the bedsheets, her nails catching in fine linen. She had underestimated Jane Bennet. Had dismissed her as merely pretty, merely kind, too gentle to pose any real threat, too stupid to even notice that her sister had been replaced by an impostor. But Jane's appearance at Hunsford had not been the coincidence she had pretended, Anne realised now. Some how, some way, Elizabeth had summoned her sister and convinced her of the truth. Jane must have moved heaven and earth to procure those ingredients, must have brewed the reversal potion herself following instructions in the grimoire that Anne had not had an opportunity to remove from Rosings.

Stupid. She had been stupid to leave the grimoire where it could be found, to assume no one would believe Elizabeth's impossible story, to think her victory was complete simply because she had spoken vows and signed documents in Elizabeth's stolen hand.

Anne threw the nearest object within reach, a crystal glass half-filled with water. It flew across the room with less force than she intended, her weak arm unable to achieve the satisfying violence she craved. The glass struck the wall and shattered, water spreading across silk paper in a dark stain that would probably ruin the expensive covering. *Good*. Let them see her rage.

A little shriek alerted Anne that she was not alone, and she turned her head to find a maid sitting on the other side of the bed, mending in her hands. The girl's eyes were wide, her gaze moving from the shattered crystal to Anne with fear. The maid was afraid of her. Thought her dangerous or mad or both.

Perhaps they all thought that now. Perhaps Elizabeth had told them some story about Anne's supposed instability, had painted her as a madwoman whose ravings should be dismissed. She had vague recollections of waking earlier to see Jane's triumphant face above her, of screaming herself hoarse with horror until a doctor was summoned to give her a sedative.

But screaming again would only confirm their suspicions. Anne forced her features into something approximating composure, her voice emerging with command that her body could not support.

"Send me Mrs. Jenkinson," she ordered, each word requiring careful modulation to avoid the breathlessness that plagued her. "And get out."

The maid bobbed something that might have been a curtsy and fled. Anne let herself slump back against the pillows, her brief show of strength leaving her exhausted. This body. This useless, failing, treacherous body that had been her prison. She had escaped it, had lived those perfect days in Elizabeth's strong form, had felt what it meant to breathe easily and walk without assistance and exist in the world without constant awareness of her own fragility. She had never been so happy in her life.

And now she was trapped again. But not permanently. Not if she could reach Mrs. Jenkinson, could convince her devoted companion to help brew another potion. The grimoire was lost, presumably in Elizabeth or Jane's possession now. But Anne remembered the ingredients, could reconstruct the potion with time and resources.

It would take weeks, perhaps months to gather everything. And this time she would be more careful, would ensure the target was properly isolated before she struck. Perhaps not Elizabeth again. Elizabeth would never allow Anne under the same roof as her again, much though she hungered to take revenge. But there were many other healthy young women in England, other bodies that could be taken and would do well enough. Forever, perhaps, it occurred to her. There was no reason why she should not simply discard each body as it began to fail and take another, younger, stronger.

She simply needed Mrs. Jenkinson's help to begin.

Anne waited, her breathing gradually settling into the shallow pattern that represented her body's best effort. Mrs. Jenkinson had been with her since childhood, was devoted to her. She understood better than anyone what Anne had suffered, what she deserved as compensation for a life half-lived in sickrooms and invalid chairs.

Footsteps sounded in the corridor outside, measured and male. Too heavy for Mrs. Jenkinson's slight frame. Anne's chest tightened with something beyond her usual breathlessness as the door opened and Colonel Fitzwilliam entered instead of her companion.

He closed the door behind him with deliberate care, the soft click of the latch somehow more ominous than if he had slammed it. His face showed none of its usual easy charm. Instead he looked grave and knowing, his eyes meeting hers with an expression that made Anne's stomach drop despite the rage still simmering beneath her ribs.

He knew.

Colonel Fitzwilliam moved further into the room but did not sit, did not approach the bed. He simply stood at a distance that suggested formality rather than familial warmth, his posture that of an officer delivering unpleasant orders.

Anne opened her mouth to speak, to ask for Mrs. Jenkinson again, to attempt whatever performance might salvage this situation. But Fitzwilliam raised one hand in a gesture that cut off her words before they could form, and something in that simple movement told Anne that performance would be useless now.

The silence stretched between them, heavy with everything unspoken. Anne's hands twisted in the bedsheets, her heart hammering against her ribs. This was wrong. This was all wrong. She was supposed to be triumphant now, supposed to be Mrs. Darcy settling into her new life, not trapped in this failing body facing her cousin's judgement.

But Fitzwilliam's expression showed no sympathy, no uncertainty. Only grim determination and something that looked uncomfortably like pity mixed with disgust.

"Mrs. Jenkinson will not be coming," Fitzwilliam said, his voice carrying none of the warmth it had always held when he spoke to Anne. "She has been dismissed from my aunt's service."

Anne felt the words strike her like physical blows, each syllable landing with precision. She opened her mouth, some protest forming. But Fitzwilliam was not finished.

"She was found to have been administering dangerous concentrations of laudanum and other substances to you," he continued, his tone remaining level. "My mother examined the bottles herself and found doses that would have rendered a healthy adult insensible. Lady Catherine has agreed that such behaviour cannot be tolerated, regardless of Mrs. Jenkinson's claimed devotion to your welfare."

That was clever, Anne had to admit even through her rising panic. They were using the tonics Mrs. Jenkinson would have administered to keep Elizabeth docile and controllable as justification for the companion's removal.

"That is absurd," Anne managed, forcing her voice to remain steady despite the way her lungs protested each word. "Mrs. Jenkinson was following instructions. My mother's instructions, approved by physicians who understand my delicate constitution."

"No physician approved those concentrations," Fitzwilliam replied, and something in his expression told Anne he knew she was lying. "Nor would any reputable doctor prescribe substances that left you too foggy to think clearly. Aunt Catherine was quite outraged when Lady Matlock and I discussed those 'tonics' with her and explained what they would have been doing to you. Or rather, to Elizabeth."

He moved closer to the bed, not quite within arm's reach but near enough that Anne had to tilt her head back to meet his gaze. His face showed no anger, no heat that might suggest his feelings could be swayed. Only cold certainty and grim purpose.

"Darcy has arranged a house for you in Bath," Fitzwilliam continued, and Anne's chest constricted at the mention of Darcy's name. Her Darcy, who should have been her husband, who should have been showing her Pemberley instead of conspiring with Elizabeth to destroy Anne's future. "You and Lady Catherine will remove there within the week, ostensibly for your health. The mineral waters are thought beneficial for consumptive complaints."

Bath. They were sending her to Bath, away from London and any chance of accessing the resources she needed.

"My mother would never agree to such an arrangement," Anne said, hearing her voice rise despite her best efforts at control. "She is far too attached to Rosings to consider residing anywhere else."

"Your mother is in complete agreement with this course of action," Fitzwilliam replied, and the gentleness that crept into his tone somehow made his words more terrible. "She is genuinely concerned for your health, Anne. Your collapse yesterday frightened her badly. She believes the stress of London society has been too much for your constitution, that you need a more beneficial environment even than Rosings, access to the best doctors who reside in Bath, caring for the invalids there."

Of course Lady Catherine believed that. Of course she had accepted whatever story they had fed her about Anne's wellbeing. Her mother had always been easy to manipulate when it came to concerns about Anne's health.

"Mrs. Jenkinson is being sent overseas," Fitzwilliam added. "India, I believe, where she has been secured a position as companion to a diplomat's wife. The voyage will take several months, and the position is expected to last for years. She will not be returning to England any time soon. And frankly, she should consider herself fortunate, but Lady Catherine was determined to do something for her, in return for her years of loyal service to the de Bourgh family."

Anne felt something crack inside her chest, some last fragile hope. India. They were sending her to the other side of the world, ensuring Anne would have no access to the one person who truly understood what she had tried to accomplish and why.

"You had no right," Anne whispered, her voice emerging raw with emotion she could no longer contain. "No right to dismiss my companion, to arrange my life without consultation, to conspire against me."

"We have every right," Fitzwilliam replied, his tone hardening slightly. "You are unwell, Anne. Your judgement has been compromised by your illness and by the desperation it has bred. The arrangements being made are for your own protection as much as anyone else's."

The words were carefully chosen, Anne recognised. Designed to sound like concern while actually announcing her imprisonment.

"The new staff in Bath have specific instructions," Fitzwilliam continued, and Anne heard finality in his voice. "They are to ensure you take only approved medications, that you are never left alone for extended periods, that any unusual requests or behaviours are reported immediately to either Darcy or myself. You will be comfortable, Anne. But you will be watched."

Anne's breathing had grown ragged, her lungs struggling to process air through the tightness in her chest. They had thought of everything. Had anticipated every possible avenue she might use to attempt another body swap and closed them all systematically. The grimoire was lost, Mrs. Jenkinson removed, her mother convinced this was all for Anne's benefit, new staff installed who would monitor her every move.

She was trapped. Not just in this failing body but in a situation designed specifically to keep her powerless, to ensure she could never again attempt what she had so briefly achieved.

Anne's hands had begun to shake, and this time the trembling had nothing to do with the weakness that plagued her. Fury coursed through her veins with heat that made her skin flush. She pushed herself upright again, ignoring the protest of muscles, ignoring the spinning in her head that warned of imminent collapse.

She would not lie here docile and accepting while they dismantled her life. Would not submit to imprisonment in Bath while Elizabeth lived the future that should have been Anne's.

Anne swung her legs over the side of the bed, her bare feet finding the carpet. She tried to stand, pushing herself up with arms that shook violently under the strain. For a moment she succeeded, her knees locked and her body upright through sheer force of will.

"This is wrong," Anne said, hearing her voice emerge too loud, too shrill, hysteria breaking through the careful control she had maintained. "You are all conspiring against me. Elizabeth has poisoned you, turned you all against someone who only wanted what she had wasted, what she took for granted."

Her voice rose with each word. "She had everything! Health, strength, a body that worked as bodies should work. She could walk without assistance, could breathe without conscious effort, could exist in the world without constant awareness of mortality hanging over every moment. And what did she do with those gifts? Nothing! She wasted them on provincial society and walks through muddy fields and impertinent refusals of men who were far above her station. She did not even like Darcy, the stupid girl, too stubborn to recognise that he loved her!"

Anne's legs began to buckle, but she fought against the weakness with everything she had left. "I would have made something of that body. Would have lived the life it deserved, would have been mistress of Pemberley and mother to Darcy's children and everything I was meant to be if not for this cursed flesh that has imprisoned me since birth. She stole that from me! She and her sister with their conspiracy to keep me trapped in this dying shell."

The words poured out of her now, unstoppable, years of resentment and rage finding voice. "Darcy was mine! He was always meant to be mine, promised to me since childhood, the one thing my mother assured me would be worth surviving for. And Elizabeth took him with her witchery and her supposedly fine eyes and her impertinence."

Anne's vision had narrowed to a grey tunnel, her hearing muffled as her strength failed, the last of it consumed by her rage. But still she continued, her voice raw now, breaking on words that emerged as much sob as accusation. "It is all her fault. She should have died in my body as she was supposed to, should have accepted the fate I arranged for her and left me in peace to live the life I earned through years of suffering. But no. She had to fight back, had to find impossible ingredients and brew impossible potions and steal back what I had claimed fairly through my own cleverness."

Her knees gave way entirely then, her body crumpling despite her desperate attempts to remain standing. Anne fell more than sat back onto the bed, her slight weight bouncing once before settling into the pillows that had been arranged to support her. The impact drove what little air remained from her lungs, leaving her gasping like a landed fish while black spots danced across her vision.

The rage that had sustained her through the outburst drained away as quickly as it had come, leaving only exhaustion so complete that even keeping her eyes open felt impossible. Anne's chest heaved with the effort of drawing breath, each inhalation bringing insufficient oxygen no matter how desperately she pulled air into damaged lungs. Her heart hammered against her ribs with an irregular rhythm that suggested it might simply give up entirely, stop beating and end this nightmare of returned imprisonment.

Perhaps that would be better, Anne thought distantly. Perhaps death would be preferable to living the rest of her abbreviated life under constant surveillance in Bath while Elizabeth enjoyed everything that should have been Anne's. At least death would be final, would end the suffering that had defined her entire existence.

"Are you finished?" Fitzwilliam asked, his voice coming from somewhere near the foot of the bed. He did not sound angry or disturbed by her outburst. Only patient, as though he had expected exactly this reaction and had waited for it to run its course.

Anne made some sound that might have been agreement or might have been simply another desperate gasp for air. Her body had begun to shake again, this time from exhaustion and oxygen deprivation rather than fury. Cold sweat beaded on her forehead.

She heard Fitzwilliam move closer. The bed dipped slightly as he sat on its edge, far enough away that their bodies did not touch but near enough that Anne could feel warmth radiating from him. It made her want to weep, that casual display of vitality that he took completely for granted while she struggled simply to remain conscious.

"Open your eyes, Anne," Fitzwilliam said quietly.

Anne forced her eyes open with effort that felt monumental, her vision still grey at the edges but gradually clearing. Fitzwilliam's face swam into focus, his expression showing none of the anger or disgust she had seen earlier. Instead he looked sad, disappointed in ways that cut deeper than fury would have.

"I need you to understand something," Fitzwilliam said, his voice soft but carrying weight. "Before you retreat into self-pity or convince yourself that you are the wronged party in this situation. Before you spend the rest of your life nursing resentment about what Elizabeth supposedly stole from you."

He leaned forwards slightly, his eyes holding hers with intensity that made looking away impossible. "You were willing, even eager, to condemn an innocent woman to die in your stead, Anne. Not metaphorically die. Not suffer some abstract harm. Actually die, slowly and painfully, in a body that was failing long before you swapped with her."

The words struck Anne like blows, each syllable landing with precision. She wanted to protest, to explain that Elizabeth's death would have been quick, that the body would have failed within weeks or months at most. But her voice would not work, her throat closing around explanations that suddenly felt hollow even to her own ears.

"Elizabeth Bennet did nothing to deserve what you did to her," Fitzwilliam continued, his voice remaining quiet but carrying condemnation. "She did not waste the health you claim she squandered. She lived as young women should live, with joy and energy and engagement with the world around her. The fact that you were denied such experiences does not make her responsible for your suffering, nor does it give you right to steal her life as recompense."

He paused, letting his words settle over Anne like a shroud. "You speak of fairness, of earning what you took through your own cleverness. But there is no fairness in condemning an innocent person to death simply because you envy what they possess. That is not cleverness, Anne. That is wickedness of a kind I would not have believed any member of my family capable of attempting. That would have been murder, in the plainest of speaking."

Anne's vision had blurred with tears she could not stop, salt water tracking down her cheeks to dampen the pillow beneath her head. She wanted to argue, wanted to make him understand how desperate she had been, how the long years of suffering had driven her to actions she might not have contemplated in calmer circumstances. But the words would not come, her throat too tight.

"The arrangements being made are not punishment," Fitzwilliam said, his tone gentling slightly though his words remained uncompromising. "They are protection. Protection for you, to keep you from attempting such wickedness again.

And protection for others who might become targets if you were left with freedom to pursue your desires unchecked."

He rose from the bed, his movement causing the mattress to shift beneath Anne's slight weight. "I am sorry for what you have suffered, Anne. Genuinely sorry. But suffering does not excuse what you attempted, nor does it make you less responsible for choices you made with full understanding of their consequences."

Anne watched through tear-blurred vision as he moved towards the door, each step carrying him further away. He paused at the threshold, his hand on the doorframe, and looked back at her with expression that mixed pity and disappointment in equal measure.

"You have lost everything, Anne," Fitzwilliam said, his voice carrying finality. "Your freedom, your access to the resources you would need for another attempt, any chance of the future you envisioned. But you have time yet to repent your sins. If I were you, I would use whatever time remained to me to pray, for the sake of my soul and what might come after this life."

He left then, closing the door with quiet click that somehow sounded louder than if he had slammed it. Anne heard the footman shift position outside, settling back into guard duty that would apparently continue for whatever remained of her abbreviated life.

She lay amongst her pillows, tears continuing to fall despite her best efforts to stop them, her chest aching with something that had nothing to do with her damaged lungs. Fitzwilliam's words echoed in her head with terrible clarity, stripping away the justifications she had built so carefully around her actions.

You were willing, even eager, to condemn an innocent woman to die in your stead. That would have been murder.

The truth of it settled over Anne like a weight, crushing in its undeniability. She had not thought of it in such stark terms while planning the body swap, had focused instead on what she would gain rather than what Elizabeth would lose. But hearing it stated so plainly, stripped of all the euphemisms and justifications she had wrapped around it, made the wickedness of her actions impossible to ignore.

Anne closed her eyes, fresh tears leaking from beneath her lids to dampen already-wet pillows. She had lost everything. Her freedom, her future, any chance of escaping this failing body that would be her prison until death finally claimed her.

The injustice she had railed against moments ago suddenly felt less clear. She was suffering, yes. Had suffered her entire life in ways that Elizabeth could never truly understand. But suffering did not excuse wickedness, did not make attempted murder somehow acceptable because the would-be murderer had experienced pain.

Anne lay surrounded by luxury and comfort that would soon be traded for careful confinement in Bath, and felt the full weight of what she had done settle over her consciousness like a shroud. She had tried to kill Elizabeth Bennet. Not quickly or mercifully, but slowly, through the gradual failure of a body that would have taken weeks or months to finally give up entirely. Had been prepared to listen to reports of Elizabeth's decline, to enjoy her stolen health while her victim suffered everything Anne herself had endured since childhood.

The realisation should have brought remorse, should have inspired some desire to atone for wickedness that even Anne could no longer deny. But all she felt was emptiness, a hollow space where determination and righteous fury had burned so brightly just minutes ago. She had gambled everything on one desperate attempt to escape her fate, and she had lost. Now there was nothing left but to endure whatever time remained in this failing body, watched constantly to ensure she could harm no one else.

Anne's tears gradually slowed, exhaustion finally overwhelming even grief. Her breathing settled into the shallow, laboured pattern that represented her body's best effort at sustaining life. Outside her door, the footman stood guard, ensuring she remained exactly where she was. Trapped. Defeated. And entirely, utterly alone with consequences she could no longer deny or avoid.

The future stretched before her, measured not in years but in months or weeks until this treacherous body finally gave up entirely. And unlike the future she had briefly claimed through wickedness and alchemy, this one held nothing but slow decline watched by guards whose job was to ensure she harmed no one else before death claimed her at last.

It was, Anne thought distantly as consciousness began to fray at the edges again, exactly what she deserved. That knowledge did not make it easier to bear. But perhaps that, too, was part of the punishment for crimes she could no longer pretend were justified by suffering alone.

Chapter Thirty-One

The drawing room at Darcy House caught the morning light differently than the grand rooms at Matlock House had done, Elizabeth noted. Softer somehow, less imposing despite the evident quality of the furnishings. She sat beside Jane on a cream damask settee positioned near tall windows that overlooked the street, her fingers tracing idle patterns on her skirts while they waited for Mr. Bingley's arrival.

A week had passed since the wedding, since potions and body swaps and impossible revelations, and life had settled into something that felt almost normal if one did not think too carefully about the strangeness of it all. Elizabeth had returned to Longbourn briefly, but her mother had asked too many questions, and Elizabeth decided it would be best to stay in London, at Darcy House, until her second wedding day arrived.

Jane sat with perfect posture beside her, hands folded in her lap with the composure that had always come naturally to her. But Elizabeth saw the tension in her sister's shoulders, the way her gaze kept drifting to the window as though she could will Mr. Bingley to arrive sooner through sheer force of attention. Or perhaps delay him. Elizabeth could not quite tell which Jane hoped for, and suspected her sister might not know herself.

Darcy had written to Mr. Bingley three days ago, a letter Elizabeth had not read but whose contents she knew. An admission of fault, an explanation of his interference in separating Bingley from Jane, and an invitation to call at Darcy House when convenient. The letter had been Darcy's idea, offered during one of their careful conversations as they navigated the strange territory of their marriage that was and was not yet fully a marriage. He had seemed genuinely troubled by his past actions, had wanted to make amends in whatever way he could.

The sound of footsteps in the entrance hall made both sisters straighten, Elizabeth's hands stilling on her skirts while Jane's fingers tightened momentarily against each other before relaxing again into studied calm.

When Bingley himself entered, Elizabeth felt her chest constrict at the sight of him. He looked exactly as she remembered, all eager energy and open expression, his fair hair slightly dishevelled as though he had run his hands through it repeatedly during the carriage ride over. His eyes found Jane immediately, lighting with pleasure so genuine and unguarded that Elizabeth felt like an intruder witnessing something too private for observation.

"Miss Bennet," Bingley said, his voice carrying warmth that seemed to fill the room. His steps quickened as he crossed toward them, his smile wide enough to show teeth. "How delightful to see you again. You look wonderfully well. London clearly agrees with you."

Jane rose with movements that suggested neither haste nor reluctance, finding some middle ground that spoke of careful control. Her answering smile reached her lips but did not quite extend to her eyes, Elizabeth noticed. Nothing like the radiant joy that had once transformed Jane's face whenever Bingley entered a room in Hertfordshire.

"Mr. Bingley," Jane replied, her voice carrying its usual gentle warmth but lacking the breathless quality it had held during his previous courtship. "How kind of you to call. Please, do sit. Elizabeth and I were just discussing how pleasant the weather has been this week."

They had been discussing no such thing, but the polite fiction served its purpose. Bingley settled into the chair nearest Jane with barely contained energy, his attention fixed on her face with intensity that made Elizabeth want to look away. Instead, she remained seated, offering her own greeting when Bingley finally remembered her presence enough to acknowledge it.

"Mrs. Darcy," he said, the title still sounding strange to Elizabeth's ears even a week after acquiring it. "I must congratulate you on your marriage. Darcy is a fortunate man. Though I confess I was surprised by the suddenness of it all."

"It was rather sudden," Elizabeth agreed, keeping her voice light despite the complicated truth beneath those simple words. "But sometimes these things happen quickly when circumstances align properly."

Bingley nodded enthusiastically, already turning his attention back to Jane before Elizabeth had finished speaking. "Miss Bennet, I had hoped I might see you again, had been considering a return to Hertfordshire, but circumstances kept preventing it."

The excuse sounded weak even to Elizabeth's ears, and she saw Jane's expression flicker with something that might have been disappointment or perhaps relief that circumstances had indeed prevented his return.

"I have barely been at Longbourn since Christmas," Jane replied, her hands folding more tightly in her lap. "I stayed with my aunt and uncle in Cheapside for a while, and now reside with Elizabeth and Mr. Darcy, to keep my sister company in these early days of her marriage."

Elizabeth watched the exchange with growing understanding. Jane's responses were perfectly polite, her manner warm enough that Bingley would find no fault with it. But there was distance there, a reserve that had not existed during their earlier acquaintance. She sat slightly angled away from Bingley rather than leaning toward him as she once had. Her smiles came a beat slower than they should, as though she had to remember to produce them rather than offering them spontaneously.

And Mr. Bingley seemed not to notice these subtle withdrawals. He spoke of his time in the north, of Netherfield which remained leased though he had not yet returned to it, of mutual acquaintances from Hertfordshire. His conversation flowed with the easy charm Elizabeth remembered, but it felt now like water running over stones rather than finding purchase in soil that might help it grow."

Elizabeth shifted on the settee, drawing Bingley's attention briefly. "Mr. Bingley, you mentioned a possible return to Netherfield. Will you take up residence there soon?"

Bingley's expression showed uncertainty, his enthusiasm dimming slightly. "I am not certain. The lease continues until Michaelmas, but I have been considering other options. My sisters prefer London, you see, and Caroline in particular has been urging me to consider properties closer to town."

The mention of Caroline Bingley made Jane's posture stiffen almost imperceptibly. Darcy had been honest with Jane and Elizabeth about Caroline's attitude towards Jane, about her unkind words, and Jane was clearly still hurt by the betrayal of someone who had pretended to be her friend.

Jane rose suddenly, her movement graceful despite its abruptness. "Forgive me, I believe I left my embroidery in the morning room. I shall return in a moment."

She glided from the drawing room before either Elizabeth or Bingley could respond, leaving them in silence that felt awkward without Jane's presence to anchor it. Bingley watched her go with expression that showed confusion mixed with concern, as though he sensed something was wrong but could not identify what.

"Mrs. Darcy," Bingley said, turning to Elizabeth with boyish enthusiasm that seemed almost desperate. "I cannot tell you how delighted I am to see Miss Bennet again. She is just as lovely as I remembered. More so, perhaps. Time has only enhanced her beauty."

Elizabeth felt sympathy stir in her chest despite everything. Bingley's feelings were genuine, his affection for Jane real even if he had allowed himself to be influenced away from her. But Jane's feelings had clearly changed, had cooled in the months of separation until what remained was respect without the warmth of love.

"Jane is indeed lovely," Elizabeth agreed carefully, choosing words that would not encourage false hope. "She has many admirers in London."

The statement was true enough, though Elizabeth had not intended it as a warning until the words emerged. Bingley's face fell slightly, his enthusiasm dampening as he processed this information.

"I see," he said quietly. "I had hoped... that is, I had thought perhaps..." He trailed off, unable to complete whatever confession he had been building toward.

Jane's return interrupted the moment, her embroidery basket in hand and her composure fully restored. She settled back onto the settee beside Elizabeth, resuming conversation with Bingley as though the interruption had never happened.

They spoke for another quarter hour, the talk ranging over safe topics that required no particular intimacy or understanding. Bingley maintained his enthusiasm throughout, but Elizabeth saw it begin to waver as Jane's polite distance continued. He must have sensed it eventually, must have recognised that something had changed.

When Bingley finally rose to take his leave, his movements lacked the energy with which he had entered. He bowed over Jane's hand with less assurance than he had shown earlier, his smile not quite reaching his eyes.

"I hope we may meet again soon, Miss Bennet," he said, the words carrying question rather than assumption.

"It is always pleasant to see friends," Jane replied, her tone warm but noncommittal in ways that made the answer's true meaning unmistakable.

Elizabeth walked with Bingley to the drawing room door, offering her own farewells with genuine kindness despite the melancholy that had settled over the visit. She watched him depart down the hall toward the entrance, his shoulders slightly slumped in ways they had not been upon arrival.

When she returned to the drawing room, Jane remained on the settee, her embroidery forgotten in her lap and her gaze fixed on the window. Elizabeth settled beside her sister, waiting for Jane to speak first.

"I feel terrible," Jane said finally, her voice soft with genuine distress. "He came here full of hope, and I could give him nothing but polite conversation."

Elizabeth took Jane's hand, squeezing gently. "You were kind to him, Jane. That is all anyone could ask."

"But I do not love him," Jane continued, the admission emerging with quiet certainty. "Not anymore. Perhaps I never truly did, or perhaps the feelings simply faded during our separation. But watching him today, listening to him speak..." She paused, drawing a shaky breath. "My heart did not race. I felt no particular joy at his presence beyond the pleasure one feels at seeing any agreeable acquaintance again. And that is not enough, Lizzy. Not for marriage, not for a lifetime."

Jane had moved on, Elizabeth realised, had recognised that what she felt for Bingley no longer justified pursuing a match between them. And in that recognition lay freedom, space for something genuine to develop if the right person appeared.

"Then you did exactly right," Elizabeth said firmly. "Being honest about your feelings, even through polite reserve, is better than encouraging hopes you cannot fulfil."

Jane nodded slowly, tears gathering in her eyes though none spilled over. "I still respect him. He is amiable and good-hearted. But amiability is not love, and good intentions do not create the depth of feeling required for marriage. I see that now."

They sat together in silence, hands clasped while morning light shifted across the drawing room floor. Outside, the sounds of London continued their familiar rhythm, carriages and pedestrians and street vendors going about their ordinary business while inside, two sisters navigated the complicated territory of changed hearts and uncertain futures.

Rain struck the study windows with steady persistence, each drop tracing paths down glass already blurred with moisture. Darcy stood watching the patterns they made, his hands clasped behind his back while his mind worked through complications that had nothing to do with estate management or business correspondence. The afternoon had been difficult, watching Bingley's hopeful arrival and subsequent disappointed departure. Elizabeth had told him about it afterwards, her expression troubled as she described Jane's polite distance and Bingley's oblivious enthusiasm.

He had invited Bingley believing he was giving his friend a second chance at happiness with the woman Bingley claimed to love. But watching his friend leave with shoulders slumped and enthusiasm dampened had made Darcy question whether his interference had truly ended or simply taken a different form.

The study door opened behind him, admitting his cousin with a quiet click of the latch. Darcy turned from the window to find Fitzwilliam standing just inside the threshold, his expression showing conflict that immediately put Darcy on alert. His cousin typically wore his feelings more openly than Darcy managed, but this level of visible uncertainty suggested something significant weighed on his mind.

"Come in," Darcy said, gesturing toward the chairs positioned before his desk. "You look as though you need brandy and conversation, possibly in that order."

Fitzwilliam settled into one of the offered chairs with heaviness that spoke of more than physical fatigue. "Brandy would not be unwelcome," he admitted, accepting the glass Darcy poured from the decanter kept on the sideboard for just such occasions.

They drank in silence for a moment, rain continuing its percussion against the windows while Darcy waited for his cousin to find whatever words he had come to speak. Fitzwilliam had been a frequent visitor this past week, ostensibly calling to discuss Anne's removal to Bath and ensure Mrs. Jenkinson was put on the ship to India. But Darcy had noticed how Fitzwilliam's gaze followed Jane Bennet's movements with attention that went beyond polite interest.

"I need to speak with you about a delicate matter," Fitzwilliam said finally, setting down his glass with care that suggested he needed something to focus on beyond Darcy's face. "Something that concerns your wife's sister, Miss Bennet."

Darcy nodded, unsurprised. So his observations had been correct, his cousin's increased visits not merely about family obligation but about Jane herself. He leaned back in his chair, adopting a posture of receptive attention rather than speaking immediately. Whatever Fitzwilliam needed to confess would come more easily without interruption.

Fitzwilliam's hands tightened on the arms of his chair, his jaw working as though testing words before allowing them to emerge. "I have developed feelings for her," he said at last, the admission emerging with quiet intensity. "For Miss Bennet. Jane. I have tried to suppress them, particularly knowing you had written to Bingley. I had thought, if he and Miss Bennet rekindled their attachment, that I would step aside. That his prior claim took precedence over my more recent regard."

He stood abruptly, moving to the window where Darcy had been standing moments before. Rain obscured whatever view he sought, but Fitzwilliam seemed to need the distance, the excuse to turn away from Darcy's scrutiny.

"She has a depth of character I have rarely encountered," Fitzwilliam continued, his voice low and earnest. "Genuine kindness without pretence, intelligence without displaying it for effect. She listens when others speak, truly listens rather than simply waiting for her turn to talk. And her composure under extraordinary circumstances." He paused, clearly thinking of Jane's role in reversing the body swap, in helping Elizabeth when everything seemed impossible. "She remained steady when most would have collapsed into hysteria. That suggests strength I find deeply admirable."

Darcy set down his own glass, rising to join his cousin at the window. They stood side by side, both watching rain blur the London street beyond the glass while Darcy considered his response. Fitzwilliam's feelings were genuine, that much was clear. And Darcy had observed enough of Jane's manner around his cousin to suspect those feelings might be returned, or at least had potential to develop into something mutual.

"Bingley's visit did not go as he hoped," Darcy said quietly, choosing words with care. "Elizabeth tells me that Jane was polite but distant, that her feelings for him have cooled significantly during their separation. I do not think you need worry about prior claims or stepping aside for his sake."

Fitzwilliam turned to look at him, hope and uncertainty warring in his expression. "You are certain? I would not wish to pursue Miss Bennet if she harbours feelings for Bingley, regardless of whether those feelings are currently reciprocated."

"I am certain," Darcy replied firmly. "Jane Bennet is not the sort of woman to encourage one man's attentions while pining for another. If she has shown you warmth, if she has responded positively to your company, then her feelings for Bingley have indeed faded, and from what Elizabeth told me, Jane was clear, if kind, in demonstrating that to Bingley this afternoon."

He clapped his cousin on the shoulder, feeling genuine pleasure at the prospect of this match. "She would make you a wonderful wife, Richard. And you would make her an excellent husband. Better than Bingley would have done, I think. He is amiable and good-hearted, but you have depth he lacks. Maturity born of military service and genuine trials. Jane deserves someone who can appreciate her strength rather than simply admiring her beauty."

Fitzwilliam's expression showed gratitude mixed with remaining uncertainty. "But what of Bingley? He is your friend, and I do not wish to cause him pain."

Darcy considered this question with the seriousness it deserved. Bingley was indeed his friend, had been for several years now, and Darcy still harboured guilt over his role in separating Jane and Bingley in the first place. But friendship did not require sacrificing his cousin's happiness to preserve Bingley's hopes, and Darcy's guilt had no bearing on the choices of Jane Bennet's heart.

"Bingley is young," Darcy said finally. "He will recover from his disappointment. His feelings, while genuine, did not have time to deepen into the sort of lasting attachment that would make loss truly devastating. He was separated from Jane for months without any apparent decline in his spirits or health.

That suggests his feelings, however real, are not so profound that their frustration will cause lasting harm."

He moved back to his desk, gesturing for Fitzwilliam to retake his seat. When both were settled again, Darcy leaned forward with his elbows on the desk, his expression showing the earnestness he reserved for matters of true importance.

"We must talk practicalities, though," Darcy continued. "You are a second son, and while I know your father will not see you left entirely without, I know the Matlock estates are mostly entailed and they hoped you would marry well. Where do you propose to live, if you marry Jane Bennet?"

Fitzwilliam reached into his coat pocket, withdrawing a letter whose paper showed wear that suggested it had been read multiple times. "That is something I meant to tell you. Part of why I felt emboldened to consider courting Miss Bennet despite my position as a second son." He smoothed the letter on his knee, his expression showing satisfaction mixed with continuing disbelief. "My maternal grandparents have made me their heir. The estate is in Nottinghamshire, not grand by your standards but respectable. Four thousand a year once my grandfather passes, and in the meantime, they have settled a thousand pounds per annum on me immediately."

Darcy felt his eyebrows rise with genuine surprise. "Richard, that is excellent news. Why did you not mention this sooner?"

"I only received the letter three days ago," Fitzwilliam replied, tucking the paper back into his pocket. "My grandfather's health has been declining, and he wanted to settle his affairs while he retained full capacity. They had no wish to see the property broken up or sold after their deaths. They had only daughters, no sons, and of their several grandsons, I am the only one without significant fortune of my own. Making me their

heir both secures my future and ensures the estate remains in the family."

He looked up at Darcy with expression that showed both pride and remaining vulnerability. "So you see, I can offer Miss Bennet a comfortable life. Not luxury, perhaps, but security and respectability. A good home, connections that would not shame her, and genuine affection from a husband who values her for more than simply her beauty or amiability."

"Then you should court her," Darcy said firmly. "With my blessing and, I suspect, with Elizabeth's enthusiastic support once she learns of your intentions. Jane deserves happiness with someone who truly appreciates her character, and you deserve happiness with a woman who can meet you as an equal rather than simply an advantageous match."

Fitzwilliam's face showed relief so profound that it transformed his features, years seeming to drop away as tension released. "Thank you, Darcy. Your support means more than I can adequately express."

A knock at the door interrupted their conversation, a servant entering to announce that dinner was ready to be served. They rose together, Darcy feeling satisfaction settle over him as they moved toward the door. His cousin had found genuine affection with a woman worthy of that affection. Jane would gain a husband who appreciated her strength and character. And perhaps, in some small way, this match would help atone for the harm Darcy's interference had caused months ago in separating Jane and Bingley.

Elizabeth sat in Darcy House's elegant parlour with Georgiana, their needlework spread across their laps while they spoke in quiet tones that seemed appropriate to the peaceful atmosphere. This had become their habit over the past few days, spending an hour or two together each afternoon while Darcy attended to business matters in his study, and Jane went for a walk or drive with Colonel Fitzwilliam. Elizabeth found she genuinely enjoyed her new sister's company, appreciated the gentle sweetness that lay beneath Georgiana's painful shyness.

Georgiana's fingers moved across her embroidery with swift skill, creating delicate patterns that would eventually become a handkerchief for her brother. Elizabeth's own needlework showed less precision, her stitches adequate but hardly exemplary. She had never possessed the patience for detailed handwork. But the activity provided pleasant occupation for hands that might otherwise remain idle, and the rhythmic motion of needle through fabric created a meditative quality that made conversation flow more easily.

"I received a letter from Mrs. Reynolds at Pemberley this morning," Georgiana said, her voice carrying the soft hesitancy that characterised most of her speech. "She writes that the rose garden is in full bloom now, that it smells heavenly when one walks through it in the evening."

Elizabeth smiled at the mention of Pemberley's housekeeper, about whom she had heard much from both Darcy siblings. "I look forward to seeing it. Your brother has told me the gardens are extensive, that they were particularly dear to your mother."

"They were," Georgiana agreed, her expression showing fondness mixed with old grief. "Mama spent hours there, planning new plantings and rearranging existing beds."

They worked in companionable silence for a few moments, needles flashing in the afternoon light. Elizabeth found herself thinking about Jane, about Bingley's disappointed visit the day before and Fitzwilliam's confession to Darcy. Her husband had told her about the conversation in his study, had shared his cousin's intentions and asked whether she thought Jane might be receptive to Fitzwilliam's courtship. Elizabeth had confirmed what Darcy suspected, that Jane's feelings had indeed shifted away from Bingley and toward the Colonel.

"I understand Mr. Bingley called here recently," Georgiana said, her voice dropping to near whisper. "To see your sister Jane."

Elizabeth glanced at her companion, noting the way Georgiana's cheeks had coloured slightly, how her fingers had stilled on her embroidery despite her attempt to appear unconcerned. "He did. My husband wrote to him, explaining his part in separating Mr. Bingley from Jane last autumn. Mr. Bingley came hoping to renew their acquaintance."

"And did he succeed?" Georgiana's question emerged with studied casualness that did not quite mask the genuine interest beneath it.

"Not in the way he hoped," Elizabeth replied carefully, watching Georgiana's face for reaction. "Jane was polite but distant. I think their separation cooled feelings that might have developed into genuine attachment had they been allowed to continue naturally."

Georgiana's shoulders relaxed slightly at this information, a reaction she quickly tried to conceal by bending more intently over her needlework. But Elizabeth had seen it, had noted the relief that flickered across her new sister's face before proper composure could be restored.

Understanding dawned with sudden clarity that made Elizabeth want to laugh at her own blindness. *Of course*. Georgiana had met Bingley during his friendship with Darcy, had likely seen him on various occasions over the past few years. Bingley, with his open manners and easy charm, was precisely the sort of man who might draw out someone as shy as Georgiana.

"Georgiana," Elizabeth said gently, setting aside her own needlework to give her full attention to the girl beside her. "Did you perhaps hope that Mr. Bingley would not renew his courtship of Jane?"

Georgiana's hands stilled completely, her face flushing deep pink that spread from her cheeks down her neck. She kept her gaze fixed on her embroidery, her fingers tracing the pattern she had created without actually resuming her stitching.

"I know it is wrong of me," Georgiana whispered, her voice trembling with obvious distress. "Jane is your sister, and you must want her happiness above all things." She finally looked up, meeting Elizabeth's eyes with expression that showed guilt mixed with helpless hope. "But I confess I would have been quite sorry if Mr. Bingley had married your sister."

Elizabeth felt her heart squeeze with sympathy for this painfully honest admission. Georgiana had clearly been carrying this secret, had tortured herself over feelings she believed were inappropriate or wrong. The girl's distress was written plainly on her face, in the way her hands twisted the embroidery in her lap with enough force to wrinkle the delicate fabric.

"There is nothing wrong with your feelings," Elizabeth said firmly, reaching out to still Georgiana's restless hands with her own. "You cannot control whom your heart finds appealing, and Mr. Bingley is certainly worthy of admiration. He is amiable and kind, handsome and cheerful."

Georgiana's eyes widened at this matter-of-fact acceptance, as though she had expected censure or mockery rather than understanding. "But he loved Miss Bennet. Or thought he did. And I should not have wished for that to end simply because..." She trailed off, unable to complete the confession.

"Simply because you harbour feelings for him yourself?" Elizabeth supplied gently, keeping her voice free of judgment. "Georgiana, having feelings does not make you wicked or selfish. Acting on those feelings inappropriately might, but simply possessing them is perfectly natural and human."

She squeezed Georgiana's hands before releasing them, settling back against the window frame with small smile. "I believe he is very amiable," Elizabeth continued, deliberately echoing Georgiana's earlier assessment. "And I think he would be fortunate indeed to gain the regard of someone as genuinely kind and accomplished as yourself."

"But..." Georgiana's voice emerged barely above a whisper, her face still showing distress despite Elizabeth's reassurances. "But I am so shy, so awkward in company. I cannot make clever conversation or draw attention in a room. Mr. Bingley would surely prefer someone more vivacious, someone who could match his energy and enthusiasm."

Elizabeth considered this assessment, recognizing the self-doubt that lay beneath it. Georgiana had been comparing herself to others and finding herself lacking, had convinced herself that her natural reserve made her somehow deficient or unworthy of notice.

"Perhaps what he truly needs is someone whose gentleness can balance his enthusiasm, whose quiet strength can provide stability his nature lacks," Elizabeth said finally. She felt a smile tug at her lips as an amusing thought occurred to her. "You know, this means that Caroline Bingley might get her alliance with the Darcys after all, though certainly not the one she originally wanted."

Understanding dawned on Georgiana's face, followed immediately by a laugh that transformed her features with genuine amusement. The sound was delightful, unguarded in ways Georgiana's usual careful demeanour never allowed. "Oh, Caroline would be furious," Georgiana said, her eyes sparkling with mirth. "To gain the connexion she sought but through circumstances that would give her no particular standing or advantage. She could hardly claim precedence over me in my own home."

Elizabeth laughed as well, pleased to see Georgiana's distress giving way to humour. "Indeed not. Though I suspect she would try regardless. Miss Bingley's capacity for self-delusion where social standing is concerned seems nearly limitless."

They dissolved into giggles that would have been unbecoming in more formal company but felt perfectly appropriate here. The tension that had characterised the beginning of their conversation had dissipated entirely, replaced by warmth and genuine affection that made Elizabeth grateful for the strange circumstances that had brought her into this family.

Elizabeth found herself thinking about Caroline Bingley's likely reaction if Georgiana and Bingley did indeed form an attachment. The woman had been relentless in her pursuit of Darcy, had schemed and manipulated in hopes of becoming his wife. To see her brother marry into the Darcy family while she remained Miss Bingley would be a blow to her consequence that Elizabeth could not help but find satisfying.

But beyond the amusing thought of Caroline's discomfiture lay something more significant. Georgiana deserved happiness with someone who could appreciate her gentle nature, who would not be put off by her shyness or mistake her reserve for coldness. And Bingley, for all his tendency toward precipitous attachment, possessed genuine kindness that would serve him well with someone as sensitive as Georgiana.

They would need time, of course. Georgiana was still young, not even officially out in society yet, and Bingley needed opportunity to recover from his disappointed hopes regarding Jane. But given time and proximity, given the natural connexion their families would maintain through Elizabeth and Darcy's marriage, something real might develop between them.

Elizabeth found a good deal of satisfaction in that thought.

Chapter Thirty-Two

THE CHURCH AT MERYTON smelled of beeswax and roses, the familiar scents taking on new meaning as Elizabeth stood in the vestibule with her father's arm beneath her hand. Through the open doors, she could see the church filled to capacity, every pew occupied with well-wishers.

The Bennets occupied the front pews on the left, her mother already dabbing at her eyes with a handkerchief whilst simultaneously beaming with such radiant satisfaction that Elizabeth half-expected her to stand and proclaim her triumph to the assembled crowd. Kitty and Lydia sat with unusual stillness, their behaviour remarkably restrained. Elizabeth had seen them eyeing Colonel Fitzwilliam's uniform with obvious appreciation as they entered, whispering to each other behind their fans, but they had settled into proper decorum once the ceremony began to draw near.

Mary sat beside them with her prayer book open, her expression showing solemn approval of the proceedings. Even she seemed caught up in the significance of the day, her usual stern piety softened into something approaching genuine pleasure.

On the right sat the Matlocks in prominent position, Lord Matlock's austere features showing what might have been approval as he surveyed the full church, Elizabeth's friends and neighbours all turned out in their Sunday best to see her wed. Lady Matlock smiled warmly, her expression genuinely kind as she caught Elizabeth's eye. Beside them, Georgiana fairly beamed, her happiness for her brother evident in every line of her posture. The girl's usual shyness had been overcome by joy so profound it transformed her features.

The Gardiners sat near the front, her dear aunt and uncle. Mr. Gardiner caught her eye and nodded with quiet encouragement, his steady presence a comfort. Beside him, Mrs. Gardiner smiled with tears already gathering, her expression showing the genuine affection she had always held for her niece.

And there, scattered throughout the remaining pews, were all the familiar faces of Meryton. The Longs and the Gouldings, Sir William Lucas holding forth despite his daughter Charlotte's obvious attempts to quiet him. Charlotte herself sat in prominent position beside her husband, Mr. Collins, whose obsequious expression suggested he was already planning the fawning congratulations he would offer at the wedding breakfast.

Mr. Collins and Charlotte were staying a t Lucas Lodge, of course, but Mr. Collins had attended Longbourn yesterday, his effusive expressions of delight at witnessing his patroness's nephew's wedding delivered with such excessive enthusiasm that Elizabeth had been driven to escape to her room to avoid prolonged exposure. He was clearly hoping to curry favour with Darcy, to establish some connexion that might elevate his own consequence despite Lady Catherine's conspicuous absence from the proceedings.

But Elizabeth's attention moved inexorably to the man standing before the altar, and everything else faded to insignificance.

Darcy stood waiting for her, his dark coat impeccably tailored, his expression showing none of his usual reserve. Instead his face was open, vulnerable in ways she had rarely seen, his eyes fixed on her with an intensity that made her breath catch. Behind him stood Colonel Fitzwilliam, his role as groomsman apparently less important to him than the frequent glances he directed towards Jane, sitting in the Bennet pew.

This was different from London. That hasty ceremony had been spoken by an impostor whilst Elizabeth watched helplessly, trapped in Anne's failing body. This was real. This was hers.

The organ swelled with music she had known all her life, the familiar hymn that had accompanied countless Meryton brides down this same aisle. Her father's arm tightened beneath her hand.

"Ready, Lizzy?" Mr. Bennet asked quietly, his voice carrying emotion he rarely displayed.

"More than ready, Papa."

They began their measured walk down the aisle. Elizabeth was aware of the watching crowd, of her mother's barely stifled sobs of joy, of the whispers that followed her progress. But her focus remained on Darcy, on the way his expression transformed as she drew nearer, warmth flooding his features until he looked years younger.

When they reached the altar, Mr. Bennet placed her hand in Darcy's with careful solemnity that suggested the moment held deep significance for him. His fingers were warm and steady, closing around hers with gentle pressure that steadied her nerves.

Mr. Bennet stepped back to join his wife, but not before catching Elizabeth's eye one final time. His expression showed everything words could not convey, the deepest pride and profound affection. She saw him mouth silently, "My Lizzy," before turning away, and felt tears threaten despite her determination to maintain composure.

The vicar began the ceremony, his voice carrying through the church with ceremonial gravity. "Dearly beloved, we are gathered together here in the sight of God, and in the face of this congregation, to join together this Man and this Woman in Holy Matrimony."

Elizabeth heard the words properly this time. Heard them directed at her, spoken for her benefit rather than for an impostor wearing her face. Each phrase settled into her consciousness with significance the London ceremony had lacked.

"Marriage is an honourable estate," the vicar continued, "instituted of God in the time of man's innocence, signifying unto us the mystical union that is betwixt Christ and his Church."

The familiar words washed over her, beautiful in their antiquity and gravity. Elizabeth had heard this service countless times throughout her life, had attended weddings of neighbours and distant relations where these same phrases were spoken. But hearing them now, knowing they applied to her, transformed their meaning entirely.

"I will," Elizabeth said when the vicar posed the question to her, and felt something settle into place in her chest. These were her words. Her vows. Spoken freely and with full understanding of what they meant, with her own voice and her own will, uncoerced and genuine.

"I, Elizabeth Bennet, take thee, Fitzwilliam Darcy, to my wedded husband, to have and to hold from this day forward, for better for worse, for richer for poorer, in sickness and in health, to love and to cherish, till death us do part, according to God's holy ordinance; and thereto I give thee my troth."

"Those whom God hath joined together," the vicar proclaimed, his voice ringing with authority, "let no man put asunder."

The ceremony complete, Darcy leaned down to kiss her with tenderness that made Elizabeth's eyes sting with tears she refused to shed. When they drew apart, his smile was radiant, transforming his usually serious features into something approaching pure joy.

They processed back down the aisle together, Elizabeth's hand tucked into Darcy's elbow. The congregation rose in a rustle of fabric and murmured congratulations. Behind them, Colonel Fitzwilliam offered Jane his arm to escort her from the church.

Outside in the churchyard, well-wishers pressed forward immediately. Elizabeth endured the attention with as much grace as she could muster, Darcy's steady presence at her side making it bearable. Mrs. Bennet's voice could be heard above the general commotion, proclaiming her daughter's excellent fortune to anyone within earshot.

"Ten thousand a year!" Mrs. Bennet was saying to Mrs. Long, her voice carrying despite her apparent attempt at discretion. "And such a fine estate in Derbyshire! My Lizzy will want for nothing, I assure you!"

Mr. Collins pushed through the crowd with determination that bordered on aggressive, his expression showing such exaggerated delight that Elizabeth braced herself for the inevitable effusiveness.

"Mrs. Darcy!" he exclaimed, bowing so deeply that Elizabeth worried he might actually topple forward. "What felicity! What unparalleled joy to witness this most auspicious union! I am quite overcome with delight at seeing my patroness's esteemed nephew allied with one of my own cousins, however distant the connexion may be. Lady Catherine would be in raptures, I am certain, were circumstances not keeping her in Bath with poor Miss de Bourgh. Though I assure you, I shall write to her immediately with a full account of the ceremony's magnificence!"

"How very kind of you, Mr. Collins," Elizabeth managed, her tone suggesting the exact opposite of appreciation for this promised correspondence.

Darcy's hand covered hers on his arm, squeezing gently in silent sympathy. "Mr. Collins," he said with polite but firm dismissal, "you must excuse us. There are many guests waiting to offer their congratulations."

Mr. Collins bowed again, releasing them with more flowery protestations, but Elizabeth was already moving away, grateful for Darcy's intervention.

A figure in military dress uniform caught her attention, and Elizabeth recognised Colonel Forster from the militia approaching through the crowd. He bowed over her hand with respectful courtesy before turning to Darcy.

"Mr. Darcy, Mrs. Darcy, forgive the intrusion," Colonel Forster said quietly, his tone suggesting the matter was of some importance despite the celebratory atmosphere. "I did not wish to trouble you on such a happy occasion, but I thought you would want to know that Mr. Wickham has been committed to the Fleet."

Elizabeth felt Darcy's arm tense beneath her hand, though his expression remained carefully neutral.

"The debts he accrued were substantial," Colonel Forster continued, keeping his voice low enough that nearby guests could not overhear. "And with his dismissal from the militia for falsified references, he had no means to satisfy them. He will remain imprisoned until such time as he can pay what he owes, which I suspect will be a considerable duration. Years, most likely."

"Thank you for informing me, Colonel," Darcy replied, his voice steady though Elizabeth felt some of the tension ease from his frame. "I appreciate your diligence in the matter, and your discretion in bringing it to my attention."

Colonel Forster bowed again and withdrew, melting back into the crowd. Elizabeth squeezed Darcy's arm, understanding what this news meant. Wickham could harm no one else, at least for now. Georgiana was safe from any further schemes he might have attempted, and so were Elizabeth's vulnerable younger sisters. The man who had caused so much pain to the Darcy family was finally facing consequences for his actions.

"One more threat neutralised," Elizabeth murmured, low enough that only Darcy could hear.

"Yes," Darcy agreed softly. "Though I find I care less about Wickham's fate today than I would have thought possible. There are far more important things demanding my attention."

His eyes met hers with warmth that made her breath catch, and Elizabeth felt a smile tug at her lips despite the solemnity of Colonel Forster's news.

"Come," Darcy said, guiding her towards their waiting carriage. "Your mother will be devastated if we are late to the breakfast she has worked so hard to arrange. And I confess I am eager to begin celebrating our marriage properly, surrounded by friends and family who actually know the woman I married."

The reference to the London ceremony, to Anne's deception, was subtle enough that no one else would catch it. But Elizabeth understood, and felt grateful for Darcy's acknowledgement of how much this day meant to her.

Longbourn's dining room and drawing room had been transformed for the wedding breakfast, every surface laden with delicacies that represented Mrs. Bennet's finest efforts. Cold meats and raised pies, syllabubs and jellies, fruit tarts and iced cakes, all arranged with attention to presentation that would have done credit to far grander establishments. The house buzzed with conversation and laughter as guests filled every available space, helping themselves to the impressive spread whilst offering toasts to the happy couple.

Mrs. Bennet moved through the crowd in a state of such elevated delight that Elizabeth worried she might actually faint from the excitement. Her face was flushed, her fan working frantically, her voice carrying above the general din as she accepted compliments on the arrangements with barely contained triumph.

When Lady Matlock approached their hostess with warm congratulations on the excellence of the breakfast, Mrs. Bennet's joy reached heights that made her nearly incoherent.

"Your Ladyship is too kind!" Mrs. Bennet exclaimed, her voice trembling with emotion. "I only wished to do justice to the occasion. My Lizzy marrying so well, you understand, it deserves proper celebration! I wanted everything to be perfect."

"You have succeeded admirably," Lady Matlock replied with genuine warmth that suggested she found Mrs. Bennet's enthusiasm endearing rather than vulgar. "You have done Elizabeth proud, Mrs. Bennet. And your home is most welcoming. Mr. Darcy is fortunate indeed to be joining such a warm and loving family."

Elizabeth watched her mother receive this praise with satisfaction that went beyond mere social triumph. Mrs. Bennet had worked tirelessly to make this day perfect, had driven Cook and the servants to distraction with her exacting standards and constant changes to the menu. Seeing her efforts recognised by someone of Lady Matlock's standing clearly meant the world to her, validation that all her planning and fretting had achieved its purpose.

"You are too good, my lady," Mrs. Bennet managed, tears gathering in her eyes. "Too good indeed. I am quite overcome. To have such illustrious company honouring our humble home!"

Across the room, Elizabeth noted Colonel Fitzwilliam in quiet conversation with Jane, their heads bent close together in a way that suggested the discussion was of a decidedly private nature. The Colonel's expression showed a tender regard that made Elizabeth's heart warm with hope for her sister's future happiness. His hand rested near Jane's shoulder on the back of the settee where they sat, not quite touching but close enough to suggest intimacy that would have been improper without the promise of courtship between them.

Jane's face had coloured slightly, but her smile showed genuine pleasure at whatever the Colonel was saying. Elizabeth saw

her sister glance towards their mother, then back to the Colonel with an expression that suggested she was seriously considering whatever proposal he might be building towards.

Georgiana had been claimed by Kitty and Lydia, who were peppering her with questions about Pemberley and London with enthusiasm that might have overwhelmed someone less patient. But Georgiana seemed to be managing admirably, her natural shyness overcome by genuine interest in her new sisters.

"Is it true that Pemberley has more than a hundred rooms?" Lydia was asking, her eyes wide with fascination.

"And that the ballroom can accommodate two hundred guests?" Kitty added, practically bouncing with excitement.

Georgiana answered their questions with gentle patience, her responses encouraging rather than discouraging their enthusiasm despite its somewhat vulgar intensity.

Mr. Collins had cornered Darcy again, his obsequious manner reaching new heights as he expounded on the condescension of Lady Catherine. His hands gestured wildly as he spoke, his expression showing such exaggerated respect that it bordered on farcical.

"My esteemed patroness has been most generous in her attentions," Mr. Collins was saying, his voice carrying across the room despite his apparent attempt at discretion. "Most generous indeed! Why, just last month she condescended to advise me on the arrangement of my shelves, and her insights were invaluable. Invaluable! I am certain you must feel the loss of her guidance most acutely, Mr. Darcy, now that circumstances have taken her to Bath."

Darcy's expression showed polite tolerance, though Elizabeth could read the irritation beneath his careful courtesy. His jaw had tightened slightly, his responses to Mr. Collins's effusions growing briefer and more clipped.

Elizabeth moved to rescue him, slipping her hand through his arm with proprietary ease that still felt novel but increasingly natural. "Mr. Collins, you must excuse us. I believe my father wishes to propose a toast."

Mr. Collins bowed deeply, releasing them with flowery protestations about not wishing to monopolise the groom's attention. "Of course, of course! How inconsiderate of me! Though I hope we might speak further later, Mr. Darcy. I have several thoughts regarding the management of parish affairs that I would value your opinion on, given your evident wisdom in such matters."

Darcy inclined his head with minimal courtesy and allowed Elizabeth to guide him away. His hand covered hers on his arm, squeezing gently in silent gratitude.

"Thank you," he murmured quietly. "Another few minutes of his obsequious flattery and I fear I would have said something regrettable."

"I could not allow my husband to commit murder at our wedding breakfast," Elizabeth replied with amusement. "It would quite spoil the festivities."

Mr. Bennet did indeed call for attention, raising his glass with ceremonial gravity that suggested genuine feeling beneath his usual sardonic manner. The crowd quieted, all eyes turning towards the master of Longbourn as he prepared to speak.

"To my daughter Elizabeth," Mr. Bennet began, his voice carrying clearly through the suddenly silent rooms, "and her husband Mr. Darcy. I have known Lizzy impertinent since childhood, have watched her develop a liveliness of mind that bordered on impudence and a wit that often tested the lim-

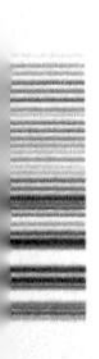

its of proper courtesy. These qualities made her my particular favourite amongst my daughters, I confess, for she was never insipid or vapid or content to simply accept what others told her to think."

He paused, his eyes finding Elizabeth's across the room. "I wish her every happiness with a man who has proven himself worthy of her particular brand of impertinence."

Elizabeth felt tears gather despite her best efforts to contain them. Her father had known that something was not right with his favourite daughter when she came to London, rushing to marry a man she had always expressed dislike of. He had mentioned something of it to her a few days ago, quietly, with a question in his eyes, and she had hesitated only briefly before telling him the whole. He had embraced her lovingly, telling her that he believed her.

Mr. Bennet had read enough accounts of utter strangeness to know that there were things in the world that could not be explained by ordinary means, and he was only sorry his daughter had been the victim of one of them. They had talked long into the evening, Mr. Bennet seeking to assure himself that she truly wished to be Mrs. Darcy, but Elizabeth had been able to assure him that she did. That she truly believed Mr. Darcy to be the best of men, and however their union might have come about, she was the furthest thing from sorry about it.

"May their union be blessed with happiness, health, and the wisdom to appreciate the extraordinary good fortune they have found in each other," Mr. Bennet concluded, raising his glass higher. "To Mr. and Mrs. Darcy!"

"To Mr. and Mrs. Darcy!" the assembled guests chorused, raising glasses in enthusiastic agreement.

The celebration continued for hours, guests lingering over food and conversation whilst Elizabeth and Darcy accepted congratulations from what felt like every resident of Meryton and beyond. By the time the gathering began to disperse, Elizabeth felt exhausted but deeply satisfied. This had been everything the London wedding was not, real and joyful and entirely her own.

Late afternoon sun slanted through the carriage windows as they departed Longbourn, the familiar landscape rolling past whilst Elizabeth settled against the seat with a sigh of contentment. Darcy sat beside her, Georgiana opposite, all three of them pleasantly weary from the day's festivities.

The farewells had been protracted, with Mrs. Bennet dissolving into tears whilst simultaneously beaming with such radiant joy that the contradiction seemed not to trouble her in the slightest. Jane had embraced Elizabeth with fierce affection, whispering congratulations and promises to write soon. Even Mr. Bennet had shown unusual emotion, his eyes suspiciously bright as he handed his daughter up into the carriage.

"I am glad we did this," Elizabeth said softly, her hand finding Darcy's on the seat between them. "The second wedding. It made everything feel real in a way the first ceremony never could."

"I am glad as well," Darcy replied, raising her hand to his lips with gesture that had become familiar over the past weeks. "You deserved a wedding that was truly yours, with your family present and your own vows spoken freely. I only regret that circumstances required it at all."

Georgiana smiled at them both with such open happiness that Elizabeth felt her heart squeeze with affection for her new sister. "It was beautiful," Georgiana said, her voice soft but

carrying genuine emotion. "I have never seen my brother look so happy. And your family is wonderful, Elizabeth. So warm and welcoming. Even your younger sisters, though they are rather... spirited."

Elizabeth laughed at the diplomatic phrasing. "Spirited is certainly one word for Lydia and Kitty. I hope they did not overwhelm you too terribly with their questions."

"Not at all," Georgiana assured her. "They were very kind, and their enthusiasm was rather endearing. I think I shall enjoy having sisters, even if they are a bit more lively than I am accustomed to."

They travelled in comfortable silence for a while, the gentle rocking of the carriage and the steady rhythm of hooves creating a peaceful atmosphere. Elizabeth found herself thinking about the past weeks, about everything that had happened since that terrible morning when she woke in Anne's body and discovered the full extent of the scheme against her.

Anne was in Bath now, under constant supervision, her schemes for body-swapping thoroughly thwarted. Mrs. Jenkinson was on a ship bound for India, sent far enough away that she could never assist Anne in another such attempt. Even Wickham was in debtor's prison, facing consequences for his lies and manipulations. All the threats to her and Darcy's happiness had been neutralised, all the immediate dangers resolved.

What remained was simply life. A marriage to build, a household to run, relationships to nurture and develop. The prospect felt both daunting and exciting, full of possibility rather than predetermined fate.

"What are you thinking?" Darcy asked quietly, his thumb brushing across her knuckles in the gentle circles that had become his habit.

"That I feel properly like Mrs. Darcy at last," Elizabeth replied, meeting his eyes with a smile that felt entirely genuine. "Not legally for the first time, but genuinely. In my heart as well as on paper. This marriage is mine now, not something that happened to someone else whilst I watched helplessly."

His answering smile was brilliant, transforming his features with joy that made him look years younger than his actual age. "I am very glad to hear it. Though I confess I have felt you were truly my wife since the moment you agreed to give our marriage a chance, regardless of how it began. Your courage in facing such impossible circumstances, your determination to reclaim what was stolen from you, only confirmed what I already knew. That you are extraordinary, Elizabeth, and that I am the most fortunate man alive to call you my wife."

The carriage rolled on towards Pemberley, carrying them towards their future together. Elizabeth leaned against Darcy's shoulder, his arm coming around her in gesture that felt both protective and welcoming. Through the window, she watched the countryside change as they moved further north, leaving Hertfordshire behind for Derbyshire and whatever awaited them there.

She was Mrs. Darcy now. Truly, completely, irrevocably. Not because an impostor had spoken vows in her voice, but because she herself had stood before God and congregation and freely chosen this path. The knowledge settled over her with quiet certainty, bringing not anxiety but anticipation.

Whatever came next, she was ready.

Chapter Thirty-Three

In a beautifully appointed sitting room at Pemberley, a room which had once been the domain of Lady Anne Darcy, Elizabeth sat at her writing desk, the grimoire resting before her. She ran her fingers across the cover one final time, tracing the de Bourgh crest embossed in the lower corner, before lifting it and placing it carefully in the drawer she had designated for things that required safe-keeping.

The key turned with satisfying click, metal sliding into place with finality that made something in Elizabeth's chest ease. She had debated what to do with the grimoire for weeks after returning to herself, after the second wedding at Longbourn and the journey to Pemberley. Destroying it had seemed wrong somehow, despite the dark uses to which Anne had put its recipes. The knowledge itself was not evil, merely dangerous in the wrong hands. And there might come a time when understanding such things once again proved necessary, when knowing how a spell was constructed could help undo damage wrought by someone else with similar knowledge.

But she would not use it unless in case of great need. Would not be tempted by shortcuts or magical solutions to ordinary problems. The grimoire would remain locked away, a reminder of choices made and consequences faced, but not a tool she would ever willingly employ.

Elizabeth withdrew the key and tucked it into the small box she kept in the drawer above, beneath correspondence and calling cards and other ephemera of her new station. Settling back in her chair, she let her gaze drift across the sitting room that had become her private retreat in this grand house.

The room was smaller than most at Pemberley, which she appreciated. Darcy had given her free choice of any chamber for her personal use, and she had selected this one for its eastern exposure and its view of the rose garden below. He had been obviously pleased by her choice, telling her it had once been his mother's favourite room. The furnishings were elegant without being ostentatious, comfortable chairs upholstered in blue damask positioned near the windows to catch the best light for reading. Her books lined shelves along one wall, a growing collection that included volumes from her father's library at Longbourn alongside new acquisitions from Pemberley's extensive collection and purchases made during their wedding trip.

A knock at the door interrupted her contemplation. At her call to enter, one of the housemaids appeared with the morning post arranged on a silver tray.

"The post, ma'am," the maid said, setting the tray on the desk at Elizabeth's elbow. "Mrs. Reynolds said to tell you that the

guest rooms are ready for your inspection whenever you find it convenient."

"Thank you, Mary," Elizabeth replied. "Please tell Mrs. Reynolds I shall come down within the hour."

The maid departed, and Elizabeth turned her attention to the correspondence. Several letters lay arranged by what she assumed was the butler's assessment of their importance. On top rested a thick missive bearing her father's distinctive scrawl, which made her smile with anticipation of his sardonic observations about neighbourhood gossip. Likely, its thickness was due to letters enclosed from her mother and some of her younger sisters as well. Beneath the packet from Longbourn lay letters from her aunt Gardiner and from Charlotte Collins.

But it was the letter at the bottom of the stack that caught and held Elizabeth's attention. The Bath postmark and the quality of the paper suggested its source before she broke the seal.

Elizabeth unfolded the letter with fingers that trembled slightly despite her best efforts at composure. She had written to Lady Catherine twice since leaving London, formal notes expressing hope for Anne's recovery and offering what comfort she could despite knowing her words would likely be received with suspicion or outright hostility. Lady Catherine had not responded to either letter, and Elizabeth had assumed her overtures would continue to be ignored.

Elizabeth's eyebrows rose as she read, realising that Lady Catherine now knew what Anne had done. Anne must have confessed all to her mother at some point.

Mrs. Darcy,

I write to inform you of my daughter's condition, as you have expressed interest in such matters through your previous correspondence. Anne's health continues its decline. The Bath waters have provided no relief, and the physicians can offer nothing beyond palliatives that ease her discomfort without addressing the underlying deterioration of her constitution.

Her mind remains sound, though her spirits vary greatly from day to day. Some mornings she wakes with something approaching contrition, speaking of regrets and acknowledging the wickedness of her actions. On such days she asks after you, wonders whether you have recovered fully from your ordeal. She seems genuinely distressed by what she attempted, by the harm she caused in pursuit of desires she now recognises as shameful.

But other days bring only resentment and bitterness. On those occasions she rails against fate, against the frailty that plagues her, against all of us who have failed to understand her suffering. She insists she would do it all again if given the opportunity, that you were unworthy of the blessings you possessed and that she had every right to claim them for herself.

I confess I do not know which version of my daughter represents her true feelings. Perhaps both do, warring within her as her body fails around them.

She demands my assistance in creating another potion, finding another body to inhabit before this one fails her entirely. I will not be a party to such wickedness. Interfering in the natural order of things is abhorrent, and had I known what Anne intended, she would never have had the opportunity to harm you. You have my word that I will not allow her to harm anyone else.

The physicians believe she has only weeks remaining now, at best. I thought you should know. I will, of course, remain with my daughter until the end.

Lady Catherine de Bourgh

Elizabeth set down the letter with hands that had gone cold despite the summer warmth filling her sitting room. Weeks to

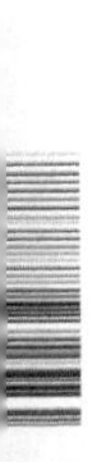

live. Anne de Bourgh, who had stolen her body and spoken vows in her voice and trapped her in a dying prison of flesh, would soon face the final consequence of her choices. The knowledge sat heavy in Elizabeth's chest, complicated emotion that defied easy categorisation.

She should feel satisfaction, perhaps. Justice being served, the villain facing appropriate punishment for her crimes. But Elizabeth found she could not summon such simple vindication. Instead she felt only a profound sadness for the waste of it all. Anne had possessed intelligence and determination, qualities that might have been directed toward genuine accomplishment had circumstances been different.

Elizabeth drew a fresh sheet of paper toward her, dipping her pen in the inkwell and pausing to think. The words she needed would not come easily, required thought and precision to convey sympathy without condescension, concern without claiming false friendship.

Lady Catherine,

Thank you for informing me of Anne's condition. I am genuinely sorry to learn of her continued decline, and I hope the physicians can at least ensure her remaining time is free from unnecessary suffering.

Please convey my regards to Anne on her better days, when she is capable of receiving them. Tell her that I bear her no lasting ill will, that I understand desperation can drive people to actions they would never otherwise contemplate. Tell her that I hope she finds peace, whatever form that peace might take.

If there is anything I might do to ease her final days, you need only ask. I would be willing to write to her directly if such correspondence would bring her any comfort.

I know our families' relationship has been complicated by recent events, but I hope you will accept my sincere wishes for Anne's comfort and your own strength during this difficult time.

With genuine concern,

Elizabeth Darcy

She read over the letter twice, weighing each phrase against her true feelings. The words were honest, she decided. She did hope Anne found peace, did wish for her comfort in dying as she had not experienced comfort in living. And she bore no desire for vengeance or further suffering beyond what Anne's own choices had already wrought.

Elizabeth folded the letter, sealing it with wax and pressing her new seal into the soft surface. She set the letter aside for the afternoon post, then rose from her desk and moved to the window.

Below, the rose garden spread toward the south lawn, blooms ranging from white to pink to deep red. The scent drifted up through her open window, sweet and slightly heady in the warm air. This was her home now, this beautiful estate with its elegant rooms and extensive grounds. She was mistress here, responsible for its management and the welfare of everyone who lived within its bounds.

The thought still struck her with wonder sometimes, that this was truly her life now. That the impossible circumstances which had brought her here had resolved into genuine happiness, into a marriage that grew more comfortable and affectionate with each passing day. Darcy had been patient beyond measure, had given her the time and space she needed to feel that their marriage belonged to her rather than to the woman who had stolen her form.

And she did feel that now. Felt that she had chosen him, chosen this life, even if the path to that choice had been extraordinarily strange. They were building something real together, she and Darcy. Something that had nothing to do with magic or coercion but everything to do with mutual respect and growing affection freely given.

Elizabeth touched the window frame, feeling the warmth of sun-heated wood beneath her fingers. Tomorrow Jane and Colonel Fitzwilliam would arrive for a visit before their own wedding at Longbourn next month. The Gardiners would come as well, eager to see her settled so magnificently and to explore the beauties of Derbyshire. The house would fill with laughter and conversation, with the comfortable chaos of family gathering in celebration.

But for now, this moment of quiet reflection felt right. A pause before the happiness to come, a space to acknowledge what had been survived and what had been learned. Elizabeth let her gaze rest on the roses below, breathing in their scent and feeling the summer sun warm her face through the glass.

Life moved forward. Hearts healed. And sometimes, despite the strangeness of how they began, things turned out exactly as they should.

The rose garden smelled of summer, that particular combination of warm earth and blooming flowers and sun-heated stone that made Elizabeth want to breathe deeply and hold each breath as long as possible. She walked beside Georgiana along the gravel path that wound between carefully tended beds, their parasols casting dappled shade across their shoulders while bees hummed among the blooms with industrious contentment. The afternoon had reached that perfect temperature where warmth felt pleasant rather than oppressive, where slight breeze provided just enough cooling to make outdoor activity comfortable.

Georgiana had grown increasingly at ease in Elizabeth's company over the past weeks, her painful shyness gradually giving way to something approaching genuine comfort. She no longer startled when Elizabeth entered a room, no longer kept her gaze fixed on her hands throughout entire conversations. Progress came slowly, but it came nonetheless, and Elizabeth found herself genuinely fond of this gentle girl who was her newest sister.

They paused beside a bush bearing white roses, the blooms so perfect they seemed almost artificial in their symmetry. Elizabeth bent to inhale their scent, finding it sweet without being cloying, delicate without being insipid. These were the roses Mrs. Reynolds had told her were the ones particularly beloved by Darcy's mother. Lady Anne had tended these plants herself, had spent hours in this garden planning and pruning and simply sitting among the flowers she loved.

Elizabeth found comfort in that connection, in knowing she walked where Darcy's mother had walked, tended beauty his mother had created. It made her feel less like an intruder and more like someone taking up a legacy that had been waiting for the right person to claim it.

Georgiana's voice interrupted her contemplation, soft and hesitant, but far less than it had once been when she addressed Elizabeth, her confidence grown in the past few weeks. "May I ask you something, Elizabeth? Something that perhaps I should not wonder about, but which has been troubling my mind regardless?"

Elizabeth straightened, turning to face her. "Of course, Georgiana. You may ask me anything."

Georgiana's hands twisted the handle of her parasol, her gaze dropping to the gravel path beneath their feet. When she spoke again, her voice had dropped to barely above a whisper, as though she feared being overheard despite their isolation in the garden. "Do you believe in magic and such? In things beyond what natural philosophy can explain?"

The question struck Elizabeth with force that made her breath catch, surprise mixed with understanding and a complicated swirl of emotions she had no easy way to process. She had wondered when this question might come, or something like it. Georgiana was observant despite her shyness, intelligent beneath her reticence. She must have sensed something strange in the rapid sequence of events surrounding Elizabeth and Darcy's marriage, in Anne's sudden illness and equally sudden removal to Bath, in small inconsistencies that never quite added up to a coherent whole.

Elizabeth considered her answer carefully, weighing honesty against discretion, truth against the necessity of protecting knowledge too dangerous to share freely.

"I believe," Elizabeth said finally, speaking slowly to ensure each word carried the weight she intended, "in choices, and in their cost. Every action we take, every decision we make, creates consequences that ripple outward in ways we cannot always foresee or control. Some people seek shortcuts, try to bend the world to their will through means that seem to offer power without requiring the usual sacrifices. But such power always demands payment eventually, often in currencies far more dear than those who sought it anticipated paying."

She turned to look at Georgiana directly, seeing confusion mixed with dawning comprehension in the girl's face. "What we call magic might simply be knowledge that most people do not possess, understanding of how certain elements combine to create effects that seem impossible to those who have not studied such matters."

Georgiana's expression showed she was thinking through Elizabeth's words with care, trying to parse their meaning beyond the careful phrasing. "Then you do believe such things exist? That there are ways to achieve the impossible, if one is willing to pay the cost?"

"I believe," Elizabeth replied, choosing her words carefully, "that what we think of as impossible often simply means we do not yet understand the mechanisms by which it might be accomplished. But understanding how something *might* be done is different from believing it *should* be done. Some knowledge is better left unused, some prices better left unpaid. That is what I believe."

The sound of gravel crunching under boots announced Darcy's approach before Elizabeth saw him. She turned to see his expression showing the warmth it always carried now when looking at her, the reserve that had once characterised his manner almost entirely absent when they were private or in family company. He had caught the end of her words, she realised, had heard her speak of knowledge and prices and choices.

"And in second chances," Darcy added quietly, joining them beside the white roses. "I believe in second chances, and in the possibility of building something genuine from even the strangest of beginnings."

His hand found Elizabeth's where it rested against her skirts, his fingers intertwining with hers in gesture that felt both intimate and comfortable, as natural as breathing. She looked up at him and felt her heart do that peculiar squeeze it performed with increasing frequency lately, that sensation of affection mixed with gratitude mixed with growing certainty that this marriage was indeed becoming everything she had once feared it could not.

"As do I," Elizabeth replied softly, squeezing his hand with pressure he returned immediately. She smiled up at him with happiness that needed no artifice or pretence, that came from genuine contentment with her life and her choices and the man who stood beside her now as partner rather than merely husband in name.

Georgiana watched this exchange with expression that showed understanding beyond her years, a small smile playing at the corners of her mouth as she observed the obvious affection between her brother and his wife. Whatever she had suspected, whatever questions had prompted her inquiry, seemed to find sufficient answer in this demonstration of genuine feeling freely given.

The sound of trotting horses and carriage wheels on the drive interrupted the moment, the rattle of an approaching vehicle carrying clearly across the summer afternoon. Elizabeth felt Darcy tense slightly beside her, his attention shifting toward the house with instinctive alertness to arrivals. But Georgiana's reaction was far more pronounced, her entire face lighting with pleasure so genuine and unguarded that Elizabeth felt her own smile widen in response.

"The Bingleys," Georgiana breathed as the carriage came into view, her voice carrying excitement she made no effort to conceal. Her cheeks had coloured prettily, her eyes bright with anticipation as she took an involuntary step toward the house before catching herself and resuming proper composure. But the damage, if it could be called such, was already done. Her feelings were written plainly on her face for anyone with eyes to see.

Elizabeth exchanged a glance with Darcy, seeing understanding and resignation mixed with affection in his expression. He was aware of his sister's growing attachment to Bingley, she realised, though she had not spoken to him of it, wanting to keep Georgiana's confidence. But he showed no disapproval, only the protective concern of a brother who wanted his sister's happiness while fearing for her vulnerable heart.

"Shall we greet our guests?" Elizabeth suggested gently, offering her free arm to Georgiana while maintaining her hold on Darcy's hand with the other. They would walk to meet the Bingleys together, the three of them, presenting the united front of the family that they had become despite the extraordinary circumstances of their assembly.

As they moved along the gravel path toward the house, Elizabeth found herself reflecting on how strange it was that things had turned out so well. That from body-swapping and dark magic and desperate schemes had emerged genuine happiness for nearly everyone involved. Jane would marry Colonel Fitzwilliam and settle into comfortable contentment as mistress of his inherited estate. Georgiana would have opportunity to explore whatever feelings existed between herself and Bingley, with time and proper courtship to determine whether girlish admiration might mature into something lasting. And Elizabeth herself had found in Darcy a partner who valued her mind and respected her independence, who showed his love through

patience and consideration rather than grand gestures or empty flattery.

Even Anne, dying slowly in Bath, had found moments of contrition according to Lady Catherine's letter. Perhaps that counted as its own form of redemption, recognition of wrongdoing and genuine regret even if such feelings came too late to change the trajectory of her fate. Elizabeth hoped Anne's final days would bring her peace, hoped she would find some measure of contentment before the end.

Elizabeth could see Bingley's fair head through the carriage window as it halted before the house, could hear his cheerful voice calling something to his driver. Opposite him sat Caroline and Louisa, their faces showing the careful neutrality of women preparing to be pretend a graciousness they did not feel.

But none of that mattered, Elizabeth realised. Caroline's disapproval and Louisa's condescension carried no weight here at Pemberley, where Elizabeth was mistress and her word carried absolute authority. They would be polite because propriety demanded it, because offending Darcy's wife would cost them more than maintaining pleasant fiction. And that was enough.

Georgiana's hand tightened on Elizabeth's arm as they approached the carriage, her nervousness evident. Elizabeth gave her newest sister's hand a reassuring squeeze, offering silent support and encouragement. Whatever developed between Georgiana and Bingley would do so naturally, without interference or manipulation, with time and proper courtship to determine its course.

The carriage door opened and Bingley descended with his characteristic energy, his face breaking into a wide smile as he caught sight of them waiting to greet him. "Darcy! Mrs. Darcy!

Miss Darcy! How wonderful to see you all looking so well. Pemberley is even more beautiful than I remembered."

Elizabeth felt Darcy's hand tighten briefly on hers before he released it to step forward and greet his friend with genuine warmth. She remained standing with Georgiana, watching the reunion while the summer sun gilded everything with golden promise and the scent of roses filled the air with sweetness.

This was her life now, she thought. Darcy, Georgiana, Pemberley, these quiet moments of domestic happiness punctuated by visits from loved ones and simple pleasures of gardens and conversation and building something real from impossible beginnings. It was not the life she had imagined for herself a year ago, not anything she could have predicted or planned. But it was good, genuinely good, in ways that required no magic to create or maintain.

Just choices, and their cost, and the willingness to pay that cost honestly. Just second chances, and the wisdom to recognise them when they appeared. Just love, growing slowly from respect and patience into something that she believed could last a lifetime.

Elizabeth smiled as Bingley turned his enthusiastic greeting toward her, as Georgiana stepped forward with shy pleasure and a bright smile to welcome him to Pemberley. Yes, she thought. Despite everything, despite the strangeness and terror and impossible magic that had brought them all to this moment, things had indeed turned out exactly as they should.

Also By Catherine Bilson

The Blushing Brides Series

An Earl For Ellen
A Marquis For Marianne
A Duke For Diana
A Captain For Clarissa

The Bookshop Belles series (co-written with Ebony Oaten)

Estelle's Ardent Admirer
Marie's Merry Gentleman
Louise's Christmas Champion
Bernadette's Dashing Doctor
Matthew's Willing Widow

The Brides of Belle Haven series

A Bride For Belle Haven (prequel novella)

Good Golly, Miss Molly
Miss Clara and the Marquess
Miss Anna's Mistake
Miss Eliza Takes Charge
Miss Charlotte Makes A Mess
Miss Laura In Love
Miss Louise Meddles

Regency Novels

His Darling Duchess

Phoebe And The Pea
Kidnapping Lord Blaymire
The Captain's Runaway Bride
The Wassail Wager
The Bride Said No
St. George and the River Horse
Christmas Courting (collection of novellas)

American Pioneer Romance

Coming From California
Returning From Rhode Island

Pride & Prejudice Variations

The Best Of Relations
Infamous Relations
Mr Bingley's Bride
A Christmas Miracle At Longbourn
Grief and Grievances

The Second Mrs. Bennet
A Loss At Longbourn
The Meddling Matlocks
Possession and Prejudice
Lydia and the Colonel (forthcoming)
The Secret Diary of Anne de Bourgh (forthcoming)

The Crime & Consequences Trilogy

Malice and Misfortune
Rivalry and Ruination
Intrigue and Inheritance

Sign up to the Shenanigans Press newsletter to find out about our latest new releases!

www.ingramcontent.com/pod-product-compliance
Lightning Source LLC
Chambersburg PA
CBHW030350310726
48979CB00001B/244

* 9 7 8 1 9 2 3 1 9 5 1 8 9 *